"*Danki*. I don't know what we would have done without—"

"Neighbors help neighbors," Leanna replied primly.

He understood no thanks were expected, but he also didn't like the idea of being indebted to the Waglers when he'd brought so much pain to Leanna and, through her, to her whole family.

There were many things he wanted to say to her, but he had to be content with "I wanted you to know Michael and I really appreciate your help."

"I'll pass your thanks on to Annie and Grossmammi Inez."

"Danki," he said again, though he wanted to ask why she wasn't accepting some of his gratitude for herself.

The answer blared into his head when the door closed behind her, leaving him alone with the twins. To acknowledge his appreciation would risk re-creating an emotional connection between them, one he'd thought would last a lifetime. She wasn't ready to take that chance again, and he shouldn't be, either.

So why had images of them walking together or riding in his courting buggy never stopped filling his mind during the day and his dreams every night?

Jo Ann Brown has always loved stories with happily-ever-after endings. A former military officer, she is thrilled to have the chance to write stories about people falling in love. She is also a photographer and travels with her husband of more than thirty years to places where she can snap pictures. They have three children and live in Florida. Drop her a note at joannbrownbooks.com.

Growing up on a farm, **Jocelyn McClay** enjoyed livestock and pursued a degree in agriculture. She met her husband while weightlifting in a small town—he "spotted" her. After thirty years in business management, they moved to an acreage in southeastern Missouri to be closer to family when their eldest of three daughters made them grandparents. When not writing, she keeps busy hiking, bike riding, gardening, knitting and substitute teaching.

JO ANN BROWN

The Amish Widower's Twins

&

JOCELYN McCLAY

The Amish Bachelor's Choice

LOVE INSPIRED
INSPIRATIONAL ROMANCE

Recycling programs for this product may not exist in your area.

LOVE INSPIRED®
INSPIRATIONAL ROMANCE

ISBN-13: 978-1-335-40245-5

The Amish Widower's Twins and The Amish Bachelor's Choice

Copyright © 2021 by Harlequin Books S.A.

The Amish Widower's Twins
First published in 2019. This edition published in 2021.
Copyright © 2019 by Jo Ann Ferguson

The Amish Bachelor's Choice
First published in 2019. This edition published in 2021.
Copyright © 2019 by Jocelyn McClay

This edition published by arrangement with Harlequin Books S.A.

For questions and comments about the quality of this book, please contact us at CustomerService@Harlequin.com.

Harlequin Enterprises ULC
22 Adelaide St. West, 40th Floor
Toronto, Ontario M5H 4E3, Canada
www.Harlequin.com

Printed in U.S.A.

CONTENTS

THE AMISH WIDOWER'S TWINS

Jo Ann Brown

For Angela Mathews.
Thanks for being such a blessing in our lives.

Remembering mine affliction and my misery,
the wormwood and the gall.
My soul hath them still in remembrance,
and is humbled in me.
This I recall to my mind, therefore have I hope.
It is of the Lord's mercies that we are not
consumed, because his compassions fail not.
They are new every morning.
great is Thy faithfulness.
—*Lamentations* 3:19–23

Chapter One

"Do you sell the *milch* from your goats?"

Leanna Wagler raised her left hand to acknowledge the man's question as she continued milking Faith. The brown-and-white doe was the herd's leader and most days waited patiently while Leanna squirted *milch* into the small bucket on the raised platform. Today, the goat had taken it into her head that she didn't want to stand still.

"Just a minute," Leanna said without looking back. "I'm almost done."

It took less time than that. Drawing the pail out from under the goat, she patted Faith on the haunches, the signal the goat should jump down. Leanna set the pail on the ground and smiled as Charity, the goat who always wanted to be milked after the herd's leader, stepped up onto the platform.

"Sorry," Leanna began as she turned in the direction of the man's voice.

She didn't finish.

Instead, she stared at the man standing on the other side of the fence.

How could it be Gabriel Miller, the man who'd held her heart in his hands when she lived in Lancaster County? He'd tossed it aside to marry another woman without letting Leanna know of his plans.

It had to be Gabriel. Who else had unruly red curls that refused to lie flat in a plain haircut? His ruddy beard, still patchy, followed the strong line of his jaw. Dark brown eyes, which she had once believed were as sweet and loyal as a puppy's, widened as his gaze swept from the top of her *kapp* to the rubber boots she wore while milking.

She fought her fingers, which wanted to wipe goat hair and stains off her apron. She didn't need to try to look her best for a man who'd dumped her.

A part of her didn't want to believe the man who'd invaded her dreams, turning them to nightmares, stood in front of her. Before she could stop herself, she asked, "Gabriel?"

At the same moment, he asked, "Leanna?"

Her heart somehow managed to leap and sink at the same time. The sound of her name in his deep, rumbling voice confirmed what she'd been trying to deny.

The red-haired man in front of her was Gabriel Miller, and the *boppli* he held…

Shock pierced her again as she looked from him to the little one who had his bright red hair. Gabriel had a *kind*? She shouldn't be surprised. He'd been married for about a year and a half. The baby looked to be about six months old and regarded her with curious eyes as brown as Gabriel's.

As brown as the *boppli*'s *daed*.

Her heart broke as it had the day she'd learned he was going to marry Freda Girod.

"*Gute mariye*, Gabriel," Leanna said.

Her cool voice seemed to startle him. What had he expected? Had he thought she'd throw her arms around him or dissolve into tears? That she was tempted to do both was something he must never know.

As emotions rushed through his eyes, she waited for him to reply. He must know, as she did, that what he said next would set the tone of their future interactions. Interactions? What an unfeeling word! Yet such words would keep distance between them.

"I didn't know your Waglers lived on this farm," Gabriel said.

"We've been here over a year." She raised her chin as if she could cut the differences in their heights, for he was almost a foot taller than she was. "Are you visiting someone here?"

Please say ja, she begged silently.

"No, we've decided to become part of this new church district."

It took every bit of strength Leanna possessed to keep her shoulders from sagging at the thought of having Gabriel, his wife and their *boppli* as her neighbors. She hadn't been successful in banishing him from her thoughts. Now—seeing him at least every two weeks for church—he'd be a constant reminder of the worst betrayal she'd ever endured.

God is our refuge and strength, a very present help in trouble. That psalm, which had offered her comfort, whispered in her mind.

"Did you say something about goats' *milch*?" She remembered what he'd said, but she didn't want to talk about why he and his family had come to Harmony Creek Hollow.

He looked relieved, but didn't give her the smile that used to make her heart yearn to twirl about with joy. He remained somber as he answered, "The *doktor* suggested goats' *milch* for my *bopplin*."

She heard a bleat from the milking platform. Charity had gotten tired of waiting and thought Leanna should know it, but Leanna couldn't move.

Couldn't speak.

Couldn't think of anything but what Gabriel had just said. He had more than the one *boppli* he held with the ease of an experienced parent in the crook of one arm?

She shouldn't be surprised. Like her, he was a twin, but unlike her and her sister Annie, he and his brother weren't identical twins. Twins were more prevalent in some families, so him being the *daed* of twins wasn't unexpected. It was a reminder, however, of how far his life had changed since the last time they'd spoken…and how little hers had.

She'd moved with her *grossmammi* and siblings, as well as her older brother Lyndon's family, from Pennsylvania to northern New York. She'd bought and now tended a herd of goats that made her laugh with their antics when she wasn't frustrated with their attempts to sneak through the fence. She had jobs cleaning houses for *Englisch* neighbors to help provide for the household.

She remained unmarried, the sole member of the friendship group she, her sister and two friends had laughingly named Harmony Creek Spinsters Club to not find a husband after moving to the new settlement. The only romance in her life, other than a few attempts by her sister at matchmaking, were the novels she read before she went to sleep each night.

She told herself to stop feeling sorry for herself. She had a *gut* life with a loving family and kind friends. She was a member of a devoted *Leit* who came together to worship and praise God.

"…would be better for their digestion."

Realizing Gabriel had continued talking, Leanna struggled to listen past the roar of the windswept ocean that had taken up residence in her head. He was going to be living in Harmony Creek Hollow, so she must get used to him being nearby.

But how?

Gabriel Miller wondered why nobody had warned him Leanna was part of the Wagler family living down the road from the farm he'd bought with his brother. Because the surname was common in Lancaster County, he hadn't given a second thought to his new neighbors.

He should have. And maybe a third and a fourth thought. He had no idea how he was going to get used to having pretty Leanna right next door. When they'd lived in Lancaster County, it had been an hour drive from his house to hers. The last time they'd spoken, he'd asked her to meet him at an ice cream shop in Strasburg, which was about halfway between their homes. That had never happened. Instead, he'd married Freda.

Every time he walked out his door now, there would be a chance he'd see the sheen of Leanna's black hair in the sunlight or hear her soft voice lilting with laughter and kindness. Two years ago, that would have been a cause for celebration. Now nothing was.

A cry came from the *boppli* in his arms, and he gave

Harley a teething biscuit. The little boy chomped on it, appeased. It was a sharp reminder, though, how Gabriel had to forget about the past and think about Harley's and his twin sister Heidi's suffering. The little girl managed better than her smaller brother, but last night both had been awake all night with stomachaches and vomiting. What they did get into their stomachs went through them so fast Gabriel was having a hard time keeping up with the laundry.

Thank You, Lord, he'd prayed as he had washed out diapers, tiny clothing and soiled bedding, *for having these troubles come to us in May. I don't know how we would have handled it in the middle of the winter.*

"Do you sell the *milch* from your goats?" he asked as he had before. The sooner he got his business completed, the sooner he could get out of Leanna's barnyard.

"Ja." The word seemed to spark a change in her because she lost her baffled expression and met his eyes.

For the length of a single heartbeat, it was as if he'd been thrown back in time to when he'd seen her blue-green eyes crinkling with a smile across a hay-strewn barn. *Forget that!* He couldn't let his mind get caught up in what had been. It was too late to change it anyhow.

Again he had to force himself to focus on the stumbling conversation. How easily they'd once chatted! Today, he had to weigh each word before he spoke it. Otherwise, he might utter something stupid, like the truth he had promised never to reveal.

"I'm looking to buy enough for both *bopplin*," he said. "Around three pints a day. Do your goats give enough so you can sell me that much?"

"Ja, but you'll have to pick it up. I don't have time

to deliver *milch* to you." She hesitated, then asked, "Where's your farm?"

"Next door, but closer to the main road." He didn't miss how she flinched. "Michael and I purchased the farm and moved in a couple of days ago. I'd assumed I could find formula for the *bopplin*, but everything seems to upset their stomachs."

Her gaze focused on Harley again. "They may be bothered by you using different water here. Are they eating solid food?"

"Some, but we're relying on bottles for the most part. That's why it's important I get something they can keep down."

"Goats' *milch* is easy to digest." Her voice sounded normal. He wished his did. "It has less sugar and trace amounts of the protein that causes troubles for those with sensitivities to cows' *milch*. If you're going to use it as a formula substitute, though, you'll need to add in a few minerals and vitamins."

"You know a lot about this."

"My goats aren't pets. When I decided to start a herd, I did a lot of reading to know what I was getting into. I've got several customers who purchase *milch*, though they're adults, not *bopplin*."

"Gabriel…Miller…is…that you?"

He looked over his shoulder to see who was speaking in a halting manner. Again he was astonished. He'd met Inez Wagler, the matriarch of the Wagler family and Leanna's *grossmammi*, several times at haystack dinners and mud sales. The last time he'd seen her, two years ago, she'd been as spry as a grasshopper.

Inez Wagler, once a powerful oak, looked like an ancient tree stripped by a storm. She leaned on a cane as she crossed the yard toward them. Her gray hair was thin beneath her *kapp*, and wrinkles were gouged into her face. Yet, when she smiled, hints of her vibrant personality were visible.

"Gute mariye, Grossmammi Inez.*"* He caught sight of Leanna's eyes narrowing before she turned to calm the goat vying for her attention. He shouldn't have used the name she always used when she spoke of her *grossmammi*. That suggested he was a member of the family, which he most definitely wasn't.

"It…is…you." She paused in front of him and rested both hands on top of the wood cane. "Are you…our new…neighbors?"

Gabriel wondered why Inez spoke in gasps. He flicked a quick glance toward Leanna and caught her unaware. Dismay was displayed across her face. As he watched, she rearranged her face into the same crisp, false smile she'd offered him.

"Grossmammi," Leanna said, "if you needed something, you could have gotten my attention from the porch."

"A soul…likes fresh…air…once in…a while." She smiled at Gabriel. "Ain't so?"

He raised his left hand as he kept Harley secure in his right arm. "I may be a new member of this settlement, but I learned long ago never to get in the middle of a disagreement between two strong-willed women."

Inez laughed and, to his amazement, Leanna did, too. He hadn't meant it as a joke.

"Who…is this…with you?" the old woman asked.

"My son, Harley." He offered her a smile, but suspected it looked as fake as it felt. "His twin, Heidi, is at home. It's a boys' trip out to buy some *milch* from Leanna's goats."

His son seemed fascinated by Inez, who spoke to him in a gentle, soothing voice. Chewing on his teething biscuit, he stared at her.

"He's…never seen…anyone…as old…as me." Inez's chuckle turned into a gasp as she struggled for breath.

Gabriel reached out to her, but she waved him away, telling him she was fine.

He didn't believe it, not when he saw the concern on her *kins-kind*'s face. Leanna's hands were clenched into impotent fists at her sides as if she were battling with herself not to climb out of the goats' pen and come to her *grossmammi*'s aid.

"Welcome…to…Harmony…Creek. We hope… you'll…like it…here." She looked at her granddaughter. "Ain't so?"

Color rushed up Leanna's face, and he realized how pale she'd been since she discovered him on the other side of the fence. When Leanna nodded and remained silent, her *grossmammi* headed to the house. Inez halted partway and asked Leanna to come in when she was done with him.

Gabriel halted himself from saying Leanna had been done with him a long time ago. Why bring up the past when she'd made it clear with her curt comments that she hadn't forgiven him for marrying someone else?

Why should she? She hadn't replied to the letter he'd sent her before he took his marriage vows, so he'd known she hadn't been ready to grant him the forgiveness he'd asked for. She must believe he was heartless. He couldn't change her opinion, because he couldn't share the truth with anyone.

Once her *grossmammi* was out of earshot, Gabriel asked, "Why does she sound the way she does?"

"We're not sure." Leanna pushed aside the goat poking her with its head. "Her *doktor* thinks it may have something to do with one of her heart valves, so he's sending her to a cardiologist."

"I never imagined her so weak she'd need a cane."

"Me, neither." Leanna became all business, and he knew she didn't want to say more about her *grossmammi*. She told him what she charged for a quart of *milch* and what containers he would need.

"I leave for work by ten most mornings," she said, "so please be here before then. Until school is out, *Grossmammi* Inez is here by herself, and it'd be better if she wasn't disturbed."

Though questions about where Leanna worked demanded answers, he didn't ask them. "I'll make it a priority to be here before you head out. If I can't be, we'll work out something else. I appreciate you helping me, so I want to make this as easy as possible for you."

"Danki." She glanced at the black goat on the milking platform, and he knew she and the doe wanted him gone.

Had she guessed he hadn't been speaking just about picking up the *milch*? When he'd made the decisions he had almost two years ago, he'd hoped there would be a way to avoid hurting Leanna. He'd spent hours working on that letter to her, praying God would give him the right words. God hadn't listened to that prayer, as He hadn't so many others in the past year. Somehow, in the midst of his chaotic life, he'd lost his connection with God, and he wasn't sure how to find it again.

"No, I should be the one saying *'danki.'* If you didn't

have *milch* to sell, I don't know where I could have found some." He backed away a couple of steps.

"There are several people around here who sell it. If you want, I can give you their names and addresses. That way if you want to check prices or—"

"I'm sure you're giving me a fair price, Leanna, and I won't find any place more convenient than next door."

"True."

When she didn't add anything else, he began to walk toward his gray-topped buggy. It'd been delivered that morning, and he had other errands before he headed home and continued unpacking enough so they could get through another day.

"Gabriel?" Leanna called.

Facing her, he asked, *"Ja?"*

"If it's easier, your wife is welcome to *komm* and pick up the *milch* for your *bopplin*."

It was his turn to flinch.

She must have seen because she hurried to say, "Gabriel, it's okay. Tell her she and the *kinder* are welcome here anytime."

"I can't." He kept emotion from his face and his voice as he added, "I can't, because she's dead."

Chapter Two

Leanna stood by the fence and watched Gabriel's buggy drive out of sight along the curving road. She wasn't sure how long she would have remained there, frozen in the warm sunshine, if Charity hadn't voiced her impatience again.

Milking the rest of the goats took Leanna less than an hour, and she carried the *milch* into the house in two large pails. As she'd expected, her *grossmammi* was sitting at the comfortable kitchen table.

Grossmammi Inez looked up from her mending as Leanna walked past her to pour the *milch* into storage containers. Most of it went into the refrigerator to wait for customers to pick it up, but she kept some to freeze in plastic containers for when she made soap on Saturdays. She did that every other week, when a church Sunday didn't follow, because she doubted anyone would want to sit for three hours beside her when she reeked of the fragrances she used in her soap mixtures.

"Are you still going to have enough *milch* to make soap?" her *grossmammi* said, halting to take a breath after every word.

"I may have to go to a schedule of making soap once a month." She sealed the plastic containers and marked the date on them with a wide-tipped felt pen before putting them in the freezer. "I've been making soap since I started milking the goats this spring. I should have enough to set up a table at the farmers market for June and July." She calculated in her head. "It'll work out fine, though Gabriel wants to buy three pints every day."

"With two *bopplin*, he'll need that. *Bopplin* depend on *milch* when they're young."

"He said something about them eating some solid food."

"How old are they?"

"I'd say from looking at Harley that they're around six months, but I don't know." She put the buckets in the sink and began to rinse them so they'd be ready for milking the next day. Some people milked their goats twice a day, but she'd opted for once. That allowed her time to work and help her sisters take care of the house.

"Twins usually look younger than other *bopplin*. You and your sister needed some time to catch up." *Grossmammi* Inez gave a half laugh that turned into a cough. "Not that you ever grew very tall."

"Gabriel didn't get married that long ago."

"*Bopplin* come when they want, and twins are often raring to be born. You and Annie weren't eight months in the womb before you decided you had to come out. Your *mamm* always said Annie dragged you with her because you've always had so much more patience than she does."

Leaving the buckets by the sink to dry, Leanna looked across the kitchen to where *Grossmammi* Inez's needle dipped in and out, mending a tear across the upper leg of a pair of her younger brother Kenny's barn pants. Most of her brother's work clothes were crisscrossed with repairs.

"*Grossmammi?*"

As she raised her eyes, her smile faded away. "Something is wrong, ain't so? You look bothered, Leanna. Is it because Gabriel and his family have moved in next door?"

"Partly." She couldn't imagine being anything but honest with her *grossmammi*.

During Leanna's childhood, *Grossmammi* Inez had taken them in twice. The first time had been following Leanna's *daed*'s death, and then the *kinder* moved in again during the horrible days after her *mamm* and beloved stepfather were killed in a bus accident on their way to a wedding in Indiana. Not once had her *grossmammi* complained about having to raise a second family in the cramped *dawdi haus* attached to her son's home.

"Then *was iss letz*?" asked the elderly woman.

"*Grossmammi...*" She wanted to say what was wrong was that two tiny *bopplin* would never know their *mamm*, but the words stuck in her throat. She'd never met Freda, whose family lived in another church district. Even so, sorrow surged through her at the thought of the *bopplin* growing up without their *mamm*. Crossing the room, she sat beside her *grossmammi*. She folded her hands on the table and drew in a steadying breath. As soon as she spoke the sad words, it would make them more real.

"Say what you must," *Grossmammi* Inez urged. "Things are seldom made better by waiting."

Leanna stumbled as she shared what Gabriel had told her before driving away. Tears burned her eyes, and she blinked them away. "He didn't say when Freda died, but it couldn't have been very long ago."

Her *grossmammi* regarded her steadily before saying, "You know your feelings had nothing to do with God's decision to bring Freda Miller to Him, ain't so?"

"I know." She stared at her clasped hands, not wanting to reveal how hearing Freda connected to Gabriel's surname always sent a pulse of pain through her. She'd imagined herself as Leanna Miller so many times.

Why did the thought of Gabriel married to someone else remain painful? Leanna frowned. She shouldn't be thinking of herself, only the *bopplin*. The poor woman was dead and her *kinder* were growing up without her.

"Are you upset because you think Gabriel Miller has come to Harmony Creek Hollow specifically to look for a wife to take care of his *bopplin*?"

Leanna's head snapped up at the sound of her sister's voice coming from the back door. Trust Annie, her identical twin, to get right to the heart of the matter. Her twin never hesitated to say what was on her mind.

Deciding to be—for once—equally blunt, Leanna asked, "How long have you been eavesdropping?"

"Long enough to find out who moved into the empty house next door." Annie stooped to give *Grossmammi* Inez a hug. "I came in to pick up a different pair of shoes." She pointed to her paint-stained ones. "I put the wrong ones on when I left for the bakery this morning. Before I go, though, you haven't answered my question, Leanna. Are you worried Gabriel Miller is here solely to find a wife to take care of his *bopplin*?"

Being false with her twin would be like lying to herself.

"Ja."

She watched as Annie and their *grossmammi* exchanged a glance, but couldn't read what message they shared.

Getting up, she hugged them. She retrieved her *milch* buckets from the sink and took them out to the shed before hitching the horse to their buggy. Today was her day to clean Mrs. Duchamps's house, and she needed to hurry or she'd be late.

The questions her family had asked were a wake-up call. She must not let the lingering longings of her heart betray her more than Gabriel had.

What was he doing wrong?

Gabriel looked from the handwritten recipe on the battered wooden counter to the ingredients he'd gathered to make formula for the twins. Realizing he'd missed a step, he added two tablespoons of unflavored gelatin. As he stirred the pot, he frowned. Something wasn't right. The color was off, and it was getting too thick too fast. He tried a sip. It tasted as it was supposed to, which was without a lot of flavor. He guessed, once they sampled this mixture, the twins would be more eager to eat solid foods.

A quick glance across the crowded kitchen reassured him the *bopplin* were playing on the blanket he'd found at the bottom of a box marked "kitchen" and "pots and pans." Friends had helped them pack, and he guessed one person had filled the box and taped it closed before another person labeled it. Bath supplies had been discovered in a box marked "pillows." True, there had been one small pillow in it, but the majority of the box had been stuffed with shampoo, toothpaste and the myriad items the *bopplin* required, including extra diaper pins.

The house, which would need his and his twin's skills

to renovate, was stuffed with boxes. He and Michael had brought the barest essentials with them, including their tools. However, two *bopplin* didn't travel without box after box of supplies and toys and clothing.

He should be grateful the boxes covered up the deep scratches in the uneven wood floors. Other boxes were set to keep the *kinder* from reaching chipped walls and floor molding. An old house could be filled with lead paint.

Eventually, it would become a *wunderbaar* family home, because the rooms were spacious. Large windows welcomed the sunlight. There were three bathrooms, one on the first floor and two more upstairs amid the six bedrooms. One toilet upstairs had plumbing problems, but the water had been turned off before damaging the floors or ceilings. Some furniture had been left behind by the previous owners, but, other than the kitchen table and chairs, it needed to be carted to the landfill because it reeked of mold and rot.

Gabriel paused stirring the formula as Heidi began to clap two blocks together and gave him a grin. Her new tooth glittered like a tiny pearl. Beside her, Harley lay on his back, his right hand holding a teething biscuit while his other hand gripped his left toes. He rocked and giggled when his sister did. With their red hair and faint beginnings of freckles across their noses, they looked like a pair of *Englisch* dolls. Their big brown eyes displayed every emotion without any censoring.

Had he ever been that open with others?

It seemed impossible after the tragedies of the past couple of years.

"What a *schtinke*," said his brother, Michael, as he walked into the kitchen through the maze of unpacked or half-unpacked boxes. Pausing to wave to the *bopplin*, who giggled, he added, "I hope it tastes better than it smells, or the kids won't drink it."

"I sampled a bit of it, and it doesn't taste as bad as it smells."

"I don't think anything could taste that bad." He reached for the *kaffi* pot.

Gabriel motioned for his brother to pour him a cup of *kaffi*, too. He was becoming dependent on caffeine. When was the last time he'd gotten a full night's sleep? "If this doesn't work for them, I don't know what will."

"Why not be positive? Isn't that what you always say?"

He watched Michael fill the cups and add a touch of cream and sugar to each. He and his brother weren't identical twins. There never had been any trouble telling them apart, but the physical differences had grown more pronounced as they grew older.

Michael's hair wasn't flame red. Instead it was a darker brown with a faint tinge of russet that became, in the summer sunshine, more pronounced. He was several inches taller than Gabriel and had a nose someone once had described as aristocratic. Gabriel wasn't sure what that was supposed to mean, but he'd always admired his brother's strong profile, which was not softened by a beard, for his brother remained a bachelor. Like Gabriel, he had hands calloused from work. His fingers, which were broader than Gabriel's, could handle a plank of wood as delicately as if it were glass. He'd worked as a finish carpenter in Pennsylvania while Gabriel had focused on rough-in work.

There were more subtle differences, too. Gabriel was the steady one, the person anyone could go to when things were getting rough. He'd give them a well thought-out solution after deliberating on it. Michael jumped into any situation. As a boy, Gabriel had read comic books with an *Englisch* friend, and Michael had reminded him of a superhero who never hesitated to run toward trouble. Gabriel saw himself more as the person picking up the pieces after the super-villain had been defeated.

"Here you go," Michael said, holding out a cup.

"Danki." Gabriel continued stirring the goats' *milch* formula while they talked about the job they'd been hired for next week.

The small project, rebuilding a garage in the tiny town of West Rupert, Vermont, about six miles east, was a beginning. They'd need as much work as they could get because they'd arrived too late to get a crop in this year.

Gabriel stared into the pot. "I don't think it's supposed to be this thick."

"You should ask the person you're getting the *milch* from. Maybe he'll know."

"She. Leanna Wagler."

His brother's brows rose in surprise. "The same Leanna Wagler you met in Pennsylvania?"

"One and the same." He didn't add she'd wandered through his daydreams almost every day since he'd last seen her. "I knew she'd moved with her family away from Lancaster County, because her brother was eager to get out of that meat-processing plant and wanted a farm of his own."

"And she was eager to get away from you."

"Ha ha," he said without humor. He didn't want to give his brother's teasing comment any credibility although, with a sinking feeling, he wondered if it were true.

No! He wasn't going to add another layer of guilt to the burden he carried.

Michael whistled a long note. "Talk about coincidences! Who would have guessed you'd find the one who got away here?"

"She's not the one who got away."

"Okay, she's the one who let you get away when you decided to marry Freda instead." Slapping Gabriel on the shoulder, he asked, "Do you think Leanna wants you back?"

"No." The answer burst out of him.

Seeing Michael's *gut* humor become astonishment, Gabriel didn't want to hear another lecture on how he should get on with his life. Why did everyone seem to think they could tell him what to do? How many people had told him the *bopplin* needed a *mamm*? He was fumbling through each day, trying to be a competent *daed* as well as a *gut* business partner for his brother. He wasn't succeeding at either because he snatched only a few hours of sleep each night. Even on the nights when the twins slept through, his conscience kept him awake with questions about how he could have failed to notice Freda's despair before she died.

He set the pot aside to cool, then joined his brother at the table, selecting a seat where he could keep an eye on the *bopplin*. Wanting to talk about anything but Leanna, he asked, "Have you found the rest of our tools yet?"

"Most of them. I dug the nail gun out of a box marked 'curtains.'" He laughed. "That's not close!"

Michael didn't seem to notice when Gabriel remained silent. Had his brother gotten accustomed to Gabriel's inability to smile and laugh? Gabriel hadn't been able to remember the last time he'd done either; yet, seeing

Leanna today resurrected memories of the times they'd shared a laugh together. It was shocking to think a part of him had died along with Freda, and he hadn't realized that until he'd looked into Leanna's *wunderbaar* eyes and recalled when his biggest concern had been if he'd have the courage to ask her to let him drive her home.

"Have you found someone to take care of the kids while we're at work?" Michael asked, yanking Gabriel out of his thoughts.

"Not yet."

"Our job begins a week from yesterday."

"I know."

"It's going to take two of us to get that foundation straight again. Or as straight as we can get it after the garage has been leaning for the past fifty years."

"I know," he repeated.

"Benjamin Kuhns—he and his brother run the sawmill—mentioned his sister used to be a nanny for an *Englisch* family. Maybe she'd be interested in the job."

"Maybe." He hated the idea of leaving Harley and Heidi with a stranger.

"How about Leanna? You know her. Do you think she'd be willing to watch the kids?"

"She said she already has a job."

"Doing what?"

"I didn't ask."

Michael arched that expressive eyebrow again. "What did you two talk about? Certainly not about old times."

"We talked about her selling me her goats' *milch*."

Harley let out a cry and Gabriel jumped to his feet, almost grateful for the interruption despite being worried about why Harley was crying. The *boppli* was far quieter than his sister, who wanted everyone to know when she was upset.

His anxiety eased when he realized the tiny boy had lost his hold on his toes and was frustrated with trying to capture them again. Kneeling, Gabriel guided Harley's foot toward his fingers. The *boppli* grabbed them and gurgled with contentment. Gabriel gave the *kinder* kisses before standing again.

"You're going to spoil them," Michael said with a fake frown. "Aren't *daeds* supposed to set rules for their *kinder*?"

He mumbled something in response. It must have satisfied his brother because Michael turned the discussion to the list of supplies they'd need before they began their first job.

Gabriel went to check on the formula. He kept his back to his brother, not wanting his expression to give any hint to the truth nobody living except him knew. He wasn't the *bopplin*'s *daed*.

Chapter Three

Leanna shouldn't have felt so proud of herself. She was well aware of the fact *hochmut* was wrong for a plain person, but she couldn't help congratulating herself for treating Gabriel as she would have any customer.

For the past four days, Gabriel had come to the house every morning to collect *milch* for his *bopplin*.

For the past four days, she'd asked him how the *kinder* were, and if he and Michael were getting settled in their new home.

For the past four days, he'd given her trite answers and she'd accepted them before watching him leave.

All nice and as indifferent as if they'd met for the first time when he came to inquire about purchasing *milch*. Because, the truth was, she wasn't sure if he was the same man she'd known two years ago. The thought almost brought an ironic laugh from her as she finished milking the last goat in the pen.

If she'd known Gabriel as well as she'd thought she had two years ago, she wouldn't have been blindsided by him marrying someone else.

Hearing the rattle of buggy wheels, Leanna pushed

her way out of the pen. She put down the buckets to double-check the gate was secured. Goats were escape artists, and she didn't want to give them any opportunity to sneak out.

Either she was late this morning or Gabriel was early. Usually she had the *milch* portioned out before he arrived.

She waited to cross the driveway until he'd slowed the black horse pulling his buggy. When he stepped out, he didn't wave to her. Instead, he turned to look inside the vehicle. Had he brought the *bopplin* with him? If so, it was the first time since he'd come to see if she'd sell him *milch*.

Setting the buckets on the back porch, she went to the buggy. Two car seats had been secured to the back bench. She could see tiny wiggling feet, but not their faces because the seats were set so the *kinder* looked toward the rear. Families carried their littlest *kinder* on the laps of parents or older siblings. She'd never given any thought to how *bopplin* would travel with only a driver.

"May I see the twins?" she asked.

"Sure."

She unlatched the door and started to raise it. When she stood on tiptoe to stretch it over her head, he took it and lifted it up to its full extent. Having him stand so close threatened to sweep her breath away, and she had to focus on breathing in and out so he wouldn't notice he still had that effect on her. She didn't want him to think she was a *dummkopf* for not ridding herself of her attraction for him. If only it were as easy to turn off as the lights on his buggy...

"Oh, my!" she gasped when she saw the *bopplin*. Both

had inherited Gabriel's red hair, and they regarded her with big, brown eyes so much like his. "They're cute!"

"I think so."

"Of course *you* do. You're their *daed*."

"*Ja*, there's that."

She tore her eyes from the adorable youngsters to look at Gabriel. When he didn't smile, she wondered if she'd offended him with her praise. He'd never been stiff-necked before. He'd been an open book when she first met him.

Her smile vanished as she reminded herself that wasn't true. She'd fooled herself then about him, believing she'd known him when she hadn't. Otherwise, why had she assumed he cared about her?

How wrong she'd been!

She blinked hot tears as she focused on the kids again. Harley was dressed in a loose garment that would make changing his diapers easier. The little girl wore a white *schlupp schotzli*, a tiny pinafore apron, over a dark blue dress. The little girl grinned and made gooing sounds. Leanna was lost as the *boppli*'s smile warmed her heart, which had been as cold as winter since she'd heard about Gabriel's plans to marry.

Not waiting to ask Gabriel's permission, Leanna reached in and began to unbuckle the little girl. He started to do the same for Harley. Both kids bounced with their excitement at being released from the seats.

Leanna cradled the little girl for a moment before the active *kind* wanted to sit up. Balancing the *boppli* on her hip as she once had done her youngest sibling, she let herself enjoy the moment. Kenny was twelve now. She'd held plenty of other *kinder* since then, but there hadn't been the same knowing that having this *kind* in her arms was meant to be.

Until now.

"Her name is Heidi," Gabriel said, helping her shove away the thought that should never have come into her mind.

"Harley and Heidi. Those aren't common names."

"My *daed*'s *grossdawdi* was named Harley, and my *mamm*'s great-*aenti*'s name was Heidi. From what I've been told, she was given that name because it was her *mamm*'s favorite story growing up."

Curious why both twins had been named for Gabriel's family instead of one for Freda's, Leanna didn't want to ruin the moment by reminding him of whom he'd lost. "Keeping a name alive in a family is a nice way to honor those who came before us. Annie and I were named for *Grossmammi* Inez's favorite *aentis*. It created a connection for us though they died before we were born."

She stiffened as she realized what she'd said.

He cupped her shoulder with his broad hand, creating another unexpected connection. "Don't think you have to choose every word so it won't remind me of Freda's death. I can't forget it."

"I'm sorry. I know it's impossible to forget such a loss."

Gently squeezing her shoulder, he said, "*Danki*. I'm sorry you, too, learned about such losses when you were young." He lifted his fingers from her shoulder, and the bridge between them vanished. "Can we get the *milch*? I know you don't want to be late for work."

Leanna motioned for Gabriel to come inside. He lowered the buggy's back and latched it, then followed her. She paused by the steps and looked at the forgotten *milch* buckets. Her mind was in such a turmoil she couldn't think of how to handle both of them while she held Heidi.

"You get one, and I'll get the other," Gabriel said from behind her.

"Danki."

She used the time it took to walk up the steps and through the mudroom to try to compose herself. When she entered the kitchen where her family was finishing breakfast, *Grossmammi* Inez looked past her to smile at Gabriel. Annie arched a single brow and remained silent.

Juanita, who at fourteen was already taller than her older sisters, came forward to take Heidi so Leanna could divide up the *milch*. Cooing at the little girl, Juanita and Kenny made faces to make the *bopplin* laugh.

Leanna's arms felt empty as she put her pail next to the one Gabriel had carried into the house. She poured out the *milch* and stored the amount she had left over for making soap in the freezer. She put the small containers she'd filled for Gabriel on the counter.

He reached for them, then halted. "I need some advice on making the formula. When I follow the recipe, it comes out so thick the *bopplin* have real trouble sucking it from the bottle."

"Do you have a bottle with you?"

He held up a finger, then rushed out of the kitchen. Returning before she'd finished rinsing out the buckets, he checked the room to see who was holding his *kinder*, and his shoulders relaxed when he saw they were still being entertained by Juanita and Kenny. He was a *gut daed*.

Then his eyes caught hers. So many questions raced through his gaze, questions she wasn't ready to answer.

To do so would upset the fragile status quo, and doing that could make the situation more uncomfortable.

If possible.

Gabriel cut his eyes away before Leanna discerned too much about the secrets he hid. She'd always known what he was thinking and feeling before he did. Before, it had been charming. Now it could destroy the rickety sculpture of half-truths he'd built to protect those he'd promised he'd never hurt.

"Let me see the bottle," Leanna said, holding out her hand.

He gave it to her and watched as she tilted it and tried to sprinkle the formula into the sink. Nothing came out. She righted the bottle and walked into the living room. She got a needle from a sewing box beneath what looked like the beginning of a quilt top, and he recalled how she'd talked about quilting. She'd been especially fond of patterns that were challenging for a left-handed needleworker.

What else had he forgotten about her in the mad rush to become a husband and a *daed*?

Hearing Heidi squeal with delight from where she sat on Inez's lap while the woman who must be Leanna's twin held Harley, he relaxed again.

"You need a bigger hole in the nipple," Leanna said, pulling his attention to her, "so the *bopplin* don't have to work so hard to get the *milch* out." She used the needle to demonstrate, sticking it in and wiggling it about to enlarge the hole.

"That's a *gut* idea." He took the bottle and tried getting the formula out again. As before, nothing emerged. "It's still too small."

Her forehead threaded. "It should have worked. It's what others have done when their *bopplin* have had trouble with formula. Are you sure you're making it correctly?"

"I'm following the recipe I was given by the *doktor*'s office." He fished a copy out of his pocket. He'd been carrying it with him in the hope he could find someone to watch the twins before he had to go to work in West Rupert in a few days. So far his search had been unavailing.

"Let me see it. Maybe I can figure out if there's a problem."

At Leanna's words, laughter burst from everyone in the kitchen.

When Inez's laugh was cut short by her uneven breathing, Gabriel found a glass and filled it with water. He set it in front of her, far enough away that Heidi couldn't grab it.

"Danki," she said in a raspy whisper. She flashed a loving smile toward her *kins-kind*. "You don't want to ask Leanna to help mix up the formula."

"Why not?"

"What my *grossmammi* is saying," Leanna interjected with a wry glance at Inez, "is that I don't cook."

He was shocked. He'd never met a plain woman who made such a claim. Most Amish families considered the kitchen the center of family life, and the women wanted to fill it—and those who entered it—with delicious food.

"Not at all?" he asked.

"Not much. Despite what the rest of the family thinks, I can cook a few things. My sisters have always enjoyed cooking, so while they've made our meals I've handled other chores around the house. However…" She flashed a jesting frown at her sisters and brother. "I can read a recipe."

More laughter swirled around the kitchen before her younger sister and brother left to get ready for school. Footsteps pounded up the stairs at the same time the first-floor bathroom's door closed.

Despite their teasing, when Leanna took the recipe and began to prepare the formula, she seemed far more competent than he was. He wondered if he was supposed to help her or if he should offer to take over for Inez and Annie, who were feeding the twins small bites of oatmeal from a bowl set between them. He halted himself before he warned them about the *bopplin* eating cows' *milch*. They knew that.

Leanna put water in a pot and reached for the box of gelatin. She spooned out two small spoonfuls.

"No," he said. "That's not enough."

"What?" She pointed to the recipe. "It's the right amount. This says two teaspoons."

He stared at the piece of paper. "Teaspoons? I thought it said tablespoons."

"No wonder the formula is so thick. You put in three times too much gelatin."

"That would do it, ain't so?" Shaking his head, he wondered what other mistakes he'd made when he was too tired to think straight.

Inez pushed herself to her feet. Keeping her hands on the table to hold herself steady, she said, "You're a busy man, Gabriel." He wanted to hug her for comprehending what he couldn't bring himself to say. "If you want, I can make up the formula and send it with Leanna each day."

He looked at Leanna. For a moment, he thought she was going to protest, but she was silent, not wanting to gainsay her *grossmammi*. Leanna always had been careful of what she said, thinking before she spoke. Another thing that hadn't changed, which pleased him. He'd respected her for not reacting to everything said or done around her, as others did.

But someone had to this time.

"That's not necessary, Inez," he said. "I can stop by and get it."

"Nonsense! She drives right past your house on her way to work."

"Where do you work?"

"I do housecleaning for several *Englisch* families in Salem," Leanna replied. "I'll be able to drop off the formula every day, except Sunday, as long as I can have access to your refrigerator."

"I'll make sure whoever I get to watch the *bopplin* knows you're coming by."

"Watching the *bopplin*?"

"You didn't think Michael and I are taking them to work with us, did you?"

When Leanna looked at him with hurt in her eyes, he knew he should have been more like her and thought before he blurted out. Rather than question her, he should have been grateful that she'd agreed when her *grossmammi* had volunteered her. Not having to go to the Waglers' farm every morning would allow him to spend a few extra minutes with the twins.

"Who's doing that?" *Grossmammi* Inez asked.

"I'm not sure," he had to admit. "Do you know someone who would be *gut* with them? I'd heard about a couple of people, but they can't help now."

"Let me think and ask around."

"Danki." He prayed Inez would find someone, be-

cause he wasn't sure what he was going to do when Monday rolled around and he had to be at work in West Rupert.

The door was barely closed behind Gabriel and Kenny, who'd offered to carry one of the *bopplin* out to the buggy, when *Grossmammi* Inez sighed and said, "That poor man needs help. Someone must step up."

"I will," Juanita said as she reached for her bonnet so she and Kenny could head to school once he returned from helping Gabriel.

"You've got to graduate first." Leanna put her arm around her sister's shoulders.

"I will be soon!"

"I know. It's *gut* of you to offer, but he needs help now."

"True, but who's going to help him?" her younger sister cried out in frustration.

"I will."

Leanna clamped her hands over her mouth as everyone in the room turned to stare at her. She'd never said anything about her attraction to Gabriel to her family, because that was a topic never discussed until a wedding was announced. Still, everyone in her family had to have been aware of how she wanted to be with Gabriel. Nobody could have missed how she'd deflated when tidings of Gabriel's plans to marry Freda were announced.

"You?" Annie asked, wiping her hands on her apron. "Are you sure about this, Leanna?"

"He needs help. Those *kinder* have to have someone to watch over them. I can do that." *I may even be able to find a way to forgive him.* Pretending she didn't care about him and was interested in marrying someone else hadn't worked to end the disquiet in her soul. Maybe letting go of her anger would ease the blight burning inside her and eroding her happiness.

"What about your cleaning jobs?" Kenny asked as he walked in and picked up his plastic lunch container.

"What about your goats?" Juanita grabbed her own lunch box.

"What about *you*?" Annie grasped Leanna by the shoulders. "Are you going to get more involved with Gabriel and his family?"

"Enough!" *Grossmammi* Inez tapped her cane against the floor. "God guided Gabriel to Harmony Creek. It must have been because He knew there would be people here to assist Gabriel with his twins. We can't step aside when God gives the opportunity to be His servants in helping our neighbors."

Leanna flushed. "I didn't offer because—"

"Why you offered matters less than that you did offer, Leanna. Fixing the details can wait. Get Gabriel in here so we can talk about it with him." She waved a wrinkled hand toward the door. "Hurry! I hear his buggy leaving."

Leanna obeyed, though every cell in her body protested chasing after Gabriel's buggy. As she ran out of the house, she wondered if someone falling off a building felt like she did. She couldn't fight the idea she was rushing headlong into her doom, but how could she do nothing when those adorable *bopplin* needed someone to watch them?

She doubted she would have caught up enough for him to hear her shouts over the clatter of the wheels on the stones if their puppy, Penny, hadn't raced past her, barking.

When Gabriel slowed the buggy so he didn't hit the

dog, Leanna shouted. He drew in the horse. As the buggy rolled to a stop, she ran to the driver's side.

"Is something wrong?" he asked. "Is it your *gross-mammi*?"

"She's fine." She panted between each word. "She sent me to ask you to come back."

"Why?"

"Let's talk in the kitchen."

Her younger brother and sister nudged each other and grinned as they walked past the buggy. They thought she'd stepped up to help because she had a crush on Gabriel. Would they understand if she explained she saw this as a way to get him out of her heart?

Leanna hoped Gabriel hadn't noticed her siblings' silliness. He motioned for her to step out of the way so he could turn the buggy toward the house.

Minutes later, she was holding Harley in the kitchen while Annie kept Heidi entertained with a game of peek-aboo. Gabriel stood by the table and looked from her *grossmammi* to her, perplexed.

When *Grossmammi* Inez motioned, Leanna said, "Gabriel, we know you need help with your *kinder*. We've come up a solution we hope will work for you. Juanita wants to help once school is out."

"When's that?"

"A little over two weeks. Until then," she said quickly before *gut* sense halted her, "I'm willing to step in. I can milk my goats before I go to your house, and I can find someone to take over my cleaning jobs."

"The rest of us will pitch in," Annie said, not pausing in her game with Heidi. "So do you want Leanna's help now and Juanita's later?"

"I do," he replied, his voice thick with relief.

Leanna blinked back abrupt tears when she heard Gabriel speak the words she had longed to hear him say, though not standing in her family's kitchen with his two *kinder*. She had to forget that absurd fantasy of having a happily-ever-after with him if she wanted to make this temporary situation work. She wasn't sure how she was going to let that dream go, but she must.

Chapter Four

Four hours of sleep…

He would have settled for three.

In a row.

Gabriel stared at the blackened pan and wondered how he could have fallen half-asleep standing by the stove. The four eggs he'd been frying looked as if they'd been dunked in soot. Smoke hung in the air, though he'd opened the kitchen window over the sink. Beneath heavy eyelids, he considered the stacks of dishes waiting to be washed. Maybe the smoke couldn't find its way past them.

Now there was another to add to the ones he needed to scour. He should have known better than to offer to make breakfast when he couldn't string two thoughts together.

Freda would have been horrified by the state of the kitchen. His late wife had jested over and over she wanted a house where a speck of dust wouldn't feel at home. After she'd died, Gabriel had wondered if she'd been joking. She had insisted on everything being in its place. A single glass askew in a cupboard had bothered her so much she couldn't eat before straightening it. The slightest disruption in her day sent her into a dark mood he couldn't draw her out of until she was ready to emerge.

When he and Michael had first gone to live with Freda's family after their own parents died, Freda Girod had been a happy little girl. Like her daughter, Heidi, she'd always found fun in every experience.

The Girod family had lived on the neighboring farm, so it had been a simple transition for the Miller twins to move next door. When the Miller farm was sold, the community had assumed the money would be used to raise the eight-year-olds. Instead, Aden Girod, Freda's *daed*, had put the funds into the bank and brought up the two boys along with his daughter, who was four years younger.

The money, which Aden had called their inheritance, was to be put toward buying a farm for the twins to share. He'd refused to let either Gabriel or Michael use it to help offset his medical bills piling up on the small table in the kitchen. The cancer treatments would be covered by the community, and Aden wanted "his boys," as he'd always called them, to have a *gut* start in life with a farm of their own.

Then, one night, Aden had asked Gabriel to take a walk with him along the line of trees separating the Girod farm from the one where the Miller twins had been born. He had something he wanted to discuss with Gabriel. Jumping at the chance to talk alone with the man he considered his *daed*, Gabriel had decided it would be the perfect time to tell Aden about his hopes of marrying Leanna Wagler.

He never had the chance.

Aden had opened the conversation by saying if Gabriel married his daughter, the Girod farm would be his when Aden died from his cancer, as his *doktors* feared would happen within the year. The inheritance money from the twins' parents could then be Michael's, and perhaps he could find a nearby farm so the brothers could raise their *kinder* together.

When Gabriel asked why Aden was making such an extraordinary offer when he had a daughter to inherit his farm, he'd answered, "Because I want my *kins-kinder* to grow up on a family farm as my daughter did. There's not much time left to make sure that happens."

"The *doktors* have been wrong before," Gabriel had begun.

"I'm not talking about my cancer. I'm talking about Freda's situation." His voice had dropped to a whisper. "I know I should have been stricter with her when her *rumspringa* friends started spending time with *Englisch* boys."

Gabriel had almost asked when that had begun but didn't, ashamed to admit he'd been so caught up with his courtship of Leanna he hadn't been paying much attention to anything else. "You're a *gut daed*, Aden," was all he'd been able to find to say, eager to finish discussing Aden's daughter and move the conversation to discussing asking Leanna to marry him.

"If I'd been a better *daed*, maybe Freda wouldn't be pregnant."

"Pregnant?" That had stopped Gabriel in his tracks.

"The *Englischer* who she says is the *daed* has refused to marry her." He turned to face Gabriel. "How can I accept God's will that I soon will depart from this world when I have to leave my daughter in such a predicament on her own?"

"I'm so sorry." Then he'd spoken the words that shattered his dreams. "If there's anything I can do to help, ask."

"I'm glad you feel that way. Will you marry Freda and give her *kind* a name?"

The earth seemed to sway in every direction as Gabriel had stared at the old man's face. Seeing the last remnants of hope there, Gabriel hadn't been able to ask why Aden hadn't talked to Michael instead of him. Maybe Aden had. No, he'd corrected himself. Aden understood the Miller boys well, and he'd known Michael wasn't interested in farming.

Gabriel had found what he wanted, too: a life with Leanna.

But everyone said Aden Girod hadn't hesitated to take in two orphans when he'd buried his own wife a few years before. How could Gabriel say no to what might be a dying man's final request?

Nobody had seemed surprised when Gabriel and Freda's wedding plans were published at the next church Sunday. If there were whispers about how they were married outside of the usual wedding season in the late fall, he'd never heard them. That they remained at the Girod house instead of traveling to visit friends was accepted, too, because Aden's condition didn't improve, and he would need their help more than ever.

Leanna had vanished out of his life. The letter he'd written to her to explain why he'd done what he had— though he'd never mentioned Freda being pregnant because Aden had asked him never to tell anyone, not even his twin brother— hadn't brought any response. Had it been delivered? Should he have sent another?

He hadn't had a chance to decide because Aden had

taken a turn for the worse, and Freda's morning sickness hadn't abated. He'd thought about talking to his brother about his concerns, but hadn't because Michael would urge him to pray to God for strength. Faith seemed so simple to his twin. To be honest, it had seemed simple to Gabriel, too, before his whole life started spiraling downward after the *bopplin* were born. Freda had become withdrawn, and he'd assumed it was because she was exhausted from giving birth and having to take care of the twins only weeks after her *daed* had succumbed to the cancer he'd been fighting for five years.

Gabriel had offered to get a *boppli* nurse to assist Freda, but she'd refused, saying she didn't want anyone coming into her house and changing things. His insistence the girl would do as Freda requested hadn't changed his wife's mind. When she had burst into tears the third time he made the suggestion, he gave up, fearing he was causing her more distress with his persistence.

That had been his first mistake, but he believed his second had been his assumption God was going to help Freda. Instead, she'd died, and Gabriel had been left with two tiny *bopplin* and a wagonload of guilt. One thing Aden hadn't ever spoken of, because it didn't need to be said, was his deep wish his *kins-kinder* be raised with two loving parents as neither Freda nor Gabriel and his brother had.

When Michael had suggested they move to the new settlement where they could leave the grief behind them, Gabriel had agreed. Anything to get away from the familiar sights that were tainted by sorrow.

Now…

A quiet knock came from the back door, jerking Gabriel out of the vicious circle of his memories. He looked up to see Leanna waiting on the other side. A quick glance at the clock over the stove told him she was right on time as usual. He'd wasted too much time reliving the past when he should be focused on the future for his family.

Leaving the blackened pan on the stove and picking up Heidi before she could crawl out of sight under the table, he was glad that while he was lost in his thoughts she hadn't decided to go into the front room again and try to lift herself up on the stack of unpacked boxes. If they fell on top of her, she could be hurt, but there was no way to explain the danger to a young *kind*. He saw Harley was right where Gabriel had put him before starting what was supposed to be breakfast. At least one of the twins was a content *boppli*.

He hoped no signs of his recent thoughts were visible when he opened the door. As he did, smoke whirled in a crazy dance through the kitchen. He couldn't help seeing how Leanna grimaced as the stench of burnt food struck her. He wanted to assure her the place didn't always look and smell so bad, but he didn't have the energy.

He said, "*Komm* in."

Waving away wisps of smoke trying to exit around her, Leanna entered. She set down a basket holding formula bottles before she lifted off her black bonnet. Her crisp white *kapp* popped into its heart shape, which accented her pretty face. In her neatly pressed pale pink dress and black apron, she seemed out of the place in the chaos. He thought he remembered seeing the ironing board in one of the unused bedrooms upstairs, but it was useless without an iron. Did he have any idea which box it might be in?

She looked well rested, too. Like his brother and the

bopplin, who somehow had figured out how to make short spurts of sleep work. He had to be happy the only mirror in the house was the tiny one over the bathroom sink he and Michael used when they shaved. Michael complained about its size, but, for Gabriel, who only had to shave his upper lip and cheeks, it was fine. He wouldn't have wanted to see his sleep-deprivation next to Leanna's neat appearance this morning.

Had he'd remembered to shave this morning? He ran his fingertips over the stubble on his left cheek. No, he'd forgotten again. Unlike men with darker hair, his russet beard was uneven and resembled an unshorn sheep losing its winter fleece. And combing his hair? He'd forgotten that, too, which meant clumps stood up as if he'd tried to catch a bolt of lightning.

"Gute mariye," Leanna said with a smile for Heidi, who returned it with a giggle. "You look ready for trouble this morning."

"She is." Gabriel was relieved Leanna acted as if she hadn't been surprised to discover him looking unready for the day. He could play along, too, though he hated the idea they were pretending instead of living their lives honestly. "Harley is a *gut boppli*, happy to play where he's put. Heidi is our explorer. I've had to keep a close eye on her to make sure she stays away from unpacked boxes."

"Maybe she wants to help." Leanna smiled, but her expression froze when he didn't return it. Walking past him, she went to the refrigerator. She opened it and put the bottles of formula inside. She glanced at the stove and the pan where he'd burned breakfast.

He wanted to kick himself. Would it have hurt him to give her a smile? Maybe, because it could have opened him up to feelings he shouldn't have for her any longer. Those feelings were another secret he couldn't share. How many more secrets could he keep before he burst wide open and revealed the web of half-truths he'd created?

"Where's your brother?" Leanna asked, breaking the silence.

"He went into Salem to check on our order at the hardware store. We need to make sure it's delivered on…" His words faded into a yawn. When she looked over her shoulder, he apologized.

"There's no reason to say that," she said so quickly he had to wonder if she was talking about his yawn or their combined pasts. "You've got every reason to be tired. You've just moved in, and you have two *bopplin* to take care of. I don't think anyone will be running to the bishop with complaints about you yawning in the middle of a sentence."

"Or having a house that looks as if a tornado came through?"

"Last I knew, dirty dishes in the sink aren't a sin." Again she smiled.

Again he didn't.

Walking toward him, she stopped more than an arm's length away. "Why don't you go and take a nap?"

"At this hour of the morning?"

She shrugged as she took Heidi from him. "I've never heard there's a particular time for a nap. You're asleep on your feet."

"If I'm asleep, then why do I feel so tired?" He didn't try to halt another yawn.

"Maybe because you're on your feet. Go on, and get

an hour or so of sleep. I'll keep the *kinder* as quiet as possible."

"I could sleep through an explosion."

"Go!" She motioned with her free hand. "Get some sleep."

He nodded, took a single step toward the front room and the stairs, then asked, "So having you here today isn't a dream?"

He wanted to retract the words he'd meant to be a weak jest, but it was too late. The faint pink in Leanna's cheeks vanished as she whirled to pick up the scorched pan and put it on top of the other dishes in the sink. Muttering a *"danki"* under his breath, he strode out the door, letting the rusty screen slam in his wake.

How could he have spoken so foolishly? He couldn't blame it on his lack of sleep, because he'd guarded his words before. Maybe the sight of Leanna in his new home had torn down the walls he'd built around his battered heart the night he'd agree to marry Freda. Had seeing Leanna in his kitchen been enough to evoke the dreams he'd decimated when he stood before the *Leit* and vowed to be Freda's husband?

If so, he had to make sure it didn't happen again. He'd hurt her too much to risk doing so again. He must keep the boundaries in place between them.

Always.

Leanna flinched at the sound of a door closing upstairs a few minutes later. Gabriel must have come back in the front door so he could avoid her. Offering to help him until Juanita graduated from school had been a mistake.

A big mistake.

She had to find someone else to take her place. She shouldn't be here, because being around Gabriel brought too many futile hopes to life. He'd made his choice, and she had to accept that.

Her working at his house wasn't about her and about Gabriel. If it had been, she never would have volunteered to help him. The *bopplin* needed her to be there to feed them and change them and play with them.

And you need them.

The thought should have startled her, but it didn't. How often had she imagined having a family of her own? More than once, she'd thought about how much fun it would be to have twins so she could watch them grow up and grow close to each other as she and Annie had.

Harley and Heidi wouldn't be hers, but she could spend time with them in the years to come because they'd be part of the small community along Harmony Creek.

"How about something to eat?" she asked the little girl she held.

Heidi answered with nonsense sounds and grinned, dancing in Leanna's arms.

Seeing two high chairs set beside boxes waiting for someone to open them, she set the *boppli* on the blanket beside her brother. Leanna had moved one chair before she noticed Heidi crawling at a remarkable speed and intent toward the front room. Scooping up the *kind*, she put her in the high chair.

"You're a cute little monkey looking for trouble, ain't so?" Leanna made a silly face at the tiny girl.

"Be careful," replied a voice even deeper than Gabriel's. "Your face might freeze that way, and it'd be a shame."

Her eyes widened when she saw a dark-haired man

standing in the doorway. He was taller than Gabriel, and his prominent nose would have dwarfed a face with gentler planes. Hints of red glistened in his hair when sunlight rippled across it.

"Gute mariye?" She hadn't intended to make the greeting a question, but she wasn't sure who the man was.

As if she'd asked that question, he said, "You must be Leanna. I'm Michael, the smarter twin."

Leanna smiled in spite of herself. She'd never met Gabriel's twin, and she was surprised how different the two men looked. Not just their coloring, but how Michael smiled easily while Gabriel remained somber even when she made a joke.

Gabriel used to laugh and smile. A lot. In fact, it had been his grin that first caught her eye during a Sunday evening gathering. He'd been on the opposite side of the barn, but when the enticing rumble of his laugh caught her ear, she had turned toward him. Her eyes had been captured by his dark brown ones, and a sensation she'd never known rushed through her like a rising wind before a thunderstorm. It was filled with warmth and anticipation and a hint of possible danger.

At the time, she'd been delighted by the instant connection between them. That had been before she'd come to understand the hint of danger was real and aimed at her heart.

"It's nice to meet you," she replied when Michael got the other high chair.

She set Harley in it and bent to tie a bib around the *boppli*'s neck.

"I hear you're a twin, too," Michael said as he leaned a shoulder against a cabinet.

"Ja."

"Are you the older or younger twin?"

"I'm sure I knew at one time or another. There are only five minutes between when we were born, so it doesn't matter."

Michael chuckled. "I guess twin girls aren't as competitive as male twins are. Gabriel never has let me forget he's almost an hour older than me. Of course, I tell him God gave him a head start because He knew Gabriel would need it to keep up with me."

Leanna laughed. As she motioned for Michael to help himself to a cup of *kaffi* while she cooked him and the *bopplin* some breakfast, she told him Gabriel was catching a quick nap.

"Gut," Michael replied. "He's a danger to himself and to everyone else if he tries to work when he can't keep his eyes open."

"Aren't the *bopplin* sleeping through the night?"

"Don't ask me. I wouldn't hear them if they came into my room and shrieked in my ears. Once I'm asleep, I don't hear anything." He opened the refrigerator and shifted the bottles before pulling out a pitcher of cows' *milch*. Pouring some into his cup, he grinned at her. "Sometimes, it's great to be oblivious."

She handed each of the *bopplin* a hard cookie to chew on, then went to the stove to crack some eggs into a fresh pan. She listened as Michael talked about the project the two brothers would be working on, and though it was a simple job, he sounded excited about doing it, especially the interior carpentry. He made jokes that had her laughing, though she tried to keep the sound low so she didn't wake Gabriel. She set a handful of fried-egg pieces on the trays of the two high chairs. She wasn't sure if the *kinder* would eat them, but the food would keep them entertained while she worked. When she put a plate with fried eggs and toast in front of Michael before returning to the stove to get bacon, he sat and dug in with the fervor of a man who hadn't eaten in a year.

"Slow down," she cautioned.

"Why? It's delicious."

"You two must not be very *gut* cooks, because I'm not. My sisters are the skilled cooks in our house."

He tapped his plate with his fork before scooping up another piece of egg, "If your sisters are better cooks than this, point me to them. I'll propose today."

She laughed. "One is going to be married this fall, and the other is fourteen and still in school."

"I'll wait if her cooking is better than this." He gave her a wink, then reached for the strawberry jam to lather it on his toast.

Leanna walked to the stove. Gabriel's brother was charming.

As Gabriel used to be.

That thought sent a chilling wave of sorrow over her. She'd lost any chance to win Gabriel's heart, but it seemed Gabriel had lost himself since the last time she'd spoken to him in Lancaster County.

She couldn't think of anything sadder.

Chapter Five

Sitting on the floor beside Heidi and Harley, Leanna wiped first one *boppli*'s face, then the other's. She tried not to smile when they scrunched up their mouths, making it longer to get them clean. However, she'd learned to wash them quickly so they didn't have time to cry. Harley could turn on the tears within seconds, but Heidi seemed to suck in air for almost a minute before a cry of dismay or pain or anger burst out of her. The first time it had happened, it had taken all of Leanna's willpower not to laugh at the little girl's reaction to being told she couldn't crawl up the stairs.

In the two days since she'd started babysitting for Gabriel, she'd discovered Harley and Heidi were already developing personalities as divergent as hers and Annie's. Heidi was the more adventurous one. Harley could be kept content for hours playing with his fingers and toes. He didn't show any interest in exploring the floor and the stairs as his sister did. *Ja*, the *bopplin* were twins, but each of them was also his or her own person.

She gave in to her urge to grin as she thought of the many times people had assumed she and Annie were alike because they looked so similar. More than once she'd switched places with her sister at school when a distracted teacher gave them the opportunity.

Heidi flopped over to her stomach and pushed herself up to crawl again. Watching her, Leanna was amazed anew. The little girl's physical skills seemed too advanced for a six-month-old.

Grossmammi Inez's voice echoed in her mind, reminding her twins appeared younger than they were. Still, Heidi acted more advanced than she could possibly be.

Again Leanna counted on her fingers as she had several times already since she'd learned about the twins. No matter how she calculated, the twins had to be around six months old. Maybe a couple of weeks older. It seemed odd Heidi should be crawling and pulling herself up to stand.

"You're someone who can't wait, ain't so?" she asked as she picked up the *boppli* and cuddled her.

Heidi chuckled a deep belly laugh and squirmed with delight at the attention. She never acted upset when Leanna curtailed her explorations. Only when she was hungry did she lose her cheerful demeanor. Leanna had discovered that when she put the *bopplin* in their high chairs and didn't have something for Heidi to eat.

Sliding along the floor to where Heidi's brother was watching them and grinning, Leanna asked, "You're a bit more patient, ain't so? A bit."

Harley arched his back as if asking to be picked up, too, wriggling on the well-worn quilt on the floor. He already resembled his *daed* with his red hair, though his was more orange than Gabriel's.

Leanna set Heidi beside her, then bent over as she

lifted Harley's white shirt, already covered with teething biscuit crumbs. She blew on his belly, and he giggled. The sound was different from his sister's. Instead of deep and joyful, it was more high-pitched. Each laugh seemed to include a gulp at the end. If he were drawing in that much air, he could end up with a tummy ache.

Raising her head, she murmured, "We don't want that."

He held up his arms to her.

"Later," she promised as she stood. "I need to warm up some bottles for two ravenous *bopplin*. Do you know their names? I'll give you one hint. Their names start with the letter *H*. Any guesses?"

She kept up a steady patter as she got two bottles from the refrigerator and put them in a pot of hot water to warm. She made a quick peanut butter sandwich for herself. She found some potato chips, grateful again that Gabriel had told her, after her first morning's arrival, not to bring her lunch. He'd assured her he and Michael preferred different foods so she should always be able to find something she liked in the kitchen.

I have. You, her heart had wanted her to call out to him as he'd turned to leave with his brother to go to work.

She hadn't expected that her recalcitrant heart would help her understand how impossible it was to control her feelings. Had it been the same for Gabriel? Had he walked out with her, hoping something would grow between them, until his heart had demanded he heed it and marry Freda?

Giving the bottles to the *bopplin* and making sure they were settled on the quilt, Leanna ate her lunch. She hadn't finished her sandwich before Heidi chucked her empty bottle aside and pushed herself up to sit. A large burp resonated through the kitchen.

"That sounds *gut*," Leanna said as she stooped to pick up the discarded bottle. "How are you doing, Harley?"

She frowned when she noticed what appeared to be a bluish tint around his lips. She bent closer and scooped him up, holding him almost upright so he didn't drop the bottle. Examining him, she decided the light and shadows had deluded her, because his color appeared normal. She was being anxious when it was clear by how he was sucking on the bottle that he was fine.

Telling herself not to look for trouble, she cleaned up the *bopplin* and carried them upstairs. She no longer felt as ill at ease as she had the first day when she had wandered around Gabriel's house. It wasn't as if she were snooping.

Everything was scattered about, but that wasn't a surprise when the family had moved in a couple of weeks ago. Or maybe it was because the house was home to two single men and two *kinder*. She had to resist the temptation to put away the towels on a chair outside the bathroom door. Her arms were already full with the twins.

Both had to be changed, and she did that as soon as she reached their bedroom, which was big enough for two identical cribs, a changing table and a dresser. Once they were in fresh diapers and their faces clean again, she put them down for a nap.

Leanna headed downstairs. She glanced at her purse, hanging over a kitchen chair. A romance novel she was partway through was tucked inside, but as she took a single step into the kitchen any idea of reading a chapter or two while the *bopplin* slept vanished from her head.

Her sneaker stuck to something on the wood floor.

Gabriel had said her job was only watching the *kinder*, but she couldn't stomach the idea of the *bopplin* crawling on such a dirty floor. Picking up the quilt, she put it on the bench by the table. She filled a bucket with soapy water and went to work on the kitchen floor. She was pleased to see it wasn't as dirty as she'd feared, though she found several other spots where someone must have dropped something sticky.

The floors in the other downstairs rooms were worse than she'd guessed. In the bathroom, the linoleum was so worn the pattern had vanished and brown spots showed through the top layer. It might once have been white or tan. The front room and the two bedrooms being used for storage sent her to the sink several times to dump out filthy water and get fresh.

Peering into the open boxes on the top of each pile, she saw a mishmash of household items and baby clothing. She hoped neither Gabriel nor Michael would be angry with her, but she began to unpack the boxes. She found places for dishes and cooking utensils in the kitchen, and put towels and washcloths in the bathrooms. Laundry supplies found a home on the wide shelves over the wringer washer.

Her next discovery was a pile of dirty clothing tall enough to reach her waist. She went into the laundry where more unpacked boxes waited. After checking that the washer was connected to water and a drain, she tossed in enough dark clothes to fill the tub. For the next two hours, she did laundry. She was glad to find a freestanding clothesline outside the laundry room door. Her shoulders and back ached from wringing out clothing, but she smiled when the clean items were flapping in the warm breeze.

By that time, the *bopplin* were awake and making sounds from their cribs. Leanna wasn't sure if they were calling to her or talking to each other. They chirped with excitement when she walked into the small bedroom. It had been the only room, other than the kitchen, not filled with unpacked boxes.

Had Gabriel and his brother been pulling out what they needed? It appeared that way, because she couldn't see any rhyme or reason to what had been unpacked. Though the *bopplin*'s small white room with its single window had no boxes, their clothing was piled on top of an overflowing dresser. She wondered why the tiny garments and diapers hadn't been put into the closet.

She got her answer when she lifted the old-fashioned latch to open the closet door. The narrow space was jammed from floor to ceiling with more boxes. Most were marked for the *bopplin*'s room, but she saw one labeled "kitchen" near the top.

"Lots more work to do, ain't so?" she asked the twins.

Before she could add more, the *bopplin* began to cry so loudly she wanted to put her hands over her ears. What was wrong? She rushed to the cribs, checking one and then the other. Neither needed to be changed, and it was way too early for their next bottles. She picked each of them up, trying to soothe them.

Nothing she did helped. Their cries rose to shrieks. Again she checked to make sure diaper pins hadn't come loose and were poking the twins. Were they suffering from teething pain? The biscuits were downstairs.

She bent to lift Harley out of his crib, then went to pick up Heidi. Balancing them, each tiny body stiff with fury, she turned toward the door.

Gabriel burst into the room. "Are you okay?"

Was he shouting to be heard over the *bopplin*'s screeching? She stared at his wild eyes as they scanned the room. She'd never seen him so upset.

Before she could reply, he said, "*Gut*. You're okay." His breath exploded out of him in relief, and his shoulders sagged as he put a hand on the door frame. "Thank the *gut* Lord."

Leanna bounced both *bopplin* as she asked, "Are *you* okay, Gabriel?"

He started to answer, then paused. While the *bopplin* continued to howl, he looked everywhere but at his *kinder* and her. "On the day Freda died, I came in and heard the twins crying. I called to her, and she didn't answer."

"You called to me today when you heard Harley and Heidi crying?"

He nodded.

If her arms hadn't been filled with *bopplin*, she wasn't sure she could have halted them from sweeping around him as she offered him comfort. She couldn't ease the pain of losing his wife, but she could show she understood how it felt to lose someone precious. When her parents had died, she'd learned pain loitered in her heart, ready to leap out at any moment. How much worse would it be to lose the *mamm* of your *kinder*?

Her tears blurred his strong face in front of her, and she bit her lower lip to keep her sob from slipping out. The tears fell, hot as acid along her cheek.

"May I?" he asked as he stepped toward her and raised his arm.

"*Ja.*" She started to turn to hand him Heidi but froze when his fingers settled on her cheek, wiping away the tears.

The past seemed to reappear, taking them back to the night when she'd told him about how she was grateful to her *grossmammi* for sharing her small home with the orphaned Wagler siblings. She'd cried then, opening herself to him as she'd never done with anyone, and the first tendrils of love had emerged from her heart.

Leanna was pulled into the present when Michael shouted up the stairs to his brother. He needed help with some boards, and the urgency in his voice was clear.

"Go," she urged. "I've got these two."

"Leanna, I—" Gabriel choked on whatever he would have said next. Pushing off from the door, he strode away.

At the sound of his boots on the treads, she looked at the twins and forced a smile. "What am I going to do with you?"

She kept up a steady chatter of nonsense that seemed to break through the twins' distress. They calmed. She discovered they needed a diaper change and wondered if their stomachs had been bothering them. Deciding to be like the *bopplin* and forget they'd been crying a few minutes ago, she redressed them.

Yet she couldn't keep from thinking of how Gabriel's face had been shadowed by a panic she'd never thought she'd see there. Why hadn't she realized it was likely he'd been the one to discover Freda after her death? She wondered what other secrets he hid, secrets too appalling to bring into the light of day. Were those what she'd sensed? She couldn't ask, because she didn't want to risk seeing his haunted expression again.

Propping one twin on each hip, Leanna went down to the kitchen. Michael was sitting at the table, wiping a soiled kerchief against his sweaty forehead. Gabriel was about to sit as well when Leanna walked into the room. Jumping to his feet, Gabriel held out his hands toward her.

"Can I help?" he asked.

"I've got them." Squatting, she put one twin, then the other, on the quilt she'd replaced on the floor. "Much easier when they're in a *gut* mood."

"You've got to teach him how to do that," Michael said with a laugh. "That way he won't have to depend on me."

"It just takes practice." Leanna stood and smoothed her apron over her skirt. "I learned how to handle more than one *boppli* when I helped with the younger *kinder* on Sundays."

"Show me?" Gabriel asked.

"Later." She motioned for him to sit beside his brother. He'd clearly decided to act as if their previous conversation hadn't happened, so she'd do the same. "I'll get you some lemonade."

"Lemonade?" His eyes widened. "I didn't know we had any mix in the house."

"It's freshly squeezed. I brought some lemons with me this morning."

"I told you that you didn't need to bring food with you," Gabriel said.

"Stop chiding her, and be grateful." His brother grinned. "You had time to do all that laundry hanging outside, make lemonade and take care of the *bopplin*? Are you sure there aren't three or four of you?"

"No," she replied with a laugh as she bent to pick up Harley. "Just two *bopplin* who took a longer nap than usual this afternoon."

Setting the little boy in one high chair, she smiled as Gabriel put Heidi in the other high chair. She tied bibs around the *bopplin* and handed each of them a teething biscuit before Heidi could begin wailing.

"Lemonade?" she asked.

Michael held up his hands. "*Danki*, but I'll have my lemonade without something to chew on." He hooked a thumb toward the *bopplin*, who were chewing on the biscuits.

His joking reminded her of how Gabriel used to do the same when they were walking out together, though expecting him now to be amusing when he was mourning his wife would be wrong.

Leanna filled three glasses and served one to each of the men before taking a sip out of her own. They downed them and she refilled their glasses, leaving the pitcher in the middle of the table.

After finishing his third glass, Michael stood. "I'll get the rest of those boards in the wagon, Gabriel, while you have some family time."

Gabriel nodded, and she wondered how much he'd told his brother about what had happened upstairs. Another question she must not ask.

Topping off his glass and her own, Gabriel looked at the crumb-covered twins, who were jabbering as they chewed on their biscuits. "They seem to understand each other."

"My *grossmammi* said Annie and I were talking to each other long before we invited others into our conversations." She lifted one shoulder in a casual shrug though she was too aware of each motion either she or Gabriel made, as well as any sound and aroma in the room. It was as if every sense was filled with as much anticipation as the *bopplin* had while waiting for their bottles. "*Grossmammi* Inez also said she believed, as

twins, Annie and I used our own special language before we were born and just never stopped. We switched
to *Deitsch* before we went to school."

"Do you know what your sister is thinking or feeling
when she isn't nearby?"

"Sometimes." She wiped her hand on the dish towel,
then hung it up to dry. "I can do that with any of my siblings. It must come from living together and sharing so
many experiences. Do you and Michael have more than
a normal ability to do that?"

"I don't know what normal is, because he's my only
sibling, though sometimes at work each of us knows
what the other needs. People have asked if, as twins,
we can read each other's thoughts. They seem to believe that's something all twins can do. I'm grateful it's
not true for us."

He looked away, and she knew he'd come close to
saying something he hadn't intended. About Freda or
something else?

"How's the job going?" she asked, latching on to an
innocuous subject.

"All right. Michael loves carpentry work. His plan is
to focus on that while I get the farm up and running. He's
never liked milking or working in the fields."

"So why did he come here?"

"Because we're his family," he replied as if that should
explain it.

It did. Her younger siblings had been shocked at the
abrupt announcement from their older brother, Lyndon,
that they were moving to northern New York, but they
hadn't quibbled. As for Leanna, she'd been excited to
leave. She'd hoped being away from the past would help

her forget what had happened since she'd heard Gabriel was marrying someone else.

Her gaze went to where Gabriel was lifting Heidi out of her chair and onto his lap. How could she have guessed her past would follow her? God must have planned for her to discover something by planting her past right on her doorstep, but what? To forgive? She should do that, but offering forgiveness without her heart being behind it was hypocrisy. God couldn't want her to do that, could He?

Do You? She aimed the prayer heavenward along with the hope she'd get an answer before she made the wrong decision.

Finally, with Leanna's help, Gabriel learned to balance one twin on each knee. Part of it was the twins were able to sit without help, though Harley kept a cautious handful of Gabriel's shirt gripped in his fingers. The rest was because he'd grown more confident in handling the *bopplin* each day.

As he watched Leanna warm bottles for the twins, her final task before she left for the day, he admired her easy efficiency. She had asserted several times she wasn't a *gut* cook, but she appeared to know her way around a kitchen. No motion was wasted, and her shoes didn't stick to the floor as his boots had that morning.

Looking down, he was surprised to see the wood gleaming in the sunlight. She must have mopped the floor. Not only the kitchen one, but the living room floor, too, he realized. His eyes widened. The stacks of boxes were gone. Only two remained.

"I hope you don't mind I unpacked some things while the *bopplin* were napping," Leanna said.

His eyes cut to where she stood by the sink wringing her apron.

"You didn't need to do that." He wasn't sure what else he should say, then added, "I appreciate what you did. Michael will, too. *Danki.*"

"I wasn't sure where some things go, so I left them in those two boxes. I knocked down the other boxes and put them in the laundry room. I hope that's okay."

"It's fine, but I don't expect you to clean the house on top of watching the twins."

Turning to the stove to lift out one bottle and testing the heat of the formula on her wrist, she said, "I'm glad to do it. I'm not used to sitting and doing nothing in the middle of the day." She lifted the pan and switched off the burner. She took out the bottles. Handing him one, she said, "Give Harley to me." Taking the little boy, she added, "It's your turn to be fed first, ain't it?" She looked at Gabriel, smiling. "There's no reason they can't be fed at the same time when we're both here."

"How did you convince Heidi to wait?" he asked as he tilted the little girl back in his arms and offered the bottle. She clamped her mouth on the nipple and put both hands on the bottle as if afraid he was going to snatch it away. "If I don't feed her first, she starts crying at a low level, but it quickly becomes a shriek."

"I give them their bottles lying on the quilt."

"I never thought of doing that."

"They're big enough to hold their own bottles, but if I end up giving Harley his first and I don't want Heidi to be upset, I talk to her."

"Talk?"

She smiled as she sat on the bench facing him. "*Ja,*

talk. I'm finding Heidi can be distracted from what she believes is her due if she's diverted by talk or a toy."

"That has never worked for me."

"So far it has for me, but it may be because I'm some-one new and different. Once she gets accustomed to me, she may not be so willing to be diverted."

"They seem to be doing well with the goats' *milch*." He watched Heidi drinking the formula almost as fast as he had his first glass of Leanna's delicious lemonade.

"They can be weaned onto soy *milch* or almond *milch*, but they may never be able to drink cows' *milch*."

"Imagine that. A dairy farm whose *kinder* can't drink his *milch*."

"You wouldn't be the first. Or the last."

"True." He shifted the little girl in his arms, which were beginning to ache from his long hours of nailing over his head. "Your *grossmammi* mentioned you sell your soap at the farmers market in Salem."

"I did last year, and I've been planning to this year. Each day when I milk my goats, I set aside a small por-tion of the *milch* to make soap. I have almost enough for another batch, which I'll sell later in the summer. The soap I'll be selling when the farmers market opens is already made up. I need to wrap the bars, so they won't stick together when the sun's heat is on them."

"I'm surprised."

"That I make soap?"

"*Ja*, a bit. I thought you'd sell your quilts. You used to talk about quilting a lot."

She shrugged, and he wondered if he'd upset her with his comments about the past. No hint of that tainted her voice as she replied, "People coming to a farmers mar-ket are looking for small things because most of them have walked there. They don't want to tote a big quilt home. Besides, I can sell any quilted articles I make at Caleb's bakery."

"That's the one out of the main road?"

"*Ja.* He's taken some of my items on consignment. Even there, small table runners and wall hangings sell better than a full-size quilt."

"You've stopped making big quilts?"

She shook her head. "No, I recently finished one that a lady at the fire department's mud sale asked me to make for her. She'd bid on the one I donated, but didn't win it, so I agreed to make her a similar one for the cost of the materials if she'd donate the difference to the fire department."

Gabriel nodded, knowing he shouldn't be surprised. Leanna wouldn't think twice about making such an offer when it would help someone else.

He was sorry when Heidi finished her bottle, followed by Harley. Leanna rinsed them out and put them in her cloth bag to take home so she could refill them with formula.

Setting the bag on the table, she said, "I left a casserole in the oven for your supper." She paused as she reached for her bonnet. "Don't worry. I didn't cook it. Annie made two for us last night, and she asked me to bring it over here for you."

"*Danki.* I don't know what we would have done without—"

"Neighbors help neighbors," she replied primly.

Had he insulted her? Everything he said, no matter how well-intentioned, came out wrong. But it also seemed wrong not to acknowledge how the Waglers had gone beyond neighborly and had taken on the burden of looking after the Miller family. He understood no thanks were expected, but he also didn't like the idea of being indebted to them when he'd brought so much pain to Leanna and, through her, to her whole family.

There were many things he wanted to say to her, but he had to content himself with, "I wanted you to know Michael and I really appreciate your help."

"I'll pass your thanks on to Annie and *Grossmammi* Inez."

"Danki," he said again, though he wanted to ask why she wasn't accepting some of his gratitude for herself.

The answer blared into his head when the door closed behind her, leaving him alone with the twins. To acknowledge his appreciation would risk re-creating an emotional connection between them, one he'd thought would last a lifetime. She wasn't ready to take that chance again, and he shouldn't be, either.

So why had images of them walking together or riding in his courting buggy never stopped filling his mind during the day and his dreams every night?

Chapter Six

The village of West Rupert was so small it barely deserved the name. A dozen houses spread along the narrow road, a white church set next to a cemetery, a fire station and a general store with antlers mounted over the door comprised the whole village. Small farms edged the roads leading in and out of town. The fields were sloped on one side and flat along a meandering stream on the other. The road continuing to the east led over Rupert Mountain and to the ski resorts along the spine of the Green Mountains.

Gabriel balanced on the top of a ladder leaning against what he guessed had originally been a storage barn for *milch* cans. Looking past the rafters he and Michael would finish rebuilding this morning, he stared at the meandering creek. It either was the same one or connected with the creek that ran through Harmony Creek Hollow and on down into the center of Salem.

His mind went with the water toward the fields he'd be planting next year. The mountains that rose around him were so different from the rolling hills where he'd grown up in Pennsylvania. The background to his days had changed in as spectacular way as his life had. He and Michael now owned a farm, and he had a family to raise there.

And Leanna was in his home, watching over his *kinder* as if she were their *mamm*. A double pulse of regret surged through him. Freda should have been the one tending to her twins. Leanna should never have been hurt by the promise he'd made to Aden. He wasn't sure which situation he rued more.

He was grateful Leanna had gone along with his intention of ignoring what had happened when he'd panicked at the *bopplin* crying so hard and nobody answering when he called out. If she'd asked questions about the day he'd come home to learn Freda was dead, he wasn't sure if he could have withheld the whole truth.

About how Freda had given in to her depression and committed suicide. About how he had failed to notice she was suffering from more than what she'd assured him were "*boppli* blues."

How, God, did I miss the signs right in front of me? Why did You let her suffer when I could have helped if You'd opened my eyes and my heart to what she needed?

Those questions had raged through him from the moment he realized Freda wasn't asleep, that the empty pill bottles had taken her away from the *kinder* he'd believed she loved too much to abandon. He wished they could have found the love a man and wife should have, but she'd been inconsolable from the moment her *Englischer* turned from her. The *Englischer* whose photo was beside her on the bed the day she died. She'd accepted Gabriel's offer of marriage and never asked for more, because she had given her heart to another.

As you did.

He closed his eyes, wishing he could reach out to God in something other than frustration and anger.

"Hey, are you asleep up there?" called Michael from the base of the ladder.

"Waiting on you to stop wandering around and get to work." He was grateful to be able to tease his brother, letting Michael's laughter sweep away his dreary thoughts.

"I'm here. Let's get going." He hefted a board up along the side of the garage, where any hint of paint had vanished years ago.

Gabriel grabbed the top and guided it to where he could put it in place. He aimed his hammer at the nail at the end of the board. With a pair of quick swings, he drove that nail and another in to hold the two sides of a rafter together. He appraised how the final rafter aligned with the others.

"Looking straight," Michael shouted.

"It should." Gabriel descended the ladder, glad Michael kept one hand on it. "You measured it over and over before cutting the angle."

"I wanted to make sure it was right when there will be two skylights in the roof."

"Making those calculations are something we can do in our sleep."

"Maybe I can, but when's the last time you slept through the night? I heard you pacing last night. What's going on?" He gave a terse laugh and answered before Gabriel could. "It's her, ain't so? Having Leanna at the house every day has you agog."

"I wouldn't say that," he hedged.

"Then what would you say?"

Gabriel was spared from answering when the homeowner, an *Englischer* named Don Fenton who planned to turn the building into an art studio for his wife, walked toward them. Talking to Don wasn't easy because the *Englischer* knew less about carpentry than Gabriel knew about sending a man to the moon. While Gabriel explained what they were doing—and why—his brother went to the stack of lumber.

Mrs. Fenton wandered out and began asking about flower boxes on the three windows the gray-haired lady wanted on each side. Gabriel listened and made a few suggestions, though it was the first time he'd heard about flower boxes. Maybe she'd mentioned them to Michael, and his brother had forgotten to say anything. No, that wasn't likely. Michael wrote down every detail of a project in the notebook he shared each night with Gabriel. Nothing had been in there about flower boxes.

It wasn't a problem. They could use a few pieces of leftover wood to make what she was looking for.

"Are you going to bring your twins here one of these days?" Mrs. Fenton asked, startling him out of his thoughts.

"Not while work is going on." He tried to keep his voice upbeat, but the beginnings of a headache was building between his eyebrows. "Too many things here are too dangerous for little ones."

She laughed. "I understand. When my children were small, they could find trouble where there shouldn't have been any. I do hope you and your brother will bring the babies and join us when we inaugurate my new studio."

"Of course." What else could he say? A party for a storage barn getting a new roof, windows and paint? Sometimes he found *Englischers* incomprehensible.

Gabriel talked for a few minutes more with the Fentons, then returned to work. His brother had estimated it would take them a month to complete the repairs and paint the building inside and out, but they might be finished sooner than that, so he and Michael needed to look for more jobs. Whether they worked together on the project or took two separate ones, he knew the money they'd make on this job wouldn't last long.

By the time the sun was high in the sky, Gabriel was ready to eat. He washed his hands with a hose attached to the main house before joining his brother, who sat at a nearby picnic table. They bowed their heads in silent thanks before reaching for the tuna sandwiches Michael had made that morning while Gabriel was giving the twins their morning bottles.

Gabriel's first bite warned him his brother had added too much mayonnaise. He tried not to grimace, but Michael did and put the sandwich down.

"That's disgusting," his twin said. "You shouldn't let me make lunch."

"I told you I'd do it." Gabriel took a huge bite of his own sandwich, swallowing it almost whole so he didn't have to taste it.

"And when would you have had the time?"

"I could get up earlier."

Michael's frown deepened. "You're half-asleep on your feet most of the time. Maybe you need to rethink Leanna's *grossmammi*'s offer to send over food for us."

"They're doing enough for us already."

Standing, Michael grabbed a handful of pretzels and his thermos of iced tea. "We need help. You might thrive on stress and drama—"

"I despise it."

"For someone who despises drama, you sure seem to surround yourself with it."

Gabriel's fingers clenched on his sandwich. Forcing them to ease off their death grip, he scowled at the mayo oozing around his fingers. He reached for a cloth to wipe his hands before saying, "Because lots of things have happened doesn't mean I wanted any of them to happen."

His brother's face fell, and he looked stricken. "I didn't mean… I wasn't talking about Freda dying."

"I know." He kneaded his forehead where the small headache was becoming the thunder of stampeding horses.

"I was talking about Leanna Wagler."

"I know," he said, wondering why his brother was stating the obvious.

"Has she said anything?"

He gave a humorless snort. "She's said a lot."

"You know what I mean. You spent hours working on that letter you sent her, and you never got an answer. Has she explained why?"

Standing, Gabriel stuffed his unfinished sandwich into the plastic lunch box they shared. "She doesn't owe me any explanation."

"There you go again. Drama." Michael sighed. "At least it won't be forever. Her sister graduates soon. It'll be different when Juanita is watching the twins."

"You're right."

He *hoped* his brother was correct. Though Leanna wouldn't be at their house each day, she'd be next door. How was he supposed to ignore her when his heart kept reminding him of the dreams it once had harbored? Once? With a silent groan, he knew those dreams of having her as his wife and the *mamm* of his *kinder* hadn't vanished.

* * *

Leanna glanced from the road to her *grossmammi*, who sat on the passenger side of the family's gray-topped buggy. *Grossmammi* Inez was staring straight ahead. Her lips moved, but no sound emerged. Guessing the older woman was praying, Leanna added a few silent pleas of her own.

The appointment with the cardiologist, who came one day every other week to the medical offices in Salem, hadn't gone the way either of them had hoped. Leanna knew her *grossmammi* hadn't really believed her shortness of breath had anything to do with the last winter's cold, but *Grossmammi* Inez hadn't expected to hear there was a problem with her heart.

Leanna had listened to the *doktor* explain in simple terms how one of her *grossmammi*'s heart valves had become constricted, making it impossible for her heart to get enough oxygen into her blood.

Tests would confirm the *doktor*'s diagnosis, so another appointment was made to confer with the cardiologist after those were done. The office had told Leanna to check in at week's end to find out when those tests could be run, and had alerted her that *Grossmammi* Inez would need to travel to the clinic—almost thirty miles away—for the tests.

That meant contacting Hank Puente, who made his large, white van available to the plain community. The short, jovial man was retired, and Leanna guessed he enjoyed the company of his neighbors more than the small amount he charged to drive them to places too far to go in a buggy. Once she had the day and time of the appointment, she'd have her twin sister call Hank from the phone in Caleb's bakery.

That part was easy.

What wasn't was knowing something was wrong with her *grossmammi*'s heart. She'd realized *Grossmammi* Inez's gasping for breath meant something wasn't right, but right up until the moment the cardiologist started explaining his findings, Leanna had hoped it was something simple. Something that could be healed with a round of antibiotics.

More than once during the half-hour ride from the village, Leanna thought about starting a conversation to break the silence. Each time she'd halted herself.

She sighed with relief when she drove into the Waglers' dooryard and stopped the buggy. Jumping out, she considered walking around it to help her *grossmammi*. Again she stopped herself. *Grossmammi* Inez had refused her assistance to get into the buggy at the *doktor*'s office, announcing loudly enough for everyone on the street to hear that she wasn't an invalid.

Leanna delayed unhitching the horse and walked with the older woman toward the house. When *Grossmammi* Inez held on to the railing along the steps, Leanna's breath caught in her throat. The motion warned her *grossmammi* might be suffering more than Leanna had guessed.

Inside the house, her siblings, including Lyndon with his family, were waiting. School was out, and it was, Leanna was shocked to realize, long past time for supper. The appointment had been late in the day, and she and *Grossmammi* Inez had sat in the waiting room for over an hour waiting to see the cardiologist.

The receptionist had suggested Leanna take an appointment early in the morning, but Leanna had made today's so she could work her regular hours at the Millers' house. Gabriel had been pleased he wouldn't miss much time at work. She wondered what he'd say when she told him she'd need time to take her *grossmammi* for testing.

A pang cut through her when she realized that by the time the testing was scheduled, she might no longer be watching the Miller twins. Juanita would have taken over the job by then, and Leanna would return to cleaning houses. All too soon she wouldn't be spending each day with those adorable *bopplin*.

Until supper was on the table and silent grace had given them time to thank God for the food and family with them, nobody asked a single question about the visit with the cardiologist. The pot of Annie's delicious beef stew and platters of buttermilk biscuits were passed around, and still nobody spoke.

Leanna's eyes were caught by her twin's, and she saw her dismay reflected in Annie's blue eyes. She mouthed the word *later* before taking a bite of stew. She chewed and chewed, but found it impossible to swallow. She noticed the only one eating was her *grossmammi*. Even Lyndon's young *kinder* seemed too antsy to do more than nibble at their biscuits, getting more crumbs down the front of them than into their mouths.

Grossmammi Inez glanced around the table. "You might as well spit out what you've got to say. Maybe then you can eat your supper."

Questions came from around the table. Leanna listened while their *grossmammi* answered with a reassuring smile. When the elderly woman paused between every word to gasp for breath, her family's worried expressions deepened.

"Don't look so upset," *Grossmammi* Inez said with an uneven laugh. "Remember the *doktor* said I might be able to take pills to help me." She didn't look in Leanna's direction. "Let's get that peach pie Annie brought from the bakery. Juanita, glasses of *milch* all around would be *wunderbaar.*"

While her twin went to slice the pie, Leanna followed. She whispered a quick overview of what their *gross-mammi* had omitted from what the cardiologist had said. Leanna saw more questions in her sister's eyes. Those would have to wait until after *Grossmammi* Inez went to bed.

They ate their dessert, which Leanna assumed was delicious because everything from the bakery was, whether Annie or Caleb made it. Tonight, the pie was tasteless. That Kenny didn't ask for seconds showed he was pretending as much as she was that everything was normal. Her younger brother loved peach pie and always had a second—and sometimes a third—slice.

Instead of lingering over their meal to chat about their day, everyone was up as soon as they'd finished. *Grossmammi* Inez excused herself and headed to bed, exhausted from the day. Lyndon herded his family out, and the kitchen grew silent.

Ten minutes later, draping the damp dish towel over the last of the dishes set in the drainer, Leanna joined her siblings in the front room. She sat next to Kenny on the light brown couch. That allowed her to face Annie who was rocking by the unlit woodstove. Juanita perched on the edge of a footstool in front of the chair where *Grossmammi* Inez used to sit and read the Bible aloud to them. The older woman had stopped when talking became too difficult.

"Tell us," Annie said.

"The *doktor* acted as if this condition wasn't anything

unusual for a woman her age," Leanna said, taking care not to use her *grossmammi*'s name. She doubted their lowered voices would wake *Grossmammi* Inez, but she didn't want to take any chances.

"So it's possible taking pills could solve the problem?" asked Kenny, looking younger than his twelve years.

Leanna put her arm around his quaking shoulders. He was struggling not to cry. Sometimes, because he matched their older brother step for step working on the farm, she forgot he was still a *kind*.

"We have to wait and see what the tests reveal," she said, giving him a squeeze. "While we wait, we need to pray for God to guide the *doktors* so they can help *Grossmammi* Inez."

When her siblings rose to seek their own beds, because they'd be up with the sun in the morning, Leanna didn't follow them toward the stairs.

"I'll be up in a minute," she said. "I want to make sure the goats don't get out. There have been sightings of coyotes around the area, and the kids could be vulnerable."

Annie gave her a taut smile. "Sleep well."

"I'll try. You, too."

By the time Leanna had checked her goats and returned to the house, she was too restless to sleep. She poured herself a glass of water and walked onto the front porch. As she sat on a rocker that had little of its original green paint, the mountains to the west were backlit by a flicker of lightning. The dull rumble of distant thunder faded away. Overhead stars glittered, but clouds gobbled up a few as she watched.

"Leanna?" came a voice from the darkness closer to the ground.

She gave a soft cry as she almost jumped out of the chair.

Gabriel stepped into the dim light shining from the living room. "I'm sorry. I didn't mean to startle you. I figured you'd heard me coming up the walk."

"I was watching the storm. Lost in thought." Her voice sounded as breathless in her ears as *Grossmammi* Inez's did.

"I wanted to find out how Inez's appointment went."

She knew she should invite him to come up on the porch and sit, but the words wouldn't form. Then she told herself she was silly. What had happened had happened, and she couldn't change it. She motioned for him to take the chair beside hers.

When he had, she stared again at the sky. It was easier than looking at him. If she saw sorrow on his face, she might lose her grip on her emotions. She didn't want to break down in front of him.

"The appointment went as well as can be expected," she said after explaining what the *doktor* suspected was wrong. "They want to run a few tests to confirm the diagnosis, and then they'll decide what to do."

"When are they doing the tests?"

"Soon. I'm supposed to check in at week's end to find out when they've scheduled her to come in."

He frowned. "They don't seem to be in any hurry."

"I know, but I have to accept they know what they're doing. They deal with patients all day long."

"But this patient is your *grossmammi*." A gentle compassion eased into his voice.

"Ja." She wrapped her arms around herself. To ward off the cold the thought of surgery sent through her? Or to halt the warmth surging forth at his heartfelt words?

She didn't want to delve too deeply. "And I can't help worrying the process is going on too long. On the other hand, if there's a way she can avoid surgery, the delay will be worth it. The *doktor* said some people can be treated by taking a pill. It depends on what the tests show. We have to trust in God's plan."

He gave a rude snort, shocking her as much as his arrival had. "God's plan?"

"You don't believe God has a plan for each of us?"

"Oh, I'm sure He has a plan." His voice hardened. "I'm also sure it doesn't have anything to do with what we want or need."

Leanna bit her lower lip as she heard the pain he couldn't conceal. Not so long ago, he'd buried his wife and her *daed*, a man who'd raised Gabriel and his twin as if they were his own sons. He'd been left to raise his *kinder* without a *mamm*, something he'd experienced himself so he knew about the void that would leave in the *bopplin*'s hearts.

Sympathy for him and his family threatened to overwhelm her. She didn't want to dim what happiness he had left.

A smile tilted her lips. She had just the way!

"I have something to show you." She stood. "Wait here."

"What have you got to show me?"

She smiled. "I've always heard patience is a virtue."

"I've heard that, too." He cocked an eyebrow at her. "I'm not sure I believe it, because satisfying my curiosity is always a blessing."

Leanna almost gasped. Had Gabriel made a jest? If so, it was the first time she'd heard him do so since the last time they'd walked out together. Maybe he hadn't changed as much as she'd believed.

Alarms sounded through her head. If he hadn't changed into the dour man he'd acted, then the danger to her heart was greater than she'd guessed. She'd fallen in love with the amusing man he'd been in Lancaster County.

So had Freda Girod.

She rushed into the house before her face revealed what she was thinking. A moment later, she wheeled a small red wagon onto the porch. "I thought you could use this to pull the *kinder* around in. That way, you don't have to try to carry both by yourself if nobody else can help you."

"They're young to ride in a wagon," he said as he came to his feet. Surprise widened his eyes when he looked from the wagon to her.

"That's why I had Lyndon put these wooden insets on each side." She ran her fingers along the panels that were about six inches high and encircled the wagon.

He knelt to examine them. "I've seen wagons like this before. I always wondered what the slits were in the sides."

"The boards will keep Harley and Heidi from tumbling out."

"And Heidi from climbing out."

She shook her head. "I'm not so sure about that. I'm beginning to think your little girl is planning to be a mountain climber when she grows up. If she waits that long."

"This is remarkable, Leanna." He stood, and for a second she thought he was going to smile.

It must have been a trick of the poor light. Telling

herself she should be grateful he hadn't smiled, because she was unsure she could resist that, she replied, "I remembered we had a little wagon for Kenny when he was a *boppli*. I found this one at the thrift store by the old courthouse and cleaned it. I think it'll make it easier for them to go for an outing."

"You never said anything about it."

"I wasn't sure when Lyndon would be able to get around to building the panels."

He arched an eyebrow at her. "My brother is a carpenter. Remember?"

"I know, but it might not have been a surprise if I'd asked him."

"Michael is pretty *gut* at keeping secrets."

For a moment, she was tempted to ask if Michael was as skilled at hiding things as Gabriel was. She didn't say anything because that would ruin the simple happiness of being able to present him with this gift from the whole Wagler family.

"Well," she said, "now he can be surprised, too."

"I'm overwhelmed." He put his fingers on her arm. "*Danki*. The *bopplin* will love it, I'm sure."

"*Gut*." She edged away so the buzz emanating from the spot where his skin touched hers eased and allowed her to think. "And *danki* for stopping by. I'll let *Grossmammi* Inez know you called."

He stared at her for so long she wondered if he'd turned into a statue. He started to speak once, then a second time. Finally he said, as he picked up the wagon, "*Gut nacht*, Leanna. *Danki* again."

"*Gut nacht,*" she replied, resting her hand on the porch support as she watched him walk down the steps and disappear into the darkness.

Thunder rolled, much nearer than it had been before. She was astonished she hadn't noticed how the storm was approaching. Lost in the wonder of Gabriel's touch, chaste though it'd been, had made her unaware of everything else. What would have happened if she hadn't stepped aside when he'd brushed his fingertips on her arm? If she'd, instead, moved closer?

She let her head loll against the porch column as lightning sewed a brilliant seam between the clouds. She had done the right thing to protect her heart from being hammered again, so why did she feel so lousy?

Chapter Seven

Sunday dawned with the promise of a lovely day to come. The sunrise painted the eastern sky with astounding colors that couldn't be found in a box of crayons. Spring kept the air a bit crisp and lighter than it would be when the middle of summer battered them with heat and humidity.

Leanna finished pinning up her hair and set her *kapp* in place before going to stand by the single window in her bedroom. Looking down at her goats, who were gathered near the gate as they waited for her to come to feed, water and milk them, she smiled. She was glad the services in Harmony Creek Hollow were close to their house so the family could stay to enjoy the company of the other members of the *Leit* before evening chores.

The Sabbath was set aside as a day of rest except for tending to their animals. No cooking or baking or housework allowed. Only the necessary tasks of taking care of those who couldn't take care of themselves. Leanna wrapped her arms around herself as she thought of how they'd be allowed to nurse *Grossmammi* Inez on a Sunday. No, she didn't want to think of a time when her *grossmammi* couldn't manage simple tasks on her own.

Nobody else was downstairs when she returned from milking her goats. She'd heard voices from the main barn, so she knew Lyndon and Kenny were milking. What a blessing it was her younger brother could do everything he had before that accident during the winter! He'd healed but not fast enough for an impatient boy who'd been hit by a skidding car while he was skiing behind a fast-moving buggy along a snowy road. She hoped he'd be less of a risk-taker the next time he and his friends got such a ridiculous idea in their heads.

Leanna put the fresh *milch* in the refrigerator on the far right side. That would keep it separated from the *milch* Kenny brought from the cow barn. She had to shift a few of the *bopplin*'s bottles to find room for her metal *milch* container. Yesterday *Grossmammi* Inez had made a double batch of formula for the Miller twins, so they didn't have to prepare any today. Later she would put the leftover *milch* into the freezer. It should give her enough to make up a batch of soap for the farmers market.

Ignoring the dread bubbling up in her as she thought about having to talk to strangers who were interested in her soap, she focused instead on filling cups with the *kaffi* Annie had prepared. Her *grossmammi* and her siblings drank as if they'd crawled across a desert. Biscuits left from last night's supper were topped with different types of butter, including apple and peanut.

Church was being held at the Bowmans' farm, which was closer to the main road that ran from Salem to the Vermont state line. *Grossmammi* Magdalena, who oversaw the Bowman household, had held a work frolic earlier in the week to make sure everything was ready for the service and the *Leit*. As it'd been held during the Miller *bopplin*'s nap time, Leanna hadn't taken part. However, she knew the Bowman farm well because they'd held services there a couple of times already. The number of households in Harmony Creek Hollow was small, so each family hosted church more often than in bigger districts. No one minded, because it was an honor to provide space for the *Leit* to worship together.

Though the house was a short distance away, Leanna and Annie insisted on taking the buggy. It was too far for *Grossmammi* Inez to walk. Lyndon's younger *kinder* rode with them, excited to have a chance to spend time with their beloved great-*grossmammi*. The rest would walk.

The Bowmans' house was the smallest one in Harmony Creek Hollow, so the service would be held in a barn. The double doors had been thrown open wide, and the sun shone in to banish the shadows to the deepest corners. Benches had been put in place, two sets so the men could face the women during the service. Tarps beneath them would protect clothing from grit left by years of driving farm vehicles in and out.

Grossmammi Inez went to join the other older women who had gathered in the shade of a pair of huge maple trees. Annie and Leanna watched while their brother's *kinder* skipped across the grass to join their *mamm*. When Annie said she'd be right back, Leanna wasn't surprised she walked at a much more sedate pace toward where Caleb Hartz was getting out of his buggy. Nobody would be surprised when the two published their plans to marry in the fall.

Turning to join the other women, Leanna couldn't keep her eyes from focusing on Gabriel, who held the handle of the wagon she'd given him. His bright red hair was hidden beneath the black church hat that matched the *mutze* coat and trousers he wore. Her breath caught against her pounding heart when she noticed how broad his shoulders appeared.

He looked in her direction, and their gazes collided. It was almost a physical impact, and she was surprised she wasn't rocked back on her heels. Her breath stuck over her heart, which seemed to be trying to break a speed record. Its thud hammered like a cloudburst in her ears.

Leanna dropped her gaze, hoping her face hadn't displayed—in that ever so brief second—how her heart hadn't changed in spite of his choosing another over her. She walked past a group of twittering teenage girls and ignored their speculation about which of the available *maedels* Gabriel should consider as a wife. Her name wasn't mentioned, and she tried not to let that bother her. Though she'd never guessed when her sister and their friends started the Harmony Creek Spinsters Club that a year later she'd be the only one with no plans to marry.

Shaking her head, she kept walking. She would marry if—and only if—God's plan for her included marriage. As she tried to talk sense to her aching heart, she wondered if Gabriel realized how much talk there was among the unmarried women about his need for a wife.

He did, she discovered, when instead of handing off the twins to sit with the women and other small *kinder*, he kept both *bopplin* with him while he sat next to his brother on the men's side. She wasn't surprised when Gabriel got up twice and Michael once more with the *bopplin* when they became fussy or needed to be changed during the three-hour service. Though it was unusual for a *daed* or *onkel* to handle such chores, she knew Gabriel had been wise not to ask any of the women to take care of his *kinder*. Such a request would have been seen as a possible invitation to become better acquainted.

She fixed her mind on the service, but her eyes kept shifting toward Gabriel. It was startling to realize they'd never worshipped together before this. They'd spent hours talking about everything, including their faith, during the time they'd walked out together.

At the end of the service, Leanna rose and joined the other women getting the cold sandwiches and preserves waiting in the kitchen. The men shifted the benches to make tables for the meal the *Leit* would share. As always, the oldest men moved to the table first.

Leanna emerged from the house with a platter of sandwiches and set them on one end of the table. She was about to go for another plate when she saw Gabriel pull the wagon up to the table and heard a wail from it.

Heidi!

Moving to where Gabriel was trying to calm the little girl, Leanna said, "I'll watch them while you eat."

"You don't have to do that. We can—"

Michael interrupted, "*Danki*, Leanna. I, for one, appreciate your offer." He aimed a steady look at his brother. "That's true, ain't so, Gabriel? No need for any *drama* today, ain't so?"

What was exchanged between the twin brothers was beyond Leanna's comprehension, but she was sure she'd heard the slightest emphasis when Michael said *drama*. That meant something to the brothers, and she doubted Gabriel would want her probing into what was going on.

Leanna picked up Heidi and crooned, "There, there. So much noise from such a tiny mouth. What's going on with you, *boppli*?"

The *kind*'s face softened from its scowl, and she began to gurgle. Relief eased the lines in Gabriel's brow.

"I owe you one," Gabriel said.

"Nonsense." Leanna cuddled the little girl and tickled her belly. "I'm glad to help."

"I know you are, but I still owe you one."

Michael chuckled. "Don't bother to argue, Leanna. I learned years ago it's a waste of breath. Let him owe you one. And don't worry about him forgetting it. Gabriel always keeps his promises." He winked at his brother. "That's one thing you can count on. Once Gabriel Miller says he's going to do something, he does it. That's right, ain't so?"

Gabriel's shoulders stiffened as he'd been about to reach for his son. "I guess so."

Leanna glanced from one brother to the other. Again some message she wasn't privy to had passed between them, but she wasn't sure which of Michael's words bothered Gabriel. It had to be more than his brother complimenting him.

Gabriel mumbled something that she guessed was *"Danki."* To his brother or to her?

Gathering up Harley after Michael walked away to speak with their minister, Eli Troyer, she said, "Gabriel, there's a question I've been meaning to ask you."

"Go ahead."

"Are you okay with me taking the *bopplin* off your farm while I'm watching them?"

"Of course." His familiar frown returned. "Why would you ask such a thing? Don't you think I trust you?"

"No, that's not it. I know you trust me. You wouldn't have asked me to watch your *kinder* if you didn't trust me." She edged away one step, then another. "You're their *daed*, and I thought I should check with you before I do anything different with them."

She sounded like a *dummkopf*, babbling as if she couldn't stop. She clamped her mouth closed before she said something she'd regret for the rest of her life.

When Leanna looked away, Gabriel understood what she was trying to avoid saying. It wasn't a matter of him trusting her. It was about her not trusting *him*. And why should she? He'd betrayed her once.

At least that was how she must see it.

It was how *anyone* would see the events that had occurred. If he could be honest with her, maybe she would have forgiven him. He rued the letter he'd written, because it must have seemed ridiculous to her when he couldn't explain the truth of why he'd agreed to Freda's *daed*'s proposition. Knowing how Leanna cared for her own family, he guessed she might have forgiven him if he'd been able to tell her why he'd stood her up and married someone else such a short time later.

The truth burned on his lips, begging to be spoken. How many times had Aden reminded him, Michael and Freda that the truth would set them free? He'd told them being honest kept them from being bound by ropes of lies that would grow tighter with each layer added.

So why, Aden, did you bind me to a promise that keeps me from being honest with Leanna?

"Where do you want to take the *bopplin*?" Gabriel asked.

"I thought they might like to visit my goats."

"That's not dangerous?"

"Do you think I'd do something to put the twins in

danger?" Her blue-green eyes snapped, and he knew he'd upset her again.

He wasn't sure why he kept doing things to distress her. Was keeping a chasm between them a way to prevent him from having to think about what they'd shared in the past? If so, it wasn't working.

"No, of course not. I know you love Heidi and Harley. But I know these two *kinder*. I know they will go looking for trouble whenever possible. Or at least Heidi will."

"She's curious about things. Like her *daed*." Her smile for the *bopplin* was warm, and it widened to include him, as well.

He couldn't smile because her words were a slap in the face. A reminder of the truth he wished he could share with her and close the chasm between them.

He couldn't let that happen. He'd failed as a husband once. He couldn't risk doing that again.

Monday evening, Gabriel came home to an empty house. He found a note in the middle of the kitchen table. It was from Leanna and told him she and the *bopplin* were at her family's farm. She asked him and Michael to meet them there for supper.

He handed the note to his brother before heading into the bathroom for a quick shower. Tomorrow he and Michael would paint the Fentons' art studio, so they'd spent the day smoothing joint compound on the new walls. A glance in the mirror as he waited for the water to warm up showed how much plaster dust covered him. Now he knew what he'd look like when his hair and beard were more white than red. He rushed through his shower. Coming back into the kitchen, he let Michael know it was his turn to clean up.

"I'm heading next door to get the twins, " he said as he reached for his hat.

"In a hurry to see our pretty neighbor?" asked Michael, dropping his suspenders over his shoulders as he walked toward the bathroom.

"Ja."

The honest answer surprised his brother, halting him as he was about to close the bathroom door. Gabriel didn't blame his brother.

It didn't take Gabriel long to find Leanna and the twins at the Wagler farm. She'd told him she wanted to bring the *bopplin* to meet her goats. Going to the pen where the animals were kept, he held his breath, not wanting to interrupt the scene in front of him.

Leanna sat on the box where she milked her goats. Heidi was perched on Leanna's knee and bounced with excitement while Harley sat in the wagon, staring with big eyes at the goats, which must seem huge to such a tiny boy. Heidi's fingers were outstretched and wiggled as if she could lure the goats to her with the motion.

Leanna made a soft, clicking sound, and the goats looked toward her, their ears up. One brown-and-white goat edged forward. It was, he guessed, the one she'd been milking the first morning he'd come to the Wagler farm.

"This is Faith," Leanna said with a smile that seemed to encompass the *boppli*, the goat…and him. "Faith is the boss, and she never lets any of the others, including me, forget it. Once she's your friend, they all will love you, too."

He realized she was talking for his benefit because neither Heidi nor the goat could comprehend her words.

She was trying to reassure him again the *bopplin* would be safe with her goats.

His heart softened as he watched Heidi touch the brown-and-white goat. The little girl snatched back her fingers before reaching out again. Her deep laugh swelled into the afternoon when she buried her fingers in Faith's coat. She leaned her cheek against the goat's head, then patted the goat's face, attention that he was surprised the animal accepted as her due.

"See?" Leanna asked without looking over her shoulder. "The *kinder* are safe with the goats and me."

"I should never have doubted that." He resisted stretching out as Harley patted the goat's haunch. When Leanna lifted him from the wagon so he could explore Faith as his sister was doing, Gabriel added, "You've always been cautious. You're someone who looks before you leap."

"Almost always." The words were so soft he wasn't sure if he'd heard her right.

Regret flooded him anew. She had to be referring to walking out with him. If only he could be honest with her...

Leanna stood and put the *bopplin* into the wagon. The goat wandered off to join the rest of the herd.

After closing the gate, she pulled the wagon around so the *kinder* could see him. They held up their arms, and he knelt and gave each a hug and a kiss on the head. The *bopplin* babbled with excitement, and he wondered if they were trying to tell him about the goats. Heidi was bouncing as she had on Leanna's lap while Harley leaned against the wagon's panel and grinned up at him.

"I'd say the visit to the goats was a success," Gabriel said, standing.

"They took to the herd as if they'd been around goats their whole lives." Leanna smiled. "Heidi astonishes me. She's curious about everything while Harley is content to observe his world. Was Freda like Harley?"

He flinched, unable to halt himself. Why was Leanna asking about Freda? Had he exposed the truth he wasn't the *bopplin's daed* without realizing it?

As if he'd asked aloud, she said, "Maybe you don't want to talk about Freda. I understand that, because it's been such a short time since she died. However, I don't know anything about her because I never met her. I see how much Heidi resembles you, and I'm curious whom Harley takes after because they seem to have such different personalities."

"More like Freda's *daed*." He warned himself not to overreact to what was an obvious question. In fact, he was amazed Leanna hadn't asked about Freda sooner. "Freda was a lot like Heidi. I remember when she first started school. She wanted to poke her nose into every book there, even ones she wouldn't be using for years."

"*Ja*, that sounds like Heidi." Her smile fell away. "When you hugged Harley, did you notice his wheezing?"

"He seemed to be breathing harder, but I assumed it's because he's excited. Do you think he's allergic to your goats?"

"He drinks their *milch*, but they're dusty, so he might be allergic to dust."

"I never noticed that, and our house was thick with dust before you started keeping it clean."

"You may want to mention it to his *doktor* the next time you take him in."

"I'll try to remember."

"*Gut*. If—"

"Gabriel!" called Juanita as she jumped off the porch. Running to where they stood, she grinned. "You're coming to school on Friday, ain't so?"

He almost asked what Friday was, then wondered how he could have forgotten the eighth-grade graduation. Last week, he'd been counting down the days, the hours, the minutes until Juanita would be done with school so she could take Leanna's place watching the *bopplin*. He was startled. He hadn't done that during Leanna's second week at the farm.

He resisted the longing to ask her to stay on, because he guessed the people she cleaned houses for would be anxious for her to work for them. In addition, Juanita having a responsible job would satisfy the vocational study requirements the State of New York had set for plain scholars who didn't attend school until they were sixteen as *Englischers* did.

"I wouldn't miss it," he said.

"*Gut!*" Juanita clapped her hands as if she were as young as the twins. "We've been practicing our pieces for the past month. Not just the two of us graduating, but all the scholars. It's going to be a *wunderbaar* ceremony, and we want everyone in the hollow to attend."

"I'm sure most will." Leanna gave her sister a quick hug. "It is our first school graduation from our brand-new schoolhouse."

With a wave, Juanita rushed back into the house. The screen door slammed in her wake.

"You don't have to feel obligated to attend." Leanna stared at his boots.

"It will be a chance to see inside the school where the twins will be scholars in a few years."

"All right."

His fingers tilted her chin up before he could halt them. Astonishment bloomed in her eyes, and he hoped he hadn't made a horrific mistake. Since he'd touched her on the porch the night she'd given him the wagon, he hadn't been able to stop thinking about how much he longed for another chance to do so.

"Is everything really all right?" he asked.

"Everything is as it should be."

"You're avoiding answering my question."

"That's my answer." Her breath brushed his face as he leaned toward her.

"That everything is as it should be?"

"Ja."

"I wish I could believe you believe that, Leanna."

"You can."

Would she say the same thing if he asked if he could kiss her? He'd kissed her once. She'd been soft in his arms, her fingertips curved along his face as if she wanted to memorize it. Her lips had been welcoming, and his tingled at the memory.

"Gabriel!" she gasped.

"What?"

"You're smiling." She stared at him in disbelief.

"I guess I am." He felt his lips tip more.

She flung her arms around him as she whispered in his ear, "I've been praying you'd be happy again. *Danki* to God for opening your heart to joy again."

He was saved from having to answer when his brother came up the driveway and her sister called from the house at the same moment. As she hurried to help with whatever needed to be done inside, Michael stopped next to the wagon.

"Be careful, brother," he said without any other greeting. "Don't forget you broke her heart once already."

Gabriel tore his gaze from the porch and met his brother's eyes. "I can't ever forget that. Not ever."

Chapter Eight

The farmers market was held every Saturday morning during the summer in a small park at the center of the village of Salem. People still talked about the night the building that had stood there burned. It had held four shops and two apartments, and the fire began at 6:45 p.m. on a Tuesday. Because the fire siren was tested every Tuesday at 6:50 p.m., too few of the volunteer firefighters had realized there was an actual fire until the alarm was activated for a second time. By then, the fire had gained control of the old Victorian building, sending the residents fleeing with the clothes on their backs. The next morning a charred foundation and puddles filled with ashes were all that remained.

When it became obvious nobody was going to re-build, the village took over the property. A gazebo was set in the center, and trees and flower beds planted. Narrow sidewalks crisscrossed the park. Many of the village *kinder* had learned to roller skate there, safe from vehicle traffic and pedestrians.

During the week, the benches were empty, but on

Saturday mornings from May until September when the farmers market was held, no empty seats could be found.

Along with shoppers and those who'd come to talk and browse, *kinder* and dogs on leashes had gathered for a contest. They wore costumes, and Leanna wasn't sure who was fidgeting more: the *kinder* or the dogs, which came in a wide variety of shapes, sizes and colors. She guessed the dogs were supposed to be other types of animals. One was a black-and-white cow, because she could see a pink udder hanging down. Another one, a black pug, was showing off her rabbit ears and a tail made out of cotton balls.

Leanna couldn't wait for the market to close for the day. Each time she spoke with a stranger, it was a strain. She couldn't be like the other vendors who called out to neighbors, urging them to come and check out their wares. Instead, she sat behind the table she'd covered with a white cloth. Stacked on it were the bars of soap she'd made during the winter. A single hand-lettered sign listed what she had to sell and for how much. Since she didn't have an awning as many of the other sellers did, she'd been relieved to discover her spot was in the shade of the neighboring building.

A blonde stopped in front of the table. She looked close to Leanna's twenty-five years, but it wasn't always easy to tell with *Englischers* who wore makeup. Her close-cropped curls framed her round face, and she smiled as she asked, "Is this right? You made soap out of goats' milk?"

"That and other things like oatmeal and scents."

The woman picked up the bar and held it to her nose. "Oh, lavender. That's my favorite."

"I think it's a relaxing scent for enjoying a bath after a long day's work."

"Exactly." The woman grinned. "I'll take three bars."

Leanna told her the total price while putting the bars into one of the paper bags she'd collected during the winter. Handing the bag to the woman, she made change.

"Are you here every week?" the woman asked.

"I hope to be, but it depends on how my goats cooperate."

The woman laughed. "I can see how that could be a problem." Her eyes widened as she glanced past Leanna. "Your family is here to help, I see."

Looking over her shoulder, Leanna's greeting to her siblings vanished when she saw Gabriel pulling the twins in the wagon she'd given him.

He surveyed the market booths with the same curiosity his daughter did.

"Good morning," he said to the blonde, then switched to *Deitsch*. "*Gute mariye*, Leanna."

The blonde grinned broadly before she walked to the next booth, but turned and winked.

Had it been aimed at her or Gabriel? Had he noticed as he bent to settle Harley in the wagon?

"What are you doing here?" she asked, horrified by how anxiety heightened her voice.

Gabriel chucked Harley under the chin before facing Leanna. He suspected she was doing well at the market. Only a few bars of soap remained on top of the table, and the pair of baskets by her black sneakers were empty. Her hands were clasped in her lap, making her look ill at ease while other sellers and customers bustled through the space between the small square and the road.

"I decided to see what all the talk about the farmers market is about," he said.

"And what do you think?"

He glanced around the score of tables and the people milling between them, stopping to talk with vendors and other shoppers. "I think," he said, realizing Leanna was waiting for him to answer, "I need to find the place where they're selling the fudge I see some kids eating."

"Third table to the left." She pointed.

"I'll make sure I don't miss it while we're walking around." He glanced at the wagon. "This design is truly clever."

"I thought they'd enjoy it."

"No question about that." He gave a wave and pulled the wagon up a cut in the curb.

As he wandered around the tables, talking with people he recognized and answering questions about the twins from people whom he hadn't met, he kept glancing at Leanna. He was pulled to her like a yo-yo, dancing on its string. No matter how interesting the articles were on the other tables, his thoughts returned to her.

He gave in to those thoughts and returned to her table. When Leanna asked how he'd liked the fudge, he realized he'd forgotten to sample any.

Rather than admit that, he asked, "Would you like some ice cream?"

When she smiled and nodded, he was glad she wasn't thinking about the last time he'd invited her to join him for ice cream. His heart lurched as he couldn't keep from wondering what she would have said that day if he'd asked her—as he'd planned—to become his wife.

"Are you planning to share with the *bopplin*?" she asked as she stood and began to fold the white tablecloth.

"A bite or two at least."

"Then we should get sorbet. It'll be less likely to bother their stomachs."

"I didn't think of that," he said before he could halt himself. He must sound like the world's worst *daed*.

She smiled. "It's hard to remember everything that contains cows' *milch*."

"Ice cream should be easy to remember."

The wrong words, because her smile wavered, and he knew she was thinking of how they had been going to meet in Strasburg on what should have been a special day for them.

"Maybe someone makes ice cream out of the *milch* from goats," he said, unable to bear the silence between them.

"Unlikely."

"You can't make ice cream from it?"

"You can, but it's thinner than regular ice cream. If you put it in the freezer, it becomes like a slab of granite." A smile flitted across her face. "I know, because I tried a few times until my family begged me to stop using them as guinea pigs for my experiments."

He was about to ask another question, but halted. The twins were getting antsy and ready to climb out of the wagon. At least Heidi was, and it seemed to Gabriel as if Harley was egging her on. He didn't dare to turn his back on the twins while helping Leanna pack up her empty baskets and put them in the Waglers' buggy, parked in front of the grocery store up the street. It took longer than he'd expected to walk the short distance because vendors kept stopping Leanna to ask if she'd be there next week.

"Your soap is such a hit!" exclaimed an *Englisch* woman whose black braid hung past her waist. "People stop there and then at my table to look at my jewelry. Maybe we should consider a cross-promotion."

"It's something to think about, Iris." With a wave, Leanna crossed Main Street during a break in the Saturday morning traffic.

"Do you think the bishop will be okay with you doing promotion for your products?" Gabriel asked while she stored her supplies in the buggy.

"No, but Iris is a nice woman, and I didn't want to say no without checking."

"You're a nice woman, too, Leanna Wagler."

A blush rose up her cheeks, and she bowed her head to hide her face. He wanted to tell her such a motion was useless. After hours of re-creating her expressions while he stared at the ceiling, he could imagine how lovely the color looked against her black hair.

She checked to make sure her horse was all right. When she walked with him to the sidewalk, she began to talk about the farmers market as if it were the most important subject on the planet.

He listened as they strolled past the bank in a grand Victorian house and toward the hardware store, knowing this was her way of dealing with his compliment. Thinking back to when they'd been walking out together, he knew he must have praised her at least once.

Hadn't he?

He realized he had...though only in his mind. He hadn't wanted to embarrass her. It shocked him to discover that, before Aden asked him to save his daughter's reputation, Gabriel hadn't been honest with Leanna. He'd thought she was the loveliest, kindest, most fun girl he'd ever spent time with; yet he'd never hinted that to her.

No wonder she'd thought the worst of him when she

learned he was marrying Freda. How could he fault Leanna for not responding to his earnest letter when he'd never told her how he felt about her?

He hadn't changed his mind about Leanna, and, as he listened to her lilting voice and saw her smile when she paused to speak with vendors packing up after the farmers market, he knew he must be careful. If he spoke the truth to her about anything, he might slip and reveal everything.

The twins crowed with delight as two large dogs walked past them. He slowed the wagon, after asking the dog owners' permission to pet the dogs.

"They're fascinated with dogs," Leanna said. "You should get them one."

He shook his head. "No."

"*Kinder* love dogs."

"I know."

Her smile vanished at his clipped tone. "What is it, Gabriel?"

"What do you mean?"

"I know that expression. You wear it when you're thinking about when you were young and everything in your life changed. Did you and Michael have a dog?"

"Ja." He should have guessed he couldn't hide from her keen eyes. He might as well tell her, so he could stave off her curiosity with more recent events. "We had a dog before we moved in with Aden. Red didn't get along with the Girods' dog, so he was given to another family. We never saw him again."

"I'm sorry. You must have been heartbroken."

"We were. It'd seemed, at the time, a sorrow as great as losing parents." He took a deep breath and released it. "That's why I think the twins are better off without a dog."

"It's not a decision you have to make today."

Smiling in response to her kind words seemed the most natural response. When she stared at him, astonished, before she returned his smile, he knew why he hadn't given in to his yearning to smile before. The emotion arcing between them was invisible but as powerful as the sunlight burning through his straw hat.

His fingers tingled in a silent plea to reach them out and take her hand. He tried to ignore them. Such a public display on the street busy with *Englischers* and a few plain folk would reflect poorly on Leanna. He couldn't risk that.

Gabriel stopped before they reached the intersection at the heart of the village. "Here we are."

The building was three stories high. The upper floors were painted pale gray. The dark red trim around the windows matched the color of the ground floor. Rolled red-and-white-striped awnings hung over the two sets of storefronts. Large windows flanked the doors. A third door between the stores led to the apartments on the top two floors.

The left-hand shop sold fabrics, and the other was their destination. Gold letters arched in the windows announced the shop sold candy and ice cream and other treats. Double screen doors at the top of three steps were open to catch the late-spring breezes and invite passersby in to enjoy a snack.

When he pulled the wagon to one side of the steps where it wouldn't be in anyone's way, he wasn't surprised Leanna picked up Harley at the same time he reached for Heidi, who held her tiny arms up to him. He and Leanna had learned how to work in concert to take care of the twins. Would he develop the same easy rapport with Juanita as he had with Leanna?

Impossible!

Though in some ways it would be much simpler to have the teenager around his house. He almost snickered as he wondered if he were the first adult ever to have such a thought.

Juanita would do a *gut* job for him, and the drama that annoyed Michael would be gone. It was for the best.

It was!

If that was the truth, why couldn't he think of anything but how he'd miss the sound of Leanna's voice? He'd be sorry not to view the brightness of the *bopplin's* eyes when they saw her and the scent of her floral shampoo and the twinkle in her own eyes before she said something outrageous and… The list went on and on.

"All set?" Leanna asked.

Relieved to be freed from his thoughts, he settled Heidi against him so she could look past his shoulder and not miss anything. "All set."

Gabriel let Leanna precede him up the steps. Inside the shop, the wood floors might once have been polished or painted, but any hint of finish had been worn away. On one side, two great glass cases displayed wares the store would have sold when it first opened its doors. He glanced at boxes for candies that were no longer produced, and then his gaze was caught by the magnificent soda fountain.

A marble slab was set atop a carved bar more than ten feet long. Six cast-iron stools with bright red vinyl seats marched in front of it. Beyond the bar were the goose-necked dispensers for soda water and flavored drinks.

The preparation area ran the full length of the bar, large folding doors on top of the freezer for the containers of ice cream. Smaller compartments must hold toppings and other supplies. Fluted dishes for sundaes were arranged before a huge mirror that reached to the ceiling. One corner of the mirror had a crack about as long as his hand, but the rest looked as pristine as the day it'd been put up, which he guessed must be close to a century before.

"This is amazing," he said in a whisper.

"Isn't it?" Leanna laughed. "You'd never guess this was in here if you drove past. Who'd imagine a little farm town would have such a fancy ice cream parlor?"

A cheerful man behind the counter gave them a big grin. "What can I do for you today?" He wiped the counter with a cloth though it looked clean. "Maybe an ice-cream soda? A banana split? An egg cream?"

"What's that?" Gabriel asked.

"It's soda water and cream and flavoring. I can make chocolate, vanilla or strawberry for you."

"No eggs?"

The man laughed. "Not a one. And don't ask me why they're called egg creams. Nobody seems to know, but they're good."

"It does sound *gut*, but we've got two lactose-intolerant twins here, so we need to skip anything with cream in it."

"We were thinking sorbet would be okay for them," Leanna added.

The man nodded. "It's your best bet." He pointed to a list over his right shoulder. "Those are the flavors we have."

Gabriel scanned the list. "I'll have raspberry. A medium. What about you, Leanna?"

"Strawberry. Small for me."

"A cone or a dish?" asked the man behind the counter.

"A dish for me." She smiled at the twins. "I think it'll make it easier to share."

"For me, too," Gabriel said.

The man grinned and went to fill the order. The servings were more generous than Gabriel had expected, so he was glad he hadn't ordered a large bowl. He paid for their treat, then led the way to a small metal table and pulled out two of the metal chairs. The metal backs had been twisted to match the heart shape of Leanna's *kapp*. Setting his dish on the white tabletop, he sat and settled Heidi on his lap. She quivered with excitement when she saw the colorful sorbet in front of him.

He gave her a little bit on a spoon, and her nose wrinkled. "Don't you like it?"

"Give her another bite." Leanna was offering a bit of her own to Harley. "That's not her 'I don't like it' face. It's her 'I don't know what it is because I've never had it before' face."

When he held up the spoon to Heidi again, she opened her mouth. She giggled when the sweet flavor rushed down her throat.

"You're right," he said.

"I've learned most of her expressions. Heidi doesn't hide anything about the way she feels. She wants the world to know. Harley is more circumspect, like you."

He took a bite of the sorbet to hide his reaction. It was simple with everyone else, even his brother, to hide the truth, but it was difficult not to share it with her. If only Aden hadn't asked him not to reveal the truth about his daughter…

"Da-da-da-da," Heidi said, patting his chest with each impatient repetition.

"Ja." Leanna smiled. "That's your *daed*. Aren't you going to answer her, Gabriel?"

"She's making nonsense sounds," he argued, holding out the spoon to Heidi again so he didn't have to look across the table. "She does that all the time."

"She does, but not that sound. She's talking to you, *daed*."

He readied a curt retort, but the sound wouldn't emerge past his lips as he stared at the *kind*. She believed he should understand what she was saying.

His throat filled with emotions, too many to examine a single one, as he wondered if she really was trying to say *"daed."* Once the *bopplin* began making sounds, he had been curious when one would come out with a real word. He never once allowed himself to imagine that word would be a *boppli*'s version of *daed*.

The enormity of the future swarmed over him. Heidi and Harley would grow up calling him that. At some time, he needed to be honest with them. When and how? Would they see his letting them think he was their *daed* as a deception or would they accept the truth and go on with their lives?

A bit of ironic laughter surged in his clogged throat. How would their lives change when he spoke the truth? He couldn't keep it from them forever.

Soft fingers settled on his hand fisted around the spoon. Raising his gaze from her hand to Leanna's compassionate eyes, he heard her speak a single word.

"Don't."

"Don't what?"

"Don't go wherever you went with your thoughts,"

she said. "Whether it was the past or the future, don't go there. *This* is a happy moment. Stay here with us."

"There's nothing else I'd rather do."

His sincere words brought a scintillating smile from her. *"Gut,"* she said before offering Harley another bite of her sorbet.

She was right. He was going to enjoy this special time with her and the twins because he wasn't sure if there ever should be another.

As he listened to Leanna teasing both *kinder*, he knew there were a lot of things about his future he needed to consider. He must be careful before he hurt the people he cared about.

Again.

Chapter Nine

Leanna looked up at the clock on the kitchen wall. It was only ten, but she felt as if she'd put in a day's work. Nothing had gone right. She'd overslept and had to rush getting dressed. Somehow, she'd failed to put all the pins in her hair and her *kapp*, so now she had to keep pushing both into place each time she moved.

When she'd arrived at the Millers' farm, Gabriel had been curt. Not just to her, but to his twin and his *kinder*. Michael had given her a quick shrug before he followed Gabriel out the door, showing he didn't know what was bothering his twin.

The *bopplin* acted as out of sorts as their *daed*. Harley spit out every bite of oatmeal she tried to feed him. Heidi refused to eat or play with her toys. The little girl kept rubbing her eyes and yawning as she alternated between crying and whining, and Leanna wondered if the whole family was exhausted by everything that had happened since they'd left Lancaster County.

A knock came at the door, and Leanna considered ignoring it. The kitchen was a mess, the *bopplin* were covered with bits of food, and she must look a sight with her *kapp* threatening to fall over her right ear. Taking a deep breath, she opened the door.

"Miriam!" She hadn't expected to see her friend at the Millers' house.

"You look as if you're having a dandy of a day." The tall blonde walked in and surveyed the kitchen. Without saying anything further to Leanna, she picked up Heidi and asked, "What's bothering you so much you have to tell the whole world about it?"

The *boppli* regarded Miriam with curiosity. Sticking her thumb in her mouth, Heidi became silent.

"You should have come earlier and convinced her to be quiet." Leanna lifted Harley out of his chair. "Do you have time to stay and visit for a while? Once I get him cleaned, I can put on the teapot."

When Leanna faced her friend, Miriam gave her the stern look she usually aimed at a recalcitrant scholar. "You can't have forgotten!"

"I could, because it seems I have." She resisted a yawn of her own. Too many dreams of Gabriel opening his arms to her—last night's had been in a new location: in front of the ice-cream shop—had jolted her awake in the middle of the night. After almost too many nights of various versions of the sweet fantasy, she had no idea if her dream-self had ever accepted his invitation to hug or not. It was as if her mind didn't trust her with that information because it feared she would give in to her yearnings to be near him when she was awake.

She'd never expected her brain to have to protect her from her heart. It was unsettling to think about.

"Didn't Juanita and Kenny remind you this morning?" Miriam's question saved her from her disconcerting thoughts.

"They may have, but I arrived here this morning in time to discover the *bopplin* were refusing to take their bottles. And then the morning got more frantic after that." Even in her own ears, the excuse sounded weak, but how could she speak of her tumultuous thoughts to her *gut* friend Miriam?

"Today is the school picnic down by the creek." Miriam grinned at Heidi, who gave her a shy smile in return. "I know *you* want to go and have fun with the other *kinder*. How about you, Leanna?"

"Of course I want to go." She rolled her eyes. "I can't believe I forgot the school picnic. Juanita and Kenny have been talking about it nonstop."

"You've had a few other things on your mind."

"*Ja*, these two."

"And their *daed*? Annie told me yesterday at the bakery that you and Gabriel walked out together before he married the *bopplin's mamm*."

"We did." She took Harley to the sink to wash thick blotches of oatmeal off before it hardened on his clothes. With her back to her friend, she added, "It didn't work out as either of us hoped when we first met."

"I'm sorry. Is it uncomfortable for you taking care of his *kinder*?"

"It was at first. It's not now." Leanna was amazed to realize that was the truth. She never would have imagined she could become accustomed to the crazy situation in which she and Gabriel had found themselves. Yet when they'd taken the *bopplin* for sorbet on Saturday, it had seemed natural to be with him and his family.

"I'm glad to hear that."

"Me, too." And that was almost the truth. She wondered if it was possible ever to fall out of love with someone. The hopes she'd savored during those few months had left a permanent shadow on a corner of her heart, something she'd decided should be filed under "older but wiser" experiences.

Not wanting to think about that, she left Miriam playing with the twins. Leanna concentrated on collecting extra clothing, food and bottles for the *bopplin*, as well as some of their favorite toys. She put two small quilts in the wagon, then added a pair of towels because the picnic would be beside the water and the *kinder* loved splashing in their baths. Because she knew Gabriel would be concerned if he came home and they weren't there, she left a note on the kitchen table explaining where they were.

As she pulled the twins' wagon behind her, Leanna was relieved Miriam spent the five minutes it took for them to walk along the road talking about her scholars. Though Miriam was looking forward to the opportunity to spend time at home with her husband, Eli, and his nephew, Kyle, she admitted she'd miss teaching. She'd stayed on an extra year and had been training the blacksmith's sister, Grace Streicher, to take her place. The girl had moved from Canada to manage her brother James's house a month ago, and she'd agreed to help at the school when it became obvious there was nobody else who could.

Leanna pulled the wagon down the narrow path from the road. Stones and tree roots jutted out of the ground at odd angles, threatening to tip it. She edged to the side to let four scholars surge past her. Knowing they had their sights set on the creek at the bottom of the hill, she doubted if they'd noticed her much slower passage along the rough path.

She heard the waterfall before she saw it. Only about

five feet high, the cascade sent water into a deep pool in the otherwise shallow creek. No wonder the *kinder* had claimed the area for a swimming hole.

The open glade along the creek's bank was beautiful. Trees surrounded it and lined the far side of the creek, but no underbrush crowded the shore. Gravel edged the pool, offering a place for the younger *kinder* to play beside the water. Someone had mowed the grass enough for the *mamms* to spread out blankets. Sitting there, they could keep a close eye on the pool and the waterfall dropping into it.

Leanna smiled when she saw the other two members of the Harmony Creek Spinsters Club, her sister and Sarah, sitting in the shadow of some ancient trees that stretched their branches over the creek. The leaves filtered the sunshine, setting it to dance on the water flying over boulders farther down the creek.

Sarah had hair as red as Gabriel's and wore new glasses. When Sarah explained she'd taken a tumble off a horse and broken her old ones, Leanna was glad that was the only damage her friend had suffered. Sarah always told amusing stories, something she'd learned in order to entertain four *Englisch kinder* when she was their nanny. She soon had everyone sitting around her laughing about how a beaver had helped itself to some of the trees her brothers had chopped down and planned to cut in their sawmill.

"For some reason, nobody wants wood that's already been gnawed," Sarah finished. "Menno was annoyed, but Benjamin reminded him the beavers were getting revenge for the two of them breaking up a new dam on the farm pond. The dam had blocked the flow of water, and my brothers need it to get big logs from the woodlot to their sawmill. Also, far more important to Benjamin is that the dam meant losing *gut* fishing."

"Has Menno calmed down?" asked Leanna, knowing Sarah's two brothers had once tried to run her life. That had changed, but her elder brother Menno had little patience with anyone or anything else.

"I have faith he will...eventually."

That brought more laughter as the rest of the scholars and their *mamms* and younger siblings joined them beside the creek. Everyone pulled out food to share, and the conversation was interlaced with recipes, as well as for calls for the *kinder* to be careful in the water.

As she chatted with her friends, Leanna was kept busy chasing Heidi to keep her from the water. After they'd finished picking up from their picnic, she decided to take the *bopplin* to enjoy the water.

"Before you go..." Miriam said as Leanna threw the towels over her shoulder and bent to pick up the twins. "I have some news, but you can't share it with anyone. Not your husbands, not your families."

"What is it?" Annie's eyes twinkled. "Is it what I think it is?"

"Promise first. No telling anyone."

After all three vowed they'd keep Miriam's secret, she put her hands around her abdomen. "The secret's right here."

"You're going to have a *boppli*!" Leanna exclaimed as the others grinned. "When?"

"In November. Around Thanksgiving time." Her voice was flush with joy. "My timing was off. I wish I'd been done teaching school before I had to deal with morning sickness."

Sarah laughed. "We're going to have to change the

name of our group to the Harmony Creek Spinsters, Newlyweds and New *Mamms* Club. Who would have guessed our lives would change so much in a year?"

Leanna forced a smile when the rest joined in with Sarah's laughter. It was true their lives had changed. She wished she knew what her life was changing into. Gabriel was in it, but not in any way she would have imagined when she'd first heard of his wedding plans. She'd always been sure of what she wanted. A *wunder-baar* romance with an exciting man like in the books she used to read.

Odd… She couldn't remember the last time she'd picked up a novel and let herself be drawn into the story of two people falling in love. Was that because she wasn't sure if such a tale would ever come true for her?

Gabriel wiped sweat off his nape as he edged down the already well-worn path toward the creek. The sound of happy voices drifted through the thick leaves, but he couldn't see the water or any of the people gathered there. Stepping around a blackberry bush, being careful to avoid its thorns, he saw a clearing below. The only thing in it was the red wagon Leanna had given the twins.

He'd been surprised when he got home after finishing a hard morning's work on the studio in West Rupert to find a note from Leanna on the kitchen table. She hadn't said anything to him before about taking the twins on a picnic. It wasn't like her to be so secretive.

"No," his brother had said, "that's what you are, Gabriel."

Michael's words continued to ring in his ears, another reminder of how much he hated being restrained by the promise he'd made. Gabriel had considered going to Eli Troyer, their minister, to seek his advice but hadn't. How could he explain to Eli how he no longer believed God heard his prayers?

Those thoughts vanished when he rounded a corner on the path and caught sight of Leanna squatting by a pool. The sunlight glistened with blue fire on her black hair and added warmth to her cheeks, which were a shade lighter than the dark rose dress puddling around her bare feet. Beside her, Harley sat close enough to slap his hands in the pool. Each time his palms hit the water, he chortled with delight. Leanna was holding Heidi up so she could stamp her tiny feet, sending drops in every direction. When a few hit her brother, Harley shook his head and just kept playing in the pool, too.

It was an enticing sight, a view of a woman spending time with two *kinder* she loved. He paid no attention to the older *kinder* lining up to slide with the quick current down the waterfall and into the pool. A group of women sitting on blankets beneath the trees to his right barely registered in his mind.

Walking as if drawn by an invisible cord toward Leanna and the twins, he paused behind her. She looked up, and their gazes fused. He couldn't pull his eyes away. Not that he wanted to, because he could have stayed there forever. It was a moment out of time, as it had been the night he first saw her.

"Hi," she said.

"Hi." Not great conversation, but the single word seemed perfect.

The moment was shattered when Heidi let out an impatient cry. Leanna shifted the little girl so she could splash in the water more.

Gabriel took a steadying breath, feeling as if he was waking from the best dream he'd ever had. His contentment vanished when he noticed how blue the twins' lips looked.

"They need to get out of the water," he said.

"Why?"

"Look at them! They're blue with the cold!"

Leanna laughed. "They're blue from the ice pops they had a few minutes ago." She turned Heidi so he could see drops of the same color down the front of the little girl's once-pristine *schlupp schotzli*. "I think they got more on them than in their mouths. I figured I could wash them and let them play at the same time."

More than a bit embarrassed, Gabriel said, "Let me help."

"*Danki*. Can you say hi to your *daed*?" She wiggled Heidi's hand in a greeting as she handed him a towel. "Your *daed* wants to get you cleaned up."

"Da-da-da," Heidi chanted, curling up her toes in delight.

He glanced at Harley, but the little boy seemed interested only in how much of his tiny fist he could cram into his mouth.

"Don't worry," Leanna said. "He'll talk in his own time. I've been told I didn't talk to anyone but Annie until I was almost three. I let Annie talk for us, and it looks as if Harley is doing the same with Heidi. When I did start talking to everyone, *Grossmammi* Inez said I spoke in full sentences. She said it probably was the first time I could get a word in edgewise. Don't worry about Harley. He'll talk when he's ready."

"You're right." He dipped one corner of the towel into

the water. Dabbing at Harley's face, he chuckled when the little boy screwed up his mouth to thwart him.

"You're laughing." Astonishment heightened Leanna's voice.

"I've been known to from time to time."

"Not since you've moved here."

He finished washing Harley and looked at her. "I'm sure I have—"

"Not once. You've smiled." A flush rose up her face. "I'm sorry, Gabriel. I shouldn't be teasing you when it's been such a short time since…"

He didn't need her to finish. He knew what she'd been about to say. *Since your wife died.*

She frowned at Harley. "Let me clean him up."

"I did."

"You did? His lips are still blue."

Gabriel looked at the *boppli* and saw she was right. "The water is chilly."

"He didn't go into the water. I've kept a close watch on them, so they didn't get too cold."

"He's been laughing a lot?"

"Ja."

"Well, there you go. You know he can laugh so hard he ends up coughing. It makes him short of breath. He's always fine in a few minutes."

"Always?"

"Leanna, it's been less than a month since you first met them. I've known them their whole lives. Don't you think I'm more familiar with what's going on with them?"

"Sometimes fresh eyes see things others haven't noticed."

"He's fine. Look at him." He motioned toward the *kinder*.

She started to retort, but must have thought better of it. She stood and settled Heidi on her hip before she began to pick up the *bopplin*'s toys and put them into the wagon.

"Do you want some help?" he asked.

"No, I'm fine."

He resisted the yearning to tell her he agreed. It might push her further away.

"I shouldn't have said that, Leanna."

"Said what?"

She wasn't going to make this easy for him. And why should she? He had been the one to ruin the fun they were having with the *kinder*.

"The truth is," he replied, "your question poked at a sore spot."

"Your worry that you aren't a *gut daed*?"

"How—?"

She smiled at him with as much compassion as she did the twins. "You may think you're keeping it a secret, but it colors everything you do, Gabriel. These *bopplin* are such a part of you, and you want to give them all you can so they have a *wunderbaar* childhood. Shall I tell you something else that isn't a secret?"

"Ja." If she had discovered the truth about the pledge he'd made to Aden, then it'd be better for him to find out. How had she learned about what nobody else living knew?

She crooked her finger and motioned for him to lean closer. When he did, she said, "It's no secret you're succeeding much better than you seem to think you are."

* * *

Leanna couldn't keep from smiling when she saw the amazement and then relief in Gabriel's eyes. Was he so worried about being a *daed*? He must be, and she must make sure she pointed out—in a casual manner that would not lead him to suspect she was trying to bolster his confidence—what he was doing well for his *kinder*.

Putting the *bopplin* into the wagon gave her the excuse to move away from him before she did something crazy like running her fingers along his cheek or pressing her lips to it. She must have lost her mind to be thinking of doing such things when her twin and their friends were sitting ten feet away.

Gabriel reached for the wagon's handle at the same time she did. His fingers closed over hers, and he arched his brows. Was he daring her to tug her hand away from his? *Ja*, he was!

Joy surged through her. This afternoon, he had become, for a few minutes, the man she'd walked out with, a man who chuckled and enjoyed teasing her. She'd begun to believe that man was gone and would never return. Hope filled her, something that hadn't happened in so long she couldn't remember the last time she'd enjoyed the sensation.

"Do you think it'll take two of us to pull the wagon up to the road?" he asked, his smile returning.

"We wouldn't want it to slide backward and careen down the hill and into the water."

"It might be the only way to get their clothing clean." He glanced at the twins, and love for his *kinder* blossomed in his eyes.

How could he think he wasn't a *wunderbaar daed*?

She must make an effort to confirm that for him in the few days she had left before Juanita came to the farm to take her place.

Chapter Ten

Gabriel finished shaving and reached for a towel to wipe bits of suds out of his beard. He grimaced at his reflection in the downstairs bathroom. It was vanity to be annoyed that his beard looked uneven. Curling and red, the fine hair refused to fill in.

"You look fine," teased Michael from beyond the open door. "It's not as if it's your *kinder* graduating today."

"I don't think I'm ready for teenagers yet." He tossed the towel onto the side of the sink and put away his shaving cup and razor. Pulling his suspenders up over his shoulders and into place, he added, "I don't know if I'll ever be."

"You'd better figure it out over the next twelve years because you'll be facing every growing-up phase times two."

"*Danki* for the reminder." He glanced into the mirror to make sure his collar was straight. "As if I needed it."

After going into the kitchen, he picked up his straw hat. He put it on his head before reaching down for the twins. Remembering how Leanna had taught him to pick up one, then the other, so he could carry both, he smiled at the *bopplin*.

"Let me help," Michael said.

"Danki." Gabriel motioned for his brother to take Heidi. His twin might tease him—a lot—but Gabriel was always able to depend on him to be there to help and to give his honest opinion. Honest? Gabriel wished he could be the same. *If only Aden hadn't asked him to promise not to reveal the truth that would hurt his daughter in the eyes of the community...* The words had been repeating endlessly through his head for the past few days.

Again he longed to reach out to God for guidance. At first, his anger at his Heavenly Father had been a scaffold, holding him up during the trying days and weeks in the wake of Freda's and Aden's deaths. How could Gabriel have guessed at the time he'd been using that support to build a wall between him and God?

"Don't take this the wrong way, Gabriel," his brother said as they walked out to their buggy, "but I hope you're prepared for today."

"It's not my graduation ceremony. I don't have to worry about reciting today."

Michael didn't smile at Gabriel's jest. "We've been walking on eggshells whenever Leanna's in the house. You're making such an effort to pretend you don't share a past you might as well be wearing signs that say 'Look at me. I'm over you.'" He scowled. "Of course, that would be a lie."

"Half a one maybe."

"You think you're over her?" Michael made a rude sound deep in his throat. "I still don't understand why you married Freda when you were in love with Leanna, but I've gotten tired of asking and getting the runaround. I've got *gut* eyes, and I can see you're not over her."

"I didn't say that. I think she's..." He didn't want to say the words out loud. They'd be too final, too forever.

He knew if Leanna walked out the door tomorrow and treated him with the coolness she'd shown when he'd first gone to the Waglers' farm to get goat *milch*, it would be better for them. He'd be able to keep the promises he'd made to Freda and to her *daed*, and Leanna could...

He was shocked he didn't know what Leanna wanted for the rest of her life. Marriage, he assumed. A woman who was as *gut* with *bopplin* as Leanna was should have her own. Yet, he hadn't seen any bachelors in the community paying her special attention. Were they out of their minds? Maybe Leanna wasn't a great cook, but the only way to a man's heart wasn't through his stomach.

Then his own stomach cramped. Maybe she was walking out with someone. He didn't know their neighbors well enough for them to pass along gossip from the Amish grapevine. The other unmarried men might not have taken notice of pretty Leanna because they knew one among them was courting her.

He couldn't inquire himself or get Michael to ask. His brother would refuse to become involved. He'd made it clear he didn't want to be part of what he called "the drama" any longer. To speak of Leanna to the other men in the settlement would be an announcement he was interested in her. He wasn't going to risk hurting her as he had before, and until he knew what he wanted for his family, how could he even consider making her a part of it?

He'd make a greater mess of her life than he had with Freda's. Hadn't Paul written in his letter to the Ephesians that a man should love and sacrifice for his wife as Christ loved and sacrificed Himself for the members of His church?

And Gabriel had failed to do that.

Everyone in the small plain community had gathered for the first graduation ceremony at the school that sat not far from the banks of Harmony Creek. The air of expectation sent the scholars racing from one group of adults to the next, so excited they couldn't stand still.

Leanna slowed the family's crowded buggy as she reached the small white building that was the community's school. She held her elbows close so she didn't bump her *grossmammi*. Usually there weren't more than two or three of them in the buggy at once. However, today Juanita had insisted she needed to ride because she didn't want to get dusty walking the half mile to school. Kenny had decided he shouldn't walk, either, though he wouldn't explain why.

So she and *Grossmammi* Inez sat in the front seat while Juanita and Kenny were cramped with Annie in the back. She was glad Miriam had decided to hold the graduation picnic earlier in the week instead of after the ceremony. Otherwise, there would be casseroles and desserts piled in the buggy with them.

"Hold on tight," she said as she turned the buggy off the road and onto the uneven ground where the scholars played ball.

Hearing groans from the rear, as well as laughter, she turned the horse toward where other buggies were parked. She gauged the distance to the school. It was farther than she'd hoped. Glancing at her *grossmammi*, she faltered. To say she was worried about *Grossmammi* Inez walking would embarrass the older woman.

"Waglers?" came a jovial shout.

Looking out the buggy, she saw Eli Troyer striding toward them. The man, who'd been ordained as the settlement's first minister earlier in the year, was married to Miriam.

"We saved a spot up front for you," Eli said when he came to stand beside the buggy.

"Danki." She made sure she was facing Eli when she spoke, so he could read her lips.

He'd become so adept at it that it was possible to forget he'd suffered a hearing loss in the tragic accident that had killed his sister and brother-in-law. He had to concentrate on what people were saying, but, as he'd joked more than once, it behooved a minister to pay close attention to what was being discussed.

"I don't need special consideration," grumbled her *grossmammi*.

"Of course not," Eli replied, "but we wanted to make sure our graduates' families had the best seats today. We'll never have another first graduation, so we want to celebrate it." With a wave, he motioned for Leanna to drive to the spot he'd pointed out.

"This sounds," *Grossmammi* Inez continued to complain, "like an excuse he and Miriam devised to make sure I got to the graduation on time."

"And we should always be grateful to those who treat us with unexpected kindness," Leanna said as she maneuvered the horse and buggy through the crowd. "I'm sure I've heard someone say that more than once."

"Me, too," said three voices from behind her.

The older woman chuckled and shook her head. "I

should have known my own words would come back to taunt me one day."

"*Gut* advice is…" She bit her lip as a little boy almost stepped in front of the horse before his *daed* grabbed him and pulled him out of the way.

"Always *gut*, even if you don't want to listen to it," her *grossmammi* finished with another laugh.

"I've heard that from someone wise, too."

"Me, too!" crowed her siblings in unison from the back seat.

Everyone was laughing as Leanna stopped the buggy in the spot that Miriam pointed toward with a big smile.

As they piled out of the buggy, Juanita scanned the crowd. A pucker formed between her eyebrows.

"Isn't Gabriel coming?" she asked.

"He said he was, and he keeps his word." *Usually*, Leanna couldn't help adding. She shoved the thought aside.

She needed to heed the advice she'd given Gabriel. Juanita's graduation was a special moment, and thinking about anything else could mar it.

Offering her arm to her *grossmammi*, Juanita led the family into the schoolhouse. The desks had been pushed aside, and the benches they used for church had been arranged in the center of the room.

Leanna smiled as her younger sister almost ran to join the scholars by the teacher's desk at the front. The older *kinder* took their places behind the little ones, and Leanna wondered how long Miriam and her assistant, Grace, had practiced with her scholars. It was an important day for her friend as well, because this was Miriam's graduation, too. Leanna guessed her friend couldn't wait to become a full-time wife to their minister.

Sitting near the end of bench next to *Grossmammi* Inez and Annie, Leanna scanned the room. Where *was* Gabriel? She didn't see him or Michael or the *bopplin*.

Miriam walked to her desk and turned to the scholars, who looked at her eagerly. Grace, a petite blonde, stood on the other side of the scholars, ready to help when needed. Giving them a smile, Miriam shifted to face the parents and families who'd gathered in the schoolhouse. It would be celebrating the first anniversary of its opening in July because last year there had been an extra session to make up for days lost during the time the families were moving into the new settlement.

"*Danki* for coming today for Harmony Creek Hollow's first ever graduation ceremony," she said with a hint of pride no one would begrudge her today. "Our scholars have worked hard this year, and each one will be taking on new challenges in their new grades next year… except for our two graduates." She aimed a smile at Juanita and at Eugene Yoder, the other graduate. "Juanita and Eugene will be facing challenges of their own, which I know they're eager to begin. I doubt they'll miss their deskwork, but I suspect they'll recall fondly the softball games we've had this spring."

Indulgent laughter rippled through the room, and Leanna knew she wasn't the only one remembering the fun of being a scholar.

Miriam began the ceremony by asking her husband to say a prayer. Eli stood and spoke with his simple eloquence of how they needed God's guidance at beginnings as well as endings. When he said, "Amen," the scholars squared their shoulders as a group and began a hymn Leanna had also sung in school.

Leanna resisted looking around the room for Gabriel

again. As they were in the second row, almost everyone would notice if she swiveled her head. Her nails cut into her palms, her fingers curled in frustration. She couldn't believe he wasn't going to keep his promise to Juanita. The only other reason he wouldn't be here was if something had gone wrong.

Dear God, don't let something have happened to the bopplin.

A hand on her shoulder brought her head up. Gabriel sat beside her, holding Heidi. The little girl raised her arms to Leanna, who took her before the *kind* could protest, interrupting the program.

Leaning toward her, Gabriel whispered, "I'm sorry we're late. Our horse threw a shoe, and we had to get him back to the farm."

"Is he okay?"

"He's fine, but Michael and I ended up pushing and pulling the buggy ourselves to the house."

Leanna put a hand over her mouth to keep from laughing. The sound wouldn't be welcome when the seven-year-olds were reciting the poems they'd written.

"How did you keep the twins from helping you?" she asked.

"Later," he whispered. "I'll give you the sad details."

Turning her attention to the scholars let Leanna hide how much she looked forward to their conversation after the graduation ceremony. She rocked Heidi on her lap, keeping the *boppli* entertained, though Heidi seemed fascinated with the scholars. When they sang, the little girl did her best to join in with them despite being seemingly fixated on a single note.

As soon as the ceremony was over, Miriam invited the guests to join her, the scholars and Grace outside for refreshments. The *kinder* rushed out the door, and Leanna guessed there would be one additional softball game for the two graduates to join.

Most of the men went to play with the youngsters, a special treat when crops and haying kept the *daeds* busy until dark six days a week. Michael, carrying Harley, stood on the sidelines as teams were chosen.

Gabriel was waiting by the steps as Leanna emerged from the school with Heidi. When she walked toward him, he was smiling. She wondered if she'd ever get accustomed to the *wunderbaar* sight after so many days of nothing but frowns?

"I imagine," she said with a feigned somber tone, "you're going to have sore muscles tomorrow after your workout today."

His smile broadened. "I'm glad everyone was already here, so nobody saw the dance Michael and I had to do as we pulled and pushed and checked to make sure the *bopplin* weren't trying to escape."

"It's *gut* you have those car seats in your buggy to keep them in place."

"Heidi has already managed to figure out how to loosen at least one strap. It won't take her long, knowing her as I do, for her to learn how to release them all. And Harley somehow got half his clothes off, though he was strapped in. I don't know how he manages it."

"He starts undressing whenever he's bored."

"You could have warned me."

She laughed. "Haven't you noticed how many times when you're coming in at night that I'm getting him dressed?"

"I thought he'd made a mess or something."

"No. He likes to take off his clothes and throw them at his sister. She thinks it's hilarious."

Before Gabriel could reply, Juanita raced up and flung her arms around him.

"You came! *Danki!*"

Again Leanna had to suppress her reaction. Not laughter this time, though Gabriel's expression of shock at her sister's exuberance was comical. A longing ached deep within her because she wanted to experience standing as close to him as her sister was. Would his warmth welcome her to lean against his sturdy chest?

She lowered her eyes before anyone could read her thoughts. *God*, she prayed, *You know Your plan for me. I know it's impatience that makes me ask You to reveal a bit of it to me, but I'm floundering. Please send me some guidance so I can live the life You want for me.*

"Leanna!" A shout came from across the schoolyard.

Michael ran toward her. People opened a path for him as they stared in dismay at the horror on his face.

Leanna understood why when Michael skidded to a stop in front of her and held out Harley, who was an odd shade of gray.

"He's choking on something!" Michael cried.

She shook her head. "I think he's having trouble catching his breath." Shoving Heidi into Gabriel's arms, she took the other *boppli*. She sat on the ground and put him on her bent knee. She rubbed his back in slow, gentle circles. "What were you doing before he started gasping?"

"We were playing a game of tickle."

"Was he laughing?"

"Ja." Michael exchanged a glance with his brother, and this time Leanna guessed what the silent look meant.

He was apologizing for whatever was happening to his nephew. "He was having fun and laughing pretty hard."

Beneath her fingers, Harley shuddered as he drew in one breath, released it and then pulled in a second, deeper breath. The color in his face began to return to normal. Lifting him to her shoulder, she continued to caress his back as she stood.

"He's okay." She spoke so everyone listening could be reassured, though her words were for the Millers.

"He gets so excited when he laughs that he forgets to breathe," Gabriel said as he put Heidi on the grass by his feet and took her twin. "I've seen it happen a few times before, and he's always fine afterward."

"You could have warned me." Michael released a sigh that countermanded his sharp words.

Gabriel shifted the *boppli* so he could see his son's now smiling face. "You didn't want anyone to forget you were here, ain't so?"

Leanna bit her lower lip. There must be more to Harley's breathing problem than what Gabriel seemed to believe, but now wasn't the time to question his assumptions.

Juanita ran over to them, smiling. "*Komm* and watch the rest of the game. You don't want to miss any of our celebration."

"Sounds fun," Michael said with a grin. "And in August, you'll have to come to the celebration at our house."

"What will you be celebrating?" Leanna asked.

"Birthdays."

"Weren't you and Gabriel born in January?"

"*Ja*, but the twins were born at the end of August."

"The twins will be a year old in August?" The words

came out in a squeak as she turned to where Gabriel was grabbing for a quick-moving Heidi.

He froze and looked over his shoulder at her. His face was as ashen as Harley's had been minutes ago. Dismay and a stronger emotion filled his dark eyes. Fear?

Behind her, she heard a sharp gulp. Michael began to speak, but Gabriel waved him to silence. Michael frowned and stamped away. Juanita glanced at them, then spun to run back to the game.

Leanna started to ask Gabriel to explain, but halted when she saw Heidi had somehow made it to the top of the steps on the school's porch. Jumping forward, Leanna grabbed the *boppli* before she could attempt to crawl down. She held the little girl close like a cloak to ward off the cold. The chill was inside her, oozing out of the most wounded parts of her heart.

"Danki," Gabriel said in an emotionless voice. "One of these days, she's going to fall on her nose, and maybe then she won't be so ready to explore." His attempt at humor was futile.

She walked to him. Though she was unsure she could speak louder than a whisper, she didn't want to chance anyone overhearing them.

"Is it true?" she asked. "Is their birthday in August?"

"Ja, at the end of the month," he said. "They will be nine months old next week."

"I thought they were younger."

"Lots of people do because they're small for their ages."

"So they'll really be a year old in August?" It was a stupid question, but she still couldn't wrap her mind around what he'd said.

"Ja," he repeated, and this time didn't add anything more.

After he gathered up both twins, he walked toward his buggy. He didn't slow. Would he stop if she called after him?

So many thoughts collided in her mind. The memory of *Grossmammi* Inez saying how twins were born early. The questions she had about how advanced Heidi seemed for her age.

No matter how she tried to rearrange the facts, they added up to one conclusion. Freda had been pregnant when Gabriel married her less than two weeks after the day he and Leanna were supposed to meet in Strasburg.

Chapter Eleven

After a sleepless night spent debating whether she should return to the Millers' farm or not when she could simply send Juanita and let her take over watching the *bopplin*, Leanna went through the motions of helping prepare breakfast for her family. Nobody complained about overcooked eggs and barely browned toast. Instead, they gave her sympathetic glances. She was grateful no one asked how she was feeling.

She had no idea.

She was strangled by hurt, puzzlement and disbelief. All the things she'd felt when she heard he was marrying Freda after he'd stood up Leanna and sent a letter she hadn't bothered to read. She hadn't cared what excuses he'd given her to explain why he was becoming someone else's husband without telling Leanna the truth face-to-face.

She should have been suffused with a sense of relief that she hadn't been wrong about how the twins didn't act the age Gabriel let her assume they were, but she wasn't. What was being right worth when she had to endure the pain as if for the first time?

Betrayed.

If someone had asked her how she felt, that would have been her answer. She couldn't say Gabriel had betrayed her…again. No, this time her heart had been the traitor. It had persuaded her to trust him while she welcomed his *kinder* into her heart, believing she was helping it heal.

How wrong she'd been!

She was sure her family noticed how little she said, but nobody, not even her older brother, Lyndon, who'd joined them for breakfast after finishing the milking with Kenny, mentioned it. That warned her that her silence wasn't fooling them. Usually Lyndon loved to tease her and his other siblings, but today he ate his food, talked about the weather and stood as soon as he'd cleaned his plate. He paused by the door long enough to aim a sympathetic glance in her direction.

Despite being curious about what they thought had happened, she didn't ask. Maybe they assumed she was upset because today she'd be handing over the job of caring for the Miller *kinder* to Juanita.

A terse laugh tickled her throat, but letting it escape would be a sure sign that there was something distressing going on between her and the Millers. Her family might suspect the truth, but to confirm it could cause the dam restraining Leanna's hot tears to collapse. Instead, she ate her breakfast and tried to pretend the morning was like any other.

As Leanna reached for her bonnet when breakfast was over, Juanita edged across the kitchen to stand in front of her. "You don't need to go with me this morning. I can go by myself."

"No, I told him that I'd show you around this morning."

"How difficult can it be? Gabriel and Michael have a kitchen. We have a kitchen. They've got a washing machine. We've got a washing machine. They've got a clothesline. We do, too."

"He has two *bopplin*."

"I know that! I've played with them a bunch of times." Her younger sister stood with her hands on her hips and gave Leanna a frown she'd borrowed from their *grossmammi*. "What's wrong? Did you two have words after the graduation?"

"Don't be silly."

"I'm not being silly. You are. You looked thrilled to see Gabriel when he came into the school. After Harley choked, he took off, and you acted as if he'd never showed up at all."

Leanna didn't bother to correct her sister. Harley hadn't choked, and there was no possible way Leanna could ever be unaware of Gabriel.

"You were there, Juanita. You would have heard if we'd had words."

Except for the ones ricocheting through my head, and I don't know how to silence them. How can I ignore the truth that he wasn't honest—he was walking out with me and seeing Freda at the same time?

"I don't know what's going on, but I don't like you being glum and dreary," Juanita said with a childish stamp of her foot. "If you won't tell me what happened, I'll ask Gabriel."

"You—"

Grossmammi Inez's voice interrupted Leanna. Folding her arms over her chest, she said in a voice that grew more halting every day, "You will not, Juanita Wagler, stick your nose into matters that don't concern you. Yesterday you graduated from school into the adult world, so you need to start thinking like an adult instead of a scholar. Do I make myself clear?"

"Ja, Grossmammi." Juanita hung her head before opening the door and walking out.

Before Leanna could follow, the older woman said to the otherwise empty room, "It's wrong for Juanita to intrude, but it's as wrong for you to keep punishing yourself and Gabriel."

"I'm not punishing anyone." She wanted to add that she was the one suffering, but then she'd sound as immature as Juanita.

"I want you to ask yourself two things. First, are you following God's path or your own? Second, are you acting as you'd want others to act toward you?"

Leanna lowered her head, chastised. She knew the answer to the questions, and neither answer made her comfortable. Nothing was simple, a sure sign she'd wandered away from God's plan for her. When she'd first looked for work near Harmony Creek Hollow, everything had fallen into place so quickly that Leanna had no doubts God's hand had been in the changes. Even before she put the word out that she was looking for housecleaning jobs, three women had come to her asking if she was interested in working for them. Now she was returning to that work, and she should be grateful she had jobs where she enjoyed working for people she liked.

"Danki for making me think," she said, "instead of just being emotional."

"Our emotions are there to guide us, but sometimes

we get so caught up in them they blind us to the truth. Don't forget that, Leanna."

"I won't." She gave her *grossmammi* a gentle hug, shocked anew at how much more fragile the older woman was with each passing day. The testing on *Grossmammi* Inez's heart was scheduled for Thursday, and Leanna couldn't wait for results. Surely they would lead to a treatment to make her *grossmammi* feel better.

In spite of her determination to accept the future God had mapped out for her, Leanna was uneasy as she walked with her sister to the Millers' house. She was surprised but relieved when they got there that Gabriel had already left. Michael told them a lumber supply order had come in a day earlier than expected, and Gabriel had gone to make arrangements to have it delivered to their next work site on Archibald Street in Salem. They were repairing the porches on a house that had been built almost three centuries before.

Giving her sister a quick tour of the house, Leanna tried to think of what, if anything, she'd overlooked. "If you've got any other questions, ask. If I can't answer them, he will."

"*He* has a name, y'know," Juanita said in a petulant voice. It would take her sister some time to forgive Leanna for the conversation that had led to *Grossmammi* Inez scolding them.

"I know."

"How long are you going to avoid saying it?"

Leanna didn't reply. If she said she wasn't trying not to speak Gabriel's name, it might be a lie. She didn't know why she was calling him "he." It could be as simple as she wanted to keep some distance between her thoughts of him and her aching heart.

"I think I've told you everything you need to know," Leanna said as she looked around Gabriel's kitchen.

She'd explained to Juanita how the kitchen faucet had to be turned on slowly or it sprayed everywhere. She'd shown her younger sister which burner on the stove didn't work. The goats' *milch* formula was poured into bottles and waiting in the refrigerator. Fresh diapers and bibs were stacked on one end of the kitchen table.

"I've taken care of other *bopplin*, Leanna. We'll be fine."

"I know you will."

"Then go, or you'll be late. You know how Mrs. Duchamps gets annoyed if you don't get there on time."

Leanna struggled to smile. "It's because she worries something has happened. She can find a cloud around any silver lining. One time, she convinced herself I'd had a buggy accident and was lying beside the road near death because I wasn't there ten minutes early."

"You're babbling." Her younger sister made shooing motions with her hands. "Go, or you will have that nice old lady ready to call nine-one-one."

She bent to kiss the tops of the twins' heads. Their soft red hair tickled her nose, but she didn't feel like laughing. For more than two weeks, she'd spent most of her waking hours with them, and now she'd see them far less often. *Ja*, she could offer to bounce one of them on her knee during the long Sunday service. She might run into Gabriel and the *bopplin* along the twisting road through the hollow or at a store in the village. If she came over with fresh lemonade and sat on the porch with the Millers when they returned home at the end of the workday, it wouldn't be the same as spending each day with Heidi and Harley and watching how they grew and changed.

Without another word, she left and walked home. There, she hitched up the horse and drove to Mrs. Duchamps's house, which was the easternmost one in the village of Salem. Such a short time had passed since the last time she'd been there, but it seemed as if it'd been part of someone else's life. Someone who hadn't run into her past and had it implode around her.

Mrs. Duchamps answered the front door herself. She was a white-haired woman who towered over Leanna. She carried a cane, but she stood as straight as the spruce dominating her front lawn. Always dressing in bright colors, she collected whimsical bear figurines. She had hundreds, displayed on every flat surface in the house. As well, she had paintings of teddy bears hanging on the walls and a quilt with blue-and-green bears draped over her bed.

"It's good to have you back, Leanna." She stepped to one side, letting Leanna in.

"I'm glad to be here." That was the truth.

Or at least part of it.

At Mrs. Duchamps's house, she didn't have to judge each word she spoke before she let it past her lips. She could think of the present and not worry about what had happened in the past.

On the other hand, at Mrs. Duchamps's house, she wouldn't see the twins and marvel at their endless mischief and efforts to try something new. And she wouldn't have a chance to talk to Gabriel or see one of his rare smiles. Even when he annoyed her so much that she wanted to stamp her foot and demand that he listen to common sense, she'd enjoyed watching him with his *kinder*.

"You remember where everything is?" the elderly woman asked.

"*Ja*. I'll start in the upstairs bathroom as usual."

"Your sister started in the kitchen."

"Do you prefer that?" She hadn't guessed Juanita would make such a change from the routine Leanna had given her. What would her sister alter with the twins?

"Whatever works for you, dear."

Leanna nodded, but went into the kitchen instead of upstairs to the bathroom. She'd worked long enough for Mrs. Duchamps to recognize that any comment, even one that the elderly woman said wasn't important, was a suggestion that needed to be followed.

As she collected the cleaning supplies from the shelf where she'd stored them in the pantry so they were available when she came, she tried to focus on her job. It was impossible. Her mind was filled with confusion and sorrow. If someone else was in such a state, she would have urged them to talk to the person upsetting them.

What was the point of talking to Gabriel? She couldn't ask him point-blank the one question that preyed on her mind: Why had he spent time with her when he was having a more intimate relationship with Freda? Gabriel had walked out with Leanna for almost five months, so it wasn't as if he were on the rebound from breaking up with Freda. She didn't want to think she'd been wrong— now as well as months ago—when she'd believed he was a *gut* and decent man. Yet he must have married Freda after she became pregnant.

Pregnancies that happened before wedding vows were spoken weren't unheard-of in plain communities. In fact, the bishop who'd overseen their district had a daughter who'd anticipated her vows. The girl had asked for forgiveness and been granted it. She'd gone on to marry the man she loved.

Why had it been so easy to offer forgiveness to that young woman and impossible to offer the same to Gabriel? He must have atoned to his district's *Leit* before he'd been baptized and spoken his vows with Freda.

When *Grossmammi* Inez had been reading to them from the Bible each evening, she'd reminded them of the importance of forgiving one another. "To deny others what we have been given means that we're turning our faces and our lives away from God."

Leanna didn't want that, but she couldn't let go of her anger and betrayal, either. Scrubbing the tile floor so hard she threatened to rub the pattern right off the ceramic didn't help.

She didn't pause when a phone rang. Mrs. Duchamps's muffled voice drifted to her, and she looked up when the old woman peeked into the kitchen and said the caller had asked for Leanna.

Praying her *grossmammi* hadn't taken a turn for the worse, Leanna went into the living room where the phone was. She picked it up, listened and said, "I'll be there as soon as I can." She put the phone in its cradle. Seeing Mrs. Duchamps in the doorway, she said, "I need to go. It's an emergency."

Mrs. Duchamps rubbed her hands together. "What's wrong? Is someone ill? Changeable weather in the spring brings on colds and other worse things. Or did someone get injured? There are so many ways to be hurt on a farm. It isn't your grandmother, is it? She—"

Knowing that the elderly woman could go on and on, Leanna said, "It's my younger sister. She needs help with two *bopplin*—babies—she's watching for the first time."

"Are they okay?"

"They're going to be fine, I'm sure." She wasn't certain she could say the same for Juanita. It wasn't like her younger sister to panic. "Let me check on her, and then I'll come and finish up."

"Take as much time as you need."

"Danki." Leanna gave Mrs. Duchamps a stern look. "Don't touch that bucket. It's too heavy for you."

The old woman made a sweeping motion toward the door. "I won't touch it. I promise. Go and see what's wrong with those little ones."

A dozen possibilities ran through Leanna's head as she drove the buggy at the highest possible speed along the main road before turning onto the one following Harmony Creek. Racing past the camp where Mercy Stoltzfus planned to have city *kinder* come to spend a couple of weeks in the country with horses, she saw her friend Sarah's brother jump out of the way as the buggy rushed past. Benjamin shouted a question after her, but she didn't slow.

Apologizing to the horse as she jumped out of the buggy in front of the Millers' house, she ran to the door and flung it open.

Juanita whirled to face her. Remnants of tears on her sister's face matched those on the *bopplin's*. "They stopped crying."

"When?"

"Right now." Juanita stared at her in amazement. "I heard your footsteps on the porch, so they must have, too. And then they stopped crying." She shook her head and snapped her fingers. "Just like that."

"Curiosity—"

"Has nothing to do with it. They recognized the sound

of your steps. They don't want anything to do with me. They want you."

"They're *bopplin*. They want everything."

Juanita shook her head. "No, they didn't want anything but you. Nothing I tried would convince them to quit crying. As soon as you put a single toe on the porch, they stopped."

Knowing she wouldn't get anywhere arguing with her sister when Juanita was so definite, Leanna squatted next to the *kinder. "Was iss letz, lieblings?"*

Of course, the twins didn't answer her and tell her what was wrong, but Heidi reached out and handed her one of the blocks she'd been clenching in her tiny hands.

Leanna didn't take it as she noticed Harley gasping for breath as he had the day before. She picked up the little boy and cuddled him. His uneven breathing eased, and some color returned to his face. When she held him up to her shoulder, his breaths, quick and shallow, brushed her neck. She murmured nonsense words until he calmed and wasn't shuddering with each inhalation.

He didn't cry much, she realized. She'd considered him the most content *boppli* she'd ever seen, but a sliver of worry pierced her mind. Could it be that he didn't cry because he'd come to realize how he struggled to breathe when he sobbed?

She couldn't ask a *boppli* such a question, but there was one she could ask her sister.

"Juanita, how did you call Mrs. Duchamps's house?"

With guilt blossoming on her face, her sister reached into a pocket under her apron and pulled out a cell phone.

"Where did you get that?" Leanna asked.

Her sister's cheeks grew bright red. "From Eugene.

He got it because he's working in Salem with his uncle now that he's graduated from school."

"But why do you have it?" She made sure her voice was gentler, guessing her sister had a crush on Eugene Yoder.

"He thought I might need it on my first day of work here, and he was right, ain't so?"

Leanna started to answer, then halted when the back door opened. As Gabriel walked in, her sister shoved the cell phone back into her pocket.

His hair was laced with sawdust, and a swath of dirt on the right side of his face emphasized his high cheekbones. "Leanna?" he asked, halting in midstep.

"Gute mariye," she said as if the past twenty-four hours hadn't happened. What *gut* would it do to rehash what had happened? She should be thinking of the *bopplin* and what was best for them.

"What are you doing here? I thought you had houses to clean today."

"I did. I mean, I do." She put Harley on the quilt. Getting a banana off the counter, she peeled and sliced it while she said, "Juanita couldn't stop the twins from crying, so she sent for me." There was no reason to bring the cell phone into the discussion. She handed each of the *bopplin* two pieces of the fruit.

"Are they okay?" He rushed to where his *kinder* were happily eating and making a mess with the banana. Looking at Leanna, he asked, "What happened?"

"Like I said, Juanita couldn't calm them. She called me to come and help."

"I see you've done that." His shoulders relaxed, and the wild expression of dismay faded. *"Danki*, Leanna, for helping."

"I'm glad I could." Smiling at her sister, she said, "It looks as if everything is under control. I need to get back to Mrs. Duchamps's house."

Gabriel walked with her out of the house, explaining he'd come to get some tools they hadn't realized they'd need this morning. "Mrs. Fenton keeps adding small details for the job, and Michael didn't have what he needed. When I got here and saw the buggy in the drive, I wanted to chcck what was going on."

"It doesn't seem to have been anything other than jitters from Juanita." She forced a smile. "I don't think there will be any other problems."

A shriek sent a shiver down her spine, and she spun to look at the house. Another followed. She heard Gabriel shout something, but didn't pay attention to his words as she rushed into the kitchen. As if someone had flipped a switch, the screaming stopped.

Tears rolled down small faces, and bananas were squashed between tiny fingers as the twins stared at her. Again Heidi held up her arms. Harley did as well, trying to lift himself off the floor as he did whenever he wanted her to pick him up. Beside them, Juanita looked as pale as fresh *milch*.

Coming to her feet at the same time Gabriel burst into the kitchen, Juanita raised her hands in a pose of surrender. "I told you. As soon as you leave, Leanna, they go into fire siren mode. As soon as you come back, they're okay again."

"I didn't expect this," Gabriel said.

"Me, either." Leanna knelt on the quilt. "This is a problem." She couldn't imagine leaving again when she knew Harley might choke again on his own sobs. "I don't know what's going on."

"They miss you." Juanita shrugged. "Well, it's true. They've never had a *mamm* that they remember, so you're the only *mamm* they've known. Isn't that right, Gabriel?"

Watching color drain from Leanna's face, Gabriel sighed. Once Juanita had spoken, it was obvious to him that the teenager had seen what he and Leanna had ignored. The *kinder* adored her. Not as a babysitter, but as a replacement for the *mamm* they'd never known.

"How old were the twins when your wife died?" asked Juanita when nobody else spoke.

"Five weeks old."

Both Waglers gasped at his answer.

"So young," murmured Leanna. "And such a short time with Freda."

"They were in the hospital for the first three weeks after they were born, but they seemed to be thriving," he said, staring out the window because he couldn't bear to look at Leanna when he revealed his part of the sad story. "I was so focused on them that I didn't notice Freda wasn't."

Leanna stood, but didn't move toward him. "I'm sorry, Gabriel."

"So what do we do for them?" he asked, desperate to change the subject to anything but his failure to see what Freda had needed. "Leanna has her jobs, and they're too young to understand they'll see her a lot less anyhow."

"I don't know." Leanna seemed about to add something more, but must have thought better of it.

"The answer is simple." Juanita gave them an easy smile.

Leanna frowned. "The answer to what is simple?"

"Making sure the *bopplin* don't work themselves into a tizzy as they have this morning."

"Go ahead," Gabriel said, though he had a *gut* idea what Juanita would say next.

"Leanna needs to take care of them while I do her cleaning jobs."

"Have you lost your mind?" asked Leanna in astonishment as she picked up Heidi and carried her to the sink to wash crushed banana off her hands.

"No, it's a brilliant idea." Juanita's grin broadened. "What do you think, Gabriel? Doesn't it make sense for Leanna and me to switch jobs?"

He wanted to check and make sure his ears weren't clogged or had stopped working. Or was it his brain that wasn't functioning?

"Switch jobs?" he repeated. "Are you saying Leanna would stay as the babysitter for the twins?"

"And she'd take over my cleaning jobs." Leanna didn't look at him.

Juanita did, though, and she was smiling with delight at what she thought was a simple solution. "So what do you say, Gabriel? Are you okay with it?"

Okay? He was torn between jumping up and down with gratitude or shouting out that it was the stupidest idea that had ever been conceived. Nothing he was experiencing at that moment was as tepid as an *okay*.

"If we take a week or two and wean them off my being here all day each day," Leanna said, "then they should be fine with Juanita."

"It's worth a try." He ignored how his heart did a dance at the thought of seeing her each morning and evening. "Will your cleaning clients agree?"

"They have so far," Juanita interjected. "If everyone

here is fine with this, I should get over to Mrs. Duchamps's house and finish up, Leanna."

With a weary wave, Leanna motioned for her to go.

Why hadn't he thought how tough this was for Leanna, too? He'd seen her face when Michael blurted out about the twins' upcoming birthday. She had figured out that Freda was pregnant when they took their vows, but without knowing the whole story, Leanna could only assume he'd cheated on her while they were walking out together.

If only Aden hadn't asked him to promise not to reveal the truth—

He silenced the thought before it could play out in his mind. "I'm sorry for making things difficult for you."

"I know, but we'll work this out."

Was that an acceptance of his apology? He doubted she had any idea how much he craved her forgiveness.

And how is she supposed to offer that when you haven't been honest with her?

He'd lost count of the number of times that question had rippled through his mind, but he knew how many times he'd answered it.

Not once.

Chapter Twelve

When Leanna walked into the bustling Salem Volunteer Fire Department building on Saturday morning, she couldn't utter a single word. Her throat clogged with tears of gratitude when she saw the long line of people waiting to check in for the blood drive that was being held in honor of *Grossmammi* Inez, though it wasn't certain yet that *Grossmammi* Inez would have to have surgery. Several of the men in the *Leit*, including Miriam's husband and brother, were volunteer firefighters who'd helped arrange it.

Her *grossmammi* had protested being singled out, but their minister had assured her it was common practice to give the blood drive a human face. Eli had added that was important because it brought in more people to donate the pints of blood that were always in short supply. At that, *Grossmammi* Inez had relented.

Leanna had entered the firehouse from the back and walked through the multipurpose room. She'd been there before for fund-raising suppers. At those, folding tables and chairs had been arranged the length of the room, and the firefighters, along with the volunteer EMTs, had been busy in the kitchen area. Today they were checking people in and escorting them to where they could wait on chairs in neat rows in the bay where the ambulance usually parked. In the neighboring area, the spot where the pumper was stored, screens divided the gurneys where volunteers were already donating pints of blood.

She recognized many of the volunteer firefighters who were assisting the blood bank personnel. Not only her plain neighbors, but *Englischers* who'd participated in events with the fire department. Some of them had worked at a mud sale earlier in the spring. She was sure she recognized the tall, mustached man. He had served as the auctioneer who'd sold the quilt she'd donated.

She waved to Sarah. Her friend had taken the rigorous training last fall and was now the first plain female volunteer EMT. She didn't wear trousers and T-shirts as the others did, but she'd put masking tape across the front of her black apron and written the words "blood drive volunteer" on it.

Sarah hurried over, her red hair aglow in the bright lights hanging from metal beams across the ceiling. "I was wondering when you'd get here. The volunteers from the blood service have been looking forward to meeting someone from your family."

"Isn't Lyndon here already?" Her older brother was an enthusiastic volunteer firefighter.

"I haven't seen him."

Leanna rolled her eyes. "I forgot. He had to go to Greenwich to pick up a part for his baler. He figured he could get there and back without missing too much of the blood drive."

"*Komm mol*, and I'll introduce you around."

"I want to donate, too."

"Don't worry. We won't let you leave until you've got a pint less of blood inside you." Hooking her arm through Leanna's, she led her to the first table.

Leanna thanked the volunteers while she was being signed in and answering a health questionnaire. When she was shown to a gurney, she stretched out on it and followed the instructions given to her by a young *Englischer*. He asked questions about her *grossmammi* while he inserted the needle. He laughed when Leanna told him one of her favorite stories about *Grossmammi* Inez.

She'd been with the elderly woman a few years ago when they came across a skunk in the road. *Grossmammi* Inez had put her hands on her waist, given the skunk a stern look and said in the same tone she used with her *kins-kinder* when they were misbehaving, "If you know what's *gut* for you, skunk, you'll get out of here. Now!"

Chuckling, Leanna said, "And the wildest thing is that the skunk waddled off as if it'd understood her. Didn't send a bit of nasty scent our way."

"I guess we all learn to listen to our grandparents," the young man said. "Even skunks." He put tape over the needle to hold it and the IV in place.

"That hardly hurt," Leanna said as he handed her a soft rubber ball shaped like a bright red heart to squeeze while the blood pumped into the donation bag. "I've pricked myself worse when I'm quilting."

"Glad to hear it. Call for me if you need anything or if you feel woozy."

"Woozy? Is that a medical term?"

He laughed. "One of the first they teach us in nursing school."

Leaning back on the raised head of the table while

she watched her blood ooze through the clear tube, she thanked God for the wisdom that had allowed medical professionals to know how to save lives with donated blood.

Less than a half hour later, Leanna sat at a small table enjoying some orange juice and chocolate chip and dried cranberry cookies that had been donated by the bakery where her twin worked. She smiled when Annie joined her, a small piece of gauze taped to the inside of her arm.

"Your cookies are delicious as always," Leanna said.

"Not mine. Those are Caleb's recipe. He's always trying something new." Annie's nose, so like her own, crinkled. "Ask him sometime about the peanut-butter-and-banana cookies he tried making. Ask. Don't try one!"

"I'll keep that in mind."

"What a great turnout!" Annie's grin returned. "Wait until *Grossmammi* Inez hears about this."

"She won't have to hear about it," replied a deeper voice from behind Leanna. "Not when she can see it with her own two eyes."

Whirling in her chair, Leanna gaped at the sight of her *grossmammi*, weak but as determined as ever, standing with one hand on her cane and the other on Gabriel's arm.

"*Grossmammi* Inez!" she gasped.

Everyone in the room seemed to turn at once and stare at the four of them. Volunteers rushed forward to greet her *grossmammi*. The older woman acted unabashed by the attention. She turned every comment into grateful words to each person who came up to thank her for being a part of the blood drive. She was urged to sit at the table. A fresh cup of *kaffi* appeared from somewhere, along with a plate topped by a generous selection of Caleb's cookies.

Leanna stood quickly. Too quickly, because her head spun and the room seemed to telescope in on itself. Determined, she blinked to bring everything into focus as she stepped aside to let others have a chance to speak with her *grossmammi*.

She grabbed Gabriel's arm and motioned with her head for him to follow her away from the crowd. As soon as she guessed they were out of anyone else's earshot, she said, "She shouldn't be here. The *doktor* wants her to avoid people so she doesn't pick up some bug that could do more damage to her heart."

"I didn't plan to bring her, so don't be angry with me." He raised his hands in a pose of surrender. "She flagged me down when I was driving past. If I hadn't agreed to bring her, she would have walked."

With a sigh, Leanna had to admit that Gabriel was right. Her *grossmammi* had been upset that her faulty heart valve was keeping her from visiting neighbors as she'd done the previous spring.

"Where are the twins?"

He pointed to a small door to the right. "There's a room set up as a nursery. I left them there with a few other *kinder*. I should get in line to donate, too."

"Gabriel?"

"Ja?"

"I'm sorry that I jumped to conclusions about you bringing *Grossmammi* Inez here."

"It's okay. I know you've gotten used to assuming the worst of me."

"I…" She wanted to deny his words, but she couldn't. "I'll try to change that."

He looked surprised. "You've got every right to believe as you do after what's happened between us."

"Living in the past means not treasuring gifts of the future. *Grossmammi* Inez has said that more times than I can count."

"Your *grossmammi* is a smart woman."

"I agree."

When he took her hand and squeezed it gently, she almost gasped. He strode away to go through the process of donating, and she stared at him. Had he meant to give her some sort of message by holding her hand?

If so, she didn't have any idea what he'd meant to tell her.

Leanna joined the other volunteers and passed out glasses of juice and cookies to people who'd donated blood. When the *Englisch* donors saw her plain clothing, they asked about her *grossmammi*, and she shared more stories about *Grossmammi* Inez with them. She was touched by their solicitousness for a woman they'd never met before today.

When Michael sat at one of the tables, she smiled. She handed him some juice and offered him a choice of cookies. At the same time, she glanced around the firehouse. She didn't see Gabriel, so he must be behind one of the screens in the donation area.

Thanking her for the three cookies he took, Michael said, "I've been wanting to see the inside of the firehouse, and this was my first chance." He gave her a teasing wink. "I didn't think it would cost me a pint of blood."

"*Danki* for coming today."

"It's the least I can do for your *grossmammi*, who has sent over so many delicious meals to us."

"We've been happy to help."

"And we've been happy that you've been happy to help." He gave a weak smile. "Is it usual for me to be seeing double?"

She glanced over her shoulder, hoping to see Annie. Her twin was nowhere in sight, either. "Let me call one of the nurses."

He rested his elbow on the table and leaned his head against his open palm. Tilting his head so he could see her, he said, "No, don't bother them. I was in a hurry to get up. I should have waited a few more minutes as they told me to do."

"I can still check with one of the nurses for you."

"Don't bother." He closed his eyes. "Gabriel promised me if I came and donated, he'd make sure I got home if he had to strap me to the back of the buggy."

She laughed. "I'd like to see that."

"Oh, you will." He opened one eye. "My brother never breaks a promise, which is why he's so leery of making them."

"You've said that before."

His brow furrowed. "Because it's true. I don't know what promise he made before he got married, but he changed after he told me that he'd decided to marry Freda."

Leanna murmured something about him resting. She wasn't sure herself what she said, but Michael nodded and shut his eyes again. After backing away from the table, she set the plate next to others. She walked toward the room where the older *kinder* were, she'd been told, being entertained by one of the teachers from the public school while the younger *kinder* played with simple toys.

If anyone spoke to her, she didn't hear them. If someone was in her way, they must have stepped aside before she bumped into them because she was lost in her swirling thoughts.

Gabriel had changed so much, though he was again smiling and occasionally laughing. She'd assumed he'd grown grim after Freda's death, but Michael's comment suggested otherwise. Why hadn't he been happy when he married Freda? She was the *mamm* of his *kinder*. He must have loved her, so why hadn't he been happy Freda had agreed to become his wife?

It was another question she couldn't ask, but for the first time, she wasn't sure she wanted to satisfy her curiosity. She feared knowing the truth would change her as much as it had Gabriel.

Leaving the busy donation area, Gabriel looked around. Had Leanna gone home already? He saw her *grossmammi* and her siblings other than Lyndon talking with volunteers and donors. As he thought about Leanna's brother, Lyndon rushed in to be teased by his fellow firefighters, who thought it was hilarious he was late for the blood drive held for his own *grossmammi*.

A surge of gratitude washed over Gabriel as he watched the camaraderie among the *Leit* and the *Englischers*. In the small town, they were dependent upon each other in so many ways, though the plain people kept most of their daily lives separate from their neighbors. He'd hoped their new home would be like this when he accepted Caleb Hartz's invitation to purchase the run-down farm not far from Caleb's own place along Harmony Creek.

What would have happened if he and Freda had lived here instead of Lancaster County? A few gossips there had stuck their noses into everyone's business, carrying tales, whether they were true or not, to the bishop who always took them at their word, even when it caused divisions in the district. That had been one of the reasons Gabriel had jumped at the chance to begin over again in northern New York.

Would Aden have feared so much for his daughter and the family's reputation if they'd been living among these people, instead? Not that the *Leit* in Harmony Creek Hollow or the others in Salem were perfect. No one on earth was, but he'd seen the way his plain neighbors had accepted one another's mistakes with kindness and supported each other through the difficult phase of re-creating lives in a new place laced with so many hopes and dreams.

Not seeing Leanna anywhere, he headed for the nursery. Soon it would be time for the twins' dinner, and he should get them home. He enjoyed sharing the midday meal with the *bopplin* on the weekends because during the week he didn't have the opportunity.

He entered the room and smiled. Leanna sat on the floor next to the twins, who were cuddled as close to her as they could. The *kinder* adored her, and he understood why. She never attempted to hide how much she loved Heidi and Harley. She'd brought them two of the heart-shaped balls used in the donation area. Both *bopplin* giggled when they squeezed the bright red balls. With a laugh of her own, Leanna guided the ball Heidi held away from the little girl's mouth.

Wrinkling her nose, she said, "Yucky. It's yucky."

"Ya-ya," Heidi parroted back.

Gabriel chuckled when she tried to copy Leanna's expression and ended up crossing her eyes, instead.

Leanna looked up and smiled. It seemed forced, but he wasn't going to remark on that. Still, he wondered why she wasn't wearing her customary bright expression.

"We're playing 'let's not eat the ball,'" she said.

"How do you play it?" He sat on the other side of the twins.

"Heidi and Harley try to eat the balls, and I try to keep them from doing so."

"Pretty simple rules."

"Yet it's not as easy as it sounds."

"So I see." He reached across the space between them. Tapping Heidi's nose, he grinned when she managed to scrunch up her own nose.

The *boppli* chortled and raised the ball high above her red curls before bringing it down on her knee. She repeated the motion over and over, her delight visible to everyone who walked past.

"Watch out!" Leanna warned. "Harley wants to take a bite out of his!"

Putting his fingers on the ball the little boy held, Gabriel lowered it away from his lips.

Harley opened his mouth to protest, but became fascinated when Gabriel guided his arms in the same up-and-down pattern as his sister.

"*Danki,*" Leanna said. "I was beginning to wonder if God would listen to my prayer to send someone to help or to give me a couple of extra hands so I could keep them from eating the balls. Clearly today, Gabriel, you're the answer to my prayer."

"I'm not that." Her words made him uncomfortable.

Not that she meant them as anything other than a cheerful remark, but each one reminded him of how he'd broken her heart.

"Why not? I prayed for help, and here you are. Don't you believe God hears our prayers and answers them?"

He jerked at the feeling as if she'd driven a knife into him, draining away his contentment with playing with the *kinder*. "Do *you* believe that?"

"*Ja*, with every bit of my heart."

"I wish I could."

"Why can't you?"

He met her eyes over the *bopplin's* heads. "Because, assuming God heard my prayers, He hasn't answered them."

Plucking the ball out of Heidi's mouth again, she said, "If you're talking about when Freda and her *daed* died, you know that our prayers aren't always answered in the way we want them to be. We can't see what God knows."

"I know that, Leanna."

"You don't believe it." She reached past the twins to jab a finger into his chest. "Not here."

"I prayed for Freda and Aden to be freed from their pain." He held up a hand. "Don't tell me that God answered my prayer because He took their pain away when they died."

"No, I won't tell you that. God knows what was in your heart. And it wasn't that you wished to lose two people who were so important to you. Let Him into your heart, Gabriel, and He'll show you the truth of His love."

"I don't know how to take down the wall between me and Him."

"The same way you built it, but in reverse." She gave

him a sympathetic smile. "You're a builder. You know how these things work. It's harder sometimes to take down a wall than to put it up, because you must be careful and pay attention to every step you take."

"You make it sound easy."

"No, I don't. I know how hard it is."

"Do you? Really?" He folded his arms in front of him and frowned.

"*Ja*, I've gotten angry at God, too. I ran away from everything I knew, too."

"When was that?"

"When you married Freda and I had the chance to move here." She stood, turned on her heel and walked away, not giving him a chance to reply.

What could he have said?

If only Aden hadn't asked him to promise not to reveal the truth that would hurt his daughter in the eyes of the community...

Chapter Thirteen

Leanna stopped at the bottom of the stairs in Gabriel's house the following Tuesday morning and held her breath as she listened for the *kinder*. Not a sound. She shouldn't be surprised. The twins had been more than ready for their nap when she put them down about ten minutes ago. Gabriel had warned her that Heidi and Harley had been up late last night because Benjamin and Menno Kuhns had come over to discuss having the Millers use some of their lumber in upcoming construction projects. The conversation had gone on, and Gabriel hadn't had a chance to put the *bopplin* to bed until after Sarah's brothers had left.

She was glad to hear about the two sets of brothers doing business together. She'd heard Michael complain more than once that the lumberyard where they'd been getting their supplies wasn't as dependable as he was accustomed to in Pennsylvania. Knowing how dedicated the Kuhns brothers were, she guessed they'd have the proper lengths of wood at a job site at the exact time Gabriel and Michael needed them.

She went into the kitchen and opened the bag she'd

brought with her along with her regular satchel containing the *bopplin*'s bottles of formula. She pulled out long rubber gloves and plastic protective glasses, as well as her soap molds. She'd asked Gabriel last night before she left if she could make soap today if the twins napped long enough. The task was simpler when there weren't other people around.

Simpler and safer, because the lye she used was caustic. She usually made the soap when her younger siblings and Lyndon's *kinder* were in school. With school out for the summer, it'd be easier at Gabriel's house.

She was surprised when Gabriel walked in right after she'd finished measuring and melting lard, coconut oil and canola oil. He went to the refrigerator and pulled out the pitcher of ice tea she'd made earlier.

Pouring a glass, he asked, "Do you want one?"

"Not until I'm done making soap." She gestured with her elbow. "Please stay back."

"Mind if I sit at the table and watch? I've never seen anyone make soap before. I'll stay out of your way so I won't do anything to distract you."

"All right," she replied. Didn't he realize that his presence was distracting? "I thought you'd be out all afternoon."

"Michael is at the job site. I went to the livestock auction in Cambridge."

Measuring the temperature of the oils with a handheld thermometer, she asked, "Did you buy anything?"

"A small herd of dairy cows. They'll be delivered in a couple of days. Once they're here, I can start milking the half dozen that are giving *milch*, though I'll have to buy some feed for them until I can get a full crop in and harvested next year. The grass in the pasture is growing well, and I should be able to get a first cutting by the end of the month."

The anticipation in his voice made her smile, but she didn't turn as she retrieved her frozen goats' *milch* packets from where she'd stored them in the freezer. As she chopped the *milch* into chunks and put it in a large metal bowl, she said, "It's what you've been waiting for, ain't so?"

"*Ja.* This is the next step in building a future for my family on this farm. The land here needs work to make the soil as productive as it could be, but that will come in time."

"And soon the twins will be scurrying around trying to help and getting in your way while you milk."

Her hope that he'd laugh was dashed, but he did say, "I want them to learn everything about farming so they can appreciate what we have here as much as I do."

Leanna didn't answer as she pulled on her protective gloves and goggles. Measuring out the lye, she began to sprinkle it over the top of the frozen *milch*. She stirred between each small amount. The *milch* began to melt as she added more lye.

"Why do you have the *milch* frozen?" he asked. "Wouldn't it be simpler to have it liquid and pour it into the lye?"

"The lye has to go into the *milch*, not the other way around. If I put the lye in first, it'd erupt like a volcano." She kept adding in small amounts of lye and stirring. "Having the *milch* frozen keeps it from curdling when I put in the lye."

He remained silent until she was finished with the lye and had poured in the melted oils. She put in a small amount of oatmeal and a few drops of lavender oil. Using a battery-operated handheld blender, she carefully mixed the ingredients, making sure no bubbles appeared. Again and again she paused and lifted the blender out of the soap. Once the pattern of the blade remained visible, she ladled the soap into the molds, taking care not to drop any on the counter.

She gathered up the bowls. She made sure the lye container was closed before she put it in her bag.

When she'd finished cleaning her equipment and the counter, Gabriel poured her a glass of ice tea and re-filled his own.

"Danki," she said, taking the glass and sitting at the table. "And *danki* for letting me use your kitchen to make soap today."

"It was fascinating." He sat facing her. "Do you always put in the same scents and the oatmeal?"

"Not always. Sometimes I use coffee grounds instead of oatmeal."

"Coffee grounds?"

"With them, I have a soap that exfoliates dry skin."

He held up his work-hardened hands. "Maybe I should try some?"

"I can bring you a bar in about a month because the soap has to cure."

"I had no idea that making soap was such a long process."

She smiled. "That's because the only parts of the process most people are familiar with are picking a packaged bar off the shelf and unwrapping it before using it."

"So why do you go to all this work?"

"Why are you working with Benjamin and Menno to make sure you have boards that meet your specifications?"

"Answering a question with a question is the sign of trying to avoid giving an answer."

"Why would I do that?"

"Why not?"

She laughed. This time, she was sure he was teasing her as he used to do.

Before he married Freda…

Leanna stood and walked away. While she'd been working at the counter, she'd had to focus on the soap. That had allowed her to forget, for a few precious minutes, about how Gabriel had been with Freda at the same time he'd been taking Leanna for buggy rides.

Now that she was over her initial shock at the realization of Freda being pregnant before marrying Gabriel, something didn't feel right to Leanna. Everything else she'd ever seen or heard about him proclaimed he was an honest man. If he'd been spending time with Freda, he would have said something to Leanna. Even if he'd been determined to keep it a secret, why hadn't she heard the truth from someone else? Others had ended up with their names repeated along the Amish grapevine when they had stopped or started walking out with someone new. It was an illusion nobody knew who was courting whom. The truth was it was rare for anyone to be surprised when a marriage announcement was published during a church service.

Gabriel cleared his throat. How long had she been lost in her thoughts?

"I'm sorry," she said. "My mind was wandering."

"No, I should be the one saying I'm sorry. I know I've been gruff."

"An understatement."

"Again you're right."

Why was it so easy for her to accept his apology now but not be able to forgive him for breaking her heart? She should be eager to put the past behind her so she could move on.

Instead, the question of how long he'd been seeing Freda while he was walking out with Leanna tried to slip past her lips. Again she kept the words from bursting forth. She should get his late wife out of her mind. Would it help if they spoke about Freda more? She'd seen him clamp his lips closed when someone mentioned his wife's name.

"Gabriel, we need to be straightforward with each other," she said.

Wariness narrowed his eyes. "What do you mean?"

She wanted to ask why he was looking at her as if he expected her to attack him at any moment. "I'm not sure how to act around you. I don't want to do anything to put more pressure on you. You put enough on yourself with getting the farm started, helping your brother, worrying about your *bopplin* and recovering from your wife's death. That's on top of having a wife become ill in the wake of the twins' being born, as well as a dying *daed*-in-law. That would be awful for anyone."

"I appreciate that, Leanna, but I'm fine."

"You may think so, but I know how difficult it is to have someone you love fall ill. When I was a *kind*, my *daed* died after being sick for what seemed like forever. I saw what my *mamm* went through nursing him. It took her a long time to recover her own health after that."

"I told you. I'm fine." His tone was as caustic as the lye she'd used. For a moment, she thought his bitterness was aimed at her, and then realized it wasn't.

"Leanna, can we change the subject? This is too hard to talk about."

"It's okay to admit that it was hard. We *kinder* depended on Mamm during that time, too. We were older than the twins, so I can understand how tough it was for you as she got sicker and weaker and you had to do more for her. Trust me. I do understand, and I think it'd be *gut* for you to talk to someone who understands."

Gabriel's hands clenched on the table. "You don't understand a thing, Leanna! I didn't do a single thing for her. I didn't know how sick she was until she killed herself by overdosing on sleeping pills."

Leanna blanched as she gripped the edge of the counter. "Freda killed herself?"

He berated himself for opening that door to the past he'd fought to keep closed. "I wish you could forget that I said that." He shook his head and drew in a deep breath. His heart seemed to ache more with each beat, but at the same time a weight that had been grinding down into it had lessened at the exact moment he shared the truth.

His hands fisted more tightly. If he'd relieved an ounce of his suffering, it shouldn't have been because he'd passed it to Leanna. She'd stepped up to help him when she had every reason not to, and shifting his pain and grief to her couldn't be the way he repaid her.

"I can't forget it," she whispered, "but I won't say anything to anyone else."

"Danki."

"I'm so sorry." She put her hand on top of his clenched one. "You're right. I don't understand what you've gone through, but I hope that God will show me a way to help you."

With a raw growl that came from the depths of his throat, he shook his head. "Don't you think I've asked God for help? Go ahead and try it yourself if you want. Maybe you'll get a better response than I did, which was nothing."

"Tell me what happened."

"Are you sure you want to know?"

She was still for so long that he wasn't sure if she was going to reply. Finally she said, *"Ja."*

He stood, unable to sit and face her while he recounted what had happened. Staring out the window, he said, "Freda never seemed to recover from the twins' birth. After they were born, she didn't want to pump her *milch* for them. She complained when the nurses urged her to do so. I thought once she got home, things would be better. When she was home and the *bopplin* at the hospital, she moped. I thought she missed them, but she never wanted to go and see them. I spoke with the *doktor*, and he said having two *bopplin* as a first pregnancy was extra rough." He rubbed his uneven beard, then jerked his hand away from the thing that identified him as a widower. "I listened to him, because he'd been right about everything else. He'd been recommended to us, and he took such *gut* care of Freda during what was a difficult pregnancy."

"He was wrong about this," she whispered.

Her voice touched the chafed parts of his soul that had never healed. Instead of the pain he expected, her compassion offered a cooling balm. *"Ja*, he was wrong, but so was I. When Freda had a bad day, I'd try to reassure her that things would get better as the *bopplin* grew and slept through the night. When she had a *gut* day, I convinced myself it meant the dark days were going to be over soon."

He'd failed Freda by not doing what his gut told him was the right thing. Instead, he'd let her convince him that seeing her *doktor* wouldn't help her. She told him time would bring healing.

She'd been lying to him, and he hadn't suspected.

That ate at him, though he didn't blame Freda. She'd been ill. He should have insisted she get care so he didn't have to come home and find her dead next to empty pill bottles and the picture of an *Englischer*. He should have been a stronger husband and put his foot down, taking her to the *doktor*. He'd failed her as the *daed* of her *kinder* had. Guilt swelled over him like a fever, hot and weakening him.

He took a deep breath and held it before exhaling. His guilt belonged to him and him alone. He couldn't dump it on Leanna. She didn't deserve that, though, he argued with himself, she deserved to know what type of man he truly was.

"And you came home," Leanna softly from right behind him, "to discover the *bopplin* howling and got no answer when you called to Freda." She put her hand on his back and leaned her forehead against his shoulder. "No wonder you reacted as you did the day you rushed upstairs here. I'm sorry to have made you go through that again. I had no idea."

"I know you didn't. You want me to be honest? Okay, I'll be honest. I don't want to risk my heart like that again. Not ever."

"But…" Her voice trailed away as a thin cry came from upstairs. It was followed by a louder one, an announcement that the twins were awake.

Leanna pushed away from him and hurried into the other room. As she reached the bottom of the stairs, she paused. She looked at him. Tears were luminous in her eyes.

"I understand why you don't want to chance suffering any more sorrow," she said in a broken voice.

In horror, he stared as she rushed up the stairs. She thought he'd been talking about falling in love with her. Was that what he'd meant? He wasn't sure.

Of anything any longer.

He took a step to follow, then halted. If he gave chase, what could he do but hurt her—the one person he had never wanted to hurt—more?

Chapter Fourteen

Leanna became aware of how her family was avoiding getting in her way when she stamped around the kitchen while she helped prepare supper that evening. It was as if she had an invisible cloud of silence around her and nobody was allowed to intrude. She also noticed she was chopping onions for a salad as if trying to drive the knife through the cutting board, the counter and right down to the floor.

She hadn't thought she could become any angrier at Gabriel than she'd been the day she'd found out he was marrying Freda Girod.

She'd been wrong.

When he'd told her that Freda had committed suicide, she'd offered sympathy with all her heart. He'd taken it, or at least he'd seemed to before he told her he wasn't ever going to risk his heart on another relationship.

But he never said he was ever in love with you.

She wished she could silence that thought, repeating in her mind like Heidi's endless nonsense words. Every thought, no matter how she tried to halt it, led her to Gabriel and his *kinder*. It'd been barely more than a month since he'd shown up by the pen where she kept her goats. Before that, she'd been sure she was on the road to forgetting how much he'd wounded her. Seeing his handsome face had swept aside all progress—albeit slight progress—that she'd made.

Leanna tried to focus, but it was impossible. Every motion felt as sharp as the knife she was using. During supper, the efforts her family made to act as if everything was normal seemed to emphasize how much was wrong in her life. She tried to participate in their conversations, but she couldn't seem to swim through the swamp of her thoughts and concentrate on what everyone else was saying.

At the end of a supper she hadn't tasted, Leanna offered to do the dishes because her twin was planning to take a walk with Caleb. Her younger siblings were so tired they could barely keep their eyes open, and she didn't want her *grossmammi* to help.

However, *Grossmammi* Inez remained at the table while Leanna washed and dried the dishes and cleaned up the kitchen. Other than the clatter of plates and cooking pots, the only sound in the room was her *grossmammi*'s labored breathing. Leanna considered urging her *grossmammi* to go to her bedroom and rest, but a single glance in the older woman's direction was enough for Leanna to know that *Grossmammi* Inez wasn't going to retire until she'd said what she had to say to Leanna.

"Would you like some more *milch*?" Leanna asked.

"That would be nice to sip on while we chat."

She poured a glass and carried it to the table. She set it in front of her *grossmammi* and sat beside her.

"Was iss letz?" *Grossmammi* Inez asked after taking a sip.

Though Leanna wanted to say "everything was wrong," she answered, "To begin with, I'm worried about you."

"You've been worried about me for weeks." Her *grossmammi* waved aside Leanna's words. "Something else is wrong. *Was iss letz?*"

Knowing she was wasting time by equivocating, she said, "I'm upset with Gabriel."

"I guessed that. You've been upset with him for longer than you've worried about me, but tonight's the first time you've tried to saw through the counter." After sipping again, she said, "Don't make me ask a lot of questions to persuade you to be honest with me, *kins-kind*, when I sound like an old train engine running out of steam. Just tell me what happened."

Leanna explained why she was upset with Gabriel, though she said nothing about Freda's suicide. She couldn't break the promise she'd made to Gabriel such a short time ago. When she ran out words, she closed her eyes so the tears searing her eyes wouldn't fall.

She waited for her *grossmammi*'s advice, but *Grossmammi* Inez didn't answer right away. Was it because she wanted to gather her thoughts, or did she need to fill her lungs with enough oxygen to let her to say what was already on her mind?

At last, *Grossmammi* Inez spoke. Her words were punctured by her gasps for breath, but that couldn't lessen the impact of what she said as she met Leanna's eyes.

"My dear *kins-kind*, do you want me to say it's okay for you to punish Gabriel for marrying someone else?"

"No!"

"Then you must be trying to punish yourself, because

you continue to care about him after the greatest betrayal you've ever suffered." Compassion warmed her wrinkled face. "Is that what you plan to do with your life? Are you upset with him—and with yourself—because you let yourself hope he'd turn to you and you could decide together what your futures would be?"

She was about to reply, then halted herself. Could *Grossmammi* Inez be right?

At last, Leanna said, "It's not my place to decide the future."

"*Gut.* I'm glad you're seeing sense before you destroy the kitchen."

Leanna smiled in spite of her aching heart. She was blessed to have her *grossmammi* to keep her on an even keel by reminding her of the need for faith in the One who held the future in His hands.

"I don't think it would have been all of the kitchen," she replied. "Maybe a quarter."

Grossmammi Inez patted Leanna's arm. "As it never happened, let's forget it."

"I owe you and the rest of the family an apology for being so self-absorbed."

"I know they would appreciate hearing that as much as I do." She smiled. "I know they will forgive you as I already have. And they *do* understand. All of us have had rough days."

She almost asked if any of her family had endured a day like she had with the news of Freda's suicide. The thought of her *grossmammi*'s grief when Leanna's parents died halted her. *"Danki, Grossmammi."*

After lifting her glass, the older woman drank deeply before she lowered it to the table. "Two of the most important verses to us plain people are in the sixth chapter of Matthew. Verses fourteen and fifteen. You know those verses, ain't so?"

"Ja."

"They are?"

Leanna said, "'For if ye forgive men their trespasses, your Heavenly Father will also forgive you: But if ye forgive not men their trespasses, neither will your Father forgive your trespasses.'"

"Don't you think it's time you forgave Gabriel?"

"I've tried!"

"I know you have, and I'm glad that you haven't offered lip service to forgiving him in order to placate your conscience. Forgiveness that doesn't come from the heart isn't true forgiveness. But, Leanna, you need to search your heart and find a way to forgive him. Otherwise, you won't ever be free of the anger that has betrayed you today."

Leanna stared at her *grossmammi* in astonishment. Her anger had betrayed her? If asked, she would have said today's betrayal had come from Gabriel. Yet he hadn't done anything except to be honest with her as she'd asked him to. He'd been honest with her. Did she want him to spare her feelings by deceiving her?

No!

"Let me give you another set of verses to pray with tonight before you go to sleep," her *grossmammi* said as she pushed herself to her feet. "I've found they help me when someone doesn't meet my expectations, and I'm hurt. This is from *Psalms* 55: 'As for me, I will call upon God; and the Lord shall save me. Evening, and morning, and at noon, will I pray, and cry aloud: and He shall hear my voice. He hath delivered my soul in peace from the battle that was against me: for there were many with me.'" She put her hand over Leanna's. "Sometimes our battles are with others. Sometimes they are with ourselves."

Her *grossmammi* leaned forward to kiss Leanna's cheek before she moved out of the kitchen, leaving Leanna with thoughts whirling like a tornado.

Gabriel put down his pen on Thursday evening and rubbed his eyes as he looked across the kitchen, which was lit by a single propane lamp. His brother was out, visiting the Kuhns brothers. Michael and Benjamin were becoming *gut* friends, and Gabriel suspected they might go into business together while Gabriel concentrated on the farm.

The farm…

He almost groaned as he picked up the page of estimated expenses he'd compiled for the next six months. He and Michael had found enough work to pay their bills this month, even with the extra cost for the cows delivered that afternoon. He hoped he hadn't made a big mistake by starting a herd now. Next month, the budget must include money to pay for the cows' upkeep, as well as household expenses. The twins had another visit to the pediatrician in a few days, and though the fee for the last month's visit, including medicine for Heidi's ear infection, had been lower than he'd expected, it had been enough to put a burden on their budget.

"Not that you're a burden, little girl," he said as he glanced down at where she sat banging two wooden blocks together. "Or you, either, little man." He smiled at Harley, who was watching his sister.

Both *bopplin* grinned at him, and his heart swelled with love. He was blessed by having these two *kinder* in his life. That was something he'd never regret. What would Leanna think if he could tell her the truth about why he'd married Freda?

His lips tightened, and he put the budget page on the stack of papers in front of him. He needed to keep Leanna out of his head. She'd invaded his thoughts more than usual—though he hadn't guessed that could be possible—since he'd told her about Freda's death two days ago.

He sat back in his chair and stared at the ceiling where shadows moved in rhythm with the propane flame. Everything had changed, but nothing had. Leanna had come downstairs with the twins that afternoon when he'd arrived home, and she had made sure they were fed before she left for home. She'd returned the past two mornings, acting as if he'd never said a single word about Freda. She was kind and smiled, but he couldn't miss how her face seemed shadowed by sadness. She hadn't once met his eyes during their short conversations before he left for work and when he returned at day's end.

Yet she seemed to be keeping her promise. As far as he knew, she hadn't said a word about Freda's death, not even to him.

That hadn't surprised him, but he'd expected in the past two days she'd mention something—anything— about the heartfelt letter he'd written to her before he married Freda. When he'd agreed to Aden's offer, he had been determined that Leanna would hear the news from him instead of through friends and neighbors. Though he couldn't explain in the letter the real reason he'd made the decision to become Freda's husband, he'd asked Leanna to forgive him for any pain he might have brought her.

Might have?

The urge to laugh at his own foolishness choked him. Maybe he didn't deserve to be forgiven when he'd hardened his heart to the truth of how his choice—the one he'd believed he should make to repay the debt he owed to Aden for being a *daed* to him and Michael—had injured the woman he loved.

He wished he could reach out to God for comfort and guidance, but how could he hope for help when he'd turned his back on his Lord like a petulant *kind* who hadn't gotten what he wanted?

I needed You then, Lord. Why did You ignore me? It was a prayer he had made often over the past year.

"Sometimes you're a mule-headed fool."

The voice that emerged from the darkness made him jump out of his seat. A second later, he recognized the voice as his brother's.

"Hello to you, too," he said to hide his reaction that he'd been getting an answer directly from God.

Michael set his hat on a peg by the door and crossed the room, being careful to skirt the twins.

His brother scowled. "*Ja*, sometimes you're a mule-headed fool, Gabriel, and the rest of the time you're just plain stubborn."

"So you've said. About a million times."

"Well, maybe the millionth-and-first time will be the time when you'll listen."

"I'm not going to argue with you when I don't have any idea what's got you so hot under the collar."

"I'm annoyed for the same reason you're sitting here pouting in the dark." He put his hands on the table and leaned forward. "Leanna Wagler."

"What about her?"

"Why are you doing everything you can to push her away? It's not like she's flirting with you or making your life miserable by reminding you how you tossed her aside so you could marry Freda." Michael shook his head. "Something—I've got to say—that, after having met Leanna, I can't understand why you did. Leanna is a special woman, and you were *dumm* not to marry her when you had the chance."

"It's not something I can explain."

"Yeah, yeah." Michael grimaced. "All that stuff about the heart leading the head or other sentimental garbage. I think it's an excuse for your desire for drama. If things get too quiet, you try to shake things up by shaking poor Leanna up. I can't believe you treat a woman you say you care about like that."

"I don't—"

Michael flung up his hands. "Don't tell me you don't know what you've done. Benjamin's sister, Sarah, was at their house tonight, and she was upset. She said Leanna had enough to deal with without you adding more stress to her life."

"Michael—"

"I don't want to hear it, Gabriel. You messed up the first time around with Leanna, but for some reason I can't fathom, she's stepped up to help with your *kinder*. You welcomed her into our home, so what was she to think but that you're interested in her again? What are you interested in, Gabriel? Having a make-believe family that's convenient for you?" He didn't give Gabriel a chance to answer. Putting his scowling face close to his brother's, he snarled, "What happens when it's not convenient any longer?"

"Michael, it's not what you think."

"Isn't it? Well, it doesn't look as if it'll be much longer, because you're messing everything up again. Do you know how few people get a second chance to right a wrong? And you're throwing this one away!"

His brother stormed out of the kitchen and up the stairs. As Gabriel returned to the table, he heard Michael's boots slamming on the floor upstairs.

Heidi gave a soft cry of alarm.

"It's okay," Gabriel said to soothe her and her brother. "Your *onkel* Michael likes to be loud sometimes." He made a silly face, which made the *bopplin* smile before they began playing again.

Folding his arms on the table, he pondered what his brother had said. Michael was right…from his point of view. Without knowing the whole truth, his brother saw him as a witless *dummkopf.*

And maybe he was.

Could his brother be right about him pushing Leanna away by resorting to drama?

A knock on the door startled Gabriel. Who was calling so late at night?

Whoever it was must be carrying a flashlight, for he saw it move when the person knocked a second time. He got up and opened the door.

"Leanna, what are you doing here?" he asked as he motioned for her to come in.

She took a single step into the kitchen and closed the door behind her. As she stepped into the light, he saw the raw emotion on her face that matched her broken voice when she said, "My *grossmammi* needs surgery on her heart."

Leanna's heart longed for Gabriel to take her into his arms and hold her until her fear faded away. When she'd gotten home from the hospital with her *grossmammi*, and while *Grossmammi* Inez got ready for bed, she'd spent time explaining to her siblings what they'd learned. Leanna had gone out to check on her goats, wanting time alone to unwind from the appointment, and instead, she found herself walking to Gabriel's house.

No matter how irritated she was with him, no matter how little she comprehended why he'd chosen Freda over her, there was a bond she'd never been able to explain between her and Gabriel. Something that went beyond friendship, beyond obligation and even beyond love. It was as if, in times of trouble, he was the one she must turn to.

Gut sense rallied in time, so she bent to pick up the *bopplin.* Without a word, Gabriel took Heidi from her and put his other hand on her arm. He opened the door and steered Leanna toward the rocking chair on the front porch. She didn't resist, so tired from trying to appear cheerful for her *grossmammi* that she wasn't sure how much longer her knees would hold her up.

Once she was sitting, rocking slowly, he pulled the other chair near to where she stared out across the yard toward the horizon and the faint silhouettes of the Green Mountains. She loved the view from his porch, and tonight she'd be happy to lose herself in watching the stars dance across the sky. She appreciated the reminder that she was small in the universe and that God was holding her beloved *grossmammi* in His hand.

"Inez needs surgery on her heart," he said, prompting her to speak.

Leanna cradled a sleepy Harley in her arms, the pace of her rocking increasing as she outlined what the *doktor* had said less than two hours before. "She must have a new valve to replace a clogged one. I asked about pills, but the *doktor* said it would only postpone the surgery and delaying could be stupid because the valve is getting more clogged. It's making *Grossmammi* Inez weaker and weaker. If she gets too weak, the surgery will become extra dangerous."

"So she has no choice."

"Not if she wants to feel better."

He sighed as he looked at Heidi, who was falling asleep against his chest. "Where are they going to do the surgery?"

"Albany."

"That's, what, forty miles from here?"

"More than fifty. We'll arrange for a driver, Hank if he's available, to take us there." She waved that aside as if that detail weren't important.

"What will the *doktors* do during the surgery?"

"It's almost unbelievable. They've made so many new medical advances, and what they can do is awe inspiring. They'll send the new, man-made valve through a vein in her leg, knock the old valve aside and set the new one in place."

"You're right. That sounds crazy, but I've heard about other types of procedures that use veins to reach the patient's heart. When are they doing the surgery?"

"Day after tomorrow. We've got to be there before seven, because the surgery is scheduled for around ten in the morning. Juanita will come over that day to take care of the *bopplin*. I hope they behave for her."

"Don't worry about it. I've—"

She didn't let him finish, too focused on what needed to be done to pay attention to what he was saying. "To be honest, Juanita is looking forward to it now that the twins know her better. Juanita told me to let you know that she'll be available for as long as necessary to babysit. My brother Lyndon's wife, Rhoda, as well as Sarah and Miriam, will take care of Juanita's housecleaning jobs until she can return. I don't know how long *Grossmammi* Inez will need me. Once she's home again, if you can drop off Heidi and Harley, I'll watch them at our house while I'm helping my *grossmammi*."

"I told you. You don't have to worry about the twins."

"Of course, I do. I told you that I'd babysit for you, and I don't go back on my word. If I did, then why would anyone believe what I said ever again? I…" Her eyes widened as if she'd realized that what she said could have been considered a slur aimed at him. "Gabriel, I didn't mean…that is…" With a groan, she put her hand over her face.

He took her hand and lowered it. "You don't have to apologize for speaking the truth, Leanna. I let you believe one thing, and then I did the opposite. I should be astonished that you have done as much as you have for me and my family after what I did."

"What you did was marry someone else. You didn't make any promises to me."

I wanted to make you a promise that would last a lifetime.

The words burst into Gabriel's head like an explosion. The memory of his brother's sharp words followed. Instead of helping Leanna as she was helping him, he was filling her life with more strain and uncertainty. When she should have been thinking of her *grossmammi*, she'd been making plans for childcare for him.

"Leanna, you don't need to worry about the twins," he repeated.

Her brow furrowed, creating deeper shadows in the dim light from the kitchen. "What do you mean?"

"I know you agreed to watch them as a favor, and I've taken advantage of your kindness for too long. That's why I've found someone else to watch them." He'd tried to explain that to his brother, too, but neither Michael nor Leanna had given him a chance.

"Someone else?" She stiffened in the chair, and Harley roused with a soft complaint.

"David Bowman's *mamm* has been looking for something to do now that his *kinder* are getting older, and I know you're overwhelmed with helping here along with everything else you do. She's volunteered to get the *milch* from your house and make the *bopplin*'s formula. You've mentioned several times how you worry about Inez doing that because the least little thing tires her out."

"Annie's been making the formula before she goes to work at the bakery most mornings."

"So it'll be easier on your twin, too."

And easier on me.

He bit back the words he shouldn't speak. He didn't want to admit that Michael was right, that he hadn't looked for a substitute before because he'd wanted Leanna to come to the house every day. That Gabriel liked having the woman he had almost married help him create his make-believe family.

In front of him, Leanna seemed to wilt. The strength she'd shown tonight and every day since they'd met again drained from her. What had happened? He'd thought she'd be pleased with his solution to easing her stress.

He opened his mouth, but she halted him by coming

to her feet. She handed a half-asleep Harley to him and straightened her shoulders. No warmth brightened her face as she looked down at him.

"That sounds like a reasonable solution, Gabriel." Her voice was crisp and her words clipped. "Shall I finish out the week?"

"That's not necessary. With Inez's surgery coming up in a couple of days, it'd be better if Magdalena started right away. That way, if she's got any questions, I can have her talk to you before you get involved in caring for your *grossmammi*."

Turning on her heel, she bade him goodbye as she'd done at the end of every day she'd been at the house.

Unlike then, she wouldn't be returning.

He watched her vanish into the shadows.

"So are you pleased with yourself?" Michael asked through the open door.

Gabriel didn't answer. He should be relieved. Leanna hadn't made a scene or given him more than a token argument. She'd been gracious as she always was, keeping her feelings private.

No, that wasn't true. He'd seen the flash of hurt in her eyes before she'd hidden it.

Everything had gone better than he'd hoped.

So why did he feel as if he were the greatest and most heartless *dummkopf* who'd ever walked God's green earth?

Chapter Fifteen

The morning air was close and sticky when Leanna stepped out onto the back porch. She was relieved Juanita had agreed to milk the goats this morning. Annie would be teaching Magdalena Bowman how to make the formula for Harley and Heidi, but her twin was useless when it came to milking either the goats or the cows. Annie loved animals and was always sneaking treats to Penny whenever the copper-colored pup came into the house, but she hated milking. She was happiest when she was working at the bakery, devising new recipes with the man she'd be marrying in the fall.

In spite of herself, Leanna looked across the dark fields to where she could barely see the tilting silo behind the Millers' barn through the glistening gray of morning fog lit above by moonlight. She wondered if the brothers would fix it or tear it down and build something new.

Then she wondered why she cared.

Gabriel had been pushing her away for the past week, and she'd been too *dumm* to realize it. She'd sought him out because she thought he'd offer her some comfort in the wake of her *grossmammi*'s prognosis. Instead, he'd told her that he'd found someone to replace her in taking care of his *kinder*. She shouldn't be surprised after the debacle when he decided to marry Freda, but she'd been so sure there was more to him that the self-serving man she didn't want to believe he was.

She'd been wrong.

"Ready?" asked a weak voice from behind her.

Turning, Leanna offered *Grossmammi* Inez her arm. That the older woman took it as they went down the steps warned Leanna that her *grossmammi* was feeling worse. Glad her *grossmammi* wouldn't have to suffer through another day of gasping for breath, Leanna sent a quick prayer to ask God to guide the surgeon's hands and instruments with skill.

They'd reached the grass when a vehicle turned up the driveway and came to a stop near where the buggy was parked. In the light from the porch, the van was spotlessly white, and Leanna wondered how Hank managed to keep it so clean on unpaved roads. The short man with gray hair and a beard turning to the same shade jumped out of the driver's side and came around to open the passenger doors.

"Good morning, ladies," he said, cheerful as always. He wore his usual coat that, he'd told Leanna months ago, was purple and gold to support the local high school teams. Without asking, he assisted *Grossmammi* Inez into the van.

Leanna appreciated the *Englischer*'s kindness and how he didn't make a big deal of how her *grossmammi* sounded as she breathed or how she shuffled when she walked. After climbing in to sit beside *Grossmammi* Inez, she thanked Hank when he closed the sliding door before going around the van and getting behind the wheel.

Though she'd given him the address when she contacted him, Leanna told him again that they needed to go to Albany Medical Center.

"The New Scotland Avenue entrance?" he asked.

After he'd switched on the light in the van, she checked the map among the papers her *grossmammi* had been given by the surgeon's staff. *"Ja."*

"Let's go. It's already almost five thirty." He smiled at them as he turned off the light and turned the key in the ignition. "I'm glad we're leaving so early, so we shouldn't have to worry about too much rush hour traffic on our way."

Leanna leaned against the hard seat and watched her *grossmammi* wave to their family gathered by the driveway. She knew their cheerful expressions were as false as her own.

There wasn't much traffic on the road into Salem, but the small talk she made with Hank drifted away before they'd gone ten miles. Beside her, *Grossmammi* Inez was looking out the window at the houses and barns rushing past in the strengthening light of the day.

"I haven't ridden in cars often," the old woman said as they wound through the streets of Greenwich, which were draped in the fog that had grown thicker while they followed the road along the Battenkill. "It reminds me of the motion picture I saw when I was a young girl. Everything moved so fast. I scarcely had time to see one thing before something else had replaced it."

"I didn't know you'd ever gone to a movie."

Her *grossmammi* wagged a finger at her. "I know I seem as old as these hills to you, *kins-kind*, but there

were movies fifty years ago." She winked at Leanna.
"And I know exactly how many you and your sister managed to sneak out to see with your friends. Three."

"Ja." She tried to laugh, but it sounded fake even to
her. "We never could fool you, *Grossmammi* Inez."

With a pat to Leanna's arm, she said, "Now, now,
don't sound so sad. I'm not planning on leaving this life
today. In fact, the *doktor* said replacing the valve should
make me feel two decades younger. I plan to stick around
here so I can spend a lot more time with my *kins-kinder*
and your own *kinder."*

"I know." She blinked tears away, but others rushed to
take their place and threatened to fall down her cheeks.
"I want you to know how much we appreciate what
you've done for us."

"I love you, so the rest was easy."

"You opened your home to us when first *Daed*, then
Mamm and Bert, our stepfather, died, and you raised us
when you could have been enjoying your retirement."

Her *grossmammi* made a sound that sounded like
something Heidi did when offered something to eat
that she despised. "Retirement? Sitting on the porch and
rocking and watching the sun rise and set? Such a boring life would have led me to an early grave. You *kinder*
have kept me on my toes and kept me young."

"You could have—"

"No, Leanna, there's been nothing else I would have
wanted to do. Having so much time with my *kins-kinder*
has been a *wunderbaar* blessing that I wouldn't trade for
anything." She patted Leanna's cheek. "And I refused to
let you *kinder* be separated."

"Separated?"

Grossmammi Inez waved a diffident hand. "There

was a lot of talk about where all of you would live after your parents died. You know how everyone feels the need at such times to voice an opinion. Nothing ever came of it. I shouldn't have said anything. After all these years, what does it matter? We are where God wants us to be, and that's together."

Leanna gave her *grossmammi* a gentle hug, not wanting to squeeze her and make it more difficult for her to breathe. If *Grossmammi* Inez wasn't so anxious about the surgery, she most likely never would have mentioned that there had been a discussion to place the Wagler *kinder* in different homes.

The rest of the long ride to Albany was mostly silent, though Leanna answered whenever her *grossmammi* spoke. She wasn't surprised when *Grossmammi* Inez grabbed her arm and didn't let go when the van zoomed across a high bridge. Her *grossmammi* kept holding on to her when they exited onto narrow city streets with cars that seemed to go as fast as on the highway.

"There's the hospital ahead of us," Hank said.

Leanna peered through the windshield at a tall red-brick building. Cars were jammed up in front of the entrance. She glanced at the clock on the dashboard. They would never reach the office in time to check in if they had to wait for those cars to clear.

"Don't worry." Hank glanced back with a smile. "We're going into a different parking lot. We'll have you there with plenty of time to spare, Inez."

"We can be dropped off at valet parking," Leanna reminded him.

"Even better."

The van zipped around the corner and then took a

quick right. A sign, Valet Parking Here, was a welcome sight because it confirmed they were in the right place.

She didn't wait for Hank to open the door for her. She slid it aside and stepped out to go around the van and help her *grossmammi*. She heard a frantic siren and saw a crimson ambulance race to a door about a hundred yards away.

Salem Rescue Squad was painted in large white-and-gold letters on the side.

She stared as the passenger door opened and a familiar form jumped out. She had to be wrong, but how could she mistake Gabriel Miller for any other man?

Behind her, she heard Hank draw in a sharp breath.

"Go," urged her *grossmammi*, and Leanna guessed that reaching the hospital had made *Grossmammi* Inez's stress worse. "Check…while they…get me a…wheelchair to…take me…upstairs."

"I should—"

"Go! Don't…argue…with me." Though *Grossmammi* Inez's voice was breathless, her strength of will remained powerful.

Leanna kissed her *grossmammi*'s cheek and promised to join her upstairs. The old woman waved her away before taking Hank's outstretched hand so he could help her out.

Rushing across the grass between the two entrances, Leanna reached the emergency room door as a gurney with an impossibly small cargo emerged from the ambulance.

"Gabriel!" she shouted.

He whirled and stared at her in astonishment. "Leanna?" he asked as if he couldn't believe his own eyes.

"What are you doing here?" she cried.

"It's Harley." His face was long with despair. "You were right, Leanna. There's something wrong with him. Something horribly wrong."

Gabriel pushed aside the heavy door and walked into the surgical waiting area. A half-dozen people sat in the room decorated with cheerful prints and posters showing cutaways of the human heart. His gaze focused on one person.

"May I?" he asked, motioning to the empty chair next to where Leanna sat.

She nodded and swallowed roughly. Was she trying to hold in that mixture of fear and sorrow and recriminations that threatened to gag him?

"How is Inez?" He settled himself in the uncomfortable chair and noticed how nobody other than Leanna would meet his gaze. They, like he, must wish they could be, at that moment, anywhere else in the world but waiting to hear if their loved one had survived surgery.

"She went in half an hour ago. They said they'd come and get me in about an hour or so."

"They can finish her surgery so fast?"

"That's what they said." Dampening her lips, she whispered, "Why are you in the cardiac surgery waiting room?"

"They're doing an exploratory to find out what's wrong with Harley's heart."

Her fingers slid over his on the narrow arms of the chairs and curled around them. The motion said more than any words could have, and warmth trickled through him, like the first sign of a spring thaw after a frigid winter.

"I'm so sorry," she whispered. "What happened?"

He was amazed she hadn't asked the question before. Realizing he hadn't given her a chance before he rushed into the emergency room with Harley, he sighed. "He stopped breathing."

"Oh, my!" She became even more gray with fright.

"He and Heidi were sitting on the floor, and she crawled away. He started to follow, made it a foot or so, then collapsed. I shouted for Michael, and he went for help." He stared at his clasped hands. "I picked Harley up and patted his back like I've seen you do when he's gasping. He didn't respond, so I patted harder. He began breathing, but not well. His lips were blue, and his fingertips were turning blue by the time your friend Sarah burst into the house."

"Sarah is a volunteer EMT."

"I am so thankful she was at your house when Michael went there to find out the closest place with a phone. She got Harley breathing steadily again and kept working with him until the ambulance arrived. She told me to go with him, and she'd make sure Heidi was okay. I jumped in the ambulance and came here to the emergency room. He needs surgery, which they hope will keep him from stopping breathing like that." He bowed his head. "It was terrifying. He's such a tiny *boppli*."

Fear smothered him, and he couldn't hold back the tears that had been dammed within him since the day he'd known he must break Leanna's heart in order to protect the only family he had. When she put her arms around him, he gripped her arm. He wept against her shoulder, hoping his scalding tears didn't sear her. He no longer cared there were others watching.

She didn't pull away and, instead, leaned into him, putting her cheek against his hair. She said nothing, and

he was grateful she didn't try to give him a list of plati-
tudes. He knew them. He'd probably said each of them
at one time or another.

Trust in the doktors. *They know what they're doing.*
Have faith and hope for the best.

God doesn't give us more than we can handle. That
one contradicted what he'd been told after Aden's death.
God knows when it's our time because we are each a
precious piece of His plan.

He believed those were true, but hearing them
wouldn't help. The only things he wanted to hear were
that Harley and Inez had come through their surgeries.

As the last of his tears fell, Leanna whispered, "I'm
sorry, Gabriel."

"You can say that you told me so." He raised his head
and girded himself for the sharp words he deserved, the
words she should have thrown into his face weeks ago.

She took his right hand and folded it between her
smaller ones. Meeting his gaze, she whispered, "What
gut will that do?" Her eyes were almost turquoise with
the tears welling up in them, and he knew they were for
Harley and him. "Harsh words aren't useful at the best
of times."

"Which this isn't."

"No, it isn't." She glanced at the double doors that
stood between them and the surgical area. "They told
me it wouldn't take that long for *Grossmammi* Inez's surgery, but it seems like I've sat here a lifetime already."

"Are you here alone?"

She nodded. "*Grossmammi* Inez insisted only one of
us come. As I can hand off my chores and I'm not working out of the house, she asked me to come."

Gabriel fought to swallow again. There hadn't been

any accusations in her words, but they both knew the truth. If he hadn't acted like a cowardly *dummkopf* and hired Magdalena to watch the *kinder*, Leanna would have been on her way to his house that morning and one of her siblings would have been sitting in the waiting room.

"Who's watching Heidi?" she asked, showing that her thoughts must be close to his. "Magdalena?"

"Sarah insisted on taking her to your house so she'd be nearby when I got home. Annie was there, or so Michael told me before we left." He gave her a faint smile. "I guess it takes two people to handle your job."

"More likely Sarah had planned to visit Annie today, and they'll watch Heidi together."

"Either way, I appreciate their stepping in to help, especially when your sister has to be anxious about Inez's surgery."

"And Harley's." Her face grew a bit paler. "They don't know about that, do they?"

"I've got the phone number at the bakery. I called and left a message about what the *doktors* have decided. I'll call when he's out of surgery. If you want, I can let them know about Inez, as well."

She patted her black purse. "Annie gave the phone number to me, along with instructions to call the minute I know how our *grossmammi* is doing."

"There's a phone we can use not far from the elevator."

"The cardiac unit has a phone for people who don't have cell phones. We can use it to share news with our families. One of the local church groups in Albany had it installed. I was told I could use it to call for a ride, too. If you're ready to leave when I am—"

"I appreciate that, but I can't make any plans until Harley is out of surgery."

"I know." She hesitated, then went on, "I wish I'd been wrong about Harley. However, if I'd had any idea it was so serious, I would have been insistent, even if it annoyed you."

"And I'm sorry, Leanna, I didn't listen to you. I know your concern comes from your love for the *hopplin*."

"That's true. *Danki* for understanding."

"Eventually."

She gave him a crooked smile. "Better late than never…or so I've heard."

Leanna was paging sightlessly through a magazine when the doors to the recovery area opened yet again. Each time they had, she and Gabriel—along with everyone else in the waiting room—had sat up straighter, willing that the name the nurse called to come back would be theirs. The waiting room had emptied, and other people had come in, but the ninety minutes Leanna had been supposed to have to wait had been over almost forty-five minutes ago.

"Wagler?" called the nurse, a tall, dark-skinned man who wore light blue scrubs that were almost the same shade as her dress. His name identified him as Darnell.

She suddenly was unable to move or speak. All at once the wait time seemed to be too short, because she feared what the nurse might tell her. And how could she leave Gabriel here alone when his son was on the operating table?

"Over here," Gabriel said. Turning to her, he urged, "Go ahead. Inez will be wondering where you are, and you don't want her to worry. That won't be *gut* for her heart."

"But—"

When he took her hand between his much larger ones, he looked directly at her so she couldn't doubt his sincerity. "Go ahead, Leanna. I'll be fine."

"If you hear anything about Harley…"

"I'll send word to you right away." He squeezed her hand, then released it.

"Promise?"

"I keep my word."

"I know." And she did know, though she'd tried to ignore the fact before. For those he cared most about, Gabriel would keep his word, even if it made him look bad. His brother had said Gabriel always kept his promises, and she wondered what ones Michael was talking about. Whatever they were, they'd exacted a great toll on Gabriel's soul, a price he was still paying. That he'd never once complained told her that she had never met anyone else with such strength.

God, hold him up. He loves You, too, I know. His faith is wobbly, but I know it must be at least as big as a mustard seed, and Your son told us such small faith can move mountains.

Leanna kept praying for Gabriel, for her *grossmammi,* for Harley, for herself, for the others who were in the hospital. She followed the nurse into the recovery area. There was a mixture of urgency and yet calm in the wide space that had rooms with curtains across the opening that connected them to the central space. Men and women went from one room to the next, pushing equipment she couldn't identify. It was hushed, though she heard quiet voices in the rooms she passed.

Darnell stopped in front of a curtain covering the entrance to the fourth room on the right. Opening it, he said, "Mrs. Wagler, you've got a visitor eager to see you." He gave Leanna a compassionate smile. "Go on in."

"Is she—?"

"I'm all right," her *grossmammi* said faintly.

She looked past the gurney in the center of the space to a female nurse who nodded to confirm *Grossmammi* Inez's words, and then Leanna realized *Grossmammi* Inez had spoken without all the pauses that had slowed her speech since almost the beginning of the year.

"She needs to rest here in recovery for a few hours. No getting up or moving around so she causes bleeding on her incisions." According to the tag on the female nurse's scrubs, her name was Judy. "After that, we'll move her upstairs and monitor her overnight. If everything is as it should be in the morning, you can take her home then."

"So soon?"

"Amazing, isn't it?" Judy closed the top of a laptop sitting on a shelf with items Leanna couldn't identify. She smiled as she picked up a cup and offered *Grossmammi* Inez a drink of water through the bent straw. "I see these surgeries every day, and I marvel at what our doctors can do."

After Judy left, Leanna pulled a chair to a spot where her *grossmammi* could see her without moving. She wasn't surprised *Grossmammi* Inez's first question was about Harley.

Leanna told her only that the *boppli* was being examined by the *doktors*. She didn't want to upset her *grossmammi* now, and she wasn't sure how much medication *Grossmammi* Inez was taking. The anesthesia hadn't completely worn off.

"Gabriel said he'll let us know how Harley is doing as soon as he knows."

"Ach," her *grossmammi* moaned. "Such a little *boppli*." Holding out her hand, she turned her head when Leanna took it. "We are two voices, but there must be many more in Harmony Creek Hollow raised in prayer right now. Let's join them."

Leanna bowed her head as she reached out with her heart. She heard the older woman's whispered words and repeated them. In addition, she thanked their Heavenly Father because her *grossmammi*'s voice seemed to grow stronger with each word she spoke. The pauses had almost vanished already. Leanna couldn't wait to call the bakery and share the *gut* news.

When *Grossmammi* Inez drifted to sleep, Leanna alerted Judy that she was going to call her family. She glanced into the waiting room when she walked past, but Gabriel wasn't there. Was Harley out of surgery?

She didn't hear anything from Gabriel before it was time to move her *grossmammi* to her room for the night. Judy reassured her. If Gabriel sent word about Harley's condition to the recovery unit, they would pass it along to *Grossmammi* Inez's room.

Not if, Leanna wanted to argue. *Gabriel promised to let me know as soon as he could. He never breaks promises.*

As the time passed while her *grossmammi* seemed to get better by the minute, Leanna sat in a chair by the bed and began to wonder if Gabriel had forgotten his promise. She couldn't believe that, but why else hadn't she heard anything? Was it possible Harley was still in surgery? She was going to have to return home soon because *Grossmammi* Inez must get what sleep she could. The older woman wouldn't rest while Leanna was there.

When an aide brought in a supper tray, Leanna knew she couldn't put off calling Hank any longer. She started to stand, but halted when a young man in bright green scrubs came in. His badge identified him as a nursing student.

"Miss Wagler?" He stared at her, and she guessed he hadn't ever seen a plain person before.

"I'm Leanna Wagler."

He thrust a folded piece of paper at her. "I was told to give this to you."

"*Danki*. Thank you."

Nodding, he rushed out, and she heard him asking someone at the desk why she was dressed so strangely.

"Aren't you going to open it?" *Grossmammi* Inez asked while she took the lid off a plate of meat loaf and mashed potatoes.

"*Ja.*" Her fingers trembled as she unfolded the page. It was a simple message that gave her a room number that was in a different section of the hospital and a scrawled note: *Please come. Gabriel.*

"What is the news from Gabriel?" asked *Grossmammi* Inez.

"He doesn't say. He sent me a room number. It must be where they brought Harley after his surgery."

"What are you waiting for? Go ahead," her *grossmammi* said as Gabriel had earlier. "Don't leave for home without letting me know how the *boppli* and his *daed* are doing."

"I won't." She gave her *grossmammi* a kiss, then rushed out of the room. She was already praying by the time she reached the elevator.

Chapter Sixteen

The hallway was brightly lit, and people moved with unhurried determination to complete tasks Leanna couldn't begin to comprehend. Outside the row of doors, computers displayed information that seemed to be updating constantly. The walls were decorated with pictures of animals and carnival rides and cartoon characters she'd seen at the grocery store.

The faint protest from a *kind*, quickly hushed, wafted toward her, but most of the rooms she passed were silent. She guessed the *kinder* were asleep by now. Odors of disinfectant and other cleaning supplies assaulted her senses, and she fought to keep from sneezing as she walked along the hall.

Checking the numbers on the doors, she slowed as she neared the one that matched the number Gabriel had sent her. She was shocked that everybody in the unit couldn't hear her hammering heartbeat. She took a deep breath to steady herself.

She tiptoed into the room. It was dim compared to the hall, and she paused to allow her eyes to adjust so she didn't bump into something or someone. Out of the shadows, the silhouettes of furniture appeared. A chair. A table on wheels. A crib. The soft beeping from a machine matched her anxious heartbeat. In astonishment, she realized the steady sound must be Harley's heartbeat.

As she started to thank God, she heard Gabriel speak. He stood by the crib, his hands on the rail as he gazed down at a tiny form on the mattress.

"Have pretty dreams, sweet Harley," he said. "Sleep easy tonight and for the rest of your life. I'll be here for you each one of those days that God grants me. I promise you, no matter what happens, I'll be your *daed* forever."

"Of course you will," Leanna said before she could halt herself. "Why wouldn't you always be his *daed*?"

Gabriel straightened and faced her. "How is Inez?"

"As tart as a barrel of dill pickles." She smiled as she shared the amazing news. "She's stronger and acting more like herself than she has in a year. With the new heart valve, it's almost as if she's a brand-new woman. I'd say she'll give a woman half her age a run for the money by the end of the month."

"That's *wunderbaar*."

Though she wanted to ask why he hadn't answered her question, Leanna looked at the crib where Harley was motionless. "How's he doing?" she whispered.

"Sleeping, which the nurses tell me is the best thing for him. The procedure went even better than they'd hoped, and they told me there's *gut* reason to believe it'll be the only one he'll ever need. Like your *grossmammi*, he'll have to see a cardiologist at least a couple of times a year." He gave her a half smile. "Maybe we can arrange for them to go together."

"She would love that. You know how she adores *bopplin*."

"As you do."

"*Ja.* I..." She clasped her hands behind her before she could reach out to take his. While she walked over to the window that gave a view of the building across the street, she knew he was watching her. He was waiting for her to continue, but she wasn't sure what to say.

Footsteps, hushed but assertive, came into the room, and Leanna saw a trim dark-haired woman dressed in scrubs with the some of the same cartoon characters as on the walls in the hallway.

"Hi! I'm Sally." She glanced toward the crib. "I'm the RN for that handsome young man over there." She was careful not to use Harley's name so she didn't rouse him from his healing sleep. "I'll be here for you and for your son tonight, Mr. Miller. If you've got any questions—any questions at all—don't hesitate to ask. Or ask Alan. He's the LPN here tonight."

"*Dan*—thank you," Gabriel said as he stepped aside to let Sally examine the sleeping *boppli.*

When she was finished, she said, "He's doing well. You've got a beautiful son." She checked the computer she held before adding, "And he'll be more beautiful and strong now that his heart isn't fighting against him."

"What happens now?" Leanna asked.

Sally glanced at Gabriel, who nodded that it was all right to answer Leanna's question. "Children with his condition live long and normal lives. There may be a few things you'll want to check with his doctor about before he does them, but moderate exercise and play shouldn't be a problem for him. The important thing is to keep in touch with your son's cardiologist through the years, so the problem doesn't become serious again."

Leanna moved closer to Gabriel and put a hand on

his shoulder. He glanced at her before looking at Sally and asking when his son would be able to return home.

"You can discuss that with his doctors when they make rounds in the morning. With little ones, we have to be more patient, because they can't tell us if they're feeling better. We need time to observe how he's doing before we can make that decision." She gave them a warm, professional smile. "Don't hesitate to call if you've got any questions."

Gabriel thanked the nurse. He'd lost count of how many people he'd thanked since he'd been taken to the pediatric recovery unit. The staff had been kind and explained everything to him about the surgery, which hadn't been so different from Inez's, though more delicate because Harley was such a young *kind*. There had been talk of putting him in the pediatric ICU overnight, but his vital signs had rallied and he'd been brought to this room, which contained the monitors and other devices he needed.

As soon as he'd had a chance, Gabriel had written a note to send to Leanna. He'd been reluctant to take her away from her *grossmammi*, but knowing how worried she'd become if he waited any longer, he'd arranged with one of the staff to have it delivered to Inez's room. That had been almost three hours ago, so he guessed the note had gone a roundabout route to reach her.

Now she was here, and he couldn't imagine anyone else he'd want beside him.

"Leanna," he said at the same time she murmured, "Gabriel."

"Go ahead," she urged.

"Let's sit over by the window so we don't disturb

him." Like the nurses, he didn't use the *boppli*'s name. "It'll be better to talk there. The nurse said he'll sleep through the night, even when she comes in to check him, but I don't want to risk waking him."

He let her take the rocking chair while he got a folding chair from the hall and set it beside her. Though he wanted to hold her hand as he had in the waiting room, he didn't reach for it.

"I've had a lot of time to think about a lot of things," he said. "Mostly I've been thinking about how you deserve to know the truth."

"What truth?"

"All of it." He leaned toward her. "I know you realized after Michael's remarks at your sister's graduation that Freda was pregnant when we got married." He looked toward the crib, then at her. "What I'm about to tell you nobody else alive knows. Not even Michael. I made Freda and her *daed* a promise that I wouldn't ever speak of why I married her."

"You told me she was pregnant, so I guess you married her to protect her family name."

He gave her a sad smile. "That's true, but there's more to the story than anyone, other than me, knows. I want you to know, too."

"You said you promised not to speak of it, and you always keep your promises."

"I do, and I promised to keep this one so it wouldn't hurt the Girod family, but after I prayed on it—"

"You prayed to find the answer? You reached out to God?" Her face lit with pure happiness. "Oh, Gabriel, I'm so happy you've found your way back to God."

"I am, too. I'm thrilled all I had to do was open my heart to Him, and He was there."

"He always was."

"I know." Awe warmed his voice. "Or I should say, I know that now. It's such a blessing God has patience with His most stubborn *kinder.*"

"With all of us, whether we're stubborn or not." She set her hand on his arm. "Gabriel, I'm happy for you."

Placing his hand atop hers, he was amazed how right it seemed to be sitting with her. "It was through talking to God that I realized telling you the truth won't break the promise I made. Nothing I say to you will wound either Aden or Freda, because they are safe from pain with our Heavenly Father."

"I'm listening," she said as she took a deep breath. She was, he knew, preparing herself for whatever he had to say.

He sandwiched her hands between his. "What I did was for love, but not the love of a man for a woman. I never saw Freda that way. She was always like a little sister to Michael and me. Aden made us feel a true part of their family from the day he opened his door to us. Not once did he do or say anything to make us feel that he loved us any differently than he did Freda."

"That's how it's been with *Grossmammi* Inez. She believes she's been blessed to raise another family when she could have stepped aside." She swallowed hard. "She refused to let us be sent to different family members because she wanted us raised together."

"I think that's why Aden took us in, too. Though I was very young, I seem to remember people talking about which family should take Michael and which should take me. I was terrified because I couldn't imagine growing up without my brother." He glanced toward the crib. "I pray Heidi and her twin never have to know such fear."

She drew one hand from between his and cupped his cheek. "Don't falter in your belief that he's going to be fine. The *doktors* have fixed him up as *gut* as new. Better. That's what the nurse said."

He took a jagged breath, knowing his faith needed time to grow as strong as hers. For so long he'd been hiding from people, not trusting even God, never knowing who might convince him to break his promise to Aden. With God freeing him and Leanna believing in him, he was sure he'd found the right way to go.

"When Aden came to me and asked his favor, I knew I had to agree," he said, watching her face.

"A favor? I thought he would have been upset because you and Freda had..." She colored prettily.

"We didn't, Leanna."

"But she was pregnant!" She clapped her hands over her mouth as her voice rose.

"*Ja*, she was, but I'm not the *bopplin*'s *daed*."

"What? They live with you."

"I'm raising them, but I'm not their...what's the word? I'm not their biological *daed*."

"But they've got your red hair."

"Which is why no one's questioned that they're my *kinder*. I never knew Aden Girod's wife, but I'm guessing she was a redhead, too."

"I don't understand. Why did you marry Freda, then?"

"Because the *Englischer* who is the twins' actual *daed* refused to marry her. Once we were married, the *kinder* would be seen by the community as belonging to me. Aden thought that would protect his daughter and his *kins-kinder*. He knew he didn't have much more time to live, because his lung cancer had spread throughout his body." He held his breath as he waited for her answer.

He needed her to understand why he'd made the decision he had. If she didn't, he wasn't sure he could stay in Harmony Creek Hollow and be near her day after day and never have a chance to hold her. In the past few days as she'd treated him like an employer and nothing more, the idea of watching her marry another man had become a burning poison in his gut.

"Oh." She clasped her hands in her lap. "That makes sense."

He laughed with relief. Of all the answers he'd anticipated she'd give him, that hadn't been one of them. It sounded like Leanna, sensible and caring and empathetic.

"I hope I'm as *gut* a *daed* to these *bopplin* as Aden was for me and Michael. We might not have shared a blood relation, but he was a true *daed* to us."

"As you are for Heidi and that sweet *boppli* over there."

"I wish I could have told you the truth in the letter I sent you."

Her eyes widened. "The letter?"

"I explained as much as I could within the constraints of the promise I'd made. I'd hoped you would read between the lines and know that I hadn't made the choice without realizing how much it would hurt you. Did it help you?"

Leanna cleared her throat, but had to fight to get her words to emerge as she whispered, "I never read your letter."

"What?" His eyes grew wide as his brows shot upward. "Didn't you get it?"

"I did, but I didn't read it. I threw it away unopened."

He stood and shook his head. "You threw it away unopened? I spent hours on it. I wrote and rewrote and crossed out and started over from the beginning while I tried to find the right words to ask for your forgiveness, though I couldn't tell you the whole truth." He jammed his hands into his pockets. "All this time, I've been thinking that I must have written something so terrible there was no chance you'd ever forgive me."

She gazed at him, her voice breaking. "I couldn't read it, Gabriel. To read you didn't love me as I loved you would have been like rubbing a file across sunburned skin."

"I didn't write that."

"What did you write?"

"It started out this way. 'My dearest Leanna,'" he murmured as he leaned forward and ran his fingers against her soft cheek. "I wrote at least a dozen pages, though I sent you only two. Nothing I wrote could say what I wanted to."

"And that was?"

"How sorry I was I never had the chance to ask you to marry me."

She gasped. "You were going to ask me to marry you?"

"Ja." A shy smile eased the lines of worry from his face. "I'd hoped that once I'd bought you a big dish of ice cream—"

"I planned on having a hot-fudge sundae."

"And I was planning to ask you as you finished the last bite if you'd sweeten my life by becoming my wife."

She bit her bottom lip to keep it from trembling. "I'd hoped you might, but then you married Freda, and that changed everything."

"You're right. Nothing is the same as it was the day we were supposed to meet for ice cream."

"We have moved far from Lancaster County, and you've been blessed with two *bopplin.*"

"And you've become more beautiful and your heart warmer." He walked away to look into the crib. "I know I can't ask you to be my wife."

"Because you don't love me?"

Shock emblazoned his face. "I've loved you since the night you first let me drive you home. I've never stopped loving you, and I never will. You're a *wunderbaar* woman. You deserve a man who'll be a *gut* husband for you. That's not me."

Getting up, because she was too shocked to sit, she asked, "Why would you say something like that?"

"I failed Freda by not being there when she needed me."

"You did what you could. You spoke with her *doktor,* and you listened to advice. You offered her your name and a life together."

"I couldn't offer her enough."

She crossed the room and put her hand on his arm. Stroking those strong muscles, she whispered, "You're right."

"I am?" His face lengthened again.

"*Ja.* Nothing you could have done was enough because her heart was broken, and you weren't the one who could repair it. Trust me on this, Gabriel. I know far too much about broken hearts."

Again he walked away from her, but this time she didn't follow. She watched as he paced. He must be trying to sort out what were new ideas for him. When he stopped, he stood right in front of her.

"I'm going to have to get used to you being right all the time, Leanna."

"I'm not right all the time. Nobody is."

"You're right about this. Freda had a picture of an *Englisch* man lying beside her when she died. I think it was the twins' *daed*."

"You can compare it to Harley when he's grown. Maybe you'll see something in the photo to confirm your guess."

"I can't."

"You got rid of it?" She could understand why he would have thrown away the picture of the man who'd hurt Freda so much.

He shook his head. "No, I slipped it into Freda's coffin just before the top was closed. I knew she would have wanted the man she loved with her forever as he was at her last breath."

Tears fell from her eyes. How could he think he wasn't a *gut* man? How could he believe he hadn't been the best husband he could have been to Freda, who had longed for another man? Gabriel's final loving act for the woman he'd described as his beloved little sister was to give her in death what she couldn't have in life.

Leaning her head against his arm, she whispered, "*Ich liebe dich*, Gabriel Miller. I have from the moment I first saw you and I won't ever stop."

"You're a fool to love a man like me."

"*Ja*, I'm a fool if loving a man who has opened his heart to two adorable *bopplin* and their *mamm* is foolish. I'm a fool if loving a man who honored the *daed* who raised him by granting him one of his last wishes is foolish. I'm a fool if loving a man who loves me is foolish."

"I do love you. I've never stopped loving you." He gathered her into his arms.

His lips found hers as easily as if he'd kissed her as many times as she'd dreamed he had, warm and gentle and persuasive and filled with longing. Their second kiss, which had been so long delayed, put her dreams to shame, and she melted against him. Her breath caught as he deepened the kiss. She had waited so long for this kiss, and she knew every moment of the uncertainty and sorrow had been washed away by the love swelling through her.

"Will you marry me, Leanna Wagler?" he asked. "Will you be my wife and the *mamm* of my *kinder*?"

"You know that's the first time I've heard you call the twins 'my *kinder.*'"

"Are you avoiding giving me an answer?"

She smiled as she locked her hands behind his nape. "Now you know how it feels!"

"Leanna!"

"Of course, I'll marry you. How could you doubt that for a second?"

"Because I'm always surprised by you."

A soft sound came from the crib, and they turned as one to look at Harley, who was shifting in his sleep.

Though she wanted to stay with the man she'd never believed would be hers, she said, "I should go and see how my *grossmammi* is. The *doktor* wants her to rest tonight, and she won't if she starts wondering why I've been gone so long. I don't want her heart to get beating too fast."

"Then you'd better not tell her about this." He drew her into his arms and kissed her again.

She locked her fingers behind his neck as she gazed

up at his beloved face. "I'm going to tell her and the whole world about this. No more secrets for you and me, Gabriel. We've had too many for too long."

He grinned broadly. "I agree, and, to be completely honest, I don't think I can keep how much I love you a secret from anyone anyhow."

Her laugh faded as he drew her closer again. As he kissed her, she knew he was right. Something as amazing as their love could never be a secret.

Epilogue

Leaves crunched beneath Leanna's sneakers and the wheels of the red wagon as Gabriel pulled it along the twisting road that led to the far end of Harmony Creek Hollow. Inside the wagon, the twins chortled as they tossed leaves at each other. Harley had grown faster than his sister in the past three months, and they were almost the same size. He'd surprised everyone by walking before Heidi had.

"He's trying to make up for lost time," was what *Grossmammi* Inez said. Like the little boy, she'd recovered from her surgery and seemed to live every minute to its utmost. She no longer had to gasp for breath after each word, and she had reclaimed the kitchen as her own, delighting in making meals for her family. Once again, she sat with the family in the evening and read from the Bible, so they could pray together before bed.

Leanna took a leaf away from Heidi before the little girl put it in her mouth. Heidi tried to put everything in her mouth while Harley was more intent in trying to figure out how their toys could be taken apart. He'd been tearing leaves into tiny pieces, and their clothes and hair were littered in red and gold that glittered in the last light of the day. The sun set earlier with each passing day as summer faded into fall.

Today would always be one Leanna remembered with a warm glow because today was the day she and Gabriel had spoken their vows as husband and wife in front of the community. In the morning, the four of them would be leaving to visit relatives in Lancaster County.

"I think the *kinder* will enjoy riding on the train to Pennsylvania," Gabriel said as he reached down to brush some leaf bits out of his son's hair.

"Entertaining them for eight hours will be a challenge."

"Bring plenty of cookies and books for them to color in." He chuckled. He did that more and more, and she savored each laugh. "Assuming they don't try to eat the crayons again."

"Last time they drew on each other's faces and hands."

"As they did with icing from the wedding cake?" He laced his fingers through hers as they walked together. "It was a *wunderbaar* wedding dinner."

"Between Annie's cooking and Caleb's baking skills, there couldn't be any complaints."

"Your friends seemed to find a lot of the day funny."

She hesitated, then realized she needed to be as forthcoming with him as he'd been with her the day of the two heart surgeries. "They were celebrating because the members of our older girls' club aren't eligible for it any longer."

"Why?"

"Because we called it the Harmony Creek Spinsters Club."

"Spinsters Club?" He laughed and slid his arm around

her waist. "You're going to have to pass that title on to other women."

"No, it's better to retire the name. Let others come up with a name for their groups of friends."

"Or we could have the Harmony Creek Bachelors Club now that Michael is spending so much time with Benjamin and Menno Kuhns."

"I don't think they'd appreciate being called that."

"Which makes it all the more fun to use." He chuckled, a sound she knew she'd never tire of hearing.

"I'm glad you told Michael about Freda."

He grew serious. "I am, too. What amazes me is that he wasn't surprised. He said he knew there had to be some overpowering reason why I didn't marry you in the first place."

"Our siblings know more than we give them credit for." She paused in the road. "Here we are."

"At Eli and Miriam's house? Why are we here?"

"You'll see." She took the handle of the wagon from him. *"Komm mol."*

Leanna led the way to the barn beyond the house. She smiled and waved to Miriam, who stood beside Eli's nephew, Kyle. The boy, who'd sprouted up several inches over the summer, was grinning.

"Are you ready to see them?" Kyle asked.

Enjoying Gabriel's puzzled expression, she followed Kyle into the barn and to a corner where a blanket peeked over the edge of a large wooden box. She looked in and asked, "Which one?"

"This one." The boy lifted out a black-and-white puppy and handed it to Leanna.

She carried it to Gabriel. "I know she'll never be the

dog that you had to give up when you were a boy, but I thought she'd make a *gut* wedding gift for you."

"She's the perfect gift," he said, his voice breaking. "I only told you that story once, but you remembered."

Touched by his reaction, she hurried to say, "She's too young yet to leave her *mamm*, but by the time we return from visiting family and friends, she'll be ready to join our family. Harley and Heidi are going to love her."

Gabriel took the puppy from her and knelt by the wagon. The adoration between the twins and the little puppy was instantaneous, and Leanna didn't know which one wiggled more in excitement as the *bopplin* reached out to pet the puppy's silken fur. Both twins began to giggle with excitement, and the puppy's tail wagged so hard it was a blur.

Blinking abrupt tears, Leanna sent up a prayer of thanks that Harley could laugh and not lose his breath. In the four months since his surgery, strength had flowed through the little boy as his heart pumped life along his veins.

The *bopplin* and the puppy protested when Gabriel stood.

"How about you, Leanna?" He handed the pup to Kyle. As the boy set her in the box, Gabriel said, "You're the one who'll have to train her and clean up her puddles until she's housebroken."

"Puddles! That's a cute name."

"I hope you'll think so after a couple of weeks of having three *bopplin*—two human and one puppy—in the house along with having to take care of your goats."

"I know I'm going to love everything about our home together."

Not caring that Miriam and Kyle were standing on

the other side of the wagon, because, after all, it was her wedding day, Leanna gave her husband a swift kiss. She started to step away, but his arm around her kept her close.

"If you'll excuse us a minute, Miriam," he said with a wink, "my wife and I have some lost time we need to make up for."

"You may need more than a minute." Miriam laughed and motioned to her nephew to come with her. They walked out of the barn.

"She's right," he said as he bent toward Leanna again. "We're going to need a lifetime."

"Starting now?"

He answered her with a sweet kiss, and she knew she would love every moment of the rest of their lives together. Some things, she'd learned, were worth the wait.

* * * * *

THE AMISH BACHELOR'S CHOICE

Jocelyn McClay

First, I thank God for this amazing opportunity. Thanks always to my wonderfully supportive husband, Kevin. Thanks also to my beta readers, particularly Alyson, who noted to the Iowa crew that my interest in romance novels was more than just a way of avoiding doing dishes years ago. But this is for you, Genna. I couldn't have done it without you. May there be many more to come.

For I know the thoughts that I think toward you, saith the Lord, thoughts of peace, and not of evil, to give you an expected end.
—*Jeremiah* 29:11

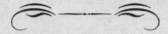

Chapter One

"I wonder if the new owner will change the name? It'd be strange to have it no longer be Fisher Furniture." Jacob's words were barely audible over the humming of the lathe.

The blood drained from Ruth Fisher's face. She hadn't considered that possibility. *Oh,* Daed, *if missing you wasn't enough, how can I bear to see your name removed from the business you built?* The end of her nose prickled as she swallowed against the lump in her throat.

Widening her eyes against threatening tears, Ruth willed her coworker not to look up from his focus on the spinning chair leg until she eliminated any trace of the effect his words had had on her. She glanced around the workshop to ensure the few others working in the extensive room weren't paying attention, before tipping her head back and blinking any telltale traces away. No one would see her cry.

The others understood her grief. Friends and neighbors as well as employees of her father's furniture business had helped her through his difficult passing and funeral. But they were moving on. When Ruth moved on, it would be away from her *daed*'s legacy. She'd made a promise. She swallowed again, this time against a flash of nausea at the reminder of her recent resolution. It took pinching the skin between her thumb and forefinger to stop any renegade tears. But when Jacob looked up, he was met with clear eyes behind her safety glasses.

"*Ach*, Ruth, I—I thought you were Isaac," he stammered, his face flushing to match his red hair.

"He was busy, so I brought the chisels over." She set them on the bench beside him.

"I—I… It was on my mind as they moved in this weekend."

Ruth didn't have to ask who "they" were. Jacob's family farm was a mile from the Yoder farmstead, empty since Atlee died last winter. Empty until the new owner of Fisher Furniture had bought it.

"My *daed* and brothers stopped by to see if they needed any help. *Mamm* and Lydia took a basket of bread and canned goods." Jacob was obviously excited at the prospect of new neighbors. "Lydia was glad to see that none of the three newcomers had beards."

Ruth could just imagine. If none of the men had beards, then they were all single. Jacob's sister was in her *rumspringa*. Potential courtship and future mates were much on a young woman's mind during her run-around years. Particularly a girl like Lydia.

"Hopefully they are good workers, beardless or no." Ruth had different priorities. Even though she'd no longer be part of the business, she wanted to see it succeed. "How are the chairs coming for the Portage order?" They had recently entered into business with a furniture dealer in one of the larger towns nearby.

Jacob's eyes lit up. "*Gut*. I like this design. Hopefully it sells well."

"*Ja*, hopefully," she echoed, forcing a smile to her face before turning to head for her own workbench.

Once there, Ruth selected a piece of oak from the neat stack on the scarred wooden surface and picked up a sanding block. She'd hoped for a number of things. She'd even had the *hochmut* to pray that someone in the district would purchase the business. The glasses slipped down her nose when she winced at the memory that she'd had the arrogance to tell *Gott* what to do. It wouldn't happen again. Ruth wrinkled her nose in an effort to push the glasses back up. Well, it shouldn't happen again. One of the tenets of their faith was *demut*. There was certainly no humility in daring to give *Gott* instructions. Thankfully, *Gott* was forgiving as well as good. He had a plan for her. But apparently it didn't include having someone she knew buy Fisher Furniture and letting her manage it. This Malachi Schrock had certainly wasted no time in taking over her *daed*'s business.

Her shoulders slumped as she ran the block over the oak. No single young woman in their district owned a business that employed four men, married and single. The bishop wasn't going to allow Ruth to be the first, even though she'd worked beside her father from the time she was tall enough to reach a workbench.

Or not tall enough, Ruth remembered with a tremulous smile. *Daed* had built her a little wooden box to stand on. First, so she could watch him work, her eyes wide with wonder at his deft movements. Then so she could mimic his actions and learn to love the wood, from its first rough surfaces to the feel of it beneath her fingers, soft as a baby's cheek after multiple cycles of sanding and varnish.

The sale of the business had been the topic of several conversations after church service two weeks ago. While gossiping was frowned upon in the Amish community, sharing of news was another thing entirely. At least three groups of folks Ruth had passed as she poured coffee for the noon meal had been discussing Miriam Lapp's nephew from Ohio, who'd purchased the business and would soon be moving into the area, along with two of his younger brothers.

Ruth was chagrined to discover, when she overheard people talking after church yesterday, that her life continued to be a subject of interest. This time, the discussion among the women, and probably some of the single men, was when she'd marry, now that her father was gone and the business sold. A few speculative glances had been cast her way when certain names were mentioned, gauging her reaction.

Ruth had made sure her normally expressive face revealed nothing.

Jacob's name was one mentioned with a side-glance yesterday. Ruth's lips twitched. According to her newly married friends, finding it hard to breathe around a man was a sign he might be *Gott*'s Chosen One for her. She had no difficulty breathing around Jacob, whom she'd known since back when she could wear buttons. He was nothing more than a casual friend, and the only time he made her heart beat harder was when she observed and appreciated his skill on the lathe. The women of the district could speculate all they want, but she wouldn't be walking out with Jacob Troyer.

Her smile faded. She wouldn't be walking out with

any Amish man now that she was leaving the community as she'd promised her *daed*.

Ruth grabbed a tack cloth and swiped it across the oak's surface, surprised she hadn't worn a hole in the wood. She stroked a thumb along the grain. Today, not even working with the wood brought her the peace and joy it normally did.

But peace required *gelassenheit*. Submission didn't come naturally to Ruth. Sometimes it didn't come at all. Putting down the cloth, she picked up the sanding block and deftly applied it. Inhaling deeply, she relished the aroma of fresh lumber inherent to the room. *Gelassenheit*. Bits of sawdust danced in the air as she exhaled slowly through pursed lips, trying to clear her mind to *Gott*'s will.

So the new owner had arrived in Miller's Creek with his two brothers. Ruth's hand paused, her eyes resting on the other occupants of the room. Her heart beat heavily as she wondered what the addition of three more men would mean for her father's loyal employees. The strokes across the wood resumed with jerky motions.

Ruth didn't know what she needed to do, but she was determined that the men would keep their jobs. Dropping the block on the counter, Ruth folded her hands in her lap and bowed her head. She would pray and accept *Gott*'s will for her fellow workers and herself. Ruth squeezed her eyes shut. Hopefully His will would journey the same road as her plans.

The horse flicked his ear back toward the buggy, probably wondering if he was going to get down now that they'd arrived at their destination. Malachi figured the gelding was glad to be hanging its head over the hitching post. He frowned at the foam-flecked brown neck. Experienced with horses, he knew the animals could feel the tension of the driver through the reins. The poor bay had completed a trip full of nervousness running down the lines. No wonder his coat reflected his agitation. Malachi resolved to keep this visit short or find a place where he could stable the standardbred. It was warm for November, but he wouldn't leave a hot horse for long out in it.

Sighing, he set the brake and stepped down from the buggy. As he passed the gelding, he paused to stroke the horse's sleek, sweaty neck. It wasn't the bay's fault. He was fine for a rented animal. Malachi ran a hand down the iron-hard leg to where the brown coat turned to black, smiling when the gelding responded by lifting his hoof.

In fact, he might buy the bay. He and his brothers would need several buggy horses. Samuel would be replacing his courting buggy as soon as they settled in, probably before. Gideon, as well. Malachi shook his head at the thought. His brothers had grown faster than the passing years justified.

His smile faded as he straightened to regard the building in front of him. At least the horse was something he could try out before purchasing. Unlike the small farmstead he'd bought sight unseen. Or the business before him, which he was now owner of. Another deep sigh lifted the suspenders that crossed his shoulders.

He wasn't impulsive. Far from it. Malachi knew himself to be like Barley, one of his father's draft horses back in Ohio. A plodder. Barley hadn't moved fast, but his steady and deliberate pace had plowed, planted and harvested many fields. The seed that'd culminated in

Malachi's move to Wisconsin had germinated long ago. Things had been getting difficult back in Ohio. Malachi was surprised he'd survived there this long. Some type of change had been needed. He'd prayed that *Gott* would provide him with direction. When he'd heard of this opportunity, he'd snatched it up like a horse snapping at an insect during blackfly season.

Hopefully this'd been *Gott*'s answer. Once he'd settled on his course, Malachi hadn't paused in his plodding forward long enough to check.

The furniture shop was a good investment. He'd reviewed numbers available on the operation before he'd made the offer. It was a well-run business and Malachi was excited to be part of it. But it was a big change. He wasn't fond of changes. This purchase had prompted several of them in his life. Walking through that door would hopefully wrap up the last and biggest one.

After giving the bay a final rub on the forehead, he headed up the stairs. A cheery jingle greeted him when he swung the door open. Malachi's tense shoulders eased slightly as he inhaled the familiar scents of wood and stain. His lips curved. This was what he knew and loved. It would be all right.

An encompassing glance revealed a well-ordered showroom. His experienced eye recognized the diverse furniture's primary wood as oak, with a few pieces of cherry, maple and walnut. Stepping farther into the airy room, he ran a hand over the back of a chair that tucked into a large dining table. Malachi nodded in approval at the smooth surface. He straightened abruptly and turned to the back of the store when he heard the sound of a door opening.

An Amish woman stepped through, a ready smile on

her face. Her auburn hair was tucked under her *kapp*, a few strands threatening to escape the confines. She headed in his direction before halting abruptly. Reaching up, she touched the safety glasses on her face, hastily pulled them off and set them on the sales counter. With flushed cheeks and a sheepish smile, she turned back to him.

"Good morning. May I help you?" she inquired as she approached, her black shoes making no sound on the glossy wooden floor.

He couldn't help returning the smile. Her grin became full and moved to her eyes. Eyes that lifted briefly to his hat before returning to his face. Malachi yanked the black felt from his head and held it in front of him. *"Guder mariye,"* he returned the greeting. "My name is Malachi Schrock. I was told to meet Bishop Weaver here this morning."

The warmth faded from her face like the temperature of a fine October day upon the approach of an early-winter storm. Malachi didn't realize how much he'd appreciated its glow until he was facing frost in her green eyes.

"Ah. The new owner. The bishop isn't here right now. If he told you to meet him, I'm sure he'll be in as soon as he can." Even her voice had changed from June to December.

Malachi raised his eyebrows. The families that'd greeted him and his brothers at the farmstead had been quite cordial. Some of the young women, enthusiastically so. Obviously, this woman worked here. Just as obviously, he wasn't welcome. He slowly shifted the brim of his hat between his hands. Hopefully this attitude wasn't the consensus of his new workforce.

Upon reaching him, the woman clasped her hands

together at her waist, regarding him coolly. The top of her head, even with the thick soles on her shoes, barely reached his chin.

"If you have any questions about the business, I'd be… I will answer them for you."

Happy had been the omitted word that hung in the silence of the room. She was *not* happy to have him here, *not* happy to answer his questions. Malachi sighed. He didn't know what he might have done already to offend her. He'd only been in the district a few days and the store a few minutes.

Malachi had never been a business owner before, but he'd run a large furniture operation for his previous employer in Ohio. To his knowledge, all those he'd supervised had been quite content with his leadership. He intended that to be the case here. Apparently, he had some ground to make up.

Glancing back toward the front door, he noted the hat rack at its customary location just inside. Malachi took a moment to put his hat on one of the pegs before turning back to the young woman. He suppressed a smile. She reminded him of a fierce bantam hen.

"What would you like to tell me about the business?"

His mild, open-ended question seemed to surprise her, but she recovered quickly. "It's a well-run operation."

Malachi nodded solemnly. "I noted that from the bookwork."

The ice in her green eyes melted slightly. A shrewd spark began to replace the frost. "The employees are extremely capable and loyal. They've all worked here for some time and are very valuable to the business."

His lips twitched slightly at her artfulness. "That is *gut* to know."

"New accounts have been established with some of the larger *Englisch* furniture stores. We are starting to get a backlog of orders. It's probably time to hire more workers." She eyed him closely, gauging his response.

So this woman knew that his brothers were joining him in the business. Even without telephones, news spread fast in Amish communities. While his brothers would work with him, he had no plans to change the workforce at this time. Not until he understood their abilities and how they benefited the operation. Malachi respected that she was trying to protect the current employees. He also recognized that she was trying to lead him. Plodder he might be, but he didn't like being pulled by the halter. "Are you falling behind?"

Her mouth opened in a perfect circle before snapping closed. "Not at all! I just wanted to assure you that there was ample work to be done."

"*Gut.* I look forward to reviewing the orders." He regarded her quietly. "You mentioned *we.* How long have you worked here?"

For a moment, her eyes clouded. "My father was Amos Fisher, the previous owner. I can't remember a time when I didn't come to work with him."

Malachi frowned in sympathy for her loss at the same time a chill ran up his spine. A managing female in the business. Just what he'd left Ohio to avoid. He continued his study of the woman in front of him. She returned his scrutiny. Malachi drummed his fingers slowly against his pant leg. Perhaps there would be one immediate change to the workforce after all.

They turned in relieved unison when the door jingled to announce a new arrival.

The tall man who entered nodded to the woman before hanging his hat and extending his hand to Malachi.

"I am Ezekiel Weaver. You are Malachi Schrock?" He continued at Malachi's nod, "Welcome to Miller's Creek. I see you've met Ruth Fisher. I'm sure she was sharing how glad we are that you're coming to live in the community."

"Something like that." Malachi's eyes returned to the young woman's. Her smooth cheeks flushed under his regard.

The bishop dipped his head in approval. "*Gut.* She can tell you a lot about the business."

"So I'm discovering." So the bishop wasn't aware of the young woman's animosity. Malachi wasn't going to be the one to share the news. Except for the situation in Ohio, where evasion had seemed the more prudent choice, Malachi addressed his own battles.

Bishop Weaver turned to the young woman. "Ruth, do you have a place where we can talk in private?"

"Certainly." She gestured to the door of a small office. The bishop entered and shut the door after Malachi joined him, leaving the young woman on the other side. Malachi winced at the expression on her face. Her exclusion from a discussion regarding the business certainly hadn't smoothed any waters for him. The bishop might be glad that Malachi was now in the community, but on the other side of the door was someone who clearly wasn't.

Chapter Two

Ruth's cheeks were so hot they had to be flaming red. Granted, she deserved the ample dose of embarrassment from her behavior toward the new owner. If her *gross-mammi* had been alive, she'd have admonished Ruth. *Keep your words soft and sweet. You might have to eat them.* Ruth could almost hear *Grossmammi*'s tranquil voice repeating the Amish proverb.

It hadn't been the words so much, Ruth recalled. The words were true. Her coworkers' jobs were on her mind. When things were on her mind, Ruth expressed them. It'd been the attitude used in delivering the words that would be hard to choke down if served back to her. And the new owner was well within his rights to serve up a banquet.

Ruth banged her head gently against the side of a nearby hutch. Her prayer *kapp* slipped farther down her hair at the contact. She couldn't have made a worse first impression if she'd tried. Reaching behind her head to address the familiar task of repinning the *kapp*, she glanced up and froze. Yes, apparently she could. For meeting her eyes through the window between the office and the showroom were the keen blue ones of the new owner. Ruth jabbed a final pin in her hair, whirled around and swept through the door into the workroom.

It wasn't the heavy bang of the door as she came through that focused all the attention in the workroom on her. They'd obviously been watching for someone to enter. Four sets of curious eyes observed Ruth as she slid her hands down the front of her apron. The noise in the room abated as machines shut down.

Benjamin had returned from collecting a load of lumber. Ruth figured he was the one who'd shared the news of the occupant in the office. He'd have passed the buggies out front, recognized the bishop's and noted the unknown rig when he'd driven the team around the back of the shop. Her suspicion was confirmed when his voice carried across the now-quiet room. "Is he here?"

Ruth cleared her throat. "*Ja.* He's in the office talking with Bishop Weaver."

"What do you think?" The questions began as the men crossed to her.

I think that my life is about to change. But Ruth knew that wasn't what these men wanted to hear. "He seems a fair man." At least she hoped so. Impressions could be deceiving. Look at the one she'd certainly left him with.

"Does he know furniture?"

"I'm not sure about that. He looked like he was admiring the workmanship on that oak table and chairs you built, Isaac."

Some of the tension in their postures reduced with their laughter at her teasing.

"He knows that it's a *gut* business, that you do *gut* work and that we have many customers to keep us busy. He is not a fool." At least, she hoped not. "I'm sure he'll meet you soon." He would, or she would say something to him about making an effort to greet the anxious men.

Ruth smiled and gestured behind her. "You can go through the door to gawk and act like you've nothing better to do, or you can go back to work and demonstrate how industrious you are, should he poke his head into the workshop today."

The four men, two bearded, two not, nodded and turned back to their tasks. If she said it would be all right, it would be all right. They trusted her judgment.

Ruth's smile faded as soon as their backs were turned. She felt the weight of that trust pressing down on her shoulders. Pressing her down into the floor until she felt like she was barefoot instead of wearing the sneakers that provided comfort for long hours on her feet. A trust she didn't know if she deserved, but one she would do her best to uphold.

If there was no one to support her, well, she was growing used to that.

Ruth wove through the benches, equipment and various works in progress, and came to a stop at the far reaches of the large room. Pressing her lips together to keep them from quivering, she quietly surveyed the rough pieces of oak neatly stacked in the corner. Another Amish proverb crept across her mind. *A man should not grieve over much, for that is a complaint against* Gott. She compressed her lips more tightly. Chalk it up to another way in which she was disappointing *Gott*, for she certainly was still grieving.

And what was over much? *Daed* had only been gone a month. *Daed*, who'd been father, teacher and companion, had left a staggering void here at the shop and in the now-echoing silence of the farmhouse they'd shared. It might've been different if her father had remarried after her mother's death when Ruth was born. But he hadn't, much to the disappointment of all the available women in the district. Instead, he'd raised numerous eyebrows rearing his daughter by himself. It'd been just the two of them. And now that it was just her, she still felt his loss like a missing limb.

It wasn't that she didn't have friends. Ruth enjoyed visiting with the other single women at church and afterward every other Sunday. Or at least she had before *Daed* got sick. But between covering for his work at the shop, keeping up their household and caring for an ill father, she hadn't had time to go to the social gatherings like quilting. As it'd meant more time with her father, she couldn't regret the trade-off. Besides, now that the new owner was here, she had all the time in the world to join in those events, at least until she left.

Crossing to a cabinet, she snagged a fresh sanding block. Ruth reached up to pull her safety glasses into place from where they usually perched on the top of her head, but her searching hand only tapped hair and her *kapp.* As her hand dropped to her side, she wondered where she might have left them. Vividly, it came back to her. They were in the showroom, on the counter. Where she'd set them before she knew who he was. When her initial thought upon seeing the blond, broad-shouldered stranger had been how attractive he was and that she didn't want him seeing her in heavy plastic glasses. Where he still might be, rightfully thinking that she was the Wicked Witch of the West from a book she'd read to her *daed* while he was sick. But she wasn't going to venture anywhere near the showroom right now.

Well, she'd sanded without glasses before. Ruth returned to the corner, pulled a stool to the nearby bench and reverently picked up a flat piece of the oak.

She closed her eyes. If she tried hard, she could still see her father's handling of the wood. It'd been the last thing he'd worked on before he died. Every year for Christmas, *Daed* would make her a piece of furniture. The rocker was to be this year's gift. He'd tried to work on it, tried to hurry when he knew his time was running out, but the illness overcame him. Whenever she wanted to feel close to her father, she worked on the rocker. With dismal results. Because anytime she tried, like now, unshed tears burned her eyes.

This would not do, especially today. Ruth reluctantly tucked the oak back with the other unfinished pieces and wiped her sleeve across her eyes. As she lowered her arm, she caught the movement of the door to the showroom opening. All eyes in the room focused on the man who stepped through. Ruth took a deep breath. Time to start a new approach and hope her previous one hadn't obliterated her coworkers' options. Another Amish proverb popped into her head. *A smile is a curve that can straighten out a lot of things.* If only it were that simple. But it was worth a try.

Normally, Malachi strove to avoid being the center of attention. *Emphatically* strove to avoid it. Today, he knew there was no possibility of evading scrutiny. He was new. He was unknown. And he had some control over their lives. Until that changed, his actions and presence would be closely watched.

Looking out over the well-ordered workroom, he briefly met the eyes of the occupants, nodding at them as his gaze swept over their locations. Four men. And her. The fierce bantam hen. The distance to where she stood at the back of the room didn't diminish the energy that almost vibrated from her.

Whereas the men immediately returned his acknowledgments, there was a heartbeat or two from when his eyes met hers and he nodded to when she returned the nod. Apparently she'd thought better of her initial greeting, because after another beat or two, a smile curved her lips. It didn't reach her green eyes as he knew it could, from her initial response in the showroom. But it was an effort at least, albeit one that looked more like a grimace. Malachi wondered if it covered gritted teeth.

Not something he intended to explore or address today. He'd come in at Ezekiel Weaver's invitation for an official meeting. Malachi didn't know why the bishop needed to make it so official when a simple visit at Malachi's new farm would have sufficed. Perhaps, in having such an obvious meeting at the business, the man was attempting to extend over the new owner some additional authority as the district's bishop. Perhaps it was to make a point to the old owner's daughter. The man surely had his reasons. Malachi wasn't going to pursue them. He would establish his own path.

He made his way into the workroom, stopping to review and admire some projects, inspect equipment and visit with his new employees. In their own way, the four men expressed their welcome and interest in working for him.

Jacob, one of the two single men, was the most talkative. He also introduced himself as a nearby neighbor. Benjamin, the other unmarried man, was quiet but quick with a nod or smile. His eyes were sharp, taking in everything without being obvious. Isaac and Nathaniel, the two married men, were congenial and accepting. All of them seemed very capable in their work. All seemed ready to give him a chance. Except her.

She didn't approach him and Malachi didn't go back to greet her. An omission that perhaps had been a mistake, he reflected, as he went down the steps to the patiently waiting gelding. *Ach.* He wasn't going to retrace his steps now. He'd already met her. The rest of the workforce was aware of that. If they wanted to speculate about what they might perceive as an exclusion, so be it. He couldn't control their thoughts. He hadn't meant anything by it.

Except, Malachi realized as he climbed into the buggy and lifted the reins, maybe he had. Maybe he'd been unconsciously indicating that he was now in charge. Malachi winced as he released the brake. That hadn't been his intent, either. He had no problem with unmarried women working. He'd worked with some back in Ohio. Most were very intelligent. He had sisters who were sharper than some of the men he'd worked with.

The truth of it, Malachi admitted as the clip-clop of the bay's hooves signaled a ground-eating trot back to what was now the Schrock farm, was that he wasn't prepared to face the buzz saw of energy that radiated from her. His lips quirked. To think he'd be intimidated by a slip of a woman whose *kapp* barely reached his chin. Malachi's gaze took in the surrounding countryside that rolled by, his countryside now.

Well, he'd learn how to deal with her, one way or another.

Chapter Three

Bess trotted down the road at her usual lackadaisical pace. Ruth couldn't summon the energy to urge the mare to go any faster. She was in no hurry to get home to an empty house where the only sounds other than what she created were cracks and groans as the old structure settled.

Jacob, Isaac, Nathaniel and Benjamin had been encouraged by the short visit with the new owner. The reins dropped farther into her lap as Ruth sighed. Malachi Schrock. She supposed she should start thinking of him by his name and not as "the new owner." He wouldn't always be the new owner. One day he'd just be "the owner."

And she'd be gone.

A black-and-white blur, accompanied by energetic yapping, darted into the road. Bess shied away from it, causing Ruth to smack herself in the chin as she jerked the reins up to regain control. Guiding an agitated Bess into a nearby field lane, she set the brake. Heart pounding, Ruth looked around to identify the problem. A border collie puppy bounced out from under the buggy and plopped his rump down a few feet from the buggy step. He looked up at Ruth with his pink tongue lolling out one side of his grinning mouth, one ear up and one down. His eyes above the black button nose sparkled, as if waiting for Ruth to respond to his actions. She couldn't help smiling.

Securing the reins, Ruth hurried down from the buggy and squatted next to the pup. He rested his front paws on her bent knees. The white tip at the end of his black tail wiggled on the gravel as he showed his appreciation for her attention.

"Oh, you sweetie." Picking up the pup, she cuddled him against her chest. His warm squirming weight fitted into her arms, and her empty heart, like a puzzle piece. Closing her eyes, Ruth hugged him and smiled as he licked her cheek. Her eyes popped open and both she and the pup turned their heads at the exasperated call from up the lane.

"There you are, you rascal. Are you all right, Ruth?" Hannah Lapp strode down the lane, a frown on her pretty face. "I'm so sorry. We can't seem to keep the little stinker inside. All the rest of the pups stay put, but this one must be some type of magician, because he keeps escaping. Much to the dismay of the chickens and the pigs and the goats, and basically everyone on the farm." She stopped beside Ruth, hands on her hips as she regarded the errant pup.

"I don't think he made a good first impression on Bess, but no harm's been done. In fact," Ruth added after tucking her chin against the pup's soft head, "he's just what I need right now."

Hannah eyed her quizzically.

"The new owner came in today." The words were

mumbled into the top of the puppy's head but her best friend heard them.

"Oh, Ruth, I'm so sorry." Hannah placed a hand on Ruth's shoulder. "I know how hard that must've been for you." Ruth had shared her feelings about the loss of the business with Hannah yesterday after church.

"Certainly made it real. No going back now."

"It is *Gott*'s will. He'll take care of you. You just have to trust in Him."

The pup wiggled to get down. Ruth reluctantly let him out of her arms. Arms that immediately felt emptier than the release of the warm weight justified. She knew her friend was right. Hannah had always had the *gelassenheit* that Ruth knew she should be practicing. But she couldn't just let things be. She couldn't help doing what she could to make things turn out the way she thought they should.

Standing, Ruth wistfully watched the puppy explore the territory around the end of the lane, the white tip of his tail waving like a flag over his chubby ebony back. Here in the abnormally warm November afternoon, the tension of the day faded as she watched the inquisitive pup. She didn't look forward to entering an empty house, but at least she could do it with a more peaceful attitude than when she left work.

The pup wandered over to sniff at the buggy's wheels. After confirming that Bess was going to tolerate the small investigator, Ruth turned to Hannah to share a grin at the puppy's antics and found her friend eyeing her speculatively.

"I think you do need him."

"What?" Ruth tried to recall the last bits of their conversations. They'd been talking about *Gott*. Of course she needed *Gott*. Everyone needed *Gott*. That was a given and one Hannah wouldn't have bothered to voice. Before that they'd spoken of the new owner. Hannah couldn't be thinking that Ruth needed Malachi Schrock, could she? A vivid image of the first moment she saw Malachi popped into her head. Her heartbeat had jumped at the sight of his tall form and intelligent eyes. It'd quickened even more at the smile he'd sent her across the show-room floor. Then her stomach had dropped when he'd said his name.

"No, I don't need him." Ruth held her hands in front of her as if to ward off the traitorously tempting thought. "We might not get along at all."

"Oh, but I think you already do." Hannah nodded to Ruth's feet, where the puppy was nipping at her shoe-laces.

"You mean the puppy?" Ruth stared blankly at the busy dog.

"Who did you think I meant?"

Ruth wasn't going to go there. "I never thought about adopting a puppy." She knelt and was immediately re-warded with the wash of the pup's tongue on her finger-tips. A great longing washed over Ruth. She looked up at her friend. "Do you really mean it?"

Hannah laughed. "We don't raise them to keep them all. We'd be overrun."

Ruth wrapped her arms around the pup and stood up. Now that the idea was planted, she couldn't let it go. "I'll pay you what he's worth," she vowed, mentally wincing at the hit to her funds because she knew the value of the border collies the Lapps raised and sold.

"I think we can work something out. Right now the greater value to us is regaining the peace that he continually disturbs. We might pay you to take him off our hands." Hannah rubbed the panting puppy's head.

"When can I take him?"

Hannah raised her eyebrows as she considered the question. "I don't see any reason why you can't take him with you today. Socks has begun to wean them. Let me get you some of the food they've been started on so you'll have something for him to eat until you can get back into town. You're sure you want to do this? I didn't mean to talk you into something you're not ready for."

Ruth bent her cheek to touch the pup's head. He twisted in her arms to try to lick her. "I may not be ready, but I can't think of anything I want more right now."

Ruth settled the pup in her lap and waved to Hannah before picking up the reins. A hastily assembled puppy survival bag rested at her feet. Bess flicked her ears toward the buggy, questioning what the new passenger was doing there. Ruth smiled as she checked for traffic before backing out of the lane. *Let the old girl pout.* Ruth was as happy as she could remember being before her father had come home from seeing the *Englisch* doctors and confirmed what was making him feel weak and lose weight was the cancer they had both quietly feared it to be. The smile stayed on Ruth's lips, curving up self-mockingly at the corners when she felt a warm wet spot growing on her lap.

The pup didn't seem to mind, as he curled into a ball and fell asleep. Ruth clicked her tongue, urging Bess to increase her speed. For the first time in a long time, she was eager to get home. Even if it was to start teaching her new roommate a few basic rules.

* * *

"I think rules are going to come easier for you than for me," Ruth admitted later that evening. "You're smart, and you should be, as border collies are one of the most intelligent breeds. I'm just afraid I'm not smart enough, or disciplined enough, to teach you what you need to learn."

Perhaps it had been a mistake to get a puppy, particularly with her plans. But after spending the evening with him—feeding him, taking him out several times, setting up a bed and later having him rest at her feet while she knit—Ruth knew she couldn't bear to part with the pup and face an empty house again.

Ruth reintroduced him to the bed they'd made together. She sat beside him as he settled into it, stroking his soft head before she slipped away. Only moments after she'd settled into her own bed, the cries started.

The whimpering tore at her heart. Leaning over the edge of the bed, she saw two miniature white paws propped up against her mother's Wedding Ring quilt.

"You're supposed to be a working dog. You will be shunned by border collies everywhere for this unacceptable behavior. You won't be able to eat from their dish. Or share treats with them. Why, I'd even be surprised if they allowed you to join them in working the sheep." While lecturing him, she lifted him to join her on the quilt. The pup licked her fingers. Ruth giggled. The sound and feeling of the long-absent action surprised her. Giggling again just because it felt good, she settled the pup on the bed. They both snuggled in, comforted by each other's presence.

Her nose was cold. The weather had obviously turned overnight. Ruth nestled deeper under the covers until a sensation swept over her that something was missing. Her eyes flew open. The pup! Quickly sitting up, she patted around the bed in the predawn dark to determine he wasn't on the quilt beside her. Swinging her feet out from under the covers, she gasped as they hit the cold floor. Lighting a lamp, she saw a puddle near the door. Apparently she hadn't woken up soon enough to suit the pup.

"How long have you been up, and what else am I going to find?" Her teeth chattered in the chilly air as she snagged her robe from the foot of the bed and shoved her arms into the sleeves.

Wide-awake now, Ruth foraged for an old towel. Locating one, she looked through the open door into the living area. Of course, the pup had found the knitting she'd set beside her chair and was doing battle. And winning. Ruth wondered how many stitches she'd lost in the confrontation.

Hearing her footfalls in the bedroom, the pup raced through the door to investigate, almost knocking Ruth over. He licked her bare toes that curled on the cold floor before they both went to inspect the puddle by the door.

"This is neither approved nor appreciated behavior," Ruth admonished as she cleaned it up with the towel. "*Housebroken* does not mean the house gets broken." The pup chased the dangling ends of the cloth as it moved. Lifting him into her arms, she rested her cheek on his downy head.

"Do you need to go outside so we can get the rules sorted out?" Slipping into her shoes, she glanced out the window to see patches of frost on the ground in the first faint fingers of light. Snagging a cape from a peg by the door, she draped it around her shoulders and stepped out into the brisk morning. A hint of rose to the east heralded the sun's future appearance. It was pretty now but could mean a weather change before evening. Might be prudent to throw an extra blanket in the buggy just in case.

The pup squirmed to get down. Ruth released him, hoping it was a sign that he wanted to do his duty. Instead, it was a sign he wanted to explore the underside of the porch.

Shivering at the wind that blew against her bare legs, she followed the pup around the yard, stomping her feet against the hard ground to keep warm. The pup was in no hurry. Apparently all he'd needed to do this morning had been accomplished already.

"If you're not going to do your business, we might as well set up a place for you during the day. Besides, it will get us out of the wind." Ruth hurried to the henhouse, abandoned since it had become more efficient to buy eggs from their neighbor instead of raising a few chickens herself. The puppy bounded along behind her, eager to investigate new territory.

The farmstead had several outbuildings. A hog house, a corncrib, a shed for machinery. All unused since Ruth and her *daed* began spending so much time at the shop that it made more sense to trade and purchase goods than grow everything themselves.

The henhouse had been one of the last buildings to empty. As soon as she ducked inside the door, Ruth sighed at the immediate relief against the whipping wind. She cast a critical eye over the dimly lit interior. Thankfully, she'd cleaned it thoroughly after the last of the hens had gone. A few adjustments and a warm bed should make it a worthy daytime home for the pup.

Ruth regarded the small run outside, considering what could be quickly done to eliminate all potential escape routes. The weave of the fence was small enough that he couldn't get out, but not so big he could get stuck, so no adjustments needed there. The pup assisted the investigation by tugging on Ruth's untied shoestrings. She bent to secure them and gave him a rub on his head. "Hannah was right—you are a rascal." Gently cupping his muzzle, she met his happy eyes. "In fact, that might be a fitting name for you. I dub thee Rascal Fisher."

Releasing the newly christened pup, Ruth stood, setting her hands on her hips. "So, Rascal. I need to get some tools and fix that hole under the gate. Hannah said you were a magician at getting out. I wouldn't recommend that today, as it looks like the weather is going to turn and I won't be around to check on you."

Worrying her bottom lip between her teeth, Ruth debated taking the pup to Hannah's farmstead. "I don't want them to think I can't handle you. I know I can, but it will just take a little preparation. And you shared a shed and a run like this with your siblings and mother. You should be all right." She worried her lip a little more. "I hope."

Turning to look for the pup, Ruth caught him in midsquat. "Good boy! That's just what we needed. Let's go inside for some breakfast while we figure the rest of this out."

By the time she secured Rascal's shelter, Ruth was running late. Bess's reluctant pace didn't help. The mare kept ducking her head against the wind that was blowing in her face. The sky was piling gray in the west. Ruth urged the mare to hurry whenever Bess's feet started to drag. She knew Malachi was going to be at the shop today. In fact, he might already be there.

Bouncing on the seat helped Ruth expend nervous energy. More important, it helped keep her warm. She was grateful she'd remembered to bring along an extra quilt and glad she'd taken a moment to roll down the curtain doors of the buggy against the wind, but she was going to be late. She had never been late for work before. Ever. The others would be waiting for her to open the door.

She'd taken a moment to stop at the mailbox of her nearest neighbor and stick in a message, asking if they'd check on the pup during the day. They had two daughters who still attended school. Ruth was hoping the girls wouldn't mind the chance to play with a puppy. Providing, she amended with another uneasy glance at the sky, they did it earlier in the day before some weather hit.

When she and Bess swept into the shed behind the woodshop, several other horses nickered in greeting. Ruth counted the bays in the makeshift stalls and her heart sank. They were all here. Plus one. Hurriedly, she unharnessed a grouchy Bess, wiped her down and guiltily gave her a offering of extra hay.

Cheeks flushed with more embarrassment than cold, Ruth dashed in the door. The recalcitrant wind took the opportunity to blow a gust that jerked the door from her chilled hands and bang it hard against the wall. Hastily shutting it, she turned to find all eyes in the workshop looking in her direction.

There were four sets of eyes she knew well. Upon seeing her, they nodded and returned to their work. But two new workers regarded her curiously. They watched as Ruth made herself walk sedately over to the coatrack, remove her black cape and bonnet, and hang them with the other coats there. They continued to observe her as she crossed to the cabinet and removed the safety glasses that she'd retrieved from the showroom yesterday—after she was sure he'd left. Since they were younger versions of the blue-eyed, blond man who also regarded her steadily, she figured they were the brothers who had come to join what had been her *daed*'s business.

Ruth put on the glasses and turned to face the new owner. Some type of barrier seemed prudent before meeting his gaze. Malachi didn't say anything, just flicked a glance to the clock over her head and raised an eyebrow before returning his impassive blue eyes to her. Even in his silence, Ruth felt severely chastised.

Swinging around to avoid his penetrating gaze, she grabbed the first project she could put her hands on and set to work. Struggling because her palms were now sweaty—not a good combination with the work she was doing on the wood—she took a moment to calm herself.

She was never late. With or without her father there, she'd always been the first one to the shop and the last one to leave.

It didn't take long before the familiar sounds and smells of the workshop lulled Ruth into her version of peace. Surprisingly, the morning went fast. Malachi didn't come near her, although he worked and visited with the men. Every time someone entered the sales shop, he looked over at Ruth, who always stopped what she was doing and went to greet the potential customer.

Having forgotten her lunch at home and not wanting to leave the shop during that break as she'd arrived late, Ruth took advantage of the empty office off the show-room to eat an apple she'd left in there when she'd been the sole resident. Looking out through the observation window into the showroom and farther to the street, she could see snowflakes joining the whipping wind. Ruth shivered. What a change in a day, but that was Wisconsin weather.

Wiping her hands with a napkin after disposing of her apple, she sighed. He still hadn't spoken to her. She wasn't sure what that meant. He hadn't come by to check the work she was doing. Did that mean he trusted her, or did it mean that it wouldn't matter what she did, so he didn't care? It shouldn't matter to her, as she was leaving. But she liked to know—no, she *needed* to know where she stood on things. Squaring her shoulders, she ran her hands down her apron. Well, if he didn't talk to her this afternoon, she'd go talk to him.

On her way back to her workstation, Ruth paused to observe the two brothers, who were preparing to bore bolt holes for the frame on an oak headboard. Malachi's siblings were a good-looking pair. *Like their brother*, she thought to herself. It said in the book of Samuel that man looks on the outward appearance, but *Gott* looks at the heart. The new owner's—Malachi's—heart was probably good, something she had yet to discover, but his appearance was…distracting. And she didn't need or want distractions. Not of that nature.

Absently watching the brothers work, she abruptly straightened. They might be good-looking, but they were boring the holes on the wrong side of the bedpost. Ruth strode over.

"They need to go on the other side."

The older one looked up from the drill he'd pressed against the wood and swiveled his head toward her. The younger one lifted his safety glasses to the top of his blond hair.

"What?" Their inquiry came at her in a duet.

"You're boring the holes on the wrong side of the post.

This headboard has beveled panels on the side facing the mattress. If you bore the holes for the frame there—" she pointed to where the drill bit rested "—the design will be facing the back of the bed, probably pressed against a wall. Benjamin did too good a job on the panels' bevels to have them adorned with cobwebs against a wall."

The brothers looked at her as if she had two heads. Ruth put her hands on her hips. Didn't they have any women with brains in Ohio? Their gazes flicked behind her. Ruth didn't have to look to know who was approaching. She could tell by the tingling that moved up her neck. Malachi must be focusing his judgmental blue eyes on her again.

"What seems to be the issue?" he asked mildly, moving into her peripheral view. She didn't turn her head.

The older brother nodded toward her. "She says we're putting it on backward." His tone implied that she couldn't possibly know what she was talking about.

Other sounds of the workshop filled the room, but their little knot was silent as Malachi's encompassing gaze swept over the headboard. Sweat gathered between her shoulders.

"She's right."

"What?" the siblings echoed again.

"There's a design on the side opposite of where you're drilling. You'd have put it on backward. If you aren't going to use your two sets of eyes, at least check things twice before you drill. Or cut. Or anything else." He looked over at her. "Thanks for the catch, Ruth."

"Even though the business won't have my father's name on it anymore, I still want it to be thought of as having superior craftsmanship and service." Ruth started for the back of the shop. She stopped abruptly. Sweet words. A smile. She sighed heavily. *Oh,* Mammi, *how wise you were.* Head bowed, she strode back the way she came until brown shoes under blue cloth pants came into view. Tilting her chin up—way up, it seemed—she met his eyes. "Thank you for your support. I appreciate it. I...I didn't mean to be...snappish."

His gaze held hers. Ruth's heart thudded in quiet beats until he spoke. "I want the business to be successful and well respected, too." He paused, as if he was going to say more, but then he seemed to think better of it and just nodded.

Ruth took that as the end of the awkward situation, turned on her heel and headed back to where she would attempt to lose herself in the wood. And to try not to worry about the business. Or the pup. Or—she glanced through the glass portion of the door at the increasing volume of whipped snow outside—the weather.

Chapter Four

Malachi's lip twitched as he watched the diminutive figure stride away. That had to have been hard for her, Miss Nothing-Good-About-Having-You-Here. But she'd done it. His eyes narrowed as he watched her expertly resume the project she'd been working on. He'd been talking with his new employees. To every query, the response was the same: "Ask Ruth. She'll know." Was there any part of the business the woman didn't have her hand in? He could tell from the tone of the unprompted responses that she was respected.

He hadn't talked with her this morning. She'd looked like a cornered badger when she'd come in late. If she thought she'd been snappish a moment ago, he was thankful he hadn't approached her then. From his conversations with the men, he'd determined that she was always the first to arrive. So something must've happened this morning. She seemed more straightforward than to slacken her efforts just because ownership had changed. The recent interaction showed she cared about the future of the business. The question remained, would she have a future in it?

"Who's she?"

Malachi turned to see his twenty-one-year-old brother watching Ruth as she assembled what appeared to be a small rolltop desk at the back of the workroom.

"The previous owner's daughter."

Samuel rolled his eyes. "Oh, no. Not one of those again."

Malachi allowed a small smile in commiseration of the sentiment. *"Ja."*

"She going to haunt your steps like the other one did?"

His eighteen-year-old brother, Gideon, joined the observation of the auburn-haired woman, who fortunately wasn't aware of the scrutiny. If she glanced up, the "cornered badger" look would return, complete with hisses and snarls, Malachi thought as his smile progressed to a one-sided grin. Actually, Malachi mused, the analogy fitted pretty well. Badgers were small in stature, protective, blunt and aggressive. Like someone he'd recently met.

"She's not as pretty as Leah."

Malachi's smile evaporated at Gideon's comment. Yes, with her blond hair and thick-lashed eyes, the daughter of his boss in Ohio had been very attractive. But for some reason, the comparison to Ruth seemed unfair.

"This one works here. It couldn't be much worse."

"Samuel, what could've been worse is if she hadn't caught your mistake and we created an error for a customer on our first day on the job. Or had to waste labor and materials to do it over." The younger men's eyes dropped before their brother's steady gaze.

"Ja. You're right about that."

"Is the quality of work something I need to be concerned about going forward?"

"*Nee.* If only to make sure that she doesn't catch us at it again." Samuel nodded toward the back of the room.

"*Gut.*" Malachi dropped a hand on each brother's shoulder. He was surprised at how muscular those shoulders had become as he gave them a brief, encouraging squeeze. "I'm glad you're with me on this adventure. It would've been harder to leave Ohio without you."

"You did the right thing." Gideon earned another squeeze with his support.

"Let's hope so." Malachi patted their backs before dropping his hands. "Let's get some work done today. Show that the Schrock brothers know their way around building furniture."

Work was accomplished, but it tapered off in efficiency as the intensity of the weather picked up. Malachi watched his employees repeatedly glance up at the encroaching darkness that dimmed the skylights, the primary source of light for the business. Or go to the window and look outside at the growing storm, usually with hands on their hips and a worried expression on their faces. All except his single female employee. She stayed at her task until he could determine the project was indeed a petite rolltop desk. With the ominous change in the weather, no one entered the showroom to distract her from the work.

It was past midafternoon when Malachi called to get their attention. He waited until the machines had been turned off and the hums and squeals of the equipment died down so they could hear him.

"We want to get the work done on time for our customers. In order to do that, we need to ensure that you are safe and sound to come in and do it. We have storms in Ohio, and I've heard that the Wisconsin ones can be quite fierce, as well. We're closing up early today so you can get home and check on your families and livestock before the storm gets worse."

Although nothing was said, Malachi could tell by the relaxation in the tense faces watching him that his new employees appreciated the early release. He wanted his workforce safe. He was also striving to establish trust as their leader. Working hard in the long run did not always mean working all the time.

The men didn't need further instructions. Workstations were quickly cleaned up and equipment and materials put away for the day. Malachi saw his brothers by the coatrack, outer gear on and obviously ready to go. He frowned. There was some work in the office he wanted to finish before he left today. Malachi walked toward them, intending to instruct them to wait a bit before they hitched up the buggy. One of his new employees, Jacob, a beardless young man with red hair, was visiting with them as he put on his coat and hat.

Practiced at reading Malachi's expressions, Samuel grimaced when he saw his brother's face. "*Ach*, you're not ready to go yet. How long must we stay?"

Before Malachi could open his mouth, Jacob spoke. "I live just a mile up the road from the old Yoder place. The house with the corncrib by the end of the lane. You two could come home with me and he could pick you up on the way by."

Obviously pleased with the offer from Jacob, whose age appeared to fall between Malachi's and his brothers', Samuel and Gideon looked hopefully at Malachi. It seemed a reasonable solution and one where they would get to know their neighbors better. Malachi nodded. "I'll see you there later."

The young men eagerly headed for the door and pulled it open. They slapped a hand to their heads as the vicious wind threatened to blow their black hats off. Gideon, the last one through, struggled to pull the door shut behind him. It finally closed with a hard click.

Malachi turned to see Ruth, whose workstation was in direct line of the gust, looking at the closed door with wide eyes and arms hugging her shoulders. They were the only ones left in the room. Tools and delicate pieces of wood were neatly arranged about her. She'd still been working.

"Time to go." Malachi tipped his head toward the door that rattled against the gusting wind.

She turned back to her bench. "I was late getting here. I need to put my time in."

Stubborn woman. Malachi strode over to the partially assembled desk. *"Nee*, not today. I won't have it said that I let you freeze in a ditch on your way home from work." Green eyes turned to him and spoke clearly that he did not *let* her do anything. Fortunately, she was prudent enough not to voice the words. He held her gaze. Really, the woman didn't need any aid in freezing. The outdoor weather would probably be ambient temperature for her.

Finally, she nodded and efficiently began putting away her work. Picking up a few pieces of oak to hand to her, Malachi ran his fingers over the smooth finish. The surface felt like silk under his experienced fingertips. He ran his eyes over the intricate joints in the desk. It was amazing craftsmanship.

"Beautiful work." He handed her the wood.

Taking it apprehensively, she flicked a look up at his face, judging his sincerity. *"Denki."* The rest of the pieces were gathered up quickly, as if to indicate she didn't need his help.

Malachi raised his eyebrows. Apparently it had been a temporary truce. The badger had returned. He wove his way through the workshop, now empty and quiet, to the showroom door. At the door, he looked back at Ruth. Once he was out of her orbit, her efforts had slowed and she appeared to be working on the desk again. Malachi frowned and jerked the door open with more force than necessary. Stubborn woman, indeed.

Deciding the tasks he'd hoped to finish could wait for another day, Malachi grabbed his coat and hat from the office and secured the front door of the store. Ruth looked up as he reentered the workroom. She scowled and had the rest of her work put away by the time he reached her.

Malachi waited while she tugged on her cape and tied her bonnet. He was going to make sure she went out the door and headed home. He frowned at the thinness of her cape as he followed her black-clad figure to the door. "I'll help you harness your horse."

"I can do it myself. Besides, I have to go to the store first."

Malachi stopped in his tracks. "What? Conditions are dangerous out there. You need to get home." The exasperation that colored his tone was a stranger to him. It'd never been there before. "Whatever it is will wait."

"No, it won't. I have responsibilities."

"So do I. I'm responsible for making sure you get home safely." He was tired of talking to the back of her black bonnet. Fortunately—or unfortunately—she whipped around and he found himself facing blazing green eyes and what looked like a few freckles on the cheeks under the encompassing brim. A dainty chin tipped up toward him above the big black bow.

"No. You are not. I've been taking care of myself for some time now. I don't need you to take care of me on your first day here. I'm going to Piggly Wiggly before I head home." Turning to jerk open the door, she almost tumbled into the wall when the force of the wind hit the portal. Recovering quickly, she bent her slight frame against the gusts and headed down the street to where Malachi had learned the grocery store was located. Her figure soon disappeared in the whipping snow. Shaking his head, Malachi locked the door and headed for the shed. Stubborn woman, he muttered to himself again. Even a badger was wise enough to get out of a snowstorm.

Ruth didn't know what made her cheeks more red, the blasts of wind that threatened to steal her breath or embarrassment and self-disgust at her behavior. Another proverb came to mind as she ducked her head against the blowing snow. *It is better to give others a piece of your heart than a piece of your mind.* She felt the staccato beat of snow pelting the top of her bonnet, like it was trying to tap the reminder into her head. Well, he had enough pieces of her mind to put together a puzzle by now. A piece of her heart? That was an amusing thought, even beyond the fact that he'd surely been baptized by now, and was therefore remaining Amish. And she wouldn't be. Therefore, not even a splinter of her heart would be allowed to consider his direction.

Besides, there wasn't room in her heart and mind for anything right now beyond fretting over the safety and security of the puppy, something she'd been doing all day. Was she responsible enough in her care for him? Was he smart enough to stay out of the weather? Unlike his new owner?

That brought her back to the abrupt discussion at the workshop. As she and the new owner were leaving, she'd had the discomfiting realization that not only would she not be the one to open the shop every day, something she'd done for years, she'd also no longer be the one to close it up at the day's end. So she'd latched onto the one thing she knew she could handle in accountability, her own care. After the way she'd lashed out at his offer, worrying about herself might be the only thing she had left to do. She might not have to worry about a job anymore, and she wasn't ready to leave just yet. *Dear Lord, please help me keep my mouth shut.*

Exiting Piggly Wiggly a short time later, she was almost blown back into the sliding doors. Ruth looked beyond the grocery store's parking lot to where the road was no longer visible and sent up another fervent prayer. *Please, Lord, I hope it is Your will that Bess and I get safely home to the puppy. Please don't let my stubbornness affect the two animals in my care.*

The relief from the blocked wind when Ruth entered the shed housing the horses was indescribable. So was her surprise at seeing Bess almost harnessed. Ruth dropped her bags by the wheel of her buggy and raced over to help. Looking up at her approach, Malachi seemed to take in the snow-crusted cape and bonnet.

"Did you get your important shopping done?" There was a curtness in his voice she hadn't heard before. Ruth winced, knowing she deserved it.

"Ja," she said breathlessly, reaching under Bess to hand him the girth. Her chilled hand touched his and

she jerked it back. He paused momentarily, as well. Bess stomped her foot, encouraging them to get on with it. Ruth hurriedly renewed her efforts, careful to keep her hands on her side of the mare. She didn't want to explore the feeling that'd shot up her arm at the touch of his cool fingers.

Lifting up the shafts of the buggy, she guided Bess between them. Malachi was doing the same to a bay gelding. Faster than her at connecting the straps and buckles that safely secured the horse to the buggy, he came around to her side to help her finish. When he saw she was almost ready, he picked up her dropped bags and moved to set them in the buggy, glancing in the open sacks as he did so.

"You went out in a blizzard to get a dog toy?"

Ruth hunched a shoulder. "I needed it." She didn't look at him as she scrambled into the buggy. But she caught a glimpse of his face before she secured the door. He was not happy.

She gently slapped the reins against Bess's back. The mare needed no further encouragement to exit the shed. Ducking her head against the blowing snow, she started a brisk trot toward home.

No nudging required for the old girl tonight. Ruth tucked the blanket about her on the seat, glad once again that she'd remembered to throw it into the buggy this morning. The mare wanted to get home to a warm barn and hay. Ruth wanted to get home to make sure Rascal was warm and safe. Getting out of the elements herself seemed like a pretty good idea, as well.

Within moments, the brown back trotting in front of the buggy was splattered with white. Ruth stared apprehensively at the road in the rapidly dimming light of the late afternoon. It was hard to believe that she'd driven in with brown and a bit of green fringing the roadside. Now she was glad to even see the sides of the country road that they'd just turned onto. Hopefully Bess's judgment was better than her own at knowing where the road ended and the ditch began.

Ruth was thankful she wasn't attempting this in the dark. She supposed she had Malachi to thank for that. And for harnessing Bess so she could head home sooner. Ruth saw motion in the small rearview mirror that jutted out from the buggy's side. A bay and buggy had just turned down her road. Recognizing the rig as the one ready in the shed before she'd left, Ruth frowned. He should've gone straight at the intersection. Why was Malachi following her home? It would take him at least five miles out of the way on a horrible night.

As the temperature dropped, the light dimmed and the howling wind rose further, Ruth became grateful for the companionship on the road. It was the only company she encountered on the long, cold trip. When the buggy lurched as Bess cut the corner short into the lane, Ruth was never more glad to see the building shapes that identified her farmstead in the swirling snow. She darted a look at the chicken coop as Bess pulled hard toward the big barn doors.

Ruth would've gasped when she partially rolled up the buggy door to slip out if the wind had allowed her enough air to do so. The driving snow stung her cheeks and tried to tug her bonnet from her head. To keep from tumbling ahead of its force, Ruth kept hold of the buggy and then of Bess as she worked her way to the doors that shook ominously in their frames.

Bracing herself for the jerk when she released the

latch and the doors suddenly became kites, she almost fell in surprise when two arms reached in front of her to pull the lever back and opened the doors in a controlled, albeit jolting, manner. Securing her attention, Malachi waved her into his own buggy. Bess needed no further instruction, driver or no. As soon as the opening was wide enough, she swept inside. Ruth hustled into Malachi's buggy. Driving the gelding into the big barn as well, she was instantly enveloped in the smell of hay and livestock. Malachi wrestled the doors shut behind them.

The sudden break from the force of the driving snow was eerie, as was the wail of the wind as it attacked the barn's walls. Ruth wobbled her way down the buggy steps, more shaken from the ride than she cared to admit.

Bess bobbed her head. Ruth knew the mare. She was saying, "I got you here. Now get me my supper." That reminded Ruth of her other charge. Dashing to the side door of the barn, she wrenched it open. There was a brief, startled call from Malachi before the howl of the wind shut out every other sound. Bowing her head against the buffeting snow, she pushed her way to the henhouse. Her cold fingers were clumsy on the door latch. Biting a chilled lower lip, she worked the frozen bolt from the latch, flung open the door and stumbled in.

Chapter Five

For a few heart-stopping moments, she couldn't see. Then her eyes adjusted to the dim light and she located Rascal on the makeshift bed she'd made him that morning. He blinked his eyes open and stretched his miniature muzzle in a yawn, showing his pink tongue. She hastened over and swept him into her arms. Her heart finally slowed to normal for the first time all day as she nuzzled her cold nose into the top of his head. Waking quickly, Rascal licked the snow from her face.

Sufficiently certain of his well-being, Ruth tucked Rascal under her cape, took a deep breath and stepped outside. By half running, she managed to keep her feet under her in the blowing wind. She reached the side barn door and struggled with it with her one free hand. "Hang on, boy. It's going to go flying when it opens." Moments later, plastered against the door by the wind, she was losing hope when it jerked open, held by a firm arm that gave her just enough room to duck through to the relative quiet of the barn.

Rascal squirmed to get down. Ruth knelt and let him loose, the puppy erupting from beneath her cape like a magician's trick. Once he had his bearings, he hurried to explore the enticing smells of the barn.

Ruth rose to face Malachi. To her relief, he was watching the dog. The tension that'd coiled in her shoulders over worries about Rascal and the nerve-racking drive home seeped away. Concerned she might not be able to stay upright without hanging on to something, she stepped over to Bess and continued the work of unharnessing the mare that her unexpected help had already started. Within seconds, she could see Malachi's impassive face and snow-spattered hat over the top of the mare as he aided her efforts.

"New?"

Ruth didn't ask what he meant. There had been so many new things in her life lately. Only one that had caused her to act more erratically than normal, though, and had just popped out from beneath her cape. "*Ja.* I adopted him last night."

Malachi grunted in acknowledgment as he unbuckled the harness from the horse collar before removing the leather harness from Bess's back. He gazed at Ruth with a questioning look and she pointed him toward the tack room. Grabbing a brush and rag from a shelf on the wall, she proceeded to wipe the damp mare down before leading her into her stall. Preliminary investigations complete, Rascal scampered over to help when Ruth set about feeding the mare. Having located the straw, Malachi scattered some additional bedding in Bess's stall for the cold night.

When Malachi stepped out of the stall and secured the gate, Rascal bounced over to make his acquaintance. Malachi knelt to the wiggly black-and-white bundle and proved himself an experienced puppy petter, hitting all the important spots until Rascal rolled over, exposing his belly in ecstasy.

Malachi glanced up to meet Ruth's watching gaze. "He's a fine one," he acknowledged as his fingers gently rubbed the silky tummy. "I suppose he's worth a toy or two." He shot a smile at Ruth before returning his attention to the puppy.

For a second, Ruth found it hard to breathe. When she remembered how, she drew in a long one, inhaling with it the comfortable smells of the barn—hay, horses and leather. The elusive feeling of peace flitted just out of her reach. She tore her attention away from the beguiling sight of man and dog and glanced across the barn to find Malachi's gelding watching her hopefully.

She hurried over to the bay, grateful for the distraction. "Oh, you poor boy," she crooned, rubbing his damp neck. "Can I get something for him?" She could hear Malachi's movements behind her. A moment later, she saw his steady form beyond the edges of her bonnet's brim.

"The rental place called him Kip. He's been a fine horse. I'm going to keep him." He rubbed the gelding's neck on the opposite side. "No point in doing anything when we're going right back into the storm, because we can't stay."

"No, you definitely cannot." Their eyes met over Kip's lowered head. "But at least let me get him a small bit of oats to eat while I fix you a thermos of coffee and warm up a brick for your feet on the trip."

Malachi scratched the bay under the black forelock for a moment. "I suppose some hot coffee wouldn't go amiss. I saw where the oats are stored. I'll slip his bridle off and feed him some while you get the coffee."

"I doubt he'll go anywhere, but there's a halter in the tack room if you want to use it." She headed for the barn door, glancing in his buggy's open door as she passed the vehicle. After a brief pause, she marched over to her buggy and pulled the quilt from its bench seat to toss it on the seat of Malachi's buggy.

"I see you don't have sense enough to keep blankets in your buggy in this type of weather."

Malachi buckled the halter and then the oat bag over Kip's head. "I've been doing a number of things over the past few days. Thinking about blankets hasn't been very high on the list."

She huffed. "Wisconsin weather will take a heavy toll on the unprepared."

He pulled her forgotten grocery bags from her buggy. "Unprepared? Like not having dog food when you have a dog?"

Ruth scooped up the puppy that trailed at her heels and crossed to Malachi, her hand outstretched for the bags. He shook his head and retained possession of them.

"I'll help you get to the house. With this wind and your small sizes, the two of you could end up in the next county."

Aware that he had a point, she didn't argue. They headed for the exit. Knowing she also owed him something more, she spoke to the wind-rattled door in front of her. "I...I want to thank you for going out of your way and following me home, even though I didn't need it."

"You're welcome." His voice was bland, but Ruth could hear a trace of smile in it. Her lips curved slightly in response as she prepared to face the gauntlet between them and the house.

Malachi held the jolting door in check as she, with

the pup again under her cape, slipped through. Ruth started for the house while he secured the latch. Stumbling against the relentless wind, she would've fallen if a firm hand hadn't grasped her elbow and pulled her upright. With one hand holding her close against him and the other pressed hard against his hat, Malachi guided them to the house. Once in the shelter of the porch, the wind dropped abruptly, as did Malachi's hand.

Ruth tried not to miss its surprisingly comforting presence as she pushed open the unlocked door to the kitchen. Malachi paused in the doorway.

"Ach," Ruth exclaimed, waving him in as she set the pup down. "You can't stay, but you can at least come over the threshold." Needing no further encouragement, Malachi entered and shut the door behind him. The ample kitchen seemed suddenly closet-size. Ruth busied herself with lighting a burner on the gas stove to make the coffee. Malachi stomped snow off his work shoes and pants before moving to the fireplace and starting a fire to chase the noticeable chill from the room.

The homey scene created a surprising ache in Ruth. She spoke quickly to dispel its unaccustomed appeal. "I'll fix a sandwich for you for your drive home. You'll have something to eat in case you get stuck in a ditch."

"I don't think starving would be my immediate issue, but that would be much appreciated." He made quick work at the fireplace and soon a small blaze lent additional light and heat to the cozy room.

After hanging up her cape and bonnet on a nearby hook, Ruth nudged a few bricks scattered in the fireplace closer to the flames. She grabbed the puppy before he could launch himself in to investigate. Malachi reached out a hand when she crossed back to the counter. After a brief hesitation, Ruth handed Rascal to him. The ache intensified.

"Anything that isn't something my brothers or I have prepared would be *wunderbar.* I'm liking Wisconsin, but there are things I miss about Ohio already, and my *mamm*'s meals are one of them."

"The way I heard it, all the women within a reasonable distance have brought over some food. The single women anyway." She kept her back to him as she cut thick slices of homemade bread.

"Ja." There was a smile in the deep voice. "We've had a few meals brought over."

Ruth took the knife to a leftover ham roast and cut equally thick slices. "I haven't quite learned how to cook for one yet. I suppose I could bring something over when the unmarried community finishes feeding you."

She heard a sound behind her. She wasn't sure if it was a cough or a laugh. "I'll keep that in mind," he responded.

Ruth got out a clean dish towel to wrap the sandwich in. It was quiet for a moment. Then she heard him wander across the dining room.

"This is a fine piece." There was reverence in his voice. Ruth turned her head to see him stroking the side of a bird's-eye maple hutch with one hand while he gently held the grinning pup in the other.

She pivoted fully to face him and the piece. *"Ya. Daed* made that for me for Christmas last year," Her tone was more melancholy than she intended.

Malachi rubbed the ears of the puppy cradled in his arm. "It's beautiful. And I'm sorry for your loss."

"No, it's a *gut* memory. It's the last piece he made me. He'd make me a piece every year. They started out small but kept getting bigger. There's that stool, the bench, the table."

Malachi studied the pieces. "The superior craftsmanship of the maker is easily recognized. Your *daed* was talented indeed."

Ruth blinked against the tears that threatened at his sincere comments. "Upstairs is a dresser, a headboard. A hope chest. This year he was making me another piece. He wanted to finish it, but then illness overtook him. I've tried to work on it, but it isn't the same. It was his project, not mine. Although I'd love to have it finished." She swung back to face the counter before she lost the battle and tears swept down her cheeks. "I'll figure it out somehow."

The coffee was boiling on the stove. Ruth turned in relief in its direction. Steam emanated from the openings as she filled a thermos she'd located in the cupboard. Gathering the thermos and the sandwich, she faced the room again to find Malachi watching her. Their eyes met for a brief moment. She was the first to look away.

"Here, I'll trade you," Ruth said brusquely, handing him the sandwich and thermos and taking the pup into her arms, careful not to touch Malachi in the transition. "I'll go back out to the barn with you as soon as I feed him." She located the grocery bags Malachi had set down upon entering the kitchen and got out the small bag of puppy food. The sooner he left the better. His comfortable presence was creating a twinge of longing and that would never do with an Amish man, particularly one who was her new boss.

"No. You'll stay in here." Malachi was surprised at his adamant statement. He was less surprised at the indignant look she gave him in response. "I wouldn't trust that you'd be able to make it back to the house with the wind. You'd blow past my buggy and spook Kip. Then who'd take care of him?" he concluded, gesturing toward the pup.

Ruth nodded as she dampened the small amount of food she'd poured into a bowl. As soon as she set it down, Rascal squirmed in her arms to join it on the floor. Once there, he needed no encouragement to eat.

"And if it's this bad tomorrow, you stay home." Malachi tried to keep a straight face. He said it just to rile her.

"I will not!" She glared at him before marching to the fireplace. Using tongs, she efficiently pulled a brick from the fire. Wrapping it in a thick quilted cloth, she strode over to hand it to him. "But I will be prepared for the trip. More so than you were tonight."

Malachi pursed his lips and strolled over to the door. He'd won the battle he'd hoped to win.

"You better be safe going home. If anything happens to you because you helped me, I'll never forgive myself."

"I think you take too much upon yourself. It is *Gott* that forgives us," he said.

"That's true. Hmm. Then I'll never forgive you."

"But we're Amish. It's our nature and responsibility to forgive," he said. "Although you're a rather unusual one."

"Well, I'll think about it, then." She met his eyes, more than a hint of concern visible in the green depths. "Very hard. Just make sure you make it safely home."

"It will be *Gott*'s will, but I'll do my best. The gelding seems a decent sort. We'll get through."

"And don't get lost on the way there. You're new around here and the roads look different in the dark and snow." Ruth was looking out the kitchen window at the wind-whipped night beyond. She clasped her hands at her waist. The knuckles showed white in the tight grip.

"I've heard that. Somehow for twenty-four years, I've managed to make it home safely." Malachi waited until she moved her attention from the window to him. "Any reason you are so worried?"

She regarded him steadily for a moment. "The business would be up for sale again. You seem to know your way somewhat around furniture. It was extremely busy managing it alone and I have other things to work on. I don't want to have to do it again so soon." She almost smiled but managed to keep her expression solemn.

"I'll do my best not to put your brick, thermos and quilt into the ditch, or get them irrevocably lost in Wisconsin."

"See that you don't." Ruth admonished, bending to pick up the now-fed puppy to keep him from darting out when the door opened.

Malachi shifted the three items to one hand, pulled open the door and shut it firmly behind him when he stepped out on the porch. He grinned, feeling surprisingly warmer from her smile and concern than from the brick, whose heat was radiating through the thick cloth. The grin slowly faded as he took in the elements churning just off the edge of the porch.

The cold air stung his nose as he drew in a long breath. The barn was barely visible from the porch in the swirling snow. For sure and certain, it wouldn't be a pleasant ride home. Malachi wondered if the gelding would find his way to his more recent lodgings, or revert to a previous shelter and leave Malachi stranded outside the rental facility. He'd shrug if he weren't concerned his shoulders would freeze in that position. As he'd told Ruth, it was *Gott*'s will.

He descended the steps and bowed his head against the bite of the wind. It would be interesting if it was *Gott*'s will that he continue to ruffle the feathers of the bantam hen. The wind tried to blow him off course. Malachi glanced up, making sure he was still heading for the barn. He brushed by the fence of the abandoned chicken coop, recently converted to a puppy pen. No, Ruth wasn't a small hen; she was a badger, with many more defenses. Malachi had thought he'd left the foolish, adolescent desire to provoke a prickly creature long behind in his youth.

Apparently not.

Chapter Six

Ruth looked out the window until she could make out the gelding and buggy emerging from the barn. Malachi's figure was barely visible when he stepped out to wrestle the barn doors shut. She continued to watch as the buggy rolled out of the barnyard and down the lane, turning back to the kitchen when the lights on the buggy disappeared in the whirling snow.

"Well, Rascal," she said with a sigh as she regarded the pup in her arms. "We may have agreed not to escort him to the barn, but we still need to go out into the snow. You have some business to attend to outside. What do you think?"

Rascal licked her cheek, making Ruth smile. A laugh was beyond her reach when her mind was focused on the conditions Malachi was facing on his ride home. Bundling up against the weather, she took the pup out on the leeward side of the house. Unfettered gusts just a few feet from where she and the pup huddled whisked away the breath vapor that rose from her encouragement. Snatching him up before he began to run off and explore, Ruth hustled back into the warmth and safety of the kitchen.

Malachi was on her mind the rest of the evening. How useful one of the cell phones that young men sometimes carried during their *rumspringa* would be tonight. Malachi could call if he got into trouble or call when he got home safe. She would say thank you, and then what? She had no claim on him. She wouldn't be working with him for long. Certainly he'd seemed much more pleasant and fun than she'd anticipated. But he was probably pleasant to everyone.

Don't go there, Ruth, she admonished herself during the many times that evening she set down her knitting to get up and look out the window. *It is highly doubtful he's part of Gott's plans for you in that matter. You might work for him a bit longer, but for romance, you're crazy. You don't want to be an Amish wife. A wife, ja. An Amish one, nee.*

But after she'd settled the pup beside her on the quilt following their last trip outside for the evening, she closed her eyes. *Please, Gott, I pray that it is Your will to keep him safe.*

When she and Bess pulled into the furniture shop's buggy shed the next day, Kip swung his head their way and nickered to Bess before returning his attention to the hay net in front of him. Ruth tossed the quilt off her lap and scrambled out of the buggy to give the gelding an appreciative rub on the neck.

"Good boy," she crooned. "I'm so glad you got home safely last night." She returned to an impatient Bess, removed the harness from the mare and settled her into her own hay. The gelding was the only other horse in the shed so far. Passing Malachi's buggy on her way to the workshop door, she noted her loaned quilt folded neatly on the seat, with the dish towel, quilted cloth and brick stacked on top. Ruth smiled and left them there.

The day had dawned crisp and clear, as if to atone for yesterday's storm. The wind had finally stopped in the early hours, with four inches of snow covering the ground in a pristine blanket. Glad to discover the wind had kept the roads mostly clear and the drifts confined to the ditch, Ruth had no problem driving a grouchy Bess over them when she'd started for town earlier than normal.

She darted a look around the workroom as she entered. Her shoulders relaxed under her cape when she noted Malachi's two brothers, Samuel and Gideon, already at work. They looked up as she came in. She nodded in their direction, slipped off her bonnet and cape and headed to her station.

A few moments later the door to the store opened and Malachi came through. As she glanced up from assembling the pieces of the rolltop desk to meet his eyes, her cheeks heated. Quickly nodding in acknowledgment, she dropped her gaze back to the oak pieces in her hands. It took a moment before she recalled which piece went where.

It was easy to get into the groove of the assembly, though, when he ignored her for the rest of the day. They were quite busy for a day after a snowstorm, and the light and buzzer on top of the workshop door kept notifying her that potential customers had come into the showroom. But it didn't take long for Ruth to discover that not all shoppers were looking for furniture.

It being a relatively small district, the addition of three single men would prompt the young single women to come out, snow or no snow. Ruth thought initially that the first two women had actually come in to shop. They'd wandered among the furniture, touching a piece here, a piece there. Ruth had stood, smiling patiently by the counter, ready to answer any questions they might have or run up a sale on the manual addition machine that served as a cash register.

Some hours later, her smile was less patient. Ruth had learned by the end of the morning that any questions the day's customers had were all related to the Schrock brothers. The young ladies would meander around the furniture, but their eyes always drifted to the door to the workroom, obviously hoping that it would open and they could see through it or, better yet, someone would actually come through.

It made Ruth feel old. Most of the girls were younger than her, in their teens as opposed to her ripe old age of twenty-two. She knew who they were, but whereas their older, mostly married, sisters might be friends, these young ladies were more acquaintances. It also made her rather sheepish about her reaction to her time with Malachi last night. Was she as obvious in her interest as these girls were? She certainly hoped not. And her reaction hadn't been romantic. It had been more of a person finally having company in the house after an extended period by herself. That was all.

Ruth rolled her eyes when she left the workroom and went into the shop for the fifth time that morning and found Lydia Troyer, Jacob's sister, accompanied by another young woman. Both watching the door to the workroom with eager eyes. She almost smiled at their disappointed faces when she stepped through.

Although tempted to leave them alone in the shop to twitter away among the furniture, she took up her post by the counter. Any counter work she'd needed to do had long since been done that morning. There was nothing at risk in the store. Even though the young ladies were certainly strong and capable enough to haul out anything should they actually make a purchase—a doubtful prospect—they'd ask for help. And at least four, possibly five, single men in the back would be willing to lend it.

Ruth vowed that even if they purchased the massive oak rolltop desk in the corner, she'd maneuver it out the door by herself. Somehow.

At least Lydia came straight to the point. She had an edge in the apparent race. "Is Jacob here?" She smiled at her companion. "My mother wanted me to give him a message."

Jacob had been getting his hat and coat from the rack when she'd headed to the front to respond to the summons from the shop. "I think he was just going out the door to lunch." Ruth would have opened the door to the workroom to check, but it was apparent that was what they wanted her to do. Folding her arms, she resolutely kept her back to the closed door.

The young ladies obviously found this welcome news. There was only one café in town, so Jacob wouldn't be hard to find. And presumably, he hadn't gone to lunch alone. "We'll just catch up with him at the restaurant," chirped Lydia, and they scooted to the exit. "All three brothers were at my house last night," Ruth heard her say before they went out the door. "The two younger ones had supper with us and Malachi…" Whatever Malachi had done or not done was lost to the closing of the door.

Ruth hoped it hadn't been "and Malachi was frozen solid after following that stubborn woman home." Cringing, she equally hoped it hadn't been "and Malachi, once he got there, determined they should all stay the night," which would have been possible in the full Troyer household, but not at Ruth's, a single woman's home. Ruth sighed. Either way, it was none of her business. Especially as Malachi himself hadn't even seen fit to speak with her this morning.

She didn't put up the sign that she was out to lunch. Having gotten up quite early this morning—worrying through the night did that to a person—she'd packed a sandwich. As she stepped back into the workroom, her breath caught when she saw Malachi exiting the back door, also presumably to go eat. He stopped when he noticed her and their eyes held for a few heartbeats.

"I'll stay if you want me to." He stepped back into the shop and pulled the door shut behind him.

Ruth drew a shaky breath as she made shooing motions. "Go ahead. I'll be fine watching the shop. I brought my lunch. Go see how Miller's Creek survived the first snow of the season."

He hesitated, but nodded and left.

Ruth returned to the store, and through the large front windows watched him walk down the street toward the restaurant. She saw Lydia and her friend turn, smiles on their pretty faces, and wait for Malachi to join them in front of the café. Malachi opened the door for the women and the trio walked in together. Surprised at the hollowness that settled in her stomach at the sight—an emptiness not of hunger, but of an unexpected longing to join them—Ruth shook her head. She'd never longed for anything but taking effective care of the business before.

Her steps were slow when she entered the workroom and crossed to where her cape hung. Pulling a parcel out of one of its pockets, she eyed the ham sandwich ruefully. She unwrapped it and took a disinterested bite. She suspected it would have tasted a lot better last night, sitting on a cold buggy bench under a quilt in a snowstorm. With a certain somebody beside her.

The animated chatter of the younger people drifted over Malachi at lunch. He limited his contributions to a few nods here and there, although Jacob's sister, seated next to him, tried numerous times to bring him into the conversation. He just wanted to finish eating and get back to work. When he'd seen Ruth enter the workroom before he'd left, he'd been surprised by the hope that had risen that she'd ask him to stay. Instead he'd been shooed away like a fly at a picnic.

The woman was confusing. While his eyes had been peeled on the road last night, he'd thought about her— her warm brick at his feet and her quilt on his lap, even her sandwich in his stomach—throughout the journey to the Troyers'.

Samuel and Gideon hadn't said anything, but he could tell they'd been worried about his late arrival and were glad to see him. The Troyers had offered the Schrocks a place to sleep for the night, but as he'd come that far and their new farmstead was only a mile away, his brothers had quickly preceded him out the door and into the buggy. There had been no conversation that last mile. They'd anxiously watched for their lane in the blowing snow, trying to keep their teeth from chattering. His brothers didn't ask where the quilt had come from; they'd just squeezed into the front bench under it and pressed their feet close to the diminishing heat of the brick.

The tired gelding had earned the good rubbing and extra measure of grain provided him when they finally got into the big barn. Kip had definitely proven himself to be a keeper.

His brothers had been much more loquacious on the way in to work today. Enjoying the crisp clearness of the early morning and the snow-covered but travelable surroundings, Malachi had listened with half an ear as they discussed the rigs they wanted to buy. They'd sold their previous ones in Ohio.

"Kip is a good horse for you, Malachi, but I want something fast. And flashy. Jacob's brother knows someone who buys horses that don't make it on the track in Milwaukee, if you tell him what you're looking for," Samuel had enthused.

"Jacob said that Reuben Hershberger is the best place around for buggies. He usually has several used courting buggies on hand." Gideon was newer to the world of courting buggies but catching on fast.

Taking in the intricate drifts from last night's blowing snow in the passing ditches, Malachi had smiled as he listened. His brothers had been apprentices since they left school after eighth grade and had labored diligently since then. They had their own money. They would buy their own rigs, regardless of any comment he might make, although they might take any advice he offered into consideration. They also knew they would be working to buy hay this winter and putting up hay this summer to feed the new horses.

He hadn't been surprised when the conversation turned from courting buggies to potential girls to be courted.

"Accommodating of you to be so late last night, Malachi. It gave us a chance to get to know Jacob's family," Samuel had commented mildly.

"You mean it gave you a chance to talk with his sisters," Gideon had corrected. "Where were you anyway, Malachi? You were much later than we figured."

"I had something I needed to do." For some reason, Malachi didn't feel like sharing that he'd followed Ruth home to ensure her safety.

"Well, they are part of his family. A rather pretty part, I might add." Samuel had always been the most outgoing of the three. He would never hesitate to expand on an opportunity to talk with a pretty girl.

"You would." Gideon had always been comfortable being in Samuel's shadow. A comfort level that might change now that he was getting a little older and women were coming into the picture.

"Convenient there's three of them, although Lydia's the prettiest."

Malachi felt the sidelong glance Samuel had sent in his direction but he hadn't responded to his younger brother's teasing observation. He'd been more intent on getting safely home than noticing any women hovering around when he'd stepped briefly into the Troyer kitchen last night to collect his brothers. Any impression he'd had was that they were all too young for him. And he'd learned from previous experience that although pretty was pleasant to look upon across a kitchen table, it certainly wasn't the only, or even the most, important trait when looking for a wife. At least for him. Samuel would hopefully discover that for himself over time.

On seeing he wasn't going to get any response from his taciturn brother, Samuel had turned his attention to Gideon. "*Ach*, well, what we don't meet in the next week or so, we'll meet after church, Sunday after next.

I'll have a buggy by then. I'll find a pretty girl to take home after singing."

"*Ja.* Only single girl we'll probably see till then is Ruth at work."

They had Malachi's full attention now. Kip flicked back his ears at the slight change in tension on the reins.

"*Ach*, she's too old anyway," Samuel said, dismissing their female coworker.

Malachi frowned. She wasn't that old. She was younger than his twenty-four years.

"Jacob said she'll probably go walking out with someone now that her father is gone. He said she ran the business as well as taking care of her father and the farmstead when he was sick. She said she didn't have much time for courting then. He figured that'd probably be changing now that the business has been sold."

Ruth had run the business while her father was sick? Malachi hadn't considered the possibility, but it made sense. Someone had to, and from what he'd heard, her father hadn't been in any condition to do so for some time. It would explain all the "ask Ruth" responses to any queries. It also made her attitude the first day he'd met her a little more understandable. He winced at the understatement. A lot more understandable. It was a good business. He wouldn't have wanted to sell it just because he was a daughter instead of a son.

Different districts had different rules regarding what was and wasn't allowed in the *Ordnung*. Apparently, ownership of that type of business by a single woman was verboten for the Miller's Creek Amish community.

On the heels of that thought, another thread from the conversation seeped in. Was Jacob Troyer interested in walking out with Ruth? There was a surprising twist in

Malachi's stomach at the idea. He'd never had two employees who worked for him courting before. And if they got married, she'd have to leave. If they got married… Malachi didn't pursue the thought.

He didn't know yet what he was going to do about Ruth in the business. As far as operations went, particularly in light of what he'd just heard, she was an asset. The bookkeeping—far from Malachi's favorite part of the operation—was exceptional, and the recently added business, lucrative. Her coworkers' attitudes toward her were respectful, as well.

But women could be a distraction, whether they wanted to be or not. Leah had been. It'd been the primary reason that he'd left Ohio. And a business that used tools that could take off a man's finger or worse was not a place for distractions. He'd have to pay close attention. If there were any indications Ruth was going to be a distraction for the single men, now that she might be open to courting, she'd have to go.

Malachi suddenly became aware of the distant clatter of silverware and dishes around him in the restaurant, but an expectant silence at their own table. He looked over to see Lydia's gaze directed at him and realized he'd been asked a question by the young woman.

"I'm sorry, I didn't catch that."

Yes, a woman could be a distraction. But the girl beside him, avidly trying to get his attention, wasn't nearly as distracting as the thought that his female employee might be open to courting.

Chapter Seven

Winter descended upon Wisconsin. The next few weeks dropped a few more inches of snow on the ground, albeit more gently than before. Ruth made sure she and the puppy were up early, and she was urging a cranky Bess down the road with enough time to be one of the first ones to work. But she never arrived earlier than Malachi.

Ruth didn't know when he'd become just Malachi, and not the boss, or the new owner, but he had. What he hadn't done was pay her much attention, although Ruth would look up occasionally from where she'd be working and find his thoughtful gaze on her. Upon meeting her eyes, he'd usually nod and go about his business, but he never attempted to approach her.

Her father had set up the workshop so a craftsman would normally work a piece of furniture through all aspects of production. That way, they learned every necessary skill of furniture making. Also, if one worker was out for any reason, the work didn't pile up at his station waiting for his return. Granted, some workers were better at certain tasks than others. They'd assist those less skilled, particularly on intricate pieces, when needed.

Ruth was relieved that Malachi hadn't changed the process. At least not yet. She thought she might lose some of the joy of woodworking if the operation became more of an assembly-line setup.

Ruth was also glad to discover the Schrock brothers were efficient and talented craftsmen. Malachi was particularly so. One of the many times she'd brought her lunch and stayed in the workroom, she'd strolled over to the project he'd been working on. It was a sideboard, which, instead of being part of a dining room set, was a stand-alone piece. She understood why as she examined the alluring design. Complicated yet sturdy, it personified its maker. Ruth had run her hand over the top, marveling at the smooth, glass-like finish. She knelt by the piece, examining the joints and details the average observer wouldn't notice. *Ja*, he was good. Perhaps not quite as good as her father, but very talented.

She wasn't surprised. From what she'd gotten to know of him, doing quiet, steady, yet beautiful work was consistent with his personality. Ruth realized he'd earned her respect, something she knew she was often miserly about granting. She still wished she hadn't had to relinquish the business, but for the first time, she acknowledged that it was pleasant not to have all the duties and concerns affiliated with owning and running a business on her shoulders.

Ruth could show up, do her work and go home. Granted, she was going home to an empty house with only a dog for company, but that could expand to visiting friends and neighbors as the weather got warmer and the daylight extended. But she'd probably be gone by then, Ruth reminded herself. Somewhere far away from the Amish community of Miller's Creek.

Instead of the peaceful sound of birds through the windows as they settled for the night, or the relaxing croaking of the bullfrogs in the nearby pond as she knit in the evenings, she might have a television. A radio would replace the charming occasional call and response of a barred owl, with their distinctive *who cooks for you*, as she worked a puzzle.

Because she wouldn't be on a farm. She'd be in a town or a city and hear none of those soothing sounds. It was what she'd always wanted, wasn't it? Taking a deep breath, she pushed to her feet. After one lingering finger stroked across the surface of the sideboard, she wandered back to her station and went to work.

Two days later, Ruth looked over to the door from her seat on the backless bench next to Hannah when the men started filing into the house, which the hosting Zook family had readied for church today. First the ministers and the older men walked in, then the younger married men, followed at last by the unmarried men and boys. There was silence where she sat among the single women, but she could feel the tense alertness as Malachi and his brothers shuffled by. Ruth pressed her lips together to keep from snorting. It was like a livestock sale, with potential buyers critically examining the new options that circled the arena. Well, there was no shopper more savvy for a bargain than an Amish woman.

Eyeing them critically herself, Ruth had to admit the Schrock brothers were a good-looking bunch. No wonder they were causing a discernible stir among the unmarried women. Ruth speculated on how long they'd be able to stay single. Gideon, the youngest, had a few years yet to grow into himself, although he seemed a

pleasant and hardworking young man from her limited
interactions with him at the shop. She shook her head at
Samuel, who'd had the audacity to wink in the direction
of the young ladies. Ruth didn't envy the girl who'd try
her hand at putting a yoke on that charmer.

And then there was Malachi. She watched as he took
a seat, nodding to a few men he might not have met
out in the barn where the menfolk gathered before the
church service. Unlike Samuel, not once did his eyes
stray toward the women. Ruth's mouth tipped slightly up
at the corners. There was a lot to admire there. His vivid
blue eyes, shared by his brothers, were approachable and
steady. His shoulders under the black collarless jacket
were broad and dependable. His hands, resting casually
on his lap, were strong and capable. With only a limited
number of families in the district, many with several
daughters, any new unmarried men were regarded with
a great deal of interest. Understandably, the unmarried
ladies of Miller's Creek would pounce on him like dogs
on a bone.

In fact, if she were looking for an Amish man, Ruth
admitted to herself as she studied him further, she might
look in that direction herself. With a heavy sigh, she
turned toward the *vorsinger* as the song leader stepped
forward to lead the congregation in the first hymn. But
she was not looking for an Amish man. If she married,
it would most likely be someone from the *Englisch* community. She'd marry into a lifestyle where she'd have
freedom to learn more than her short years in education
provided. To do things she was currently prevented from
doing because of community constraints. To be more
than what Plain living allowed for women. She'd made a

promise to her father. Ruth swallowed against the lump in her throat as she tried to keep her face blank.

But that didn't mean she didn't enjoy Amish church Sundays.

It was something Ruth strove to remind herself of two hours later. The second preacher was giving his sermon. Ruth knew the man hadn't wanted the role as minister. He was a well-respected, hardworking dairyman who'd been nominated along with other men from the district. During the selection process, he'd picked the hymnbook with the scripture note hidden inside. The whole district had shared in his dismay. Because the man was obviously more suited to milking his cows on Sunday than leading the church service. And it'd probably be more interesting watching him do so than listening to him struggle through a sermon.

Ruth's wandering eyes fastened on movement on the benches where the unmarried men sat. Her coworker Benjamin's *bruder* was nodding off. She watched him sway ever further on the backless bench across from her. Her eyes widened as he teetered forward. Benjamin's countenance was expressionless, but his eyes danced with laughter as he shot out an arm to stop his eighteen-year-old brother from planting his face between the shoulder blades of the man seated in front of him.

Only the clasp of her hand over her mouth kept Ruth from laughing out loud. Her eyes, wide with merriment, briefly met Malachi's, where he sat straight backed, farther down the row. His well-shaped lips twitched before he returned his attention to the uncomfortable speaker.

A few hours later, Ruth shared the incident with Hannah as they poured coffee for the men when they gathered to eat. Hannah hadn't seen it, as she'd adhered to the church custom of not making eye contact with others during the service. But she joined in Ruth's laughter over the story. Later, when they sat down to eat after the men had finished, they speculated on who would be successful in winning over the Schrock brothers, a pursuit obviously being planned and executed by the young single women gathered in clusters around the room.

A few were already going out the door. Hannah and Ruth watched them from the kitchen window as the girls hurried across the buggy-track-rutted snow in the farmyard toward the barn, where the men had gathered to visit.

"They're going to freeze without their capes." Hannah's eyes were concerned under her furrowed brow.

"Oh, Hannah," Ruth scoffed. "They'd look like a flock of crows with their capes on and that's not how they want the single men to see them today. The barn is full of hay and men to flirt with. They'll stay warm enough."

"You're so cynical." Hannah's soft tone was more wry than chiding.

"I've seen them come into the shop often enough. And I've watched the maneuverings for other single men over the past few years."

"You should be joining in, not watching." It was a gentle admonishment.

"You know my thoughts on that."

"I was hoping you'd change your mind, with the business now sold."

"I think I'm even more set on leaving, now that the business is no longer mine." Her stomach twisted slightly at the memory of her promise to her *daed* to pursue her choice for her life.

"Has he been difficult to work for?"

Ruth didn't have to ask whom Hannah meant by *he*. "Actually, no. He's been pretty fair." Memories of the trip home in the snowstorm made her add, "And kind." More than kind, actually. He was funny, with a dry sense of humor. Hannah didn't need to know all these opinions, though. It might give her the idea that Ruth was interested in her new boss.

Her mouth went dry. She was a coward for not telling her best friend yet that she was leaving the community.

With relief on her part, they returned their attention to the window. The focus of their discussion was leaning against the fence of the dairy lot, talking with Isaiah Zook, the owner of the farm. Probably about cows. She'd heard Malachi mention to the men at work that he was interested in picking up a few head of dairy cows.

What he didn't seem interested in were the single women traipsing past him on their way to the barn. Or reappearing to pet the standardbreds in the lot nearby. Ruth scowled. Like they'd never seen a horse before. But no matter how much the young women flapped about the yard, Malachi didn't pay them any attention, remaining more absorbed in the cows and his discussion.

"Do you think he has a girl back in Ohio?"

Ruth blinked. It was possible. Some Amish young men didn't marry right away because they didn't have money or a job that could support a wife and family. That obviously wasn't the case with Malachi. He had the means, what with him buying the furniture shop.

Miller's Creek's single women were doing their best to attract his attention and it didn't seem to be working. Amish courtships were generally kept secret until the weddings were announced in church. Her eyes narrowed. Perhaps he'd come early to the community and his future bride was going to join him later, with a wedding soon to follow. She attributed the sudden odd feeling in her stomach to indulging in too many pickled beets at Sunday dinner.

"I don't know. Could be. But even if that isn't the case, Samuel seems interested enough for the both of them."

Hannah laughed in agreement as they watched Samuel, a girl on each arm, enter the barn.

A few other men, beardless and bearded, wandered over to join Malachi and the farm owner at the fence. Ruth saw Lydia Troyer, one of the capeless girls, approach the small knot of men. A few moments later Jacob's sister was at Malachi's elbow, his head bent in her direction. Ruth didn't know what was being said in the conversation, but she wouldn't be surprised if it didn't include a hint for a ride home later.

The surprisingly melancholy thought of Malachi taking Lydia home in his buggy prompted Ruth to remember her own need to head toward hers. She'd been tempted to let Rascal stay in the house alone while she was gone, but the idea was abruptly scrapped when she'd noticed a few tiny teeth marks on the bottom of one of her father's furniture pieces. Although she still felt guilty every time she left Rascal in the chicken coop with its accompanying yard, he seemed happy enough, and her furniture was safe for the moment. But she didn't like to leave him longer than was necessary. Especially when she felt like she abandoned him every day during the week.

"I need to harness Bess and get home." She'd already stayed much later than she'd intended. She'd forgotten how much she'd enjoyed the social aspect of church now that, as the business had fully changed hands, she wasn't the subject of as much discussion among her neighbors.

Or perhaps she still was. While pouring coffee at one of the long tables during the meal, she did hear some gossip linking her and Malachi's names, with no mention of furniture. The coffeepot had wobbled a little in her hand at the surprising thought of their names together. She'd steadied it with the reminder that having an Amish husband meant being an Amish wife. And that was no life for her.

As Ruth gathered her cape and bonnet and prepared to leave, Hannah reminded her, "Don't forget you agreed to come over to my *haus* for Thanksgiving."

Ruth promised that she wouldn't as she hugged her friend goodbye. In fact, she was thrilled with the invitation. It wasn't the first time the Lapp family had invited the Fishers to join them for a meal. But this was the first holiday after her father had passed. Ruth had dreaded the prospect of spending it alone.

Feeling warmer from the genuine farewells she'd received as she headed out the door than from the black cape that draped her shoulders, Ruth strode over the rutted farmyard to the barn. Blinking a bit in the barn's dim light after the brighter light of the fading winter afternoon sun, Ruth nodded to the male acquaintances gathered there. She made out Bess among the numerous bay horses and headed in the mare's direction.

With a smile, she shook off the offers from a few men to help her harness the mare. Ruth noted they'd all been eligible, unmarried men. She attended to the bad-tempered Bess. Farther down the row of horses, she could see Malachi doing the same thing with Kip.

Apparently Samuel had gotten his own horse, as he'd certainly be staying for the Sunday night singing. An activity that was actually more about ogling the opposite sex and allowing the young people to flirt than singing. But Malachi wasn't staying. Ruth quashed the errant, happy thought as she slapped Bess's hip when the mare cocked her rear foot menacingly. She finished harnessing the cranky bay, glancing up as Malachi led Kip out to where all the buggies were parked. Perhaps he did have a girl in Ohio. He didn't seem interested in exploring who was of marriageable age in Wisconsin.

As she exited the barn herself, she noted with glee that he wasn't taking Lydia home, either. Although the girl's eyes lingered on Malachi as he passed by her, she didn't leave the group of young people she was with to follow him out.

The snow in the unused pasture where the buggies were located was deeper than the much-traveled farmyard. Leading Bess across it, Ruth felt her shoes get wetter with every step. By the time she reached her buggy, her black stockings were soaked up to her ankles. Ruth grimaced. Even with the blanket she always carried in the winter, her feet were going to be freezing by the time she got home.

To keep from dwelling on her increasingly chilly feet as she maneuvered Bess between the shafts of the buggy, Ruth entertained herself with thoughts of summer footwear. She, like many Amish women and children, went barefoot as soon as possible once spring arrived. She couldn't do that in the furniture workroom because of potential hazards there, but she spent most of the season away from the shop barefoot. Ruth wiggled her toes in her wet socks as she imagined freshly cut, lush grass under her bare feet, or toes curling in the sun-warmed, loamy earth of her garden. A small smile worked its way to her face at the pleasant distraction when a voice from over the top of Bess's back jerked her to the chilly present.

"What are you smiling about?" Malachi regarded her quizzically as he attached the harness breeching to the shaft on Bess's right side.

"I was thinking about going barefoot."

"In this?" His eyebrow dubiously lifted as he took in the snowy landscape and the churned-up slush under their feet.

Her mouth twitched further at his expression. "Would it make you think I'm stranger than you already assume?"

"I don't think you're strange." He grinned as he ran the reins into the buggy through the opening in the windshield. "For all I know, you could be normal for Wisconsin people. Which frightens me." He ducked his head just in time to avoid the hastily made snowball, which splattered against his black hat and not his face.

Ruth watched warily as she hurriedly finished attaching the harness on her side, but he didn't retaliate. After banging his hat against his leg to knock off most of the snow, he replaced it and leaned against his side of Bess. The mare craned her head around to look at him and then shifted in Ruth's direction. Bringing Malachi's lopsided grin a step closer.

"You're not staying for the singing?"

"Does it look like I am?" Ruth forgot about cold feet as she met his amused blue eyes.

"Why not?"

"For one thing, I'm too old. For another, I know what I want and it's not in there." She nodded her head in direction of the barn where the single men were currently gathered.

His eyebrow rose again, touching the bottom of his blond bangs under the hat. "You don't look that old."

"I'm twenty-two," she announced pertly, knowing that her small stature made her appear younger.

"I stand corrected," he said, reaching up to flick a few crystals of slush from the shoulder of his black coat. "You don't *act* that old."

He had her there. "You provoked me."

"You provoke easily," he countered.

Ruth did. And she knew it. But she didn't have time to dwell on the fact or respond before he repeated a question.

"Why not?"

"Why not what?"

"Why are you not interested in anything in there?" He, too, nodded toward the barn.

Ruth didn't know if it was the cold or embarrassment that made her cheeks heat up. "Because they're Amish."

Both eyebrows rose into the blond fringe this time. "So are you."

"Maybe not forever." Bess stomped her hind leg and swished her tail, the long black strands barely missing Malachi. He leaned away from the mare and patted her on the hip as Ruth scrambled up into her buggy. She didn't remember to toss the available quilt over her lap as she guided Bess away from the other buggies and down the lane. She was plenty warm for other reasons. A glance in the rearview mirror revealed that Malachi stood there watching her departure for a moment before he strode over to the patiently waiting Kip and climbed into his own buggy.

Ruth smiled. Finally recalling her cold feet, she snagged the blanket and pulled it across her lap. She toed her shoes off and reached down to peel off her wet stockings before curling her feet up on the seat under the blankct. Ruth cast another look in the rearview to see Malachi turn out of the lane.

She sighed. There had to be a girl in Ohio. It was unusual that someone as attractive as Malachi was still single. A second sigh followed. As she had said, she wasn't looking for an Amish husband. And even if she was, she certainly wasn't going to fall for a man who already had a sweetheart.

Chapter Eight

$\sim$

Malachi was ready to get back to work by the time the Monday after Thanksgiving arrived. He'd been surprised at how much he'd missed his family in Ohio on the holiday. Adjusting to Wisconsin was easier and happier than he'd anticipated, but a letter from home made him nostalgic of past holidays there.

Thankfully *Mamm* hadn't mentioned Leah in her letter. It was more than he could say for his aunt Miriam, where the Schrock men had spent Thanksgiving. The Moses Lapps—no relation to Hannah's family—had been good friends of the Solomon Kings, so it wasn't surprising that his aunt mentioned Solomon's daughter a few times. Malachi just wished Aunt Miriam wouldn't look at him so meaningfully every time she said Leah's name.

But he'd been glad to be at his aunt's home rather than accept the other invitation they'd received from Jacob Troyer's family. Samuel had lobbied for that option until Malachi had given his brother a look and advised in no uncertain terms that they were spending Thanksgiving with family. Samuel had wanted to go for the same reason Malachi hadn't: the Troyer daughters. Particularly Lydia. There'd been a lot of longing in that one's gaze, as well. And Malachi knew exactly what the red-haired girl intended.

Amish communities were relatively closed, with a limited number of families. Based on church last week, Malachi estimated this community to be around twenty families. That provided some but not numerous options when looking for a spouse. As a man with a well-established job, sometimes Malachi felt like he was hunted prey in a game preserve. He planned to marry someday, but he wanted it to be his choice. Not because he felt driven to it like a steer channeled through the barn until loaded for market.

So he was glad to be back at work. Where there was only one irksome woman to deal with. Although Samuel was finding her more irksome than Malachi this morning. Malachi observed the two preparing an eight-drawer dresser for shipment. Samuel was wrapping the piece in plastic to secure the drawers in place when Ruth stepped back to scrutinize the front of the dresser.

"The stain on those three drawers is a deeper red than the other ones." She pointed a slender finger at the ones in question. "I know we had another order for this set completed about the same time. Did we put three of the wrong drawers in this dresser?"

Samuel stopped wrapping plastic and looked at her, his normally charming smile absent from his face.

Ruth continued, her hands perched on her hips, "What does the other dresser look like? We haven't shipped it already, have we?"

Malachi watched as her diminutive figure strode to where Samuel indicated with a sullen tilt of his blond head. She critically examined the fortunately unwrapped dresser. "Yes. There they are. We need to pull those three and put them in the right dresser. How did that happen? We can't let this type of thing get out to our customers. What would they think of our commitment to quality workmanship?"

Watching his *bruder* assist her in switching out the drawers, Malachi covered his mouth to hide his smile. He couldn't disagree with her. Maybe he should think about letting his *bruder* go and keeping Ruth. He didn't know how the mix-up had happened, but the badger had ensured by her snarls and hisses that this would never happen again.

For sure and certain, it was not his style of management, but just as effective.

Malachi sighed as he looked at the numbers again and punched them into the manual adding machine one more time before documenting them in the ledger. He could do accounting, but it was his least favorite part of the business.

Tax work was done by an *Englisch* accountant, but there was still much that needed to be done at the shop. Ruth had done the majority of it the first few days after his arrival. Needing to be self-sufficient in that part of the operation, he'd taken it over. Sometimes you understood things better when you did it. Whether you did it well, that was another story.

The business was busy. He was fully cognizant of that. They were also making money—sometimes those things weren't synonymous—Malachi knew that, as well. Their success was due to the petite figure currently ringing up a sale to an *Englisch* couple at the counter. Her fingers were nimble on the counter's adding machine. Her smile and bright chatter charmed the customers.

He glanced at other ledger books under his elbow. She'd been nimble with the business, as well. Malachi knew Ruth had done most of the business management of Fisher Furniture, even before her father became ill. She'd done a good job. Malachi didn't know the exact numbers from Solomon King's operation in Ohio, but he knew enough to figure this business was more profitable. Because of the five-foot-nothing woman cheerfully escorting the *Englisch* couple to the door as she toted two child-size rocking chairs that'd just been purchased.

Malachi would've frowned at the *Englisch* husband for allowing Ruth to carry the chairs if the man's arms hadn't been full of two squirming *kinder* who'd presumably be using the chairs when they reached home. Ruth disappeared out the store door. She returned a few moments later, stomping the snow from her feet that she must've encountered when helping load the chairs in their car.

He watched her meander through the furniture in the shop, making slight adjustments to a piece here, sliding a chair farther under a dining table there. Malachi blinked when she stopped abruptly in front of a sideboard, wondering at her action until he realized that she would know every stick of furniture in the place and this was one he'd just put out that morning after he'd arrived. One he'd been working on when he found the time between bookwork and people management. She wouldn't have recognized it.

The hair on his forearm prickled as she reached out a hand to sweep it gently over the surface of the oak. Malachi swallowed hard at the action, almost feeling the sensation of her dainty fingers. Quickly looking away, he punched some numbers into the adding machine and scowled when he saw the results. He punched them in again before throwing down his pencil. When the same column of numbers came up two hundred dollars apart on separate calculations, he knew he was distracted. And being that distracted was no way to run a business.

The door to the workroom whisked open and drew the attention of them both. Samuel popped his head in.

"Hey, Ruth. You want to go to lunch with us?"

Ruth eyed him suspiciously. "Why?" she asked. Malachi didn't know if they'd interacted since the red-drawer incident.

Samuel's charming smile was in play. "It's lunchtime. And even though you're a tyrant, I'm assuming you still eat. Tyrants do eat, don't they? They'd have to keep up their strength, right?"

Sometimes Malachi wasn't sure if he liked his brother. This was one of those times. When Samuel looked at Ruth with a crooked grin and Ruth responded with a lopsided one of her own, Malachi decided he might be interested in some lunch, as well. He pushed his chair back from the desk and the onerous accounting.

"I've a feeling that in order to handle you, Samuel Schrock, a person, tyrant or not, would need all the strength they could get."

"Well, come on, then." Samuel pushed the door open wider.

"I believe I'll join you." Malachi strode to the door of the office, just in case they forgot he was there.

Ruth's eyes flew in his direction and widened slightly. A moment later, she asked, "Does someone need to stay and watch the store?"

Two sets of eyes looked expectantly at Malachi. Malachi frowned. He was the boss. And he was going along, whether they liked it or not. He didn't fully trust Samuel not to put something in Ruth's food, or to try to charm her and put something in her head. Either way, they weren't going without him. "Put the closed sign up with a note saying we'll be back after lunch."

Ruth nodded and headed to the counter to grab the sign stating they were temporarily out that they used occasionally. Samuel looked in Malachi's direction and winked before disappearing back into the workshop. After some shuffling, Ruth found the note and scurried over to the door to put it up.

"You want to go out this way?" She nodded at the door beside her.

"Don't you want your cape?"

"The café's not that far. As long as you don't plod along, I won't get too cold."

Malachi fought against the urge to smile. He didn't want any comparisons to his brother's charismatic grin. Yes, plodding was his style, a pace with which Ruth wasn't acquainted. Just to prove he had other speeds as well, Malachi hastened to the door, opened it and gestured for her to precede him.

Although scraped free of snow, splotches of the sidewalk glistened in the noon sun. Ruth slipped on her first step beyond the door and shot out an arm to catch herself. Malachi quickly grasped under her elbow and steadied her. She cast a grateful look in his direction but didn't shake off the hand. It remained during their short walk down the street to the restaurant. Upon reaching the door to the café, she lifted her arm slightly. Not much, but just enough that Malachi let his hand drop to his side. He immediately missed the feel of crisp cotton and warm elbow under his fingertips.

A flood of sounds and smells engulfed them when Malachi opened the door to the café. After reheated casseroles and some not-so-successful experiences with his brothers' cooking, Malachi couldn't keep from enjoying the smell of roasted meat and baked goods.

Amish and *Englisch* alike filled the Dew Drop Inn, the din of their conversations a constant background noise. While the establishment had a few rooms to rent, the majority of their business came from its position as the only restaurant in Miller's Creek. The employees were primarily Amish but, owned by an *Englisch* couple, the café was open more hours than those of Amish businesses. The Dew Drop served Plain, family-style meals for the Amish and *Englisch* work crews that frequented the place. *Englisch* tourists seemed to think *family-style* and *Amish* were synonymous when it came to restaurants, but the eatery served burgers and fries, as well. Malachi's stomach growled as he eyed an overflowing platter of food.

Spying his brothers in the crowd, he motioned Ruth in that direction. Two seats remained at the table that included Samuel, Gideon, Jacob and Benjamin. Samuel looked up at their approach and indicated to Malachi to take the seat with its back to the wall, knowing that was where his older brother normally liked to sit. Malachi returned his nod. As he passed the other vacant chair, he noticed a small pile of melting snow on the seat. Shooting a disgusted look at his smirking brother, Malachi swiped it off the seat. Ruth paused beside the chair. Her eyes moved from the drops of water remaining on it to Samuel, seated across the table.

"Are we even?" she inquired mildly as she pulled napkins from the nearby dispenser and wiped up the remaining moisture before sitting down.

"*Ja.* But I want it known that I didn't mix up the dressers."

Ruth kept a steady gaze on him. "I understand, but regardless of who did it, we can't let something like that get out to the customer. It would've affected two different ones, and that's not something I'll allow out to represent Fisher—" she caught herself "—I mean *Schrock* Furniture." She darted a hasty glance at Malachi.

"I won't allow it, either." Malachi's tone was mild but decisive.

It was quiet at the table while Rebecca, the young Amish waitress, poured their water. She slipped away quietly when she finished without taking their orders.

"*Ach,* I think I may have done it." The admission came from a red-faced Jacob. "I worked on it the day of the storm and was thinking more about the weather than the work. It won't happen again, I promise." His glance at Malachi was earnest and concerned.

Malachi thought of the drive home in the snow that day and the interlude at Ruth's house. He nodded at the beardless man and Jacob relaxed. "*Ja,* that was an interesting day for many of us."

A subtly hovering Rebecca reappeared at the table to take their orders. Malachi wasn't surprised when she positioned herself at Samuel's elbow. They placed their orders one by one, and she whisked away, but not before sending a smile in his brother's direction. A smile that Samuel returned. Yes, his *bruder* was a flirt, but Malachi didn't mind, as long as he limited it to women who didn't work in the business.

* * *

"You are a marvel." Ruth shook her head after watching the exchange between Samuel and the waitress. "Have you met all the women of Miller's Creek yet?"

"Only the single ones," Samuel quipped. "Have I missed any, Benjamin?"

"If you have, I'm not going to tell you." Benjamin grinned. "I'm hoping you'll leave some for me."

"And me!" Gideon and Jacob both interjected simultaneously. Laughter rippled around the table.

"Do you need all of them?" Ruth furrowed her brow at Samuel when it died down.

"Not all. Just one…or two at a time. I like women. Why not shop when there's a marketful?"

"I like knitting, but I can only work on one project at a time without confusing the instructions. And if I bought all the yarn that intrigued me, my house would be overrun."

"I didn't say I was buying, only shopping." Samuel winked.

"If there's an instruction booklet that comes with women, I hope someone lets me know where to find one." Gideon's smile was a hesitant replica of Samuel's charming one. Ruth rolled her eyes. Samuel's next question had her blinking in confusion.

"How do you like cows?"

Ruth quipped, "Grilled medium well?"

"Don't we all," Samuel said, grinning his magical grin. "But my *bruder* here thinks they ought to remain on the hoof. And he must think we don't have enough to do already. He's bought a couple of dairy cows and a steer. We're going to bring them home this Saturday. You want to join us in the cattle drive?"

Ruth blamed her sudden light-headedness on hunger and the delicious smell wafting from the food just set on the table rather than the thought of being included in a family adventure. Particularly this family. Her eyes darted to a stoic-faced Malachi.

She liked livestock. Before the shop got so busy, she and her father had kept a few cattle on their farm. Ruth had fond memories of *Daed* teaching her to milk Bossie, the black-and-white Holstein they'd had. In fact, Ruth was beginning to miss having animals around now that she had a little more time. *Get used to it. You won't be able to keep any in a backyard in town. Better enjoy it while you can.* Casting another glance at Malachi, Ruth refused to identify what "it" might be.

"*Ja.* I'll join you." Suddenly, Ruth, who'd begun to dread nonchurch weekends, couldn't wait until Saturday. She enjoyed the banter of her coworkers during the rest of the meal. The easy conversation, Samuel's teasing of Jacob and Benjamin when they declined the invitation due to farmwork commitments of their own. It was *gut* to be part of a group. She'd missed it. She'd allowed herself to drift away from the closeness of the Amish community.

As she scooped up a forkful of mashed potatoes, the thought again popped into her head. *Better enjoy it now, because you won't have this kind of fellowship once you leave the Amish community.* Ruth put down her silverware. She was finding the last bite a little hard to swallow.

Chapter Nine

After getting a humpbacked Bess to hurry down the road in order to arrive at the Schrock farm on time, Ruth attributed her cold nose to the crisp Wisconsin winter morning. But her heated cheeks were due to the casserole dish she'd handed to Malachi when he greeted her after she set the brake on the buggy.

She felt sheepish about bringing food, but Ruth figured most of the district had already delivered basketfuls to the bachelor brothers. It was just being neighborly. Malachi handed the dish off to Gideon to take to the house as he returned his attention to harnessing the Belgians waiting patiently nearby in their fuzzy winter coats. The geldings looked like enormous stuffed animals that some of the stores catering to the *Englisch* carried.

"Thanks!" Gideon's smile was as bright as the sun just topping the eastern horizon. "Food deliveries have tapered off and none of us can cook. Fortunately, it picked up a bit after Sunday."

"I'll just bet it did," Ruth muttered as he disappeared into the big white farmhouse. Remembering all the eager single women who'd eyed the Schrock brothers on Sunday, Ruth cringed that she'd joined the rush. She reminded herself the only reason she'd brought something over was because she'd told Malachi she would on the snowy night he'd followed her home. It wasn't like it was a cooking contest. So what if it was her favorite recipe? One her *daed* had often raved about after patting his stomach appreciatively. Didn't mean all men would.

Moving three head of cattle a few miles down the road from the Zook farm shouldn't take too long. Ruth secured Bess to the rail designed for that purpose and climbed aboard the back of the hay wagon, ignoring Malachi's outstretched hand offering assistance. The wagon shifted as he hopped on the end opposite from where she sat. It lurched forward when Samuel clicked the geldings into motion. Condensed breath drifted from the Belgians' nostrils and wafted over their blond manes. The wagon wheels crunched on the snow that had refrozen overnight as they rolled out of the farmyard.

Ruth's fingers tightened on the edge of the wagon as it bumped down the lane. She turned her face to the east, absorbing the magic of the rising sun on a wintry landscape. It was going to be a beautiful day. They'd had a few days where temperatures hovered slightly above freezing, always a treasure in a Wisconsin winter. This looked to be another one. It helped keep the roads clear, but the ditches and glistening white fields beyond would be soggy beneath the surface.

The beauty of the morning didn't have anything to do with the solid presence of the man whose feet dangled from the back of the wagon a few feet from hers. Or so Ruth told herself. Her hearing was tuned to that direction, but Malachi remained quiet.

Ruth forced her attention to the steadily diminishing view of the farmstead. Given the short time they'd been there and as busy as they'd been at the shop, the Schrock brothers had made significant improvements on the place. During his declining years Atlee Yoder had been stubborn and always refused community help. The place had fallen into disrepair. Evidence of the work Malachi and his brothers had done on the house, barn and pens adjacent to the barn was obvious. Come spring, when the ground softened enough to put in posts, they'd repair the dilapidated fences along the road. It'd be a beautiful place when they finished. Ruth sucked in some of the brisk morning air. Perhaps she'd drive by in a car later this summer. Just to see what they'd accomplished.

The wagon hit a bump, almost jolting Ruth from her perch. One of her boots nearly slipped off her dangling legs. She curled her toes in the black Wellington at the last moment, halting its downward slide. The boots were a half size too large, but they'd been the only size available at the store last spring. As she didn't have many outdoor chores anymore beyond taking care of Bess, Ruth figured she could make them work. The Wellingtons made sense for the morning's adventure, as she'd be walking through snow, mud and other things associated with cattle that she didn't want to step in with her good shoes. Ruth wished, though, that she'd put on two pairs of socks this morning, both to keep the boots on and for warmth. The frostiness of the morning was seeping through the rubber and her black knee-high stockings.

Ruth twisted her body to look ahead over the bobbing ears of the geldings. The dairy farm was in sight. A few miles' walk behind some cows would warm up her feet.

The Schrock brothers were quiet on the way over,

seemingly as content as she was with their thoughts and the lovely morning. As they approached the lane, they outlined the plan for getting the cattle home. There were good fences, for the most part, on both sides of the road between the dairy farm and the Schrock place. One of the cows purchased was an older one, used to a halter. Samuel would drive the Belgians back, with that cow tied to the back of the wagon. The younger dairy cow and the steer purchased to fatten for meat should follow.

Gideon would ride with Samuel, hopping off to guard the corner on the one crossroad of the journey and the far side of the road once the wagon made the turn into the lane. She and Malachi would walk behind, keeping the entourage moving and addressing any traffic that might come upon them during the short trip. A little hay was loaded on the wagon as extra incentive for the cattle to follow. Cattle were herd animals. The younger ones should follow the cow led behind the wagon. There shouldn't be any issue.

Upon observing the new purchases in the lot, Ruth could tell the young cow wouldn't be a problem. She seemed docile and stayed close to the older Guernscy the dairy farmer was currently haltering. But the short-horn steer was another story. Ruth knew by looking at him that the roan would not be easy. Head up, spooky-eyed and snorting in the chilly morning air, he waited a few moments after the cows exited the pen before dashing after them, kicking up frozen clods of dirty snow behind him.

Ruth fell in step a cautionary distance behind him, not too far back that she wouldn't have time to head them off if necessary but not too close that the already-nervous steer would bolt. The shorthorn would watch warily a few moments as she and Malachi slowly advanced on him. Then he'd trot, head and tail high, to keep up with the steadily moving cows before stopping to watch and snort again. Half a mile down the road, Ruth was already tired of his antics.

She began to think of him in terms of how she'd like to see him cooked.

"Come on, Rib Eye. Just settle in there behind the girls," she urged soothingly when the steer snorted, spun and raced after the placidly plodding cows again.

"Easy there, Hamburger," she murmured as the short-horn spooked when he saw Gideon standing a few yards down the opposing road when they turned the corner.

"We're almost there, Chuck Roast," she encouraged when he nosed the side of the road like he was thinking of checking out the ditch.

Malachi was quiet on his side of the road, content to let her prompt the steer along. Ruth was very aware of his solid presence and the slight smile touching his face.

While the Wellingtons were useful for doing chores in sloppy conditions, they weren't so comfortable walking a few miles on a hard surface. Still, Ruth supposed she could handle walking the few miles between the farms if pioneer women could walk the hundreds of miles on the Oregon Trail, as she'd learned in school.

Ruth had liked school. She'd missed it for a while but had soon started working full-time for her father in the furniture shop. That was when the business really took off. With her father's encouragement and the previous bishop's approval, Ruth had taken some accounting correspondence courses. She'd set up their accounting system. Her fingers had itched to get on a computer, as some of their customers and other *Englisch* businesses had. Ruth's eyes flicked over to the man who walked steadily on the far side of the road. When she left the Amish community, a computer course was going to be the first class she took.

A startled holler from Malachi reminded Ruth she needed to focus on the present. Perhaps the spooky short-horn understood her nicknames and figured out what his destiny would be after a few months of fattening up. Or maybe the lure of the open field was too tempting. For whatever reason, Round Steak saw the possibility of freedom and made a dash for it. Just before the final turn into the lane, the roan-colored steer swished his tail, jumped into the ditch and was through a break in Atlee Yoder's dilapidated fence before Ruth could take the first jarring step down the steep decline.

She scrambled up the far side of the ditch, using tall grass that peeped above the snow to pull herself through. Ruth clambered over the downed fence, muttering as she went.

Dashing out into the snow-covered field, Ruth ran at an angle to the steer to keep him from escaping into the woods that fringed the back part of the property. Gideon slipped over the fence behind the barn and hustled across the field to cut off the steer from that direction. The shorthorn stopped, snorting, head and tail up, before bolting to cut between them.

"Oh, you, Stew Meat," Ruth chuffed as she struggled to increase her speed across the rough field. Her boots were breaking through the recently frozen crust and getting mired in the muddier ground underneath.

"Hey!" she shouted, trying to distract the steer and send him back to the barnyard, where the docile cows waited. It wasn't working. Using one hand to hitch up her skirt, Ruth ran as fast as she could across the rough, snowy ground. Hitting another muddy patch, she stumbled when the boots didn't move as fast as her legs did. The shock of her stocking feet breaking through crusty snow had her shrieking in the next few steps but didn't stop her dash to head off the steer.

Ruth looked back to see her black Wellingtons sticking out of the field like short posts. The mud had sucked the loose boots right off her moving legs. Although her feet were colder, she was faster without the Wellingtons. As she ran, the field threatened to rob her of her socks, as well. Gideon increased his speed at her abbreviated scream. He and Ruth converged on the corner where the steer headed. The roan skidded to a halt. He looked at them warily before glancing back at the barnyard. Apparently thinking that he'd join the ladies after all, he turned and trotted toward where the cows waited, already in the pen, where Samuel had thankfully secured the older Guernsey.

Panting to catch her breath, Ruth scanned the field, looking for the black stumps of her boots. Now that the adventure was over, her feet, in wet and muddy stockings, were freezing. Hopping from one foot to the other as she tried to warm them, she figured she might as well hop like a rabbit back toward her boots. She cringed at the thought of cold wet feet in rubber boots on the long ride home.

She startled when a dark figure appeared beside her. Ruth's heartbeat slowed only slightly when she recognized Malachi, an unreadable expression on his face. He must have followed her, probably at a more sedate pace, across the field. Ruth couldn't imagine him scrambling up the ditch and running, coat flapping, across the field.

Ruth shrieked when Malachi swept her up into his arms and began walking across the field to the barnyard. Her heartbeat raced faster than the galloping steer as she felt his strong arms around her shoulders and under her knees. Hopefully he wouldn't feel it thumping against his chest. Hopefully he would think her breathlessness was from her race with the shorthorn and not from the sight of his beardless jaw just inches from her face. So close that she could lean just slightly forward and kiss him. If she so chose.

To keep from choosing to do so, Ruth curled her fingers into her palms until she could feel her nails cutting into the flesh. Wiggling for escape only caused the work-hardened arms to tighten.

"Put me down." Her command lost its impact when she could hardly find enough air to get the words out.

Malachi shook his head before dropping his chin to glance at her. "No."

Ruth's eyes widened. The drop of his chin put Malachi's well-shaped lips only a few inches from her own. Before she did something incredibly foolish, she turned her head toward the barnyard.

Her black bonnet had fallen during the run and hung by the bow still loosely tied under her chin. Fortunately her *kapp* was still secure, but Ruth could feel some pins coming loose. She could also feel the soft and steady thump of her head against Malachi's well-muscled shoulder with every step he took. Strange that the time it took to run to the corner of the field seemed a lot longer than the time it was taking to be carried back in Malachi's arms.

Samuel was standing by the pen gate, which, fortunately, the renegade steer had edged through. Ruth was surprised he hadn't spooked the shorthorn again as he was doubled over with laughter. Gideon, approaching from where he'd run to cut off the steer, looked like he was trying to suppress the mirth that'd taken over his *bruder.*

"Gideon, go get her boots," Malachi directed as he carried Ruth past.

As they approached the farmyard, Ruth's socks were getting icy from the combination of wet material and the winter wind that was kicking up. Otherwise, she was amazed at how warm she was in Malachi's arms. If she was getting frostbite, she wouldn't know it until she got home. And if she was, she currently didn't care.

When they finally reached the barn, Malachi shouldered open the gate from the field. "Samuel, quit your laughing and get that gate secured before you're the one chasing them all over."

Bess swung her head around as Malachi approached the buggy and set Ruth on the seat inside with her feet hanging out the door. Ruth sighed. She refused to interpret whether it was with relief or dismay that his arms were no longer around her.

"I don't suppose you brought other socks."

"I didn't think that I would need them." She could finally get words out, now that his lips weren't inches from hers. "What are you doing?"

"Looks pretty obvious to me. I'm taking off your wet socks before you catch a cold." Malachi looked up at her from under the black brim of his winter hat. His blue eyes glinted under his lashes. When had he gotten such long eyelashes?

"I need you healthy at work. We're having challenges filling orders in a timely manner as it is." Ruth got goose bumps when his warm fingers touched her knees. She had trouble hearing the rest of what he was saying. "Or were you really serious about this barefoot business you mentioned Sunday?"

"I try to limit that to the months of April through October." The chills that ran up her legs as he peeled down her muddy socks had nothing to do with the cold. "I can do that," she insisted, reaching down to push his hand away.

"So can I. And since you were kind enough to help me by driving cattle, I think I'll return the favor with the act of servitude by cleaning your feet." Ruth's heart thumped heavily as she looked down at his lopsided grin. How anyone could think that Samuel was the more charming brother, she didn't know. She exhaled a breath she wasn't aware of holding, relieved when Malachi turned his attention to his brother as Gideon dropped her black Wellingtons by the wheel of the buggy.

"Almost had to get a pair of pliers to pull them free." A smile still lit Gideon's face. "I washed them off at the hydrant."

"Thanks. Go into the house and get a towel and a pair of socks."

His younger brother looked surprised at the request. "Whose?"

"Doesn't matter. Any. If we have any clean ones," Malachi added drolly.

After dropping the soaked socks just inside the door of the buggy, he cupped her chilled feet in his warm hands.

Ruth almost slid off the leather seat. She searched for something, anything, to distract her from the enthralling sensation.

"So you can get them to bring food, but you can't get the single women to come over and do laundry yet?"

Malachi looked up from where he'd been examining her feet. "I'm not the one getting them to bring over food." He grinned. "But a clean load of laundry or two wouldn't go amiss." He returned his attention to where his thumbs rubbed slowly over the arches of her foot.

Ruth bit her tongue to keep from volunteering to march into the house barefoot to do laundry for him. She swallowed hard and quipped hoarsely, "You'll have to work on that."

"I suppose. But I'm not quite ready to let a woman have free rein in the house yet. Some are like a spoiled horse. You give them a little and they'll take advantage and go where they want to go. Makes it pretty hard to get control back."

Samuel's head popped into view through the door of the buggy. He took in the sight of her feet in his brother's hand. "She gonna live?"

"*Ja.* Even walk again. But for the time being, she's going to be wearing a pair of our socks." Malachi turned at Gideon's approach and took the well-worn towel and worn but intact socks from his brother. He flipped the socks over his shoulder and used the towel to further warm Ruth's feet.

"How long did you have to search before you found socks without holes?" Samuel clapped a hand on his younger brother's shoulder.

"It's not any of yours, Samuel. It's hard to tell with yours which end the foot goes in—there are so many holes on the other end," Gideon retorted. "I brought a pair of Malachi's."

Ruth flushed at the thought of wearing Malachi's

socks. Or maybe it was due to his hands gently tugging the dry socks up her now very warm feet and legs.

Malachi frowned when the socks slid back down her slender calves. After another attempt to secure them, he let them alone, much to her relief.

"You coming in to eat what you brought over?" Samuel nodded toward the house.

"Ah, no. I…I need to get back home. I left Rascal in the house as kind of a test. One I'm pretty sure he'll fail." It was as good an excuse as any. Ruth's normally tightly reined control was running amok, and unlike the recently herded beef, she didn't know if she'd be able to corral it before it escaped completely.

"You aren't avoiding it because there's something in there we should be concerned about, are you?"

"*Nee*, Samuel. Unlike you, I do unto others as I would have them do unto me," she retorted.

"It was only a little ice. Besides, it didn't work."

"That's because yours is only a little brain."

Samuel grinned at the comeback. "You'll do. Thanks for coming over and helping today, Ruth." He gave her a finger salute and tapped the edge of the buggy before turning to head for the house. Malachi watched his departure unsmilingly before returning his attention to Ruth.

"You always give folks tests you think they'll fail?" Malachi asked as he set her boots inside the buggy. Ruth smiled her appreciation, quickly pulled them on and swiveled on the seat to face the front. She didn't have an answer to that. Thankfully Gideon had untied Bess, which allowed her a hasty exit. She backed the mare away and headed down the lane with a parting wave.

Bess swung into a trot toward home, leaving Ruth free to ponder Malachi's question. Maybe she did give folks tests she expected them to fail. Was it a way of protecting herself? Somberly, she fingered the reins in her hands. If that was the case, then what kind of test would she unconsciously give Malachi?

Malachi watched Ruth's buggy turn right and roll down the road. Taking a deep breath, he headed for the barn. He tried telling himself it was to check on the cattle, but Malachi knew it was to regain his equilibrium before entering the house and facing his surprisingly perceptive brothers.

He stepped through the recently repaired barn door. The sweet aroma of alfalfa hay and clean livestock greeted him. Malachi could see through the dust motes dancing in the light let in by the midmorning sun that the two cows had their heads buried in mangers of hay. The roan steer jerked his head up from where he'd been eating and eyed Malachi warily before chewing again. Samuel had done a good job of settling them in. Malachi knew he would.

Good thing one of the Schrock brothers was thinking straight. Malachi hadn't since his heart had stopped at Ruth's scream. Maybe it'd been more of a yelp, but either way, it'd almost scared him out of his boots. He'd been climbing over the downed fence when he'd heard her shriek and was twenty yards into the field before he saw what'd caused it and slowed his frantic run. All he'd known was that Ruth was in distress.

Malachi exhaled slowly, the dust motes swirling in front of him as he eased closer to check the cattle's bedding. Later, the distress had been his own. His mouth grew dry as he recalled the feel of her slight form in his arms and her dainty feet clasped in his work-calloused hands.

He'd kissed a pretty girl or two in his twenty-four

years. He hadn't kissed Leah—that would've sealed his fate—but he'd come close, since she'd been so available. And pretty. But the thought of kissing the prettiest girl in Knox County, Ohio, hadn't shaken him near as much as the memory of the badger's surprisingly delicate foot in his hand. Malachi jerked his felt hat from his now-sweating head. He'd have a hard time avoiding looking at her heavy black socks under the hem of her dress, now that he knew what was within them. Malachi jammed his hat back on his head in disgust, startling the steer, who whirled away from his hay.

"Easy there," Malachi crooned automatically, edging back down the alley of the barn. His lips twitched as he recalled the names Ruth had called the steer during the walk to the farm. He'd almost burst out laughing several times during the trip. Only his concern of scaring the animal had kept him from doing so.

Shaking his head as he climbed into the loft, Malachi wondered what was the matter with him. In Ohio, after church the unmarried men would fall all over Leah. Some would even come into the store on some excuse in order to talk with her. Malachi couldn't have cared less, even as Leah would look over at him with big eyes. But let one beardless fellow, most recently his *bruder*, interact with Ruth, and he got all riled up.

He climbed over some neatly stacked bales, glad the recently acquired Yoder barn was half-full of quality hay and straw. Making his way over to a small window, he unlatched its wooden door and pushed it open. Lying stretched before him was the acreage he'd purchased, and the gently rolling hills of the surrounding countryside beyond. Big white houses and big barns– some white, some red—dotted the landscape.

Enjoying the view, Malachi eased down onto a nearby

bale. It was *gut* they had moved. Land in Ohio was expensive, and getting almost impossible to purchase with the growing Amish population there. Malachi still had two more brothers at home. Daniel, his youngest brother at fourteen, would inherit his father's farm, as was the Amish way. Due to the limited land, there was less and less opportunity to stay in farming, which was why many Amish young men turned to earning a living off the farm.

But farming was in his blood. So was helping take care of family. Malachi was hoping the farm and the furniture business would be successful enough that his other brother could join them. He knew Samuel and Gideon felt the same way. They might complain out loud, but they were familiar with hard work and didn't hesitate to tackle it. They'd eventually find their own ways. Thanks to the excellent management of a badger with surprisingly delicate feet, they had time to think about it. They were also in a position to have their next youngest brother, Wyatt, join them when their father was ready to let him go.

Malachi squinted into the distance, thinking about being ready. Several of his friends back in Ohio had already married. Beyond kissing girls, Malachi hadn't been tempted yet. He'd been too busy trying to establish himself at work, helping his parents watch out for his younger siblings and saving money to make a purchase such as the business and the farm. But now, he felt he was ready. For what, he wasn't quite sure. But as he rose from the hay bale and reached out to pull the Z-braced wooden door closed, he thought it might have something to do with an auburn-haired woman who didn't hesitate to run after cattle.

Chapter Ten

"*Ach*, you always make something with so many pieces." Benjamin was helping Ruth disassemble the petite rolltop desk. To confirm quality staining, they took the furniture apart to ensure the sprayed stain and sealant got into all the corners and small areas of the piece. After the staining and sealing processes, he'd help her wipe the sprayed pieces with a soft cloth to create a uniform appearance.

They'd partnered on this frequently over the years. Their actions were automatic, leaving time for easy conversation.

"Hannah said at church that you have a puppy from their dog's recent litter."

Ruth smiled at the thought of Rascal. The joy he'd brought to her life with his company and antics had been sorely missed. "Oh, yes. I'm struggling, though. There are things he could easily learn, if I just knew how to train him. And sometimes, when he does something and I know I should scold and make him behave, all I want to do is laugh."

Benjamin smiled in return as he unbolted a leg. "I

know what you mean. We had a shepherd puppy one time. Smoky was his name. Smart as a whip. But with four young boys to see to his training…" He shook his head. "You can imagine how it went."

His smile extended further over his lean, tanned face until it was a face-splitting grin. "One time, my *brieder* and I were busy in the hog pen. I think we were sorting. The puppy tried to get in and help but just kept getting in the way, so we'd tell him to go. He did for a while. But he came back. With what he was apparently hoping was a gift." Benjamin snickered at the memory. Ruth poked him in the shoulder with a slat from the rolltop to get on with the story.

"*Mamm* had been hanging up the laundry on the other side of the house. While she was hanging up some sheets…" He started chuckling again. Grinning at his contagious amusement, Ruth poked him anew, highly curious by now.

"The puppy got into the laundry basket and pulled out some of her…" Benjamin blushed and waved his hand vaguely up and down in front of Ruth's torso. Ruth's eyes widened, not at Benjamin's gesture, but at the thought of a puppy running around the yard with Mrs. Raber's undergarments in his mouth.

"The puppy made it to the hog pen and before we could stop him, he'd crawled through the fence and started chasing the hogs with it. Waved it like a white flag, only he wasn't surrendering. Not his new prize anyway. And it didn't stay white for long. He wasn't very big or agile yet, and some hogs got by him, trampling on his prize in the process. Pretty soon it got mired in the mud, and with four boys and a puppy chasing hogs around a messy pen, it got lost." Benjamin attempted to get control of his mirth, only succeeding for a moment. "*Daed* found it in the hog pen three days later and offered it to *Mamm*. For some reason, she wouldn't wear it again. The puppy stayed chained up in the backyard on wash-day ever since." He burst out laughing at the memory.

Ruth started giggling and couldn't stop. It felt so good. Her eyes watered. She wrapped one arm over her stomach and covered her mouth with the other, trying to muffle her laughter.

Her merriment drew to an abrupt halt when she heard an exclamation from across the room where Malachi was working with a jigsaw. Turning, she watched him jerk a bloodied hand close to his chest.

It was good to be able to work on a few projects, Malachi reflected as he guided the jigsaw around a curve in the design. It was Thursday and the store was closed, but with so much business, his crew still toiled in the workshop. He was taking a welcome break from the office. The more involved he got in other parts of the business, the less time he spent actually making furniture. He missed it. Finishing the board length, he lifted it to examine the cut. Blowing off the sawdust, he reassured himself that he still had the knack.

As he eyed down the line of the walnut wood, he couldn't help noticing two of his employees interacting beyond it. He could tell from their faces and postures they were deep in conversation, apparently a particularly enjoyable one. He'd seen a lot of expressions flit across the badger's animated face, but so far, not one of total delight. At least not in his vicinity. It did something to her delicate features. Which did something to Malachi's pulse.

Narrowing his eyes on the couple, he set down the cut piece of walnut and picked up the next. They were obviously very comfortable with each other, her and Benjamin. Malachi checked the wood for the design he'd be cutting and inspected it for any knots or imperfections that would affect the cutting process. He grunted. *Comfortable* and *the badger* were not words he'd normally use together. Malachi started the jigsaw over the design, eyes down, but ears perked in the direction of his employees.

He was halfway through cutting the design when he heard a sound he couldn't identify. Malachi glanced up. The next second revealed what a terrible decision that was. He jerked his hand away from the saw. Then he identified the sound. It was Ruth. Laughing. Eyes brimming with mirth. Focused on another man. Malachi didn't have to think long at all to determine, for some reason, that he didn't like it. The focus. Not the merriment. The merriment was mesmerizing.

The pain in his hand intruded. Throbbed for attention, in fact. It was bloody. Malachi stopped and abandoned the jigsaw. Grabbing the bleeding hand with his right, he pulled it to his chest.

Closing his eyes, he tried to concentrate on how many fingers he gripped in his hand. Were there enough? He could feel the accelerated beat of his heart through the digits in his tight clasp. Sliding his right thumb to the end, he counted the tips. One, two, three and a very sore—but still there—four. Malachi blew out a breath he hadn't realized he was holding.

In two quick strides, he reached a stack of absorbent wipes they kept on hand for cleaning up stain and topcoat. Malachi snagged a few from the stack without letting go of his hand. Before he could loosen his fingers to apply them, small, cool and capable hands gently cupped his from underneath.

"Let me see," Ruth murmured. The demand was gentle but urgent.

Malachi loosened his grip. Immediately blood oozed from the end of his left index finger. Ruth quickly covered it with the wipes and reapplied pressure with her own fingers.

"Can you walk with me?"

"Ja." Sure he could. He could walk by himself. But he didn't want her to move from where she was, tucked almost against his chest, the back of her *kapp* almost brushing his chin. Malachi looked over the top of the *kapp* to see the men in the workshop converging on him if they weren't already hovering nearby. All eyes were concerned, particularly his brothers'.

"I'm fine. Just a little nick. Been doing too much paperwork and not enough woodwork."

There were a few beats of silence before Samuel spoke. "You'd better keep all your fingers so you can grip a pencil. Because none of us want to do the bookkeeping, either." The tone was casual. The speaker's eyes, not so much. Malachi gave an infinitesimal nod of appreciation to Samuel as the tension began to ease from the shoulders of the surrounding men with the resulting chuckles.

"I think he's just trying to get out of work," Gideon quipped, eyes wide with concern.

"Ach, that's more your line, little *bruder."*

"I learn from the best, *ja*?"

"Well. I suppose that is me, then." Malachi smiled over gritted teeth. His finger was throbbing. There was more laughter, then the men began to drift back to their own workstations. Malachi looked at his brothers. With uncharacteristic concern still in their eyes and characteristic shrugs, they returned to their work, as well.

He matched his steps to Ruth's as she eased him over to the sink and the cabinet above it that housed the first-aid kit.

She looked back over her shoulder to him, her expression apologetic. "It needs to be washed out in case there's any sawdust in it and then have antibiotic ointment applied."

Malachi nodded. He heard the words, but they could have been a chorus from the *Ausbund* for all he understood. Although he certainly wasn't thinking of the Amish hymnal. He was thinking about how beautiful she was.

Ruth turned back around and he was again facing the stiff muslin of her *kapp*. Malachi could see over the top of her head as she pulled down, one-handed, the first-aid kit, opened the metal container and removed the materials needed. She turned on the faucet and checked the temperature of the water. Carefully pulling the now-bloody wipe from his hand, she guided the hand under the water and quickly, carefully and efficiently washed it out. She then gently dabbed it dry with clean wipes before pressing a gauze pad against the wound.

Malachi winced a few times at the resulting sting of pain. He glanced around the workshop. Only a few brief looks were cast their way, and those came from his brothers. Malachi's lips quirked in another wince and stayed in a self-mocking half smile. Well, he now had Ruth's attention focused on him. Not intentionally, and not in a manner he'd have preferred. And she wasn't laughing. Malachi recalled the musical sound. Good thing he hadn't been working with the band saw or the table saw. He'd probably have cut off his finger, if not his whole hand.

Looking down at the slight figure before him, Malachi was glad her *kapp* didn't fully cover her ear. He could see most of the dainty shell that peeked out from its edges. There were so many delicate edges on the fierce little badger. She was like the desk she was finishing. Beautifully wrought, but sturdy and businesslike. And time-consuming to properly appreciate.

Progress, particularly Malachi's, toward a satisfactory goal was measured in slow steps. He breathed in the scent of her hair that wafted through the *kapp*. Absorbing the warm clasp of her petite hand around his larger, rougher one, Malachi wondered what it would be like to be the focus of her joyful attention.

He speculated on the steps it would take to make that happen.

Ruth clamped the gauze against his finger, holding it in place while she waited and hoped the cut would soon clot. Looking down at the strong, tanned hand clasped in her smaller one, Ruth was startled to feel the hair follicles rise on her forearm. Her eyes swiveled from the goose bumps back to the clasped hands. It looked like they were holding hands.

A quick look while washing the wound had shown that, although currently bleeding steadily, the cut wasn't that long or deep. It shouldn't need stitches. She hoped. Ruth shuddered at the thought of what could have happened. Machines that cut and shaped wood could easily cut a man's hand. Malachi didn't seem the type not to pay close attention to what he was doing. She studied the calloused hand in hers. There weren't any white scars or healed abrasions that would've indicated previous accidents. That made sense with how methodical and careful he normally was. What happened today to affect his concentration?

She checked the gauze. Still bleeding. Sliding the finger of her other hand over his wrist, Ruth checked his heartbeat. Steady. Just like Malachi. She curled the wayward fingers back into her palm before they could stroke over the wrist with its light blond hairs. What was the matter with her? It was like she was the one light-headed from blood loss.

To distract herself, Ruth wondered if any blood had gotten on the project he was working on. If so, the stain should cover it. Walnut didn't come cheap. Of course, it came at a much lower cost than missing digits. Most of the blood covering his hand had come off when she irrigated the cut, but some red smudges were still visible. Ruth shuddered again, thinking of the missing fingers on some woodworkers she knew. He was lucky. He should have been paying attention.

"What were you thinking?" She didn't turn her head. Malachi was standing at her shoulder. Even with the renewed sounds of machinery starting up again after the scare, he'd be able to hear her.

There was a pause before he whispered, "I must not have been."

Ruth had never heard him whisper before. The surprising intimacy of his soft voice and the gentle wash of his breath by her ear raised gooseflesh on the back of her neck. Blinking her eyes at the sensation, she squeezed her fingers around his, only realizing her response when he flinched.

"Sorry." She quickly loosened her grip.

"'S all right," he murmured.

Ruth could feel the movement of his broad and steady chest with the brief words. She realized that if she closed her eyes, she could pretend that not just one, but both of his arms were around her again. And that his hand was entwined with hers not due to necessity but desire for her companionship. With Malachi, it could always be all right.

Ruth blinked her eyes open and the thought evaporated, leaving a feeling of longing as residue. Because she wasn't with Malachi. And never would be. She'd planned a different direction for her life, and marrying an Amish man wasn't part of it.

No, Malachi admitted, he hadn't been thinking, and he must not be thinking now. Because he was definitely feeling. And smelling. And seeing. Malachi tried to breathe shallowly, when all he wanted to do was take a deep breath to inhale the clean scent of what must be shampoo, as Amish women didn't wear perfume.

He felt the length of her arm against his, where they brushed from shoulders, along forearms, to meet at clasped hands. From his angle at her shoulder, he could see the sawdust sprinkled over the back of her delicate neck under her *kapp*, much like powdered sugar sprinkled over the top of a cake. No, he wasn't thinking when he blew a gentle breath over the surface, dislodging the golden particles until they floated in the air. The fragile strings of her *kapp* danced in the light breeze he created.

She jumped. Malachi winced, as she'd taken his hand with her on the ride.

"What are you doing?"

"You had sawdust on the back of your neck."

She huffed. "I probably always have sawdust on the back of my neck. Or stain on my fingers. At least it's better than blood." Her grip gentled as she checked the bandage again. Malachi was surprisingly content to let the cut continue bleeding. They'd barcly studied any anatomy prior to finishing eighth grade years ago in Ohio, but from what he remembered, there was a good bit of blood in his body. He wouldn't mind a little more dripping out if it meant Ruth would keep holding his hand.

And it was definitely keeping her out of conversation with Benjamin. Malachi slanted a glance over to where the dark-haired man worked. Unlike Malachi, his attention was firmly focused on his work. Concentration was obvious on the clean-shaven face as he continued to disassemble the desk.

Apparently the flow had reduced to a trickle, as Ruth efficiently whisked off the bloody piece of gauze and replaced it with a clean pad. More gauze was wrapped around it to keep it tightly in place. In the process, the remaining fingers of his left hand were bound together. Malachi sighed as she slowly let go of his hand.

"Keep that on at least overnight. Tomorrow you might be able to get by with a butterfly bandage, topped by a large Band-Aid to keep it clean. I don't think you need to be in the workshop for the rest of the afternoon," she advised primly. "You seem to have enough issues working safely with two hands. We might have to call the *Englisch* ambulance if you try it with just one."

"*Ach*, I suppose you're right. I've got some work I need

to look at in the office." It was his least favorite part of the business, the office work. Malachi was as comfortable as a duck on a pond in the workshop, with the equipment and managing the employees. But the office had been Solomon King's domain and Malachi had rarely ventured there. The office had been just off the store area, as this one was. The store had been Leah's territory. Malachi had avoided those areas as much as possible.

Ruth packed up the first-aid kit. Placing it back on the shelf, she glanced over at him. "Do you need some help?"

Malachi's heart thumped a little faster. Good thing the cut had clotted. "Probably. I'm trying to figure out your accounting system."

She scoffed. "It's easy. Didn't you look at the numbers before you bought the business?"

"*Ja*. But going over the profit and loss statements were easier than trying to read your chicken scratching."

"Ha. I'd imagine my penmanship is much better than what you've probably scribbled illegibly since then. I'd better go check to make sure it's something the accountant can read when she does the taxes." She marched toward the door between the workshop and store.

Malachi ambled slowly behind her. Suddenly, tackling office work didn't seem so irksome this afternoon.

Chapter Eleven

The following Wednesday afternoon, Ruth had half finished harnessing Bess before she noted the mare was grouchier than normal. Bess laid her ears back when Ruth buckled the girth. She rounded her back under the leather when Ruth swung her around in front of the buggy shafts.

"Are you sick?" Ruth stroked the neck of the cranky mare. Bess swung her head around and rubbed it against Ruth's shoulder, almost knocking her over. Ruth glanced at Bess's hay net. It was empty, so she'd had an appetite. Her water bucket was half-empty, indicating the mare had drunk normally during the day. A quick perusal revealed no signs of abnormal sweating in the chilly weather. Ruth rested her head against a harness-free area of the mare's belly, listening for sounds that might indicate colic. Everything seemed normal.

She couldn't ask any of the men what they might notice. She was the last to leave the shed that night, having walked to the Piggly Wiggly to get groceries after work. Since the day of his accident a week ago, she and Malachi had been leaving work at the same time, but tonight he'd had to leave early to go to the lumberyard to arrange to pick up some lumber tomorrow morning.

Brow furrowed, Ruth climbed into the buggy, watching Bess carefully as the bay grudgingly trotted down the street. The mare was sluggish, but that was normal. The exception was that Ruth didn't hurry her as she normally did. Something was off. It wasn't until they turned the corner to head down their road that Ruth identified the problem. Bess was limping slightly on her left front leg.

Ruth winced as she eased the mare into a walk. It wasn't a bad limp, which was why she hadn't seen it at first, but the leg was definitely bothering the mare. There was nothing to do now but to get home in as comfortable a pace as possible for Bess. Ruth sighed. She had a good suspicion what the problem was. It didn't bode well for her, but taking care of Bess was the first priority.

It didn't take long to determine her hunch was correct. The harness was off, Rascal was investigating the corners of the barn and Bess was munching on hay when Ruth gently lifted the mare's hoof and rested it on her bent knee. After cleaning the interior, she carefully applied the hoof tester to the sole of Bess's hoof. The mare had a propensity for abscesses, the reason for the long-handled pincer in Ruth's grasp, and why she knew how to use it. She also knew to anticipate Bess's reaction when she found the spot of the abscess.

Ruth jumped back when the mare jerked her foot off Ruth's knee and snaked her head around with laid-back ears. Setting the tester out of the way, Ruth rubbed the mare's forehead. "I know it hurts, girl. I don't know why you get these so often." The situation arose at least twice a year. Bess ignored Ruth's sympathetic crooning and went back to eating, still with laid-back ears.

Frowning at the attitude, Ruth added, "I also don't know why I keep you." She picked up the tester and patted the mare's neck as she passed. "Must be your charm." Calling the puppy to her, she took the tool to the tack room and headed to the house for the supplies she knew would be needed. Her shoulders sagged as she went up the steps to the porch. It'd be close to two weeks before Bess would be capable of pulling the buggy. Foot issues for the mare meant Ruth was without transportation. For two weeks. In the winter.

It hadn't been an issue when her father was alive, Ruth reflected as she gathered iodine and cotton balls from the house. They'd just traveled together in his buggy behind Silas, her father's gelding. But after *Daed* died, she'd sold Silas and her father's buggy. Maybe she should get a pony cart and pony for times like these. But that'd be foolish. The smarter thing would be to sell the mare and get a more reliable horse. And there were means of transportation that didn't require a horse. If she left. Ruth swallowed hard. She meant *when* she left.

But for the time being, Ruth still had her crabby mare to deal with.

Bess had personality. And Ruth wasn't ready for another loss of someone in her life. Her father had purchased Bess when Ruth had started her *rumspringa*, giving his daughter increased independence in her late teen years. Selling the mare would mean losing a little more of her father from her life. With the recent loss of the business, she wasn't ready to do that. Even if it meant she'd be walking for the next few weeks in the frigid Wisconsin winter.

She treated the mare the way the repeated visits of the veterinarian had taught her. Opening and draining the abscess, then pouring iodine into the wound and stuffing it with cotton to keep it clean. A task to be done twice a day for a while to the thankless horse, although Ruth could tell the mare already felt relief. She'd pick up an equine painkiller tomorrow from the veterinarian when she walked into town.

Others would gladly give Ruth rides in the meantime, should she ask them. But she'd taken care of herself, her father and the business for so long that she shied away from the idea of depending on others if not absolutely necessary.

Ruth and the puppy went to bed early that night. The next few days would involve extremely early mornings to get everything done and walk to work on time. She'd been late once. She didn't want it to happen again.

Malachi finished unloading the new lumber and led Huck and Jeb to the shed for a well-earned rest. The load was heavier than Kip could pull so he'd driven the Belgians into town today to pick up the lumber from the sawmill. Pleased with the geldings, Malachi ran a hand down the fuzzy chestnut shoulder of Huck, the one closest to him. They were willing, strong and a well-adjusted pair. The other horses nickered as he led the big boys into the shed.

Absently glancing over at the other horses after he'd attended to the geldings' needs, Malachi frowned and ran another quick count. It was one horse shorter than normal. His brother's high-strung filly was there, watching him warily, as were the placid bays of the rest of his workforce. All were present except Bess. Ruth's mare was missing. A rapid scan revealed that her buggy was absent, as well.

Malachi narrowed his eyes. He knew she hadn't been in the workshop while he was unloading the wood. Because he'd looked. But he'd just assumed she'd been in the store during that time. Was she here today? Ruth never missed work. Was she sick? No one had commented on her absence. With a sudden urgency in his step, Malachi headed to the front of the shop.

Ruth looked over in surprise from where she was doing some bookwork at the counter when the door burst open with a wild jangle of chimes. Hoping his reddened cheeks would be attributed to the brisk weather outside, Malachi gave her a curt nod and strode through the store to the workshop door. He jerked open that door and stepped through, taking a deep, steadying breath as he did so.

After a brief glance to see who'd come through the door, the rest of his employees returned their focus to their work. Slowing his stride to a more leisurely pace, he walked to the rack to hang his coat and hat. His eyes touched on two of his employees as another possibility regarding the missing Bess surfaced. Had one of the single men given Ruth a ride to work?

He quickly eliminated Jacob. Ruth treated her redheaded coworker as a fond but exasperating brother. But Benjamin on the other hand... Their dark-haired coworker had earned a number of smiles. And rare, shared laughter, Malachi recalled, rubbing a thumb over the still-sore injury the laughter had caused him.

Shedding his coat, Malachi studied the broad back of his employee. He supposed a woman would find him attractive. Benjamin was certainly a good worker. Talented. Reliable. He'd be a good provider. He was pleasant. Had a sense of humor and an easy smile, which women seemed to like. Malachi turned and jabbed his hat on the peg hard enough that it dented the black felt. He really hoped Ruth hadn't ridden in with Benjamin. Ruth had said she wasn't interested in being courted by Amish men, but women changed their minds. They were always changing their minds.

The door to the shop opened and she came through. Moving over to the project he was working on, Malachi watched surreptitiously as she walked through the workshop to see if she paid any special attention to Benjamin. He frowned in confusion when the two didn't even look at each other.

"Everything all right?" Malachi almost jumped when Samuel spoke at his shoulder.

"*Ja.* Of course. Why do you ask?"

"You seem a little distracted, *bruder.* I don't normally see you like this. Is everything all right with the business?"

"The business is fine." Malachi's lips twisted. "Thanks to previous management, we have even more growth opportunities than I'd expected. The challenge may be in keeping up with all the orders."

Samuel gave him an odd look. "You don't look happy about it."

"I'm happy," Malachi muttered.

"Then what's the issue?"

"I'm not sure about the possibility of hiring more employees when I don't know if I can manage the ones I have now."

"You've never had a problem with employees before."

A small smile touched Malachi's lips in appreciation for the surprise and loyalty evident in Samuel's response.

He focused on not letting his eyes slide to where Ruth turned on the belt sander. "Not until now," he agreed.

Malachi wondered all afternoon about Bess's where-abouts. Then he wondered why it bothered him so. He'd never spent so much time worrying about a horse. Ruth didn't speak with Benjamin that afternoon, or make any moves to hurry and get ready when the dark-haired young man left. When Ruth put on her cape and bon-net, Malachi was ready to go out the door behind her. To his surprise, she headed directly for the street, not the shed. Perhaps she'd ridden in with someone else in town? There was one way to find out.

"I didn't see Bess in the shed today." He fell into step beside her.

"*Ach*, she picked a fine time to have a hoof abscess. I'd rather she limit them to summer." Ruth looked up at him with a wry smile on her face. "More pleasant days for walking then."

Malachi halted, trying to absorb a strange sense of relief and the normal, growing feeling of exasperation he felt around this stubborn woman. "You walked to work today?"

"How was I to get here if I didn't?"

"That's several miles."

Ruth smiled tiredly. "*Ja*, my feet know it well." She looked in surprise at the hand he'd placed on her elbow.

"I'm giving you a ride home."

Her feet dragged a little as he pulled her gently along toward the shed. "No, you're not. It's miles out of your way."

"But Kip is used to covering miles. It won't be an issue for him."

"You brought Kip in to get the lumber from the saw-mill this morning?"

No, he had not. He'd totally forgotten that in all his thinking about horses today. "Actually, no, I brought the team of Belgians." Malachi paused briefly at the re-alization and how it affected his sudden plans. It'd be a slow trip home with the geldings. But the prospect of that much time with Ruth didn't bother him. In fact, an unexpected sense of anticipation began to grow at the thought.

His eyes narrowed. He'd be late getting back to the farm after taking her home. Well after dark on the short-ened winter days. Time wasn't the issue; it was the equip-ment. The heavier wagon was used for day work and didn't have lights that his buggy did. It could be a haz-ardous trip home in the dark with little visibility for *Englisch* drivers to see him. Hazardous for him and the geldings, too. Malachi frowned. He couldn't risk their safety. He remembered his recent inventory of the shed and smiled. The Belgians hadn't been the only Schrock horses in attendance.

"My *brieder* can take the geldings and I'll take you home in Samuel's buggy." Decision made, he continued to the shed. Ruth's slight weight was no obstacle to his firm but gentle hand under her arm.

She continued to drag her feet. "I don't know. Samuel may not let you. He seems pretty proud of that filly."

"He shouldn't be. She's a nuisance." Their cowork-ers looked up from where they were involved in vari-ous stages of harnessing their horses when Malachi and Ruth rounded the corner into the shed. Fortunately, Sam-uel was still there, adjusting the harness collar on the already-sweating filly. Malachi shook his head at the high-strung animal. A ride behind her wouldn't be relaxing, but it would get Ruth home, and both him and the Belgians off the road before dark.

"Wait here." He left her by Huck, a gentle giant of a horse. Ruth immediately started cooing to the draft gelding, rubbing the blaze on his face and running her fingers through the flaxen forelock. The big boy nodded his head in appreciation, almost lifting Ruth off the ground.

Malachi strode down the shed until he came to Samuel's filly. She jerked her head up, her eye ringed with white at his approach. Gently placing a hand on her croup on the opposite side from where Samuel was working, Malachi stroked her flinching flesh before he started helping harness the spooky animal.

"Easy, Belle," Samuel murmured to the filly as his questioning eyes met Malachi's over the tall brown back.

"Don't know why you call her Belle. According to the ownership papers that you left on the kitchen table, her name is Sour Grapes. At least one of those is correct. She's about as sour a horse as I've seen in a while."

"Don't pay him any mind, Belle. He's just jealous because you can run circles around his boring gelding."

"*Run* being the appropriate word. And if I had Kip here, I wouldn't be asking."

"Asking what?"

"Wonder if you and Gideon would take the geldings home and I drive Sour here."

Samuel blinked in surprise. "Why?"

"Ruth's mare has an abscessed hoof and she walked in. I'd drive her home with the geldings, but by the time I got home, it would be well after dark and the wagon doesn't have any lighting."

Casting an eye to where Ruth was now helping Gideon

harness the Belgians, Samuel scrutinized her from beneath lowered lids for a moment. "You and Gideon could drive the geldings and I'll take Ruth home."

"No, you won't." Malachi was surprised at how fast and firm the words came out of his mouth. From the look on Samuel's face, so was he. Now Malachi was the one being scrutinized from under Samuel's lowered lids.

"No problem," Samuel finally agreed, a smirk on his lips as he shot a sidelong look at Ruth.

Benjamin was just finishing harnessing his bay mare next to them. The subtle sounds of the shed—the muffled stomping of hooves, the quiet snaps of buckles on harnesses, the faint murmurs of the men either to each other or to their animals—hadn't obscured their conversation. "I can give her a ride. I live in that direction."

"I got it." Usually Malachi appreciated the supportive nature of the Amish community, but for some reason, tonight the offers rankled. Benjamin shrugged and backed his mare from the shed. Samuel's smirk got wider. That rankled Malachi, as well.

"Anything I should know about Sour?" He prepared to back the nervous filly out to hook her up to Samuel's buggy.

The smirk transformed into a huge smile, showing most of his brother's white teeth. "She's not Kip," was the only advice offered as Samuel sauntered over to help with the Belgians.

Malachi snorted. No surprise there, he acknowledged, taking in the sweating neck of the filly again. They'd hardly left the shed. He eased the shafts down over her, attached the harness to the shafts, called to Ruth and stepped into the buggy. Looking around the unfamiliar interior of the rig and identifying the essentials, he recognized the used buggy as reflecting his brother's more outgoing personality. The bishop might discourage things that were *hochmut*, but either he granted leniency to the young men in their *rumspringa* on what might be considered proud, or the bishop had never stepped into one of their buggies.

The squeak of an opening door preceded Ruth's entry into the buggy, an enigmatic look on her face. She sat down, hugging the door, a good six inches between where her cape draped the seat and the edge of his coat. Malachi eyed the space between them before returning his attention to the filly. He pursed his lips. Between the two females with him on the trip, he wasn't sure which one would be more distracting.

Chapter Twelve

As the temperatures were above freezing, Malachi eschewed his gloves and stuffed them in his pockets. He wanted bare hands on the reins to keep a better feel for the unknown, and most likely fractious, horse. With Ruth seated on his left side, they sped down Miller's Creek's main thoroughfare. A glance in her direction revealed a smile on Ruth's face at the brisk pace they set. He had to admit, Sour Grapes was a smart goer. Malachi was beginning to see the allure of the filly. It wasn't long ago that he'd have wanted one just like her.

By the time they were out of town and approaching the corner where the intersecting road went to Ruth's farm, lather was already flecking off the filly's neck and chest. Sour Grapes kept jerking her head forward and playing with the bit. Malachi maintained a gentle hand on the reins. Approaching the corner, he slowed her down and put on the blinker in the buggy. She fought the shortened lines, tossing her head forward to pull more rein. She knew home wasn't that way and she didn't want to make the turn. Malachi's lip curled. How appropriate.

The filly was already barn sour, wanting to get to her stall as soon as possible.

He battled her around the corner, keeping a close eye on the car behind him. Some *Englisch* drivers were very courteous in sharing the road with Amish buggies. Some were not. Malachi had a feeling the red car behind them might be one of the nots. Swinging wide on the corner, the buggy took up more than its normal share of the road. With a hard pull at the bit, Sour was speeding up. They completed the turn when, engine roaring, the red car honked loudly and accelerated down the road they'd just vacated. At the dual sounds, Sour shot forward at a gallop, every lunge jerking the buggy forward.

Malachi's hands tightened on the reins. He sucked in a breath as Sour headed close enough to the ditch that his side of the buggy tipped precariously in that direction. Malachi leaned hard the opposite way, banging shoulders with a bouncing Ruth. A powerful tug on the left-hand rein got Sour Grapes back on the road, where Malachi focused on stopping the bolting filly. Hopefully with the buggy and its occupants in one piece.

He knew, with the bit clamped in the filly's mouth, a steady pullback would do no good, so he began with alternating pulls and releases. There was no reduction in the horse's speed. At least they were more on the road now, although encroaching over the centerline. With the narrow bridge over the town's namesake getting closer with every lunge, Malachi figured this was a good thing. Or so he thought until he heard Ruth's gasp and looked ahead of the flying black mane to see a car approaching from the opposite direction.

Please, please don't honk, he beseeched the driver when it became evident they were going to meet on the

bridge. Malachi's fingers clenched the reins and he gritted his teeth as the clatter of the shod hooves changed
tenor when the filly's churning legs crossed the metal
expansion joint from blacktop to bridge. The vehicle
flashed by, the other driver's startled face only a few feet
away. The car's protruding side mirror passed within a
whisper of the buggy wheel.

Once they passed the bridge, the filly headed for the
ditch again. The buggy tilted abruptly as the wheels on
the ditch side left the blacktop. Harsh crunching sounds
resonated through the buggy as they tore through fingers
of snowdrifts that edged the road. Drifts that'd dwindled,
but had been through numerous melt-and-refreeze cycles, causing the buggy to jerk in their direction at every
impact. Even if it didn't tip, the buggy wouldn't hold up
much longer with that kind of abuse. Wincing at the pain
in his still-bandaged finger, Malachi pulled hard on the
left rein, throwing the filly off balance and getting her
back on the road.

Sour Grapes's chin tucked against her shoulder but
her jaw was locked against the bit and she was still running. The buggy was rocking as she swerved, fighting
for control. Malachi shot a glance ahead. The road was
open. Taking a deep breath, he gave the filly a little more
rein, letting her run. She'd eventually have to wind down.

Between alternate pulls on the right and left reins to
keep her off balance and varying tugs and releases to
slow her, he regained control. The filly eased into a trot
and finally a walk. Malachi pulled her over to the nearest
field entrance. The horse stood, lathered and quivering,
as Malachi's hands slowly unclenched. Blowing hard,
Sour Grapes extended her neck, demanding more rein.

Malachi gave her some, as what lay ahead of them

was an open field with a foot of snow. She wouldn't get far if she took off again. He set the brake anyway. He was shaking. Not over fear for himself, but in terror that an accident could've hurt or killed Ruth. During the ordeal, his attention had been on the bolting filly. He'd been aware of Ruth bouncing and swaying on the seat beside him, but he hadn't been able to glance at her, much less give her any assurance, through the harrowing adventure.

The reins shifted in his hands, which were now sweating. Malachi shot an apprehensive glance at Sour Grapes, but she was just dropping her head to blow some more. She wasn't going anywhere. He could see Ruth's right arm, braced against the dash. Her fingers were white-knuckle in their grip. She was probably trembling with fear. Fear he could deal with. He'd pat her hand, reassure her that everything was all right now.

If she was crying... *Ach, nee.* He'd never dealt with a crying woman before. Not even his sisters. But any woman would deserve to cry over the past few minutes, even this little badger. Bracing himself with a few deep breaths, Malachi turned to face her.

Her bonnet was askew. The normally neat bow that tied under the stubborn little chin was undone, the tails trailing down the front of her cloak. Malachi had been partially right. The face that turned to him had wide eyes, but her green eyes were wide with excitement, not fear. They matched glowing cheeks and an open-mouthed smile.

Malachi couldn't help himself. He didn't even think about it. Leaving the reins in his right hand, he leaned over and cupped her cheek, gently holding her face still for the kiss he placed on her lips. Malachi's heartbeat quickly elevated beyond its rate during the wild buggy ride.

The leather reins moved in his hand. The buggy shifted as the filly took a step forward. Breaking the kiss, Malachi reluctantly leaned back, sliding his fingers away from the silken skin of her cheek. Ruth's eyes fluttered open and held his as he regarded her solemnly. He couldn't interpret what was behind them. No surprise there. He couldn't define anything in his brain, either, at the moment. Except that he wanted to kiss her again.

The buggy shifted once more. His mind whirling, Malachi adjusted the reins to both hands and released the brake. He looked over his shoulder to ensure traffic was clear and backed the filly, now willing, onto the road. The buggy rolled smoothly along as he clicked to the filly and she swept into an easy ground-covering trot. Malachi didn't feel the anxious vibe through the reins, so hopefully Sour Grapes wouldn't take them on any more misadventures on the ride home.

Sensing the horse was now on better behavior, he transferred the reins to his right hand. Reaching out, he took the graceful, yet deceptively strong one that rested on the seat beside him. After a brief hesitation, her fingers curled around his. They stayed that way for the remainder of the journey to her farmstead. No words were spoken, but his thumb rubbed gently over the smooth skin at the base of hers during the trip.

The filly slowed her gait when they turned into the unfamiliar lane. Malachi urged her toward the barn. As the buggy rolled to a halt, Ruth tugged her hand from his. It was with reluctance that he let go. Before he could set the brake, something he'd always do with this horse, Ruth opened the buggy door and scooted off the seat.

"Thanks for the ride." Her voice was a little breathless. She hastily stepped away from the buggy.

"Open the barn door."

"What?" Ruth's face, under the still-cockeyed bonnet, popped back in the opening.

"Open the barn door. I want to take a look at Bess's hoof."

"Oh, there's no need. I can do that."

"I know you can. I don't see a lot of abscesses and I want to see how it's treated." Lifting the reins, he shifted on the seat, tipping his head to stretch his back. "Besides, I'd like to get out from behind this *idioot* filly for a bit."

Ruth shot a look at the lathered, still, but currently white-eyed bay. A smile crept across her face. "I can understand that."

She hurried to the barn door and pushed it open. Malachi drove the filly through. Sour Grapes entered hesitantly into its dim interior until she heard a welcoming nicker from Bess. Malachi secured the reins, set the brake and stepped down from the buggy. Ruth had disappeared into the side room he knew held the tack and feed, as well as other equine essentials. Before he reached Bess's stall, where the cantankerous mare had her head out, ears laid back, Ruth returned with a hoof pick, cotton balls and a bottle of iodine.

Malachi held out his hand. A Band-Aid still covered his cut finger.

Ruth hesitated. "Are you sure?"

"I learn best by doing."

"You'll get the Band-Aid dirty."

"I'll put on a new one."

She frowned but placed the items in his hand. Opening Bess's stall door, she entered and held it for Malachi to follow her through before she closed it. "When you clean out the hoof—it shouldn't be too bad as she's been on straw for the day—you'll see where the plug is. Pull out the existing cotton ball, pour iodine in the hole and plug it with a clean cotton ball."

Malachi nodded as he stroked his free hand over the mare's neck and across her shoulder before sliding it down her front leg to pick up the hoof Ruth indicated.

"Be careful, she's cranky."

"Well, that seems to be the nature of all females who live on this property." Malachi positioned the hoof on his bent leg and applied the pick.

There was a muffled snort, followed by a brush against his shoulder as a slender hand reached out and lightly back-fisted him on it. Malachi smiled as he located where the cotton ball was wedged against the hoof wall.

"You seem to forget that we are a nonviolent community."

"You seem to keep provoking me."

Malachi deftly pulled out the cotton plug, filled the cavity with iodine before handing the open bottle to Ruth and secured the fresh cotton ball in place. Bess, apparently determining that his administrations were complete, or needed to be, snaked her head around with laid-back ears.

"Look out!"

Malachi jerked back at Ruth's warning, barely missing Bess's nipping teeth. Losing his balance in his crouched position, he knocked into a bent-over Ruth, who had been closely watching the proceedings. She fell under his greater weight, the iodine bottle, still open, flying against the wall. They both tumbled into the straw.

The fall knocked Ruth's much-maligned bonnet further askew. Malachi's startled glance took in her wide green eyes under the crooked brim. She was so captivating he was tempted to kiss her again. But the confusion in those green eyes and the restlessly shifting black rear legs of the mare in his peripheral vision stopped him. Malachi thought he might deserve a kick in the head for his wayward thoughts.

He levered himself carefully off Ruth and extended a hand to help her up. Casting a wary eye on the mare's hindquarters, she placed her hand in his. Malachi pulled gently, surprised at her slight weight when she gave the impression of such strength.

Her cheeks were flushed when she glanced his way before scurrying out of the stall ahead of him. With a respectful awareness of Bess's hind legs, he picked up the almost-empty iodine bottle and cap before exiting, as well.

Ruth had taken off the bonnet, readjusted her *kapp* and was retying bonnet ribbons when he reached her. She glanced up at his approach. Malachi capped the iodine bottle and set it on a nearby straw bale. Reaching out with a thumb, he brushed at the soft cheek now dotted with a few spatters of iodine.

"You've got a few extra freckles," he murmured as he leaned in, his hand moving to tip up the petite stubborn chin. His lips touched hers. Malachi's eyes drifted shut at the contact. Seconds later, they shot open when she jerked back.

"The puppy."

It took him a moment to identify the distant barking. He heard the incessant sound, punctuated with some frustrated yips and baby howls.

"I have to go."

Malachi easily interpreted the words not as "I have to go attend to the barking dog," but as "I need to step away from this." He nodded. He needed to leave as well, even though it was not what he wanted. Dropping his hand, he drew in a deep breath and stepped back.

Ruth self-consciously scrubbed her cheek with her fingers, making no impact on the additional orange dots. "I supposed we should be glad we weren't knocked into a pile of something worse. This might be harder to wash off, but it smells better."

Malachi smiled in response, knowing that was what she'd been hoping for.

She cocked her ear toward to the puppy's relentless barking. "I need to go check on Rascal." At his responding nod, she whirled and hurried to the big barn doors, shoving them open in an obvious invitation for Sour and him to leave. Malachi didn't need to be asked more than twice. He climbed into the buggy, picked up the reins and released the brake. Fortunately, the filly was now in an amenable mood. She backed up like a champ and they whisked out of the barn. With a bemused smile and an attempt at a casual wave, Ruth sent them on their way.

Malachi clicked the filly into a brisk trot when they turned at the end of the lane. Sour Grapes seemed satisfied with the pace. Malachi almost wished the filly would bolt again. It would distract him from his now-galloping thoughts.

Ruth latched the barn doors and hustled to where Rascal waited in the repurposed chicken yard, miniature paws propped up against the wire fence. He'd ceased his barking once he'd gotten her attention and scampered over to greet her as she rushed through the gate. After sweeping him into her arms, Ruth nuzzled her nose into his warm neck.

"Thank you." She hadn't yet determined if the pup's intervention had warded off disaster, or spoiled a treasured moment. Rascal wiggled around to run his rough tongue over her cheek. Ruth doubted he'd have any success with the spots of iodine, either, but appreciated his assistance. She resolved to scrub her face frequently and thoroughly this evening. Not having a mirror—to have one might encourage vanity, and the Amish community had strong opinions against personal pride—she could only hope her efforts would be successful.

Stepping over the board under the gate that so far had kept Rascal from escaping, she set the pup on the ground. He followed her down the lane, staying in the ruts created by buggy wheels that wove through the melting and refreezing snow, as she went to collect the mail. While he scrambled along successfully, Ruth stumbled and almost fell more than a few times on the rough surface. Her mind was definitely not on the ground ahead. It was on the kisses. She drew in a deep breath of the chilly late-afternoon air, and only a small sense of self-preservation kept her eyes from drifting shut at the enticing memories.

The wild ride had made her heart race, but not as much as the feel of Malachi's lips on hers.

They had been more than she could've hoped for. As was the man. He was more…everything. Smiling dreamily, Ruth opened the mailbox door. Her smile faded. Ruth pulled out a large envelope, glancing without surprise at the return address. Her correspondence course had arrived, reminding her that her plans didn't include a husband—an Amish one anyway.

An Amish husband, at least in her district, meant her education would be over. It meant, once she had children, that working outside her home was over. Her responsibilities would be taking care of the home and *kinder*. She'd have no choice.

Ja, Ruth wanted a home, a husband and children, but she wanted other things, too, like *Englisch* women had. They had the ability to have a home and family without giving up other things they loved. It was what she'd desired since she'd reluctantly walked away from the one-room schoolhouse for the last time after graduating from eighth grade. Successfully absorbing more responsibilities at her father's business had only increased her resolve.

Her *daed* had known that. Which was why, before he died, he'd made her promise to pursue her choice. A choice he felt he hadn't had. With ambitions of being an engineer, Amos Fisher had planned on leaving the Amish community when he went to a Sunday night singing at the encouragement of some friends and fell in love with Naomi Schlabach, Ruth's *mamm*. As she was already baptized, he'd abandoned his aspirations and stayed, transitioning his dream of engineering into furniture making. They'd established a life in Miller's Creek. When she'd died during childbirth, he'd stayed, knowing the tight-knit community would provide much-needed support to a single father. But he'd nurtured Ruth's skills, encouraged her ambitions and pressed her to follow them, particularly when he'd realized he was leaving her.

It was the reason Ruth wasn't baptized. If she left before she officially joined the church, she could still visit and interact with friends and business associates in the community. If she was baptized into the church first and then decided to leave, she'd be shunned.

Ruth called to Rascal before he ventured any farther onto the road. She crossed her arms over the large envelope, holding it to her chest, and tried not to wish that her arms were instead wrapped around a strong blond man. She'd decided her future a while back, and it was not what was in the buggy she could barely see on the horizon, moving away from her.

Chapter Thirteen

"Ungrateful wretch," Ruth muttered, rubbing her upper arm after closing the stall door. Bess had taken advantage of her distraction this morning and nipped her arm. Ruth supposed she deserved it for not paying attention. *That will teach me. This is what happens when you don't stay on track. You get hurt.* She shot a baleful look at the mare, whose head was buried in the hay Ruth had provided before being bitten.

"You better enjoy that, you might not get anymore. In fact, maybe I will sell you before…" She paused and then went on, "Before I get some other form of transportation. You're not doing me any good now anyway." The pup barked and dashed in front of Ruth, almost tripping her up as he raced to the open barn door. She followed in his wake and looked out in the faint light of the sun, just hinted on the horizon.

A bay horse was trotting up the lane. A familiar one. Ruth's heart rate sped up and she drew in a shaky breath. *Remember what you decided last night.* The admonishment didn't do any good. A smile spread across her face as Kip drew to a halt in front of the barn.

"What are you doing here?" she asked as soon as Malachi pushed open the buggy's door.

"Making sure my employee arrives to work on time. We've got some orders to fill, as she keeps finding us more and more new business." Breath vapor floated away from the door as he poked his head out into the chilly morning.

Ruth didn't hesitate. "Let me put the puppy up and get my things." She called Rascal to her and they both bounced over to the chicken coop. Securing him for the day, she rushed to the house, closely monitoring the slick ground with her eyes and feet, but her mind wandered.

You're not looking for a husband! Her brain accused as she dashed through the kitchen door. *Yes, but that doesn't mean I shouldn't explore this,* she countered, grabbing her prepared lunch and changing from the Wellingtons to her work shoes. Her gaze fell on the kitchen table, covered with the correspondence course papers. Its allure was quickly supplanted by the memory of smiling blue eyes under a black felt hat. *Which one do you want to greet each morning?*

The ride into town was much less adventurous behind the sedate Kip instead of the unpredictable filly. Ruth kept her hands folded in her lap on the journey, afraid if she draped the right one casually on the seat between them, he might clasp it in his again. Much to her surprise and relief, the conversation was easy and continuous over the trip. Kip was the first one in the shed that morning. Removing a harness from a horse had never been so quick or enjoyable.

Ruth was well into her current project, a dainty but sturdy hall seat in oak with Queen Anne feet, before she noticed half the morning was gone. Of course, the morning had gone faster once she'd stopped craning her neck every five minutes to locate Malachi. He'd unconsciously made it easier for her by staying in the office to do some paperwork. As he was there, he attended the shop when the bell heralded the arrival of customers. Ruth hoped they were all legitimate customers and not single women shopping for a husband.

Turning over her sanding block, she ran a finger over the smooth surface. Time to change the paper. She needed to go to a finer grade for this next step anyway. Slipping off her dust mask, Ruth smiled as she recalled her friends' comments about finding it hard to breathe around their beaus. She was beginning to understand what they meant. It had been a rather breathless ride this morning.

She strode over to the cabinet that housed the sheets of sandpaper. Nodding at Gideon, who was changing out the paper on a belt sander, she looked for the grade she needed.

Samuel had been working on a chair leg on the nearby lathe. He shut off the generator-powered machine and rolled his shoulders, understandably stiff after some time in the same position.

"So who are you planning on taking home after the singing next church Sunday, Samuel?" Gideon queried.

Ruth smiled down at the 120-grit sandpaper in her hands. Malachi's younger brothers loved to tease each other. She enjoyed their banter. It made her wish she had siblings.

"It'll be hard to choose. There's so many of them."

Gideon snorted. "How do you know one will go with you?"

"Oh, they will. You just have to know women."

Instead of laughing as she expected, Gideon responded seriously. "Speaking of women, do you think Malachi is missing Leah? He's been acting strange lately."

The grit on the sandpaper roughened Ruth's fingertips as her hands tightened on the sheets. Who was Leah? She'd heard the name mentioned before but hadn't paid much attention. Now the name sounded ominous. In the book of Genesis in the Bible, Leah had sneaked into the wedding ceremony and married Jacob first. He'd eventually gotten Rachel, the one he'd truly wanted, but it had taken him seven more years of working hard for his father-in-law. Ever since reading the story, Ruth had never liked the name of the conniving Leah. She shuffled through a few more grades of sandpaper, her ears focused on the brothers' conversation.

"I don't know. Maybe when she and her father come visit before Christmas, we'll find out."

Ruth stared unseeing at the sandpaper. Her stomach felt like she'd swallowed a woodworking plane outfitted with fresh blades, the knob lodged right under her heart.

"I thought that was all settled before we left Ohio."

"You know Malachi. He never says much about his women."

"*Ja.* Unlike you."

A smile crossed Samuel's handsome face. "There's so much to say about mine. And so many of them to say it about."

With another muffled snort, Gideon settled his safety glasses back on his face and restarted the belt sander. The conversation was over.

So was Ruth's ability to breathe momentarily. Pulling

an entirely different grade of sandpaper from the cabinet than the one she'd intended, she slowly made her way to her workstation.

Ruth stared at the Queen Anne legs blankly before remembering what she was working on. Gathering up the pieces, she neatly put that project away. Thoughts whirling, she automatically pulled out the project that gave her comfort. The red oak rocker.

Not wanting to wreck her father's chair, she double-checked the grit on the sandpaper and then began the habitual soothing strokes down the slats that made the surface as smooth as glass. As her hands worked on autopilot, Ruth unfortunately had much time to think. Did Malachi have a girl back in Ohio? She and Hannah had speculated on the possibility. But that was before…he kissed her. Amish courtships were typically kept private until announced at the church a short few weeks before the wedding. Was Malachi betrothed to this Leah?

Ruth sanded vigorously for a moment, but it didn't obliterate the troubling thought. If he was betrothed, why had he kissed her? She vividly recalled her racing heart and the longing to wrap her arms around him.

He didn't seem like the type of man to play with a woman's feelings like that. But what did she know of men really? She hadn't walked out with anyone during her *rumspringa*. And she'd gotten adept at dissuading those who seemed interested, so they stayed just friends.

Daed hadn't remarried after losing his wife, even to help raise a child, in defiance of community expectations. At the thought of her father, Ruth slowed down her mindless stroking and fingered the fine-grained wood. *Oh,* Daed, *I wish you were here for words of advice.*

The back of her eyes prickled. Ruth blinked rapidly to prevent the telltale onslaught of tears.

Of course, Leah could be coming here to get ready for the wedding. Traditionally held during the months after harvest until Christmas, Amish weddings were now spread throughout the year. If she was arriving soon, it wasn't too late to get a wedding completed by the year's end.

Would he go back to Ohio, or would she come here to Wisconsin? Surely he wouldn't go back; he'd just bought a home and business. It made sense. He'd come first, get settled in a home and work before a new wife would join him. Setting the wood down, Ruth pressed her fingers to her eyes. It didn't stop the tears from welling up.

That is why you are not going to be an Amish wife, Ruth reminded herself. It would be the loss of hopes and freedoms. Now it was simply the loss of a man. A man she didn't have anyway.

An *Englisch* wife might start her marriage with *I do.* For an Amish wife, a wedding was the beginning of *I don't*s. *I don't get to make furniture. I don't work in the workshop or the store.* Once baptized, which was necessary before one got married, *I don't take a correspondence course.*

She had some more *I don't*s: *I don't want to be here if he's married to someone else. I don't want to see his new wife come in to visit him. I don't want to see her sitting with the married women at church. I don't want to see him growing a beard as a married man, a beard I won't look across and see every morning. I don't want to see her pregnant with his child.*

Her eyes squeezed shut but tears leaked through anyway. Her breath came in shallow pants. *I don't want to see her come in, trailed after by his* kinder. *Boys with solemn blue eyes with just a hint of mischief. Girls with blond hair that'd be curly when long.*

There was sourness in her stomach and the bitter taste of bile at the back of her throat. She was going to be sick. Ruth yanked her safety glasses off and tossed them on the bench. Tears now fell freely. She swiveled on her stool, prepared to make a hasty dash to the bathroom. And found herself facing solemn blue eyes. She couldn't read what was in his eyes at all. She'd never seen them like that. Nor heard the low, flat tone in his voice.

"What are you working on?"

Ruth swallowed hard against the acrid taste in her mouth. If she opened her mouth, she was afraid something other than words would come out.

Malachi raised an eyebrow, his eyes never wavering from hers.

"It's a rocking chair. For me." Ruth managed to get the words out, but just barely. "Something my father started."

His gaze flicked over the pieces of red oak before returning to her face. Ruth wanted to scrub her hands over the mess she knew she presented, but she kept them clenched at her sides. To fret about her looks would've been prideful. She fretted anyway. Pride was conditional on regaining control of herself. Ruth straightened her shoulders and swallowed again.

It was a moment before he spoke. "Shouldn't you be concentrating on something productive for the business during work hours? Since your efforts have made us all so busy?"

Ruth couldn't help it. She gasped. Amish might be nonviolent, but he might as well have punched her. She wished he had—she would've been less hurt. Brushing by him, she beelined for the coatrack and snagged her bonnet and cape from the peg as she swept by. Her shoulder burned from the brief contact. She firmly, but in a controlled manner, shut the door behind her before swinging the cape over her shoulders and fastening her bonnet as she headed briskly down the street.

Malachi watched the black cape swirl briefly in the window of the door before it—and Ruth—disappeared. He felt his sigh down to his brown work shoes. This was why he didn't like to interact with crying females. There was no right move. He couldn't pull her into his arms and comfort her as he longed to do. Absorbing all her cares and sorrows. Not here at work, where his brothers and other employees only had to swivel their heads to watch, if they weren't watching already.

His gaze left the door and swept around the room. Malachi raised an eyebrow at all of them and one by one the men returned to their work. Samuel was the last. He cocked his eyebrow in return, a mocking imitation of his brother. Malachi glared at his sibling. Samuel smirked, dropped his safety glasses down over his eyes and returned his attention to the lathe.

Malachi directed his gaze to the delicately wrought oak pieces at Ruth's station. It was beautiful work. Amos Fisher had been an outstanding master craftsman, and he'd taught his daughter well. But as talented as she was, and as beautiful as he knew the piece would be when finished, Malachi didn't want to see Ruth work on it. It hurt her too much. He saw the pain on her face every time she worked on the rocker.

Remembering the furniture her *daed* had already

made her and her melancholy expression when she'd mentioned this unfinished piece, Malachi stroked his finger over the silken wood. That was why he'd interrupted her. She was obviously distraught. He'd wanted to protect her from that pain. Knowing she wouldn't stop if he directly asked her, he'd decided to come at it from a different angle. An angle that supported her value to the business while getting her to stop working on something that upset her.

Malachi glanced at the closed door. Obviously it'd been the wrong angle. Casting one last considering look at the oak, he shook his head. Crying women. Safer to stick your fingers in a malfunctioning table saw. Sighing, he made his way to the office door.

Knowing Ruth brought her lunch, Malachi kept checking the workshop for her return during the lunch break. He stopped looking when Jacob returned from lunch at the café and mentioned he'd run into Hannah Lapp, who was giving Ruth a ride home as she didn't feel well. Malachi furrowed his brow. She'd been fine this morning. And very fine last night.

After everyone else left for the day and weekend, Malachi wandered into the workshop to Ruth's work area again. Eyeing the red oak pieces scattered across the bench where she'd left them in her hasty departure, he picked up a slat and gently slapped it across his palm.

It was later than usual when he left the shop. Malachi's mind was still on Ruth as he harnessed a lonely Kip in the shed. She might be able to avoid him tonight, and this weekend, but she wouldn't be able to do so on Monday. They were meeting with a customer in Portage that morning, a meeting Ruth had set up herself. Malachi didn't think she'd miss it.

They'd hired an *Englisch* driver to take them on the forty-mile round-trip to the larger town. The driver would pick them up at their homes on Monday morning before chauffeuring them to the furniture store in Portage and then back to work afterward. Beyond hanging out the window of the vehicle, there wasn't much she could do to avoid him on the trip. And perhaps he'd talk with his brothers about borrowing one of their rigs to take her home after work Monday. Bess would still be out of commission, leaving Ruth to make her way on foot. Maybe he'd commandeer Gideon's rig this time.

Malachi smiled grimly. Even with the wild ride, or perhaps because of it, Samuel's filly had done him a favor. Maybe he ought to give her another chance. Malachi shook his head, listening to the steady clop of Kip's hooves on the blacktop. He hadn't had so many complicated females to handle back in Ohio. Only a very subdued but straightforward one. Clicking to Kip to pick up his speed, Malachi determined he liked the twists and turns of the Wisconsin landscape better.

Chapter Fourteen

On Saturday, Ruth dusted every piece of furniture in the house, lingering over the items made by her father. She swept and scrubbed the floors, cleaned the bathroom, even tackled a closet and cleaned out the fireplace. An Amish proverb advised that women's work wasn't seen unless it wasn't done. Hers hadn't been done in a while. And she needed something to occupy her mind and her time.

Her cheeks flushed in remembrance of her actions yesterday. They'd been out of character. She wasn't an evader. Besides, none of that might even come to pass. She was always thinking of what-ifs in terms of the business. There'd never been a man in her life to think about. With Malachi, she'd gotten carried away.

Always pragmatic about business opportunities, she'd be pragmatic about this, as well. Malachi had never mentioned Leah. His brothers didn't know everything. As much as Samuel might think he knew women, well, he didn't. Ruth wrinkled her nose. Not that she was an expert. All women didn't think like her. Particularly those in the Amish community.

Monday she'd see Malachi. She'd ask him. They'd straighten things out. His kisses had to have meant something, right? They'd meant something to her.

That Sunday, one without church, Ruth spent time working on her accounting correspondence course. She didn't consider it work, as she enjoyed the challenge. It was what she'd always dreamed of. Today, she wasn't finding it as fulfilling as she'd anticipated. While staring at the words and numbers, she'd catch herself thinking of other things. Things like the cushiony rustle of straw under her back while blue eyes looked into hers. Or cool fingers brushing across her cheek.

By the time she finished the first assignment, she'd worn down half an eraser. Rubbing it again across the paper, she hoped the score on this assignment wouldn't permanently ruin her grade for the course.

When Rascal uttered his version of a warning bark and scrambled over to the kitchen door, Ruth was happy for the interruption. Sundays without church were used in the Amish community to visit friends and relatives. During her father's illness, Ruth had gotten out of the habit. Just getting through the workweek had tired him out. They'd stayed home on weekends so he could rest.

They had no close family in the area, as both sets of grandparents had passed away while Ruth was growing up. Although he'd been a business owner, Amos had been a private person. As Ruth grew older, she'd taken on more of the business aspects and interaction with people that were essential to the operation, and he'd stayed in the workshop. Yes, they'd been a part of the fabric of the community, hosting church services when it was their turn, supporting others in need, but they'd mostly been on the periphery. A quilt block lining the edge of the blanket as opposed to one in the center of the quilt.

After her father had died, Ruth had been so busy managing the business day to day, and then preparing it for sale that Visiting Sundays had continued to be ones of rest. Or more accurately, of seclusion. Perhaps that'd been a mistake. Perhaps it was time to become a more active part of the community. Then again— Ruth glanced at the paperwork spread over the table as she rose to her feet—it wouldn't matter if she wasn't staying.

A genuine smile lit her face when she opened the door as far as the bouncing pup would let her. *"Guder Nammidaag!"*

Hannah was standing on the porch, a corresponding smile on her pretty face.

"Good afternoon to you, too." Hannah knelt to rub Rascal's ears when the pup dashed outside to place his paw on her black-enclosed legs. "And good afternoon to you, as well. Have you been behaving?"

"There's a reason his name is Rascal." Ruth motioned her in and closed the door behind them. "I suppose all his siblings are perfectly behaved puppies."

"If they are, they're behaving in someone else's homes."

Ruth hurriedly piled her studies into a stack on the table and invited Hannah to sit down. Hannah glanced at the paperwork but didn't say anything as she took a seat. Ruth went to the stove to get them some coffee. "You've sold them all, then?"

"Ja. They were gone as soon as they could be weaned."

"I'm not surprised. You have a reputation for raising *wunderbar* puppies." Hannah changed the subject, to Ruth's dismay. "I wanted to see how you were. You seemed quite upset on Friday."

Ruth focused on the cups she was assembling for coffee. "I wanted to thank you for the ride home. And for not asking questions, when I looked pretty...questionable." She'd looked like something that had been dragged face-first after a plow. At least that was how she'd felt.

"I'm asking now." Hannah's voice was gentle. But intractable. When Ruth didn't speak, Hannah did. "Was it something to do with Malachi?"

Bringing the cups to the table, Ruth cringed. "Does everyone know?"

"No, because everyone doesn't know you. Well?"

Ruth sat down across from her friend. "I don't know. Sometimes, when I'm with him, I think..." Ruth paused and flipped her hand in a few small circles. It was hard to put into words what she thought. She glanced at the paperwork stacked on the end of the table. "Then other times, I'm unsure."

Hannah nodded, a sweet smile of understanding on her lovely face. Ruth studied her friend as Hannah lifted the coffee cup. Whereas Ruth questioned her place in the Amish community, Hannah was the epitome of a perfect young Amish woman. Filled with patience, *demut* and *gelassenheit*. The Amish discouraged photos, but if there were ever a poster of the essence of an Amish woman, it would have Hannah's picture on it. In the current state of Ruth's muddled mind, she didn't know how one could sincerely display such submission, or "letting be." A glaring omission in her own character that Ruth needed to pray about tonight. Again.

She didn't tell Hannah she was planning on leaving the Amish. Her friend wouldn't understand.

Hannah set the cup down. "Since you're going to share so much on that, I'll tell you the other purpose of my visit. I'm inviting you to the cookie exchange we're having at my family's home before Christmas. *Ach*, I can read it in your face. Don't say no." Reaching across the table, Hannah set her hand on Ruth's. "It's been too long since you've joined in any of these activities." She smiled gently. "I know you've been terribly busy for a long time, but we'd like you to come."

When Ruth didn't respond, Hannah continued, "Your quilting skills might be rather dismal for the bees, but I know you've a few cookie recipes that are edible."

Ruth squeezed Hannah's hand before she let it go and stood up. As she'd thought earlier, perhaps it was time to join in more often. Whether she stayed or left the community, it would be *gut* for her. "Since you asked so charmingly, how could I refuse?"

Hannah laughed as she also stood. "I'll get you the details later." She leaned over and patted Rascal's head before she walked to the door. "In the meantime, I hope things go well for you at work." With a meaningful smile, she left.

On Monday, by the time a blue car drove up the lane, Ruth had been ready for over two hours. After giving Rascal some extra attention, she'd focused on her coursework. As the vehicle rolled to a halt, Ruth stood with a barking Rascal by her side, looking beyond it to the red flag sticking up over the mailbox containing her completed assignment. Tying her bonnet under her chin, she stepped out on the porch. She greeted the *Englisch* driver with a brief smile.

Waving to the driver, Mr. Thompson, to stay in his

seat when he started to get out and open the door for her, Ruth opened the rear door, got in and sat down. Closing the door with a thunk, she was very conscious of Malachi's presence on the opposite side of the seat. She tucked her cape underneath her and crossed her ankles, trying to take up as little space as possible.

"Good morning," Mr. Thompson greeted cheerfully. "I hope you don't mind, I invited my wife along for the trip. She had some shopping she wanted to do in Portage. We thought we could do that while you conduct your business."

"That's fine," Ruth assured him. Mr. Thompson had driven her and her *daed* many times and she'd met his wife before. He was dependable and friendly. He was also chatty. And she wasn't feeling too chatty this morning. "You two go ahead and visit. I've got some things I want to think about."

Mr. and Mrs. Thompson seemed content with that and started a constant hum of conversation in the front seat. What, or actually who, Ruth wanted to think about, was eyeing her closely. She flashed him what she hoped would pass for a smile and focused her attention on the snow-covered landscape outside her window. If her hand drifted from her lap to lie palm down on the seat between them, and his strong calloused one slid from his lap to rest with only a short inch separating their little fingers, it was enough. For now.

Henry Morrow greeted them with a smile when the chime heralded their arrival into the Portage Emporium a while later. Hastening over, he shook their hands and took their outer garments. "I'm so glad to meet you in person. Business by phone used to seem impersonal.

When it's by fax, it gets even more so." His eyes rounded, in almost-comical shock, as if he'd just realized that what he said might sound offensive.

Ruth smiled, feeling like it was her first genuine smile of the day. She'd been through this before with the *Englisch*. They wanted Amish-crafted furniture but weren't so thrilled about dealing with Amish practices. "Don't worry. It's nothing we haven't heard before. We appreciate you working with us on what is required by our *Ordnung*." The Miller's Creek *Ordnung*, the set of rules that district members lived by, didn't allow phones to be owned by its members.

Malachi removed his black felt hat and handed it over. "In fact, Ruth has worked out a relationship with the local café where they can take phone messages for us, in case you need to communicate with more urgency than fax."

Ruth shot a glance at Malachi and raised her eyebrow at the encouraging smile. They'd had a rather heated discussion on the topic last week. Ruth had come up with the idea of offering the Dew Drop Inn one small piece of discounted furniture a month in exchange for the use of their phone and message receptions. The café could feature the item for its Amish and increasing *Englisch* customers, selling it at a profit that would cover the inconvenience of the use. The discreet tag on the piece of furniture would direct potential customers to the shop. The owner of the café had accepted the proposal with eagerness. Malachi had taken a little more convincing.

"Wonderful!" Mr. Morrow responded enthusiastically as Ruth gave him the number of the café. "We've had such interest in your furniture since we added it to our collection. Folks have asked about pieces in different stains and lead times on special orders. Being able to get information while they're still in the store would be extremely helpful. Strike while the iron is hot, you know."

He and Malachi fell into a discussion of lead times, as well as wood and stain options as Mr. Morrow led them to his office. They passed an open door. Ruth peeked inside to see a young woman doing paperwork at a desk. Returning the woman's easy smile, Ruth sucked in a breath as she took in the rest of the room. It was larger than most offices. Large enough to comfortably accommodate the child who sprawled on the carpet, busy coloring in a book, and the playpen against the wall. Ruth could see the hump of a miniature figure under a blanket and the tiny hand of the *bobbeli* that slept there. She blinked at the surprising pressure at the back of her eyes. Nodding at the woman, Ruth hurried on.

Her heartbeat picked up its pace as she followed the sound of the men's voices. This was what she wanted. All. She wanted it all. She yearned for a husband and children but she wanted more. She wanted to learn. She wanted to continue working at something more than the summer produce stands or quilt making, which were some of the only things Amish women in their district were allowed to do after they were married. To get all she wanted—the office with children a few paces back down the hall—she couldn't have an Amish husband.

She couldn't have…him. Ruth caught up to the voices. Malachi was in Mr. Morrow's doorway, his broad shoulder propped against the doorjamb. His thick blond hair showed the indentation of his missing hat, the ends threatening to curl below the crease. His lean cheek dimpled above a smile at something the store owner must have said. He turned at Ruth's approach and she sucked in another breath at the look in his blue eyes. A look that seemed to say, "I've been waiting for you. Here you are."

Ruth drifted to a halt, her heart thumping. She'd been waiting for him, as well. If she could have him, all the other things didn't matter. She had to cross her arms over her chest to stop herself from reaching for him.

Malachi furrowed his brow at Ruth. She had a funny look on her face. He was glad they seemed to be beyond whatever had been going on last Friday. All weekend she'd been on his mind, to the point where he'd almost driven over to see her. So he'd kept himself busy. Samuel had tested his nonviolent tendencies by smirking at him every time Malachi looked up. Only Mr. Thompson's occasional glance in the rearview mirror this morning had stifled the urge to clasp her hand during the trip. He wouldn't leave Ruth open to gossip.

She seemed stuck in the hallway. Malachi motioned her toward the office door. "Mr. Morrow has some questions that you could answer better than I." He stepped aside to have her enter the office and take the seat the store owner indicated. Malachi settled into the one beside it.

"We can't keep your product in the store. It sells out as fast as we can stock it. All the dining room sets were gone in the pre-Thanksgiving rush."

"That was all Ruth's doing. I was just getting into the picture then."

"Well, let me tell you, she does a fantastic job. Both as a craftswoman and as a business manager."

Ruth folded her hands in her lap. "Thanks. I've been taking correspondence courses to learn as much as possible."

Malachi raised his eyebrow. She had? That was news to him. Amish women normally didn't have formal education beyond eighth grade. And none after they were baptized.

"Well, it shows," Mr. Morrow agreed heartily. "I've been bragging on you, little lady. You ever want to move to Portage, or even Madison, folks would be lined up to hire you."

Ruth smiled demurely. Malachi's eyebrows took a dip, not knowing which he liked less in the comments. *Bragging* certainly wasn't a word used frequently in the Amish community. In fact, humility was a tenet of their faith. And he definitely didn't like the thought of anyone else, particularly in communities distant to Miller's Creek, hiring Ruth. His fingers curled around the wooden armrests of the chair. Time to hurry this conversation along.

Much like Sour Grapes, Samuel's spoiled filly, Malachi took the bit in his teeth in terms of the appointment. Further business discussions were quickly concluded. A short time and an expanded arrangement later, he and Ruth stood. Malachi touched the slender small of her back to guide her out of the office before he could catch himself. Fingers tingling from the contact, he pulled his hand back.

Waving their goodbyes after a quick tour of the operation, they stepped out onto the sidewalk to find Mr. Thompson's blue car parked along the street a short distance away.

Ruth looked at him with a smile. *"Gut?"*

If his hand brushed hers as they walked down the surprisingly busy sidewalk, it was an accident. At least that was what Malachi told himself. "Very *gut*."

"I'm glad. Increased business helps provide employment. You might have to expand."

Malachi's smile was a little brittle—his mind was still focused on the store owner's comment about opportunities for Ruth. "I think we can at least keep everyone employed."

After exchanging greetings with the waiting *Englisch* couple in the car and declining their question regarding an early lunch, they started on the ride home.

The Thompsons seemed to find a lot to talk about in the front seat. In contrast, Ruth was unnaturally quiet. But her hand lay palm up on the seat between them. Malachi extended his so his little finger bumped hers when the car bounced over some railroad tracks.

They'd just passed the sign for the city limits when Ruth spoke quietly. "Who's Leah?"

Malachi went still at the question. Eyes guarded, he swiveled his head to look into wary green ones.

He lowered his brows. "Where'd you hear that name?" If his tone was harsher than normal, well, for sure and certain, he didn't want to discuss Leah with Ruth.

"Your *brieder* mentioned her."

Malachi frowned. If his brothers made any unfavorable comparison of the two women within Ruth's hearing, he'd take them out behind the barn and be more brother than Amish. The two women were nothing alike. Which was why his feelings for Ruth were much different than any he'd had about Leah.

"Her father owned the furniture business I supervised in Ohio." That'd been the extent of the relationship. Even though Leah and her father had given enough hints that they'd be agreeable to a much closer one.

"So you know her well." Her slender shoulders

slumped a little. Malachi wasn't sure if that was the reason her hand shifted closer to the black cape. He just knew it moved farther away from his hand and out of touching distance.

Malachi thought of Leah. She'd worked in the store part of the business but always seemed to be back in the workshop, underfoot. No, *underfoot* wasn't the right word. Leah had more finesse than that. But around. Available. Sweet. Undemanding. Agreeable. All the things the woman beside him wasn't. His lips quirked. Yes, very unlike his badger.

"*Ja.* I know her very well." Ruth shot him a glance, her eyes pausing briefly on the smile before she faced the back of Mr. Thompson's head.

"She is coming here before Christmas?"

"*Ja.*" He said nothing more. There was nothing more to say. Leah and her father were coming to visit his aunt. The Solomon King and Moses Lapp families had been close prior to Aunt Miriam's move to Wisconsin years ago. It was highly likely he'd see them while they were in the area, as his aunt would surely invite his brothers and him over for supper some evening.

If Leah and Solomon were coming to Wisconsin for a different agenda, they were heading for disappointment. They weren't his guests. Malachi pressed his lips together. There was nothing more to say.

Apparently, there was nothing more for Ruth to say, either. She was quiet the rest of the journey home, her hands now clasped in her lap. Malachi surreptitiously flicked his eyes in her direction several times during the remainder of the journey, hoping her hand would rest on the seat between them so he could curl his own around it.

It never did.

Chapter Fifteen

On Tuesday, Ruth walked down to Hannah's farm and caught a ride into town with her. She'd informed Malachi of her plans Monday afternoon when they'd returned to the workshop after the trip to Portage. He hadn't said anything in response, just regarded her with solemn eyes until Ruth had to bite her tongue not to squirm.

Tuesday morning started out well. Malachi had apparently found much to do in the office and stayed out of the workshop, which was a relief for Ruth. It wasn't until later in the day she discovered there might be other things keeping him out front.

The petite rolltop desk was finished. Prior to preparing an item for shipping, it was their custom to place a discreet business card in a drawer. Ruth searched where the cards were generally stored in the workshop but didn't find any. She frowned as she walked toward the office. They needed to order more anyway. The previous ones had stated Fisher Furniture. New ones that read Schrock Brothers Furniture needed to be made. Particularly now that there wouldn't be a Fisher involved in the business much longer.

Ruth paused for a moment in front of the door. She ached a little every time she saw him. *Ach*, she ached when she didn't see him as well, but she'd work on that. And he wouldn't be witnessing his impact on her anyway. When she knew she was going to see him, she would be in control. Prepared.

Inhaling deeply, she briskly pushed the door open. Nothing could prepare her for what she saw as she stepped through. Malachi was not in the office, as she'd expected, but was in the store. With his hand clasped around the delicate one of a beautiful stranger. Ruth halted abruptly, her hand on the knob of the still-open door.

The two turned as the sounds of the workshop intruded into the store area. Ruth noted Malachi hastily dropped the woman's hand. She stepped the rest of the way into the store and turned to close the door behind her, squeezing her eyes shut as she placed one hand on the jamb and the other on the knob, pulling it secure. For a moment, it was the only secure thing holding her up.

After exhaling the breath that'd caught in her throat when she'd entered the room, Ruth turned back around. Lack of oxygen made her light-headed, not the sight of Malachi touching another woman. She nodded at the couple and stepped toward the office.

"Excuse me. I just needed to get some business cards for the back. Mr. Schrock, if you haven't yet, you might need to order some new ones with your business name on them." Ruth didn't care if they didn't hear a word she said. She darted through the office door. Jerking open a file drawer, she quickly flipped through the folders. As she'd thought, no cards, old or new. The file was as empty as her heart.

"Ruth." Malachi stood in the office doorway. Ruth stayed bent over the filing cabinet drawer, her back to him. "I'd like you to meet Leah King."

Her eyes squeezed shut. *What if I don't want to meet her?* She straightened, swallowing the bile that sprinkled the back of her throat, and turned to face his watchful eyes. Exiting the office, she bumped into the doorjamb in her effort to avoid touching him as she passed.

The Amish didn't believe in using the words *pretty* or *beautiful* to describe one another. To do so might make one *hochmut*—"proud" or "arrogant." Something definitely not of their Plain world. That didn't mean they didn't know what beautiful was. Or how attractive it was to the opposite sex. During her *rumspringa*, Ruth had purchased plenty of *Englisch* magazines. There'd been pictures of beautiful women in them.

Even without makeup, the woman before her could hold her own with the *Englisch* models.

Leah looked like a perfectly put together quilt. No stitch was out of place. The materials chosen were impeccable—the gold of the hair, the violet of the eyes, the pink of the cheeks. The design was flawless. Ruth looked like a quilt she might make, mismatched materials and sloppy stitching. She remembered the sawdust on her neck, gently blown off by Malachi. Now, instead of the memory making her smile, she wanted to cry. She was likely covered with the dust of the trade again. Ruth curled stain-shadowed fingers into her palms. She might work with him, but before her was what a man wanted to go home to.

Leah even had a lovely, serene smile for Ruth. One Ruth couldn't return. Had this been Jacob's Leah from the book of Genesis, he would've stopped after marrying her and forgone the other seven years of working for Rachel. Who needed a Rachel when you had this Leah?

If Malachi had introduced Ruth to Leah as well, Ruth didn't hear it over the buzzing in her ears. She gave a curt nod at the vision that had been holding Malachi's hand, and headed into the workshop, to a world where she belonged. Or at least, one in which she used to belong, she thought as she stiffly strode back to her workstation, clenching her tongue between her teeth to keep any expression from showing on her face.

Reaching her station, she stared unseeing at the empty workbench. What had she been doing? Oh, yes, she was preparing the desk for shipment. Ruth clasped and unclasped her hands, trying to relax. She'd been looking for a card to place in the drawer. She'd have to ask Malachi what he wanted to do since the cards weren't available. Later. She'd ask later. She certainly wasn't going back in there now.

And now was not a good time to start on another project. She'd either waste the wood, injure herself— she winced at the memory of another injury and the moments of closeness afterward—or she'd disappoint a customer with shoddy workmanship. A glance at the wall clock determined it was close to lunchtime. Interest in food was far from her mind, but escaping briefly was very tempting.

Ruth swallowed. Thankfully, her stomach acted like it was going to stay in place but she didn't want to put anything in it right now. But if she couldn't escape physically, she'd escape mentally. Even if it were into a piece that Malachi didn't approve of her working on during his time. Ruth's lips firmed. Maybe now would be the best time to work on something he didn't approve of.

Besides, working on the chair made Ruth feel close to *Daed*. Although it was painful, too, she needed that sensation now, when her heart and mind were racing and she felt on the edge of a precipice.

She turned to where she kept the red oak pieces. They weren't there. Ruth searched under the workbench and in the areas where she kept other projects. No red oak. Quickly rounding the end of her workbench, she checked workstations nearby. Still nothing. Her actions drew questioning looks from others in the workshop.

Numbly walking back to her workstation, Ruth concentrated on the last time she'd seen the chair. She went still as the memory surfaced. Friday. When she'd just learned of Leah. When Malachi had chastised her for working on it. She'd stormed out and left it. And it was now gone.

The door to the store opened and Malachi stepped through, immediately looking to her. Ruth met his gaze and didn't blink as he walked through the shop.

"Where's my *daed*'s rocker?" Ruth didn't recognize her voice when he was close enough for her to ask without shouting the question that burned through her. She did recognize the subsequent guilt she read in his face.

"You took it," she said bleakly.

He pressed his lips together but made no response.

Ruth turned away. Any energy she'd possessed swept out of her and she just felt...empty. "Just go. Please, go," she whispered to the nicked bench that filled her vision.

When she looked over a moment later, he was gone. Placing her hands on the counter, she dropped her head between her shoulders. A tear escaped from her eye, rolled down her nose and splattered on the wooden surface. How long ago was it that she'd been in this very spot, missing her *daed*, concerned the new owner would take away her chance to work with the wood, something she loved?

How ironic that here she was again, crying. Willing to give up woodworking if only she could have the new owner for her own.

Malachi walked back through the workshop. He could have sawed off all his fingers and he wouldn't have noticed. All he could feel was the pain evident in Ruth's eyes. He had no words against that kind of heartache. Maybe what he'd done was wrong, but it'd been done for her.

All morning he'd been trying to think of something to say that would breach whatever happened between them on the ride home yesterday. Something about Leah's pending visit had disturbed her. Before he could think of a way to broach the subject, the bell had jangled as the store door opened and Leah had come in. Malachi hadn't been expecting their visit this early. Correction—he hadn't been expecting their part of the visit to him this early.

He'd shaken her hand, asking after her and Solomon's well-being, when Ruth stepped through the shop door, a stunned look on her face. She'd slipped quickly into the office. Not knowing what else to do in the situation, he'd introduced the two women. From what he'd glimpsed of Ruth's face as she dashed back out the door, that'd been a mistake.

Turning to follow her, not sure what he'd do beyond wrapping his arms around her when he caught her, Malachi had felt a gentle touch on his sleeve.

"Your aunt and I came into town to do a little shopping. Miriam was drawn into a discussion at the quilt shop." Leah smiled charmingly. "I wanted to see your store. We thought you might give me a ride to the bishop's home, where my *daed* is visiting as she didn't know how long she'd be."

Malachi looked at her blankly, thinking that she'd be able to walk to the place faster than he could harness his horse and drive her there. He shot a glance at the closed workroom door. Perhaps he could ask Samuel to give Leah the ride, while he checked on Ruth. Samuel never minded driving with a pretty girl.

Good manners and appreciation for the opportunities Leah's father had given him over the years made him reluctantly nod. But, he resolved, good manners wouldn't prevent him from making himself scarce during the rest of their visit to his aunt. Good manners also didn't stop him from telling Leah to wait in the store while he checked something in the shop. Ruth.

Never, in all his years of working with furniture, had trying to make something better actually made it worse. Returning to the store after seeing Ruth—seeing her devastated for some reason she wouldn't say—Malachi noticed his hand trembling as it closed around the knob. He paused and exhaled slowly. After stepping through the door, he closed it on the normally comforting sounds of the shop and turned to see Leah watching him, a smile on her beautiful face.

"Are you ready?"

Malachi's eyes swept over her. There wasn't anything out of place. Except her presence in his business and life. *"Ja."*

If Kip was surprised about the unexpected outing in the middle of the day, Malachi wasn't. It seemed to be

Leah's way. She never outright asked. She sweetly maneuvered. With quiet, gentle nudges.

Malachi didn't like it. But he'd always allowed himself to be nudged along.

It was a primary reason he'd left Ohio. He was afraid he'd be nudged right into standing in front of the district as the bishop joined them as man and wife. It was obviously what Leah and her father wanted. As to what Malachi wanted, well, it hadn't felt right. It'd felt like a harness collar that didn't fit well. After a while the collar would wear a hole in his hide. And who knew how long the nudging would stay gentle.

Malachi took his time harnessing the gelding. It was some time later when he poked his head in the store door and advised Leah the buggy was out front. If she'd wanted to check out the shop, she'd had plenty of time. Hopefully enough so she wouldn't need to come back.

Climbing up by the wheel, he felt somewhat churlish when he didn't offer Leah assistance into the buggy. She gave him a sweet smile, but her eyes reflected surprise as she settled into the seat on his left side. A wife's side, Malachi noted sourly as he gathered the reins. Leah gracefully tucked her cape around her and Malachi signaled Kip to head out.

Malachi glanced over at the perfect profile visible just beyond the edge of her black bonnet. Returning his attention to the horse in front of him, he sighed. Yes, she was perfect, but for someone else. Not him. He clicked to Kip, who picked up his pace. Malachi's tense shoulders began to relax. The sooner he delivered Leah to her father, the better.

Kip made Malachi think of his new Belgian geldings. And another way to encourage plodding companions other than nudging. Jeb, the older Belgian, would get the field plowed or the lumber hauled in a slow and steady pace. It was his teaming with eager and enthusiastic Huck that got work done more quickly, and Malachi could tell, more enjoyably, for the pair. Malachi's lips quirked. Kind of like him. And…his badger. He could put his shoulders into the collar every day and pull willingly to accomplish things, but it was being in harness with Ruth that brought joy and passion to those accomplishments.

Malachi sat up straighter at the realization. Leah looked over and smiled. Sweetly. Gently. Her right hand gracefully dropped, palm up, to the seat between them. Malachi kept his focus on the straps of leather and brown back that moved in steady rhythm ahead of him. He could still see the hand rested on the seat. Kip's ears flicked back at the instructions that telegraphed down the reins to move faster. Malachi subtly shifted to the right until his elbow brushed the side of the buggy.

"Everything all right?"

Ruth wasn't surprised at Rebecca's question. She forced her stiff lips to smile and strove to ignore what she knew were red-rimmed eyes.

"Everything's fine, thanks," she lied to the waitress, trying not to wince as she said the words. Everything was far from fine. Which was why she was taking action. *Do not ask the Lord to guide your footsteps if you are not willing to move your feet.* The proverb popped into her head. *I'm moving my feet, Lord. I just omitted the asking part.*

A grimace edged across Ruth's face. She had no excuse not to ask *Gott* to guide her steps. It was why she always wore the *kapp*. Women covered their heads when they prayed. As they were to pray continually, the *kapp* was always worn.

But if it was *Gott*'s will that she stay, why would He make it so painful? So it must be His will that she go. And it was what she wanted, so she was keeping her promise to *Daed* that she choose her path. She was simply going to move her feet before she could change her mind.

"I just need to use the phone."

"Oh, sure," the young woman agreed before turning to the next customer with a smile. A big smile. Even in her misery, Ruth turned her head to see who was greeted with such enthusiasm, then instantly wished she hadn't. It was Samuel. Of course.

She whipped around and hunched her shoulders, trying to make herself smaller or, hopefully, even disappear before he saw her. It didn't work. She caught his quizzical glance at her before he flashed a smile that matched the one the pretty waitress offered him. Ruth waited for a minute before she picked up the phone receiver, hoping Rebecca would ring him up and he'd move on. No such luck. Samuel was in full flirt mode and Rebecca was a willing recipient. She even rang up a few other customers, who looked askance at Ruth as they passed her hovering at the end of the counter.

Sighing, Ruth lifted the receiver and dialed the number she'd memorized. As she listened to it ring, she cleared her throat several times. Maybe no one would pick up and she wouldn't have to do this. No. It had to be done. She drummed her fingers on the countertop to drown out the sound of the man's voice behind her. The voice that was too much like his brother's.

"Hello, Mr. Morrow? This is Ruth Fisher of Fisher Furn—I mean Schrock Brothers Furniture. Yes. I'm fine, thank you. How are you doing? That's *gut* to hear." She let the man ramble on for a moment. He talked even faster than she did.

"Say, Mr. Morrow," Ruth interjected when he took a breath. She hunched around the phone, dropping the volume of her voice. "When we visited you earlier, you mentioned you knew of a few people in Portage or Madison who might be interested in hiring me if I was available. I was wondering if you could provide some names and numbers."

Ruth squeezed her eyes shut as Mr. Morrow exclaimed over this request. Although not listening, she was throbbingly conscious of the conversation behind her and who was in it. "Yes, yes. I realize it's a big step. But it's one I'm ready to make. Things have changed here and I…I need to make a change, as well." A tear dripped down from her compressed eyes and splashed on the black plastic phone. Opening her eyes, Ruth hastily wiped it off.

"If you could give me a few names now, that'd be wonderful. Yes, you know we're not available at phones for a callback. Yes, I'll wait." Briefly and painfully. Her heart thumped with every second as Mr. Morrow apparently pulled up a computer screen. "Yes, I'm ready. Okay, got that. And the next? Could you please repeat those last two numbers?" She struggled to make the pen mark on the sweat-dampened note in her hand. "Okay. No, that's enough for now. Thanks so much, Mr. Morrow."

Carefully setting the receiver into the cradle, Ruth muttered thanks to a distracted Rebecca and hustled out the café door. Once outside, she flicked a quick glance back through the glass windows that fronted the café. To her relief, Samuel wasn't paying any attention to her. And as she had his attention, Rebecca wasn't, either.

Pent-up energy ebbed out of Ruth. She managed to get two storefronts down before she leaned against a hitching post, knees weak from making the call and the realization of the change in her life that she'd just implemented. She blew out a deep breath. Perhaps it was possible to go back.

The rapid tattoo of hoofbeats filtered through her bonnet. Turning her head, she saw a bay coming down the street. It was Kip. In the buggy was Malachi, his face turned in conversation to Leah, seated on his left. Where Leah would continue to sit with Malachi. Ruth watched them travel down the street and turn the corner.

No. Going back wasn't possible.

Malachi looked up from the onerous task of accounting to see Samuel prop a broad shoulder against the door frame. He frowned. Samuel never sought him out in the office. If he had something to talk about, he'd call Malachi over when he was in the workshop or wait to discuss it at home over chores or supper.

"Well, big *bruder*. I don't know what you did, but apparently you did it with your standard flair for effectiveness."

Setting his pencil down, Malachi swiveled the wooden desk chair to meet his brother full on. Something in Samuel's normally irreverent tone conveyed that complete attention was necessary. Attention that'd been fractured since Ruth had stared at him with devastated eyes.

Since returning from driving Leah to meet her father at the bishop's house, he'd thought of nothing but Ruth, which was why he'd pulled the accounting out to punish himself. Several times he'd sprung from the desk chair to pace to the workshop door, only to return and plop down in the chair again. He didn't know yet what to say to settle whatever was going on in that active mind of hers.

She was a reasonable woman. Normally. Sometimes. Maybe his drive home would provide time to consider a reasonable response. He'd leave a little early and stop by the shop where Hannah worked and let her know he'd be picking up Ruth in the morning. It was unlikely Ruth would jump out once she was in the buggy, regardless of what she thought of their conversation. It'd be a good time to talk. Maybe she'd calm down overnight, a little at least. If people started speculating from the frequent buggy rides that they were walking out—Malachi shuffled that around in his mind much as a horse might work a new bit in his mouth—maybe that wasn't a bad thing.

"She's leaving."

Malachi was confused with Samuel's flat statement. "Of course she is. She and her *daed* weren't planning to stay long."

"I don't mean Leah. I mean the other one. The one you want, big *bruder*. Ruth is leaving."

"What?" Malachi stood up so fast the wooden desk chair rocked against his leg. Its motion slowed much faster than his suddenly racing heart.

"Just overheard her using the phone at the Dew Drop. She called a Mr. Morrow." Samuel's eyes quirked toward Malachi to see if the name meant anything to his brother. Reading that it did, he continued, "She was asking about names and numbers of people in Portage and Madison that might want to hire her. She said something about needing to make a change. I think you had a change in mind for her, as well. But I don't believe it was this one."

When Malachi's gaze darted to the workshop door, Samuel straightened from his slouch against the door-jamb. "She's not there. You've got some work to do, *bruder*." He shook his head. "When I find the woman I might want to marry, I'm going to make it a lot less complicated than you."

Staring at the door, Malachi eased back into his chair. He didn't like complicated, either. How did it get to this point? How did he fix it? As he gazed unseeingly out the office window to the well-ordered showroom beyond, things finally started to fall into place like the handcrafted furniture it displayed. Intricately, seamlessly, beautifully.

He wanted Ruth for his wife. It was as simple as that. He'd come to Miller's Creek for a business and had found a match. Now if only he could make Ruth see that, as well.

Chapter Sixteen

Bits of red rubber flew across the lamp-lit table as Ruth furiously erased what she'd just written. She slumped back in her chair and tossed the now-eraserless pencil onto the table. If she hadn't already gone back and forth several times between knitting and the coursework tonight, she'd go back to knitting again. But she'd dropped two stitches on one row of the much-abused afghan and picked up three stitches the following row. Those were just the mistakes she was aware of. It was a mess. So was Ruth.

The pup lay at her feet under the table. Even he was tired of the pacing back and forth. Ruth curled her toes to keep her foot from tapping and stayed put, although her eyes returned to the mound of yarn in the rocker. She sucked in and blew out a breath in a long huff.

Usually her knitting, unlike her inept quilting, was impeccable. And calming. Nothing was calming tonight. Ruth's mind churned as much as her stomach. The challenge with the knitting wasn't just this evening. She'd been making one mistake after another on the project.

Several rows required ripping out and redoing, an exercise Ruth despised.

She frowned at the pile of dark blue. The pup raised his head at a few escaped foot taps. How far down did it need to be ripped out? The rows had been neat and organized. Until she met Malachi. No, she'd managed to keep it together beyond that. The stitching had gotten uneven when she'd fallen in love with him.

Crossing her arms on the paperwork strewed over the kitchen table, Ruth dropped her head upon them. *Experience is a hard teacher*, the old adage said. *She gives the test first and the lesson afterward.* Ruth clenched her jaw. She'd failed the test. Miserably. She'd done the opposite of what she'd planned—she'd fallen in love with an Amish man.

Ruth bit her lower lip as another unwanted homily surfaced. *Advice when most needed is least heeded.* She hadn't listened to her own advice. If she had, she wouldn't have fallen in love. And definitely not with a man who already had a sweetheart. How foolish was that?

I will not cry, she vowed as she pushed off the table, though her lips felt numb and her eyes hurt. Sitting back, she stared at the papers spread over the table's surface. The writing on the pages could be hieroglyphics for all she saw.

Apparently it was *Gott*'s will for her to leave Miller's Creek. Because she certainly couldn't stay. Not now. An Amish man had tempted her from her path. Ruth pressed her lips together to prevent a sob. But *Gott* had wisely put an obstacle in that direction. Malachi's already-chosen match. So Ruth's path must lie in another direction. One she'd finally set in motion.

Her eyes wandered around the home she'd grown up in. The one she'd shared with her *daed*. She looked at the furniture pieces he'd made. Those would go with her, of course. Even if she had to cram them into a tiny apartment with considerably less space than the rambling farmhouse had. But all her memories of her father were here or at the shop or somewhere in the community. And he wouldn't be around to make new ones in new places with her anymore.

A few shallow breaths fought off her threatening nausea. She calmed herself with the realization that she didn't have to sell the farm. The acreage could be rented, while the house remained available for her to stay in. Should she come back for a visit. Or return permanently, if the *Englisch* world wasn't all she hoped it to be.

But if she stayed in the Amish community, she'd already disregarded the other husband prospects here. She'd be an old maid. Bile crept up the back of Ruth's throat. The pain of that stigma and loneliness would be less than the ache of seeing a married Malachi every day and every other Sunday at church. Assuming she could get her job back.

Dropping her chin, she tried to focus on the rows of numbers in front of her. *Concentrate on this. This test you won't fail.* With a sigh, Ruth shoved the course-work to one side of the table. The challenge of learning didn't bring the joy it once did. The pencil rolled and dropped to the floor with a clatter, and the puppy scrambled after it.

Ruth wearily got up, amazed at how tired just trying not to cry made her, and picked up the pencil before Rascal gnawed on it with his needle-sharp teeth. Picking him up as well, she rested her chin on his head.

"Let's go to bed. I can't seem to do much else."

Rascal sensed her mood and did his business without his standard exploration when they went for their nightly trek outside.

He offered further support with his quiet, warm presence once they were in bed, when Ruth whispered, "Please, *Gott*, let him be happy. I bow to Your will, but pray that Your will is also that Malachi be happy. Even if I won't be the one to make him so."

Midmorning the following day, Ruth apprehensively stepped into the Dew Drop Inn, the piece of paper with the names and numbers Mr. Morrow had mentioned clenched tightly in her hand. She'd gone to work early to ease the guilt of leaving briefly when she hoped the traffic at the restaurant was slower. When she'd mumbled her request for an unscheduled break to Malachi, she'd kept her eyes downcast. Ruth couldn't look at him. It hurt too much. He, too, seemed more than usually subdued in his response, although he'd murmured an agreement to her request.

It was the first time she'd seen him after her call to Mr. Morrow.

Much to her surprise, there was already a note addressed to her when she reached the counter in the relatively quiet restaurant. It was from one of Mr. Morrow's contacts, wanting to talk with her. With more dismay than excitement, Ruth discovered when she returned his call that Mr. Morrow had already phoned the numbers and told them of her. The man on the line wanted to talk to Ruth about a job. He was sure she'd be an asset to his operation. He'd arrange for a car to drive her to Madison, about forty miles away. When could she come for an interview?

With closed eyes, Ruth remembered Malachi holding Leah's hand and his stilted interaction with Ruth this morning. She started to tell the man she could come up this afternoon if he could arrange the transportation, and even stay for a while. But when she lifted her eyes, she saw Hannah through the café window, exiting the shop where she worked across the street. Hannah, who'd invited her to tomorrow's cookie exchange.

Ruth's eyes darted around the restaurant and the street outside, noting the Amish people, obvious in their Plain garb, who dotted her line of sight. They were her friends and neighbors. A wave of longing washed over her. She wanted to spend Christmas in Miller's Creek. This one last time. Next year she might be putting up lights and decorations in Madison as the *Englisch* did. Or driving through Wisconsin's winter countryside in a car instead of a buggy, but this year she wanted to celebrate the birth of *Gott*'s son in the Plain way as she had all her life. She clutched the hard plastic of the phone and in a voice not much above a whisper, asked the Madison businessman if after Christmas would be agreeable to him.

After he'd happily concurred, Ruth returned to work on shaky legs. When she stepped back into the workshop, a quick glance located Malachi. He searched her eyes with an enigmatic gaze before she dropped hers and hurried to hang up her cape and get to her current project.

Malachi didn't come near her the rest of the morning. Wanting to avoid her coworkers at lunch, Ruth took her brown bag to the shop where Hannah worked and ate with her friend. That afternoon, she resisted the temptation to look up every time the door opened, just in case it might be him.

Sometime back, Malachi had told Ruth that if he was already in the office, he'd take care of customers that stopped in. Ruth didn't know if she should rejoice or regret that the practice gave her less opportunity to see him. And more for any other women who stopped by the store.

Stop it! She forced her focus to the woodwork before her. Capable hands moved slowly over the wood as she realized in them was the last piece she'd make for what used to be Fisher Furniture. At the pace she was going, she might not finish it before she left the business. And she was going to be gone tomorrow for the cookie exchange.

Ruth bit her lip when she recalled she hadn't yet asked Malachi for time off the next day. She bored the screw hole she was working on more fiercely than necessary as she justified that Amish businesses normally closed on Thursday anyway. In fact the store was closed. The workshop stayed open Thursdays, because business had increased to the point they were frequently pressed for time. Which meant Malachi could be in the workshop all day.

Ruth jutted her chin. She'd worked Thursdays for years. She deserved at least one off. Glancing around the familiar shop, Ruth took in the all the equipment she'd worked on and might never work on again, some she'd had a part in purchasing. Her chin sank in conjunction with her heart. She might as well just take the day. Her absence wouldn't matter in a short time anyway.

When the door opened again, Ruth looked up to meet Malachi's gaze. Something in her expression must have indicated that she wanted to talk, as he leisurely but steadily worked his way in her direction. With every step closer he came, Ruth's mouth grew drier and her palms more sweaty. Wiping them down her apron, she turned to face him.

"Ja?" His eyebrow quirked in his otherwise impassive face.

"I need to be gone tomorrow."

Malachi was quiet for a moment after her blunt statement. Even when she'd just met him and was determined not to like him, Malachi's eyes had always seemed approachable and steady. Now they were cold and distant.

"Seems like you're planning to be gone permanently soon."

Ruth winced. She was hoping he wouldn't know of her plans already. Without phones and electricity, news still flowed through the Amish community with the speed of a breaking dam. She recalled the lingering discussion of Samuel and Rebecca behind her in the restaurant when she'd been on the phone. Apparently the Schrock charmer had ears on him as well as a mouth. Well, delaying the news wasn't going to sweeten it any. Besides, didn't Malachi have an upcoming wedding to participate in?

"Ja. Mr. Morrow called one of his business associates. They left a message for me at the Dew Drop. They're sending a car to pick me up so I can go to Madison and talk to them."

His eyes never left hers. "When?"

It was her turn to swallow. She looked away. "I told him not until after Christmas." Ruth saw him nod in her peripheral vision. When she faced him again, he was studying the project she'd been working on.

"You can be gone tomorrow if you're in position to get this done before you leave the business."

Ruth's eyes widened. "But there's not enough time!"

"Whose problem is that? You're the one dictating the schedule." He gestured to the pieces of oak around her. "This project was contracted under Fisher Furniture. You told the customer the availability date. Everyone else is working on other pieces with time constraints. If you don't get it finished, you'll be the one responsible for disappointing the customer. If you don't like the time frame, do something about it."

Ruth glared at him. Approachable and steady? Ha! His eyes weren't cold now; they were almost as heated as hers were.

"All right. I will." Turning her back on what she'd once foolishly thought was an endearing face, Ruth returned to work with renewed vigor. Refusing to do less than her best on her craft, she worked the rest of the afternoon with almost maniacal focus. She didn't look up when the men started removing their coats from the rack and going out the door.

Feeling a gaze on the back of her *kapp*, Ruth finally glanced over, surprised to see Samuel's amused eyes regarding her instead of the blue ones she'd braced herself to meet.

"Still working?"

"No, thanks to you," she groused, returning her attention to the bench while she wondered just what level of violence was allowed on a tattletale in a nonviolent culture. Ruth shot him a glare, figuring that'd be within the limits.

Samuel shook his head. An attractive smile she

wanted to wipe off his face creased his cheek. "It'll be okay," he promised as he stepped out the door.

"Lot that you know," she muttered to the now-closed door.

It was some time later when Malachi came through the workshop. He regarded her for a few moments, wisely refraining from commenting.

"I know how to lock up," she tossed over her shoulder. Her eyes, but not her attention, were still on the project in front of her.

There were a few beats of silence. "You have a ride home?"

"I'll get there." Ruth scrunched up her face. She would not cry. Again. Turning to the row of shelves on her opposing side, she blindly selected a wooden dowel she didn't need so he wouldn't see the quiver in her lip. Fortunately it wasn't evident in her voice. "I can take care of myself."

"Never doubted it," were the quiet words she heard prior to the thud of the door closing.

Ruth replaced the dowel and sucked in a deep breath. Wishing and wanting and hoping and crying weren't going to do her any good. Neither in the short term tonight, nor the long term. Which—she heaved another sigh—seemed very long and bleak at this point. Now that things were in motion for her to leave, she understood what her *daed* had made her promise. He hadn't solicited her promise to leave the Amish community to pursue the possibilities in the *Englisch* world, as she'd always thought. Maybe she'd misinterpreted his wish because it was what she thought she'd wanted. No, he'd made her promise to consciously make a choice—whatever it was—and not just to stay due to expectations or lack of ambition.

Although he'd talked of missed opportunities, Ruth remembered the smile and the loving look in his eyes whenever he spoke of the *mamm* she never knew. He'd had a choice. He'd chosen to stay.

And she was leaving, when every fiber of her being wished that wasn't the case.

Chapter Seventeen

Casting an eye at the skylights that provided most of the light for the shop, Ruth gauged she had about another hour before it would be too dark to work by natural light. A quick search revealed the oil lanterns were still stored where she used to keep them. She grabbed a couple, confirming the oil levels were enough for her to get through the work she needed to finish tonight.

Several hours later, Ruth rolled her shoulders and tipped back her stiff neck. Fueled by hurt and anger—and the internal debate that she shouldn't be feeling those things as she was still Amish, for the next few days anyway—she'd made more progress than she'd hoped. The project would be finished before she left. After Christmas. Ruth mentally pushed out her departure a few more days. The man in Madison would surely understand.

Donning her cape, she stepped out the door and secured it. Ruth hurried toward the Dew Drop Inn, hoping she hadn't left it too late to use their phone to call for a ride. Luckily an *Englisch* business kept later hours than an Amish-owned one. Her relief was as weighty as her tired shoulders when she saw the lights were still on. Even better, the Thompsons were just cashing out at the counter. They gladly agreed to give Ruth a ride.

A short time later, she waved them off from her front step. Ruth had never been so glad to be home. She opened the door to the familiar kitchen, and as she stepped in, she was reminded that she wouldn't be returning to its welcoming walls for long. Her hip sagged against the counter. Yes, it had been lonely here lately, but not so much since…

Ruth dashed back out the door. Snow crunched under her feet as she raced as fast as she dared across the frozen farmyard to the chicken coop. In her frustration and irritation tonight, she'd forgotten all about Rascal. He was probably starving. It was long past his dinnertime.

Ruth slowed her charge when no black-and-white bundle met her at the gate. Quickly unlatching it, she rushed through to enter the coop, hoping to see the pup just waking from a nap. In her haste, she'd forgotten a lamp or a flashlight, but the silence in the dark coop told her it was empty. She called anyway, her pitch rising with each unanswered holler. Making her way to the door, she stumbled into the fenced pen, its emptiness obvious in the moonlit night.

Pressing her fist against her mouth, Ruth bit down on a frozen knuckle to keep from wailing in distress. She slumped against the fence that enclosed the small pen. The woven wire screeched in the cold night air as it gave slightly under her weight.

"Oh, Malachi. I need you. I might be able to take care of myself, but I don't want to anymore." She couldn't hold back the tears any longer. Her finger rose to wipe under her runny nose. "I'm so tired of taking care of everything. And obviously I'm not doing a good job of it." The tears didn't do any good. Neither did her cry to Malachi. He wasn't there. Even if she had a horse that wasn't recovering from lameness, he was miles away. And might not be alone.

But then, neither was she. Numbly, Ruth looked up to see the endless stars that sprinkled the winter night sky. Blurry at first, they cleared as she blinked the tears away. She felt small. But not alone.

"Gott," she whispered, absorbing the immenseness. "I've been acting for too long like I could manage by myself. And neglecting to ask Your will. Forgive my *hochmut*." Ruth winced at the many times she'd pursued her will instead of asking for *Gott*'s. "I pray for the peace You promise. For I can't do it alone. I know that now, what You've known all along."

Her gaze dropped to the pen, taking in its emptiness. "And, *Gott*, if it is not too much trouble, please look to one little puppy tonight, as well."

Ruth sagged further against the fence, her chin dropping against her chest. While her body felt drained of energy, her mind was curiously relieved. For a few moments, she just breathed. Took in the brisk, clean air, felt the cold at the end of her nose and against her cheeks where the tears had run. She didn't hear anything on the crystal clearness of the night but the beat of her own heart. And Ruth knew it would be all right. Whatever happened. For *Gott* had finally shown her *gelassenheit*. Ruth almost wept anew at the calm spirit that filled her because she'd yielded to His will and not her own.

Opening her eyes, she gazed unseeingly at the yard of the coop. Unseeing, at first. There were puppy tracks throughout the yard where Rascal romped. Paths packed down due to frequent travel. Generally, he didn't get close to the fence, except for the gate. Ruth's gaze sharpened as she took in the ground beneath the end of her cape, where the fence leaned back under her weight. Around her feet, the border of fresh snow had been kicked back. A sprinkling of dirt dug up by paws with sharp little nails topped the dislodged snow. Ruth squatted and found a small hole burrowed under an area of the fence where the bottom wire curled up. Small, but big enough to accommodate an escaping puppy.

The cold metal of the fence squealed again as she pushed off it and whipped out the gate. Dashing into the house, Ruth grabbed a flashlight and a shawl to drape over her cape. Returning to the pen, she followed puppy-size tracks from the fence until they disappeared in the worn ruts in the snow that traced over the farmyard. Heart pounding, Ruth headed down the lane, afraid of what she might find in the ditch.

A light, visible in the darkness that cloaked the rural landscape, was bobbing along the road toward her. It turned into the lane when Ruth was halfway down. In the moonlight reflected on the snow, she could see a black-and-white bundle leap from a black-cloaked figure and race the short distance toward her. Excited yips accompanied each stride.

Hurrying forward to sweep Rascal up into her arms, Ruth laughed as he licked the traces of tears from her face. "Yes! I'm very glad to see you, as well. Although you gave me quite a fright."

"*Ach*, we'll apologize for that." Ruth identified the black-cloaked forms as the neighbor girls. "He showed up at our place late this afternoon. We didn't know how he got out. We figured he'd find the same way again if we left him, so we waited until you got home to bring him over," Mary, the older of the two sisters, explained. "We thought we'd see a buggy come up the lane, but it wasn't until the car lights flashed as they turned that we knew you'd come home that way." Emma, the younger sister, nodded as she reached out to give the pup's back a long stroke.

Ruth rested her cheek against Rascal's warm head. "It's fine. I'm just glad he's safe. And you are right. He dug a hole under the fence and escaped." She waved the girls farewell and watched as they made their way back down the lane and road to their nearby farmstead.

Much as she wanted to continue hugging him to her, Ruth set the puppy, who was now squirming, down. She turned to head up the lane. "Oh, Rascal. I was so afraid. But you also helped me realize something. Something I needed to determine a long time ago. I knew it, but I didn't live it. You and me, we may think we're independent, maybe even alone, but we're not. *Gott* has always been with us. Even though I might attempt to grab the reins from Him occasionally, I'm going to try to let Him drive."

Ruth inhaled a deep breath of the crisp night air. "Especially over the roads we'll travel for the next while. In the meantime—" Ruth opened the door to the kitchen and the puppy bounded through "—we'll take care of Bess, and after that we have a lot of cookies to make before tomorrow."

Ruth waved Hannah off as her friend drove the pony cart back down the lane. Over Ruth's objections, Hannah had insisted on giving her a ride home after the cookie exchange. Although she attended church every other Sunday, Ruth forgot how wonderful it was to fellowship with her neighbors in the Amish community. Or maybe it was just her new outlook that made her so joyful. Perhaps the fact that her time with them was short had made the outing so precious. Whatever it was, she'd lingered and visited until Hannah proclaimed it was too late for Ruth to walk back and requested that her brother prepare the pony and cart.

A basket of cookies weighed heavy on her arm as she turned away from the lane. The smile that curved her lips faltered as she realized no miniature barking had greeted neither her nor the unfamiliar cart. A rapid glance revealed an empty chicken run. The basket almost dropped to the snow when she saw that the gate was open. Ruth's heart began to pound. Had Rascal gotten loose again? Or had Mary and Emma come and gotten the puppy? She didn't mind the girls playing with the pup, but she wished they'd mentioned it when they left the exchange earlier this afternoon. Ruth's eyes flew to the road in the gathering darkness to see if a light was bobbing its way in her direction.

Frantically, she rushed to the house to get the flashlight and begin a search, only slowing when she saw a glow from the kitchen window. She, like other Amish folks, never locked their homes. It could be anyone in the house. Ruth's heart rate accelerated further. No one but Hannah, who'd just left, had visited her lately. The doorknob in the chilly Wisconsin twilight was frigid in Ruth's sweaty hand. Before she pushed open the kitchen door, she looked back over her shoulder to confirm there wasn't a rig in the shadowed farmyard. There'd been little fresh snow since Bess went lame, so the tracks that crisscrossed the ground leading to the barn could be hers, or someone who'd brought her home. Whoever was in the house could have put their horse and buggy in the barn. But why? Brows furrowed, Ruth hesitantly opened the door.

The glow from the fireplace and an oil lamp on the counter outlined a figure sitting in a chair. Only a quick grab saved the basket from sliding down Ruth's arm and onto the floor. Dazedly, she set it on the counter with a soft thud. Rascal, seated on the lap in the chair, launched himself off and scurried to greet her.

Ruth crouched to the puppy that danced about her feet, gathered him in her arms and rose before meeting a gaze that regarded her warily.

"I am so glad to see you," she murmured to Rascal as she rubbed his ears. "I was so afraid when I thought you might be gone again." The room was quiet after her whisper, the only sounds the occasional pop in the cheerily burning fireplace.

"I was feeling the same way." Malachi's low baritone finally broke the silence. "I didn't know if you'd gone to Madison after all."

Ruth's heart beat faster than the little one whose rapid patter she could feel clutched against her chest. She tucked the comforting silky head under her chin and met Malachi's gaze. The pup squirmed when trapped between the deep breath she inhaled and her tight grip. "It was a *gut* day today. I didn't want to leave."

"Then why are you?" His voice was equally quiet.

Needing a moment, she placed Rascal on the floor. He shook himself before trotting over to lie down in front of the fireplace. Ruth wished she could shake things off so easily. She lifted her eyes again to his steady blue gaze. "I can't stay in Miller's Creek if you're not free." She forced a swallow. "Are you?"

Malachi didn't answer for a few endless heartbeats. "No, I'm not," he finally responded without breaking eye contact.

It was what she feared and expected. She propped an elbow on the counter to keep from sagging against it. When she thought she could speak, Ruth murmured, "Then what are you doing here?"

"I came to offer you something." In an easy movement, he rose from the chair he was in. Her eyes only for him, Ruth hadn't noticed it. Still gliding smoothly after his abrupt departure was the red oak rocking chair started by her father, a man she'd loved dearly. And now it sat where she envisioned it by the fire, finished by the man she loved more than she could've imagined.

"Oh, Malachi," she breathed. "It's beautiful." On trembling legs, Ruth moved to the chair and ran her fingers across the satiny back. Her eyes drifted shut, imagining for a moment the smooth surface she was stroking was his cheek. She would treasure the piece as she did the ones her *daed* had made. More so, as it had been made by both men.

She opened her eyes when he spoke. "That's *gut* to hear, but that's not all I'm offering." Malachi faced her, the chair between them. A faint smile touched his lips, but his eyes were still apprehensive.

"What I'm offering is my heart, Ruth. It goes with the chair." He smiled, creating a dimple in his lean cheek. "It went before the chair actually. It went when a stubborn woman came along with the furniture business I acquired." He sucked in a breath and blew it out slowly, his eyes never leaving hers. "So you see, I am not free. I belong to you."

Ruth's grip left the back of the chair. She found herself

clasping his strong, calloused, wonderful hands. "But what about Leah? She's perfect."

Malachi snorted softly. "Leah helped me learn a lot about what I wanted in a woman. And what I didn't. I didn't want perfect."

Ruth grinned. "You realize what that says about me."

Malachi smiled and squeezed her fingers gently, not letting her go. "I wanted perfect *for me*. A woman with a talent for managing and for working with wood. And for making me happier than I'd ever imagined I'd be. I know you're who *Gott* has chosen for me. He brought me here to Wisconsin in order to find you." The smile faded a bit when he added, "I'm only hoping that I'm enough for you."

He searched her eyes. When she didn't speak, he continued, "I know you have other options. I know you're capable of succeeding in them. I know that staying in the Plain life would limit what you want for yourself. But I allowed myself to hope."

His lips curved slightly. "When wanting to grow a crop worth harvesting or a furniture piece worth making, some preparations have to be made. The groundwork needs to be laid. I figured this was similar. I contacted the bishop regarding permission to set up one of the outbuildings with woodworking equipment, in case someone would consider marrying me. I'd set it up, so when *kinder* arrive, they'd have a safe place to play as well, while their *mamm* makes furniture, if she'd want to."

Ruth stared at him in surprise.

"And I've found I need to learn more about the business part of ownership. I was never much of a reader." He wrinkled his nose. "Even before I left school, my mind was already on physical work. I learn better by hearing and doing. So if I had a wife who wanted to study and learn—" he flicked his eyes toward paperwork still stacked on the kitchen table "—then maybe teach me, interspersed with a few sweet words, it might be a good thing."

Ruth skirted the rocker so nothing was between them. "I could do that. Most of it anyway." Her lips quirked. "Who's going to say the sweet words?"

"How about if I start out with this? Will you marry me, Ruth?" When she drew back and her eyes grew wide, Malachi continued, "I know you can take care of yourself. But for the few occasions that you might want to lean on someone, I want it to be me."

He let go of one of her hands long enough to dab at a tear that leaked from her eye. "It devastates me when you cry," he murmured.

Ruth sniffed. "Oh, Malachi! The first day you walked into the shop, I reminded myself that *Gott* had a plan for me. Foolish me, I tried to make His path fit mine, thinking I knew what I needed to be happy. But He knew me and, of course, knew better. His plan is so much more than I could've ever imagined. Nothing I could ever find in wood or on paper would bring me the joy of being in your arms."

A smile spread across Malachi's face. He pulled her into his warm embrace. "Well, then. Come here."

Resting her head on his strong shoulder, Ruth whispered, just loud enough for him to hear, "There's an Amish proverb that says to choose your love and love your choice." She nestled deeper into his arms. It felt like home. It felt like everything she'd ever wanted. "I choose you, Malachi."

Epilogue

"Ach," Malachi stepped through the door and quickly strode to where Ruth stood on a ladder. "You're supposed to making sure she behaves herself, Samuel."

Turning from where he was building a bench against the wall, Samuel shot Ruth a grin and a wink. "That's your responsibility, *bruder.* You're the one who chose such a stubborn, complicated wife in the first place. It's taught me to make sure I choose a biddable woman when I marry."

"That would be your loss. I couldn't imagine anyone else." Malachi carefully lifted Ruth down. As he set her on the ground, their mutual smiles lingered and his hand gently brushed over her burgeoning stomach before taking the screwdriver from her hand.

Malachi turned his attention to the sloped ceiling. "Come over here and help me with this. Might as well get a little more work out of you before your new horse acquisition business has you forgetting all your woodworking skills."

"You'll miss me. I might even miss you." Samuel

crossed to his *bruder* and climbed the ladder. "But you know horses were always my first love."

Malachi handed him the screwdriver. "I know. But you'll always have a place here if you need it."

Now relegated to the floor, Ruth watched Malachi and Samuel work on the skylight. As promised, Malachi was converting the hog house, its occupants long gone, into a workshop. Glancing around at the renovations, Ruth inhaled deeply, relishing the fresh lumber smell that permeated the airy room. She couldn't imagine being any happier. Everything was set up with safety and efficiency in mind for when she'd work out here.

And she would. But not as much as she'd thought. And that was okay. It was here when she wanted or needed it. For as much as she'd wanted and needed the woodworking, she wanted and needed her Amish husband more. Who'd have ever dreamed she'd have both?

Her lips curved as she listened to the brothers bantering as they worked. Malachi looked over at her and smiled. Ruth's heart swelled as she rested her hand on her slightly rounded stomach. A loving husband, a *bobbeli*, a close extended family, work she loved. The words of Jeremiah ran through her mind. *For I know the thoughts that I think toward you, saith the Lord, thoughts of peace, and not of evil, to give you an expected end.*

Tears prickled in the back of Ruth's eyes, ones born of wonder. Who could have expected this marvelous end for her?

Only *Gott*.

* * * * *

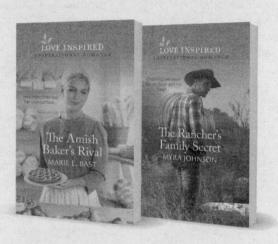

Get 4 FREE REWARDS!

We'll send you 2 FREE Books plus 2 FREE Mystery Gifts.

Love Inspired books feature uplifting stories where faith helps guide you through life's challenges and discover the promise of a new beginning.

FREE
Value Over
$20

YES! Please send me 2 FREE Love Inspired Romance novels and my 2 FREE mystery gifts (gifts are worth about $10 retail). After receiving them, if I don't wish to receive any more books, I can return the shipping statement marked "cancel." If I don't cancel, I will receive 6 brand-new novels every month and be billed just $5.24 each for the regular-print edition or $5.99 each for the larger-print edition in the U.S., or $5.74 each for the regular-print edition or $6.24 each for the larger-print edition in Canada. That's a savings of at least 13% off the cover price. It's quite a bargain! Shipping and handling is just 50¢ per book in the U.S. and $1.25 per book in Canada.* I understand that accepting the 2 free books and gifts places me under no obligation to buy anything. I can always return a shipment and cancel at any time. The free books and gifts are mine to keep no matter what I decide.

Choose one: ☐ **Love Inspired Romance Regular-Print** (105/305 IDN GNWC)   ☐ **Love Inspired Romance Larger-Print** (122/322 IDN GNWC)

Name (please print)

Address   Apt. #

City   State/Province   Zip/Postal Code

Email: Please check this box ☐ if you would like to receive newsletters and promotional emails from Harlequin Enterprises ULC and its affiliates. You can unsubscribe anytime.

Mail to the Reader Service:
IN U.S.A.: P.O. Box 1341, Buffalo, NY 14240-8531
IN CANADA: P.O. Box 603, Fort Erie, Ontario L2A 5X3

Want to try 2 free books from another series! Call 1-800-873-8635 or visit www.ReaderService.com.

---

*Terms and prices subject to change without notice. Prices do not include sales taxes, which will be charged (if applicable) based on your state or country of residence. Canadian residents will be charged applicable taxes. Offer not valid in Quebec. This offer is limited to one order per household. Books received may not be as shown. Not valid for current subscribers to Love Inspired Romance books. All orders subject to approval. Credit or debit balances in a customer's account(s) may be offset by any other outstanding balance owed by or to the customer. Please allow 4 to 6 weeks for delivery. Offer available while quantities last.

Your Privacy—Your information is being collected by Harlequin Enterprises ULC, operating as Reader Service. For a complete summary of the information we collect, how we use this information and to whom it is disclosed, please visit our privacy notice located at corporate.harlequin.com/privacy-notice. From time to time we may also exchange your personal information with reputable third parties. If you wish to opt out of this sharing of your personal information, please visit readerservice.com/consumerschoice or call 1-800-873-8635. **Notice to California Residents**—Under California law, you have specific rights to control and access your data. For more information on these rights and how to exercise them, visit corporate.harlequin.com/california-privacy.   LI20R2

HARLEQUIN

Heartfelt or thrilling, passionate or uplifting—Harlequin is more than just happily-ever-after.

With twelve different series to choose from and new books available every month, you are sure to find stories that will move you, uplift you, inspire and delight you.

Love Harlequin romance?

DISCOVER.

Be the first to find out about promotions, news and exclusive content!

f Facebook.com/HarlequinBooks

🐦 Twitter.com/HarlequinBooks

⭕ Instagram.com/HarlequinBooks

📌 Pinterest.com/HarlequinBooks

You Tube YouTube.com/HarlequinBooks

ReaderService.com

EXPLORE.

Sign up for the Harlequin e-newsletter and download a free book from any series at
TryHarlequin.com

CONNECT.

Join our Harlequin community to share your thoughts and connect with other romance readers!
Facebook.com/groups/HarlequinConnection